A Wanted Woman

This Large Print Book carries the
Seal of Approval of N.A.V.H.

LIBRARY OF CONGRESS CATALOGING-IN-PUBLICATION DATA

Dickey, Eric Jerome.
    A wanted woman / by Eric Jerome Dickey. — Large print edition.
        pages ; cm. — (Thorndike Press large print African-American)
    ISBN 978-1-4104-6746-1 (hardcover) — ISBN 1-4104-6746-5 (hardcover)
    1. African Americans—Fiction. 2. Large type books. I. Title.
PS3554.I319W36 2014b
813'.54—dc23   2014007016

Published in 2014 by arrangement with Dutton, a member of Penguin Group (USA) LLC, a Penguin Random House Company

Printed in the United States of America
1 2 3 4 5 6 7 18 17 16 15 14

A WANTED WOMAN

ERIC JEROME DICKEY

THORNDIKE PRESS

A part of Gale, Cengage Learning

GALE
CENGAGE Learning·

Farmington Hills, Mich • San Francisco • New York • Waterville, Maine
Meriden, Conn • Mason, Ohio • Chicago

To Frannie

"History is written by the victor because the loser is dead."

— *Fightville*

"Humans don't change that much in fifty years. Or a hundred. Or a thousand. It's the laws that change, the rules, the civilization. We just repeat ourselves."

— *Rectify,* Season One, "Modern Times"

"The other part of me wanted to get out and stay out, but this was the part I never listened to."

— *The Long Goodbye*

■ ■ ■ ■

REAPER

■ ■ ■ ■

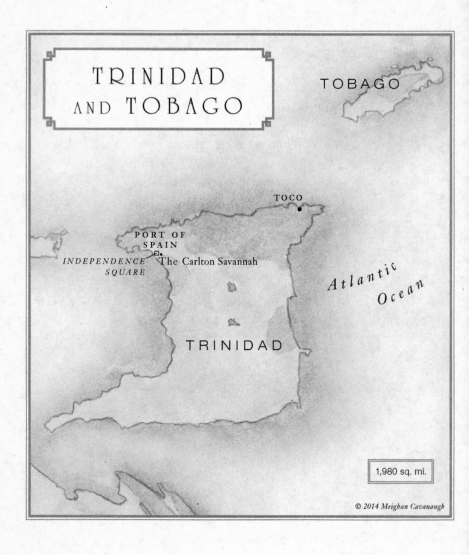

TRINIDAD AND TOBAGO

TOBAGO

TOCO

PORT OF SPAIN

INDEPENDENCE SQUARE

The Carlton Savannah

Atlantic Ocean

TRINIDAD

1,980 sq. mi.

© 2014 Meighan Cavanaugh

Prelude

Gunfire. Screams.

Four people dead within seconds.

Dozen wounded.

Dead bodyguards.

Dead bank guard.

Dead politician.

Collateral damage.

Blood flowed in two directions, the Nile reaching for the Mississippi.

The living became the dead, waiting to chat with Jesus's daddy.

Dora the Explorer many times over.

The Trinidad contract was fucked from the start.

That was the feeling I had as my Liat flight rocked through the storm and touched down on a West Indian island that I knew nothing about, only that I was dispatched there to make a living man become a dead man. Rain flooded parts of the island. Mudslides in areas named Woodbrook. Diego Martin. Glencoe. Cars were drowning in water as muddy and murky as the Mississippi River. After I landed and cleared customs, the right-hand-drive rental van was in the lot, the key hidden under the front tire. A map was in the glove compartment. No GPS, so I had to figure out the spaghetti roads on my own, everything in reverse to what I was used to in the States. Looked like the roads were designed by the British. It had taken me hours to make it northeast to the safe house, half the roads up this way changed into streams of mud as well.

I should've recognized that as an omen of how messy, how fucked-up this job would be.

Three hours of driving later, I pulled the rental van from the rocky Toco Main Road and entered a safe house in Rampanagas Village. The map said that I was in the county of St. David, the northeastern section of the island, the area also known as Rampanagas Ravine. About a thousand people lived on this section of the island, but the safe house was up a rocky road and set off to itself. It had privacy, and many fruit trees, the grounds filled with orange, Portugal, grapefruit, breadfruit, five fingers, avocado, golden apple, soursop. By then the rain had stopped and the Caribbean bugs had come out to play.

With as much as I knew about Trinidad, I might as well have been on a tropical moon. Salybia Beach, Missions Bay, Big Bay . . . many beaches were on this route, many where the leatherback turtles came to lay their eggs. I had been sent down from the United States on a death contract, not to surf and swim.

My first thought was I wished Johnny Parker were here to enjoy this paradise.

We could have done some serious fucking. It had been almost a month since Florida.

I frowned, thought about that last day in Florida, that last frantic night. I cursed.

Cellular up to my ear, I shook off that memory, focused, called the Barbarians: "I'm here."

14

"Should be a green wall somewhere in the house."

"Okay. I see the green wall. Great paint job. Who did it, a three-year-old?"

"Turn the purple light switch off and on five times."

I did. The wall opened up and revealed an armory. Thirty guns. Grenades.

I pulled down a .38, a .380, and a .22, took out a wealth of ammo.

Three two-gallon canisters of clear liquid were with the hardware, hazard symbols on each.

I asked, "How much poison is in these containers?"

"Enough to kill everyone at Madison Square Garden. Don't touch it. Top-grade."

"Okay."

"The fancy chopsticks are yours. They should be above the guns."

"I see them. Two sets."

I took one set down, turned the light switch off and on five times.

The wall closed.

I asked, "Who is the target here in Trinidad?"

"A minister who grew up in some areas called Cumana and Saline Bay."

"Minister as in clergy?"

"Minister as in government official. That kind of minister. A people pimper."

"All the same to me."

"Look at the intel and let me walk you through your assignment."

"Why haven't I been paid for the contracts I completed the last month?"

"Let's focus on this one at the moment. Was the information set up in the safe house?"

"Everything is taped to the wall. Different, but nice. The way the Barbarians have the charts set up makes it look like a CIA or FBI operation, only organized. Makes this easier for me to read."

"More photos of the target and notes are there in a notebook as well."

"Looking at the package now. The Barbarians said this was a simple job, but it looks intense."

"Page six. Info on the target starts on page six, most of it pointless."

"All that matters is when and where to put a bullet in his heart so I can exit, stage left."

The target was being protected by the organization that was labeled the Laventille Killers. The target was a charismatic man, but was noted as the symbol of bigotry, an extreme racist.

"They want him killed before he gives a speech at the Indian Arrival Day Dinner, a speech that will highlight the Muslim-Arab involvement in the slave trade. Loved by many, but people want him dead for too many reasons to count, including calling for

people of East Indian descent to boycott Tobago."

I asked, "Where will he be? The charts are
nice, but I need the specifics so I can create a
plan."

"Only the Trinidadian organization we call
the LKs has that information."

"LKs?"

"Laventille Killers. We call them the LKs.
Saves ink on paper. They know the movements of the target, are acting as his security,
and have managed to keep his location close
to their chests."

"Sounds like they're in the same business
we're in."

"Competitor. We're into legal holdings.
Drug trade helps them maintain unbelievable
capital."

"Drug and alcohol trade made the
Kennedys and Rockefellers become
Kennedys and Rockefellers. All wealth comes
from some level of corruption. Old Man
Reaper taught me that. Anyway. If that is the
case, the LKs having the GPS on the target,
how will I get that information to do the job?"

My orders were to infiltrate the Laventille
Killers. While I talked to my designated rep
with the Barbarians, I glanced over page after
page, went to the wall and did the same, read
the pages of intel.

"This is vague. How am I supposed to
infiltrate this hardcore West Indian group?"

"They're men. You're a woman. Meet one of the men and use what God gave you."

"Give me a fuckin' break. That does me no good."

"We need you to do a short version of the long game."

"A rush job. What should take days, maybe weeks, you want done in a couple of days."

He said, "One of the members, a twenty-something who grew up in Morvant, a man assigned the handle King Killer, he always goes for coffee at a place called Rituals. Seven out of seven days a week."

"King Killer. What did he do to earn that handle?"

"Five years ago he killed the top man in Laventille. A man they called the king of Laventille."

"How?"

"High noon, Port of Spain, center of town, on some strip called Frederick Street. He killed the baddest of the bad, so that made him the baddest of the bad, and some say that one act made it possible for the LKs to all but take over the slums, to take over the drug trade, and now they are a legit business, turning dirty money clean, buying police and politicians, taking over the entire island."

"Okay. I see several names highlighted here. Who's important?"

"Outside of King Killer, the name to remember is War Machine."

18

"War Machine? He's four years older than me, twenty-five. King Killer is two years older."

"Intel says that King Killer picks up sexy girls at coffee shops. That's his thing."

"I see it. But if one of the boys from the LKs is not the target, why am I dealing with them at all? Why not just let me get close to the minister or politico and figure out a way to do what I do best."

"Follow the plan. Always follow the plan that has been put in front of you, MX-401."

"Again, why can't I just break out a sniper's rifle and go for the target?"

"The political target is off-island and we have no idea where he's been sequestered."

"Thank you. That was all you fuckin' had to say."

"Less questions."

"More answers. My life is on the line, not yours. You're a fuckin' paper pusher."

"You're not winning any friends behind the red doors. You have a hard time following orders."

"Not when they make sense. I can only do what makes sense. I'm out here by myself, with no backup, so I have to look at these bullshit plans and see what works best for me."

"Follow orders. They make sense to the man behind the double red doors."

"No idea when the private plane is coming

back to Trinidad with the package?"

"LKs know when the target's coming back. He'll be back the night before the event in question. Party in his honor. They need the target dead before he gives that speech. That's the contract."

"Why not after the speech?"

"Before. After will be no good. Kill him at the Carlton Savannah the night before."

ONE

Rituals Coffee House at City Gate, South Quay, Port of Spain,
directly behind Independence Square

Fast food joints were all over. This was the main transportation hub on the island for buses and maxi taxis. It was seven o'clock the next morning in the land of steel pan, calypso, soca, chutney, and limbo, on a mountainous island renamed by Christopher Columbus. I'd come to town before sunrise to check out the area near the former Trinidad Government Railway headquarters.

By the time the sun had pulled itself from the sea, I had plotted three exits in case shit went wrong and I was forced to flee through an area that had thousands of visitors each day — that plus the thousands of locals. I walked each route three times, each time at a normal pace.

Then I left the keys in the van's ignition, driver's-side door unlocked, a Minnie Mouse sunshade in the front window. A loaded gun was under the front seat, easy to reach if I came back running.

I dressed like a University of the West Indies student, wore a T-shirt from the St. Augustine campus, jean shorts, sexy sandals, my hair short and light brown. I went for young, but mature and intellectual. Anxious, I sat listening to the rapidly changing conversations of a group of women on the way to Port of Spain General Hospital. One wore a tee that read KAMLA HAVE NO JACK TO CHANGE SHE TYRE. I listened to conversations, captured the rhythm of the tongue, picked up variations of the accent, pretty much mastered the singsong aspect, created a passable Trini accent, Chaguanas or Port of Spain, minus the proper idioms. Many had an interesting blend, a unique exoticness not seen in North America.

Despite the beauty of the people and the long lines for lattes, unrest was all around me. The newspaper spoke in volumes. Another social explosion was about to happen. Economy in decline. Frustration. Poverty. Political fallouts. IMF and World Bank called everything but the devil. Not enough to pay for housing. Not enough money to live. Barbados stealing their flying fish. School book prices high and salaries low. Teachers protesting. Nurses protesting. Police had their crimes. Army had their crimes. People losing their pensions.

And the band played on.

King Killer showed up by eight. I left my table, stood next to him as I ordered a second latte. Sat a table away from him. Sat facing him. Leg bouncing. Cleavage popping. Local paper open, pretending to read about killings, crimes, and drugs coming in from South America. The gunta didn't notice me. He wore tie clips, pocket squares, French cuffs. Charcoal-gray suit perfectly tailored, his shoes in brown hues. I watched the handsome 18-karat-gold wedding ring–wearing thug and saw that he eyed professional women. Inside of thirty minutes, he befriended five women as they came to get coffee or iced drinks — befriended them, took their cards, and exchanged fuck-you-later smiles with each as they left to rush to work. All had been well-dressed women. None had looked over twenty-five. I nodded. I understood. He was about status. He was attracted to women with smooth skin and young eggs.

The next morning I dressed like an executive: fitted, sleeveless dress, low heels, silver watch, bracelets, earrings, sat properly, was there when he arrived, a copy of the local paper on my bistro table as I sipped iced green tea and read, pretending to be interested in an article where the president of the St. Lucia Craft and Dry Goods Vendors Association was calling for heavy security ahead of the cruise season, in a bid to prevent tourist muggings in the city. Next page said that a major think tank based in Washington, DC, said that Caribbean360 had reported that gangs were stronger than the government here in Trinidad and Tobago. Now maybe the LKs were on the road to attempting a coup like the one that had happened in Trinidad and Tobago in 1990 by a small maverick Islamic group called Jamaat al Muslimeen, led by Yasin Abu Bakr. The moment had arrived. I inhaled, put the paper down, felt his hardcore energy. King Killer noticed me. We made eye contact. He grinned and nodded. I nodded in return, no grin. Hard to get.

After he ordered, he stood over me, got my attention again, and said, "Good morning."

I looked up, saw him, said, "G'day."

"How is your morning so far?"

"My morning feels out of sorts, to be honest. I'm over here feeling like it's midnight and past my bedtime, maybe because back home it is midnight, and don't you look alert and as happy as Larry."

"You have an interesting accent."

"So do you. Wee cracker of a day, isn't it?"

"Thought you might have been an English rose at best, Red legs at worst."

"Red legs" was a derogatory name for the poor whites in the islands.

I said, "New Zealand."

"A Kiwi. I'm intrigued. Here on business

24

or have you moved to my island?"

"Here on business."

"For how long?"

"Will only be here a couple of days. Pardon the yawn. I need more coffee."

"Jet lag?"

"The sixteen-hour time difference is killing me. It's morning here, but it's late night at home. By the time I am in a meeting at three this afternoon, it will be a wee bit after sunrise back home, so that will mean that I have stayed up all night again, and I'm usually in bed by nine, ten at the latest."

"Waiting on someone?"

"Not at all. My colleagues went ahead of me to the office."

"Mind if I join you?"

Not until then did I shrug and give him a curious smile, left it up to him to pursue me.

His jacket had a bulge from the weight of his gun. His pant leg caught over the backup gun he had strapped to his ankle. Hot day. Didn't take his suit coat off. Baby face with the eyes of death.

He was Trini but didn't speak with a strong Trini dialect. He sounded almost British. He had been trained to suppress or erase his accent the way Hollywood erased the accents of many.

He sat and said, "Pardon my rudeness. My name is Neziah. Neziah De Lewis."

"Neziah De Lewis. That is a beautiful

name. It sounds royal."

"It does, especially the way you say it with your accent."

"My name is Samantha Greymouth, but most people call me Sam."

"Sam it is. I will call you Sam."

"Sounds beautiful the way you say my name, Neziah."

"Likewise, Sam. The way you say my name makes it sound brand new and original."

I told him that I was in Trinidad on behalf of Australia and New Zealand Banking Group Limited.

He told me the name of his Trinidadian-based companies. I told him I had never heard of them.

Then he said, "Have you heard of Mrs. Karleen Ramjit?"

"No, afraid not."

"She is my sister. You remind me of her. You have the same powerful energy."

"Flirting with a woman that reminds you of your sister, Neziah, is that a good thing?"

"My twin sister is remarkable."

"You're a twin?"

"All women should be like Karleen."

"Women don't want to own the same dress as another woman. Being like another woman, that's simply out of the question."

He smiled. I smiled.

The newspaper in front of me caught his eye, pulled his words toward politics, the conversation starter, and maybe his way of testing my values, gauging my intelligence, seeing if I was worthy of adultery.

He said, "Too many of my people live day to day in unhappiness."

"I read most of the paper. Sounds like some sort of oppression."

"It is. Poverty is oppression. Oppression is worse than slaughter."

"Is it that bad? The sea. The sun. The sand. So lovely here."

"Oppression is why we kill one another in the streets."

"All over the world, or are you only speaking of here?"

"Eastern Port of Spain was labeled one of the most dangerous places on the planet. That was in a report. Criminal gangs. Gangster-style killings. The guns are not going away. We're close to South America. Easier to get a gun than a plate of food in some areas."

"That's horrible."

"Our country is wealthy, but there is corruption. That aspect of our island is out of control. A purification process is necessary."

I asked, "What does that mean? What is a purification process?"

"What it means, Sam, is that we will one day take charge on behalf of the people. My sister leads us. We have a plan."

"An elitist intervention?"

"No. With the people. We will one day lead the people away from the guns and the drugs. The violence among the poor will end."

"Sounds very ambitious. You make it sound very spiritual."

"Part of the journey will be spiritual. Some have become too cynical, and that has to be rectified. We are here to kill the dragon."

"The dragon?"

"A metaphorical dragon."

"I assumed."

"We want to change what is wrong and lead others toward what is right."

"Struggle is a never-ending process, Neziah. I've seen that around the world. Freedom is never really won. The battle never ends."

"We recognize that. You have to earn it with every generation. You have to build momentum and keep that momentum going. We are prepared to make sacrifices and do the hard work so our children will not have to live in the poverty we know now, not have to watch their sons and daughters and mothers and fathers slaughtered in the roads. People are afraid to leave home. You become a prisoner in your own area. You live in violence and are afraid to walk from Nelson Street to Duncan Street. Do that and you're robbed and found dead. Do the reverse, you're shot in the head, the murder posted on YouTube."

"Wicked. Sounds like parts of America I've

seen on television."

"The Americas run from Canada to the end of Argentina."

"I stand corrected. The United States. I have seen the television show *Cops,* shows like that. The rest of the Americas is twice as bad."

"And it is the same in London and Russia and countless other places on the globe. It says a lot about God's faulty creation."

"And New Zealand. Don't you dare leave my island country out. I'm also very proud to say we have drive-by shootings, stabbings, murders, carjackings like the Americans, mainly in our Brisbane area. So don't exclude us from the global madness."

He went silent.

I had fucked up.

Brisbane was in Australia, not in New Zealand.

I was ready for the killer of a king to call me on that, to sense that all was wrong, kick over the table, pull his gun, and ask me who I was.

With my fingers touching the gun inside my purse, I asked, "Are we okay?"

"Just thinking. Our island had become the Caribbean's murder capital. That makes me unhappy. That makes me very unhappy."

"Hear that?"

"What?"

"When I lean to the left, I can hear the

people in the ramshackle areas up in Kingston, Jamaica, laughing at the killings in the ramshackle areas down here. No offense, but the Jamaicans want their title back."

He laughed.

I winked at him.

He asked, "Where were you born? You've heard my story. What's yours?"

"I was born in a place called Kawerau. Eastern Bay of Plenty. Was born in the oldies' caravan."

"Oldies?"

" 'Oldies' means parents. A caravan is what you call a mobile home. Had a long drop out back."

"Long drop?"

"Outdoor toilet. Had to dig a deep hole, put a barrel at the bottom. We lived in our own type of oppression. I know poverty very well."

"You and your parents?"

"The oldies split before I was a teenager. My father left my mother when I was ten, maybe when I was nine, went to Nuku'alofa, Tonga."

"What did he do there?"

"Got a great job. Started a new family."

"How'd you get by?"

"My mum worked in a movie theater for a while, then eventually became a frock tart and worked on *Xena: Warrior Princess*. She was almost killed on the job."

"Pardon me for staring at you with such respect."

"Only if you pardon me for the same."

He grinned and said, "Your arms are so toned. You're fit."

"Netball. Hiking. Aerobics. Biking. Keep away from too much bread."

"You have the body of a dancer, Sam. No kids?"

"None. Maybe next year. Or the year after. My husband tells me that I need to be as fit as I can be before I decide to up the duff and have a rug rat or two or three or four."

He asked, "What's your religion?"

"Are you asking me if I am a member of the unquestioning, self-righteous faith against all rationalism and morality characterized by a lack of critical thinking?"

"What religion rules New Zealand?"

"I was born Christian, but I really have no interest in religion."

"Religion is about moral guidance."

"Rubbish, Neziah. The Crusades spread genocide, rape, slavery, torture, murder, animal cruelty, and some of the most insanely sadistic shit imaginable, and evil was justified by saying their version of God commanded them to do it."

"Every country, every society does horrible things, allows horrible things, for the greater good."

"Good point, but it makes me wonder."

"What does it make you wonder, Sam?"

"Maybe what we see as good is just evil that has won."

"Interesting perspective."

"If evil did win, then it would call itself good, and call what was seen as good the new evil."

"What has won, Sam, what always wins is the work of doing what is best for the people."

"Talking about religion, in my opinion, is a gerbil on a wheel, gets nowhere fast."

"You're right. I tend to play devil's advocate. If you had taken one side, I would have taken the other. That's what I do. I love intellectual stimulation. It arouses me. How moral are you, sexy woman?"

"How moral are you, married man? How moral are you?"

"I asked you first, married woman who is visiting my island."

"You're looking at me like you want to visit my island."

"How moral are you? Answer me. I asked you first."

I said, "I have to be off to a meeting soon."

"Same for me."

"So, if there is a particular direction you want this to go, if you have any hopes beyond us sharing a table while we sip coffee, let's hurry in that direction. I'm not much on small talk and chitchat and taking the long route, not when a straight line is always the

best route."

He smiled. "How long are you here?"

"Are you interested in making something happen?"

"I am. I am very interested."

"My husband is far away. Maybe you should put your wife on hold so you can hold me awhile."

"I can come to your hotel after this event with my sister. An afternoon of pleasure."

"No. I don't want any issues with my company. Illicit behavior is frowned upon, plus I've only been there for six months. I don't want to be seen as the young, wild Kiwi on the job. If we have sex, we have to fuck away from my hotel. Anywhere but the Hilton. I'm at the upside-down Hilton, by the way. So if we fuck, we can't fuck there."

"To the point. I like that. The way you say 'fuck' is erotic. It arouses me."

"Sure it's not the coffee?"

"Personal question, Sam?"

"Sure."

He asked, "When was the last time you had sex?"

"May I be honest?"

"Please."

"I'd hate to come here on a business trip and not get to sample anything outside of the doubles and curry chicken before I returned to my island country. How boring would that be? This is where I stand. I'm married, have

33

to be respectful, have to be discreet. My co leagues are also friends of my husband Understand? I can manage to slip away at night, but during the day I have to maintain a certain look for my employer."

"Tomorrow night?"

"Only free tonight, Neziah. My colleagues are going to lime on Ariapita Avenue tonight, are going to the Aria Lounge to watch a launch for Genesis or W.I.L.D., but I told them I was too tired to hit the streets and I'd sleep in a bit. Work dinner with the colleagues tomorrow night. Then I fly out the next morning."

"I have an event tonight. It's a busy day for our organization and the people of Trinidad."

"Oh well. If I'm ever this way again, or if you're ever in New Zealand, I hope to run across you."

"You'd find someone else."

"I could sit at the bar later, maybe, see what happens, who comes in, who shows interest in a lonely Kiwi drinking chocolate martinis."

I toyed with my wedding ring, played the part of the Kiwi visiting the island on business regarding holdings for a New Zealand company, a woman who needed to let the Miley Cyrus in her run free. He toyed with his wedding band. It was impressive. German-made. Expensive.

He said, "I can come for you around eleven."

"Are you sure?"

"I can cancel my date, which will be no problem, and arrange for you to come along in her place."

"Really?"

"I'd be honored to spend the evening with you, Sam."

"How should I dress?"

"Wear something easy to remove."

"Bring your frenchies."

"Frenchies?"

"Condoms."

King Killer left the coffee shop and I watched him get inside the backseat of his private car and be driven away like royalty. I stared at the man who had killed a king of the streets and paved the way for his group. Handsome. Fuckable. A wave of guilt hit me. I made sure King Killer was out of sight before I changed SIM cards in my cellular and called the man I was in love with, dialed Johnny Parker's number.

He answered on the first ring. "Hello?"

I didn't say anything. All I could do was inhale, exhale, miss him like crazy. Missed him so much my head ached and my eyes wanted to water.

He said, "Jennifer? Is this you, Jennifer?"

Last month, before this Trinidad assignment, I had an almost normal life, had used the name Jennifer, a form of the Welsh Gwenhwyfar, a name that meant "white fairy" — a little self-deprecating humor. Johnny was my boyfriend. We'd spent most nights together for four months. And had taken vacations together. The last was from Florida to Denver. During our helicopter tour of a mountain range in Colorado, we saw several snowboarders taking on the steep terrain of the couloir. The next day we both had done the same. He was as daring and athletic as I was. I had been living the perfect lie. Dates. Movies. Birthday cards. Too bad his ex-wife had become a problem that had to be dealt with.

I cleared my throat, turned on my Brooklyn accent, and said, "Parker. I miss you, baby."

Then I hung up.

Two

I had to cut away from my thoughts about Johnny Parker and regroup, had to hurry and climb into my car, become someone new, and follow King Killer to his next destination. He'd gone only a few blocks away. I knew where. I already knew about the morning event. It was in the intel. If contact had failed at Rituals, I would have gone there and tried to get in good with another member in that group. I'd become more than a little curious about this organization of LKs and its relationship to the island.

Intel said most of the members had killed, some while still in their single digits. I needed to see what kind of security and guns they had, who I was dealing with. Plus, if the target was already there and showed up, I'd take care of that. I'd do it my way, and tell the Barbarians to kiss my ass.

Hundreds, if not thousands, were out in the heat of Port of Spain, lined up outside of the business offices of the Laventille Killers, the LKs. On a day that was in the mid-nineties, a day in the middle of the rainy season, it looked like everyone from Port of Spain, San Fernando, and Chaguanas had shown up for a protest, but it was anything but. King Killer's sister was the face of their organization; that had been in the Intel. Mrs. Karleen Ramjit. King Killer had said that only a few were allowed to refer to her as Karleen; intel said only the poor of Trinidad were allowed to refer to her as Karleen, and the poor were calling out Karleen's name like she was Jesus in high heels. Classy as Elizabeth Taylor, but she was dressed in jeans and wore amazing shoes, smiled a Bollywood smile each time. Small woman. She was innocuous, desired by men, envied by women, loved by all the children. People touched her like she was Mother Teresa, hugged her like she was Princess Diana, lauded her like she was Eva Perón.

I had never seen people respond to anyone that way, not in my lifetime.

She had something that could not be bought. She was special.

If I owned fear, I would've been more afraid of her than any man carrying a gun. Men know to fear men, but the only thing more deadly than a man was a woman.

A fleet of trucks were in front of the LK offices and so were all the island's news channels. They covered Mrs. Karleen Ramjit's every move like she was the head of state. The LKs were handing out top-shelf toys to poor children. Mrs. Ramjit let it be known that her organization had bought equal amounts of toys from all Trini businesses, wanted to give something to her people and help her island's economy. Unparalleled and exquisite, Mrs. Ramjit took photo after photo, kissed babies, even invited the elderly to come up and take a toy. An old woman cried. She had grown up in Laventille, had had it hard all of her life. She was seventy and had never owned a toy. Mrs. Ramjit held the old woman, hugged her and cried with her. Cameras flashed. BBMers. Instagrammers. It looked like tomorrow's front page in the making, but after the hit tonight, that moment would have to be moved to page six.

Soon I called RCSI. That was the business name for the Barbarians.

Once on a secure line I said, "MX-401."

"Status?"

"Neziah De Lewis aka King Killer went for the Kiwi. I have access to their private party."

"Did you do your research on being a Kiwi?"

"Fuckin' seriously? Do you question men regarding their competence?"

"No room for feminism in this organization."

"I'm not a feminist. I'm a professional."

"After what you did in Florida, after the risk you created, we tend to disagree."

"That was personal."

"The man behind the double red doors still has doubts concerning your competence."

"This assignment hasn't been double verified. I need double verification."

"Hold. Let me talk to someone on the next level."

When they came back on the phone they told me the man behind the red doors wanted me to proceed. The more I read about this group, the more I had hoped the job had been pulled. These were the LKs. They killed men, women, and children alike. Most had been killing since they were nine and already had fifteen years in the business. It felt like I should've been here with a team of Barbarians.

I said, "I need a driver, someone who knows the island and these roads for this assignment."

"Denied."

I hung up, angry, nervous. Had been angry since birth, was only nervous before a job.

The man who sat behind the double red doors, only a few had ever met him. Old Man Reaper had said that the mysterious man was like a mob boss who ran Las Vegas back when Vegas was controlled by the mob. Bugsy Siegel, Fat Irish Green, Two Dumb Tonys, Frank Sinatra. He was all of them. I think that my father, Old Man Reaper, had met the man behind the red doors once.

That was one time more than the rest of the Barbarians had met him.

From what I heard.

Barbarians rarely met other Barbarians, unless one was about to be put down.

We were like sleeper agents.

Only we didn't get to sleep much.

At least, I didn't.

Where I worked, your pink slip was a bullet to the brain, pink mist in the air.

Old Man Reaper.

My father.

The day I was born.

The day he left, I didn't remember.

The day he came back, I'd never forget.

I thought about Memphis. I thought about the first time I had met Old Man Reaper.

THREE

I inherited my cynicism from my father, my insecurities from my mother's malicious and bigoted tongue, and my skin tone from a cruel joke by God. He knew I wanted to be Pam Grier and betrayed me.

Old Man Reaper showed up in South Memphis at my elementary school one hot afternoon. I had no idea who he was because I hadn't seen my father since I had been yanked from my mother's womb.

I had been pulled from the playground, told to get all my things, and sent to the office, but wasn't told why, just ordered to go. The public school system had always been short on tact and sensitivity. Back then my hair was long. I pulled my Hitchcock-blond hair back from my face, half of it in a ponytail, and took my time. They had told me to hurry, but I did the opposite. To piss them off. I entered the counselor's office sweaty, with my head down. I had scratches and scrapes, a fading black eye.

The counselor looked up from her desk and said, "Your father came to get you, Goldie."

I looked at the suited dark-skinned man sitting in the chair facing her.

I said, "I don't have a father. My mother told me that and I'm sure she's not a liar."

He stood up and nodded, said, "I'm your father."

It looked like Terry Crews and Billy Blanks and the Rock had had a baby, then God had painted him Wesley-Snipes black and given him Philip Michael Thomas hair and gray eyes that changed their color depending on the lighting and maybe his mood. The counselor smiled at him, smiled at him a lot.

In a soft voice, the Southern belle asked, "Will y'all be this way long, Mr. Reaper?"

"Not long, Mrs. Smith. We'll take care of family business and move on soon."

"It's Miss, not Mrs. You make me sound old. I'm only twenty-two and a half."

"I stand corrected, Miss Smith."

"Love your accent. Where are you from?"

"Barbados."

"So you're Jamaican."

"No. I'm Bajan."

"So, you're from Africa."

"No. I'm Bajan."

"We've never seen you around the school, Mr. Reaper."

"Was out of the country for a while."

"For how long?"

43

"Twelve years."

"Where were you?"

"Was living in the Bahamas for a while. That's not in Africa either. Nor is it in Jamaica."

"Understood."

"Then I was in England, Germany, France, Côte d'Ivoire, and Belgium."

"World traveler."

"I've seen a few places where the black man was his own king and the white man was the visitor, and I've seen places where it seemed like the black man no longer existed."

"Bet you have a few stories to tell."

"We all have stories to tell."

"I find this situation fascinating. Her mother was from Minneapolis."

"Sabina had St. Lucian roots. That's not in Africa either."

"Well, Miss Sabina never talked much."

"She was a private person."

"She always had a mean face."

"Had it rough as a child. It was her defense mechanism."

"Tall woman."

"Was teased about her height half of her life."

"And, again, she was from where?"

"St. Lucia. Castries. That's near Barbados, and neither is near Africa."

Then the woman looked at me.

She looked at Old Man Reaper again.

"How did your daughter . . . I mean . . . how?"

"If you look real close she looks like her mother."

"To be honest, I would need a magnifying glass to find the resemblance."

"Her mother was what I would call a willowy goddess robbed of her self-assurance, then turned to drink, then turned to a house of worship, and learned to praise another man's god. This side of Memphis is all churches and liquor stores and when she was depressed, she embraced both. I tried to save her from most of that. She could have been Miss St. Lucia Universe. When she came here to America, it wasn't how she thought it would be. It wasn't the way I thought it would be, so we had that hardship in common. Both of us were foreigners being called horrible names we thought reserved for the black man who was born here on this soil. It wasn't the kind America she saw in movies. The black man here has been taught to hate the black man. Cruel, racist words had did her in, murdered her self-esteem."

"Is that why you and she split?"

"That's none of your concern. Have I answered enough questions to satisfy your curiosity? I want to make sure that when I walk out that door with my daughter I won't have any issue with the police."

"Why would you have an issue with the police?"

"Every black man in America has an issue with the police simply because he was born."

"I apologize. It's just that, well . . . your daughter . . . her mother . . . your daughter have a condition?"

"Why would you ask that?"

"We have all wondered that since your child has come here. Since the first day she came here with her mother for registration. We thought the mother was her nanny. Is this a medical condition?"

"God does what God wants to do, and this is what God wanted to do. So, ask your god."

"You sure she's yours?"

"She's mine. That piece of paper has my name on it, says she's mine, so she's mine."

"And you've been gone for twelve years. Sounds like you left when she was born."

"Not going down that road, not with you. If we are good, I'll take my daughter and be on my way."

"Wait, Mr. Reaper."

"Did I fail to pass some part of this exam?"

"You were impressive."

"Then what is the issue?"

"Okay. This may seem forward, and it may be inappropriate considering the circumstances, but at some point I would love to hear about your travels, if you found the time to share them over dinner."

46

"Dinner? For more questions?"

"What I'm asking here is what the school wanted me to ask. At dinner, no questions."

"Won't be here long. We have to go . . . go see her mother. Take care of other business."

"A man has to eat sometime, no matter how much business he has to handle."

"A man does. His child will need to eat as well."

"She will."

"A man's child should eat before he does. She should get the big piece of chicken."

"Is there someone here in Memphis to make you and your daughter a home-cooked meal?"

"Not at the moment, but there is a KFC on Parkway. We'll eat there today."

"My chicken is better. Falls off the bone. My mashed potatoes and biscuits are better too."

"I'll keep that in mind. If you want to feed my daughter tomorrow, after we have dealt with the things we have to deal with, if we are in the mood for home-cooked food, that would be nice of you."

"Well, if you need anything later, and I do mean anything, feel free to contact me."

She wrote down a phone number and slipped it into his strong hand.

She said, "I'm usually awake until midnight. I become restless at night. Very restless."

"Why is that?"

"A woman feels the loneliest around midnight. God made us that way."

"Nighttime is hard on all of us."

"I have no problems with it being hard on me tonight."

"Understood."

"Where are you staying?"

"Holiday Inn off the Mississippi River. Near town and where they killed MLK Jr."

"Oh. Riverside Drive? If I had a car I would stop by there and check on you."

"Where do you live?"

"South Memphis. Blair Hunt Drive, the end by Shady Grove Missionary Baptist Church. If you found time to get away and wanted to talk after midnight, that would be fine by me, Mr. Reaper."

"Leave the porch light on."

"I'll do that. Tap three times. After that you can tap until you can't tap no more."

I'd never seen that evil bitch smile a day in my life. Old Man Reaper reached to take my chubby hand. I shook my head and left the office in front of him, headed out on Joubert Avenue.

He put me inside of a black and dirty Lincoln and drove away.

I sat back and shook my head.

He asked, "What's the problem, little girl?"

"Will you be this way long, Mr. Reaper?"

"Not long, Mrs. Smith."

"It's Miss, not Mrs."

48

"I stand corrected."

"Well, if you need anything, feel free to contact me."

"Anything?"

"Anything. No matter what the time. I would love to be able to be there for you . . . and your daughter . . . as you go through that which God has put in front of you."

"In that case, you should give me a number to reach you."

He was frozen. "How do you do that?"

"You should've just had Bible study in her office."

"Answer me. How do you do that?"

"Do what?"

"You sounded just like her. You sounded Southern and country, then you sounded Bajan."

"I sounded like you. You sound weird and I sounded like you."

"Is that what I sound like to you?"

"I can imitate almost anybody. I spend my time alone, watching television, so I get bored and imitate everybody on the television, the commercials, the cartoons, the people, everybody."

"How can you do that?"

"Just can."

"That was amazing."

I said, "So, okay, again, why do I have to leave school with a stranger?"

"I'm your father."

"Like I said, why do I have to leave school with a stranger?"

"It's an emergency."

"Something happened to Momma. You kept using the word 'was' when she is an 'is.' "

"Preacher your mother was seeing . . ."

"Was."

"Did you know him?"

"Reverend Doright. He was over last night."

"His wife went up to your momma's job this morning."

"Okay. Mrs. Doright."

"The woman started an argument."

"Okay."

"She stabbed your momma in her chest."

"The preacher's wife went down to the post office on Third Street?"

"People said the woman went berserk, showed up in her pajamas, hair in rollers."

"Okay."

"She was stabbed to death."

"Okay."

"I said 'stabbed to death.' "

"Okay."

"Your momma is gone to be with God."

"Okay."

"All you can say is 'okay'?"

"How am I supposed to get inside the house?"

"What?"

"She never gave me a key to the house."

"I tell you that your mother was murdered, and that's your concern?"

I had been mistreated and ridiculed and rejected from my first breath.

By the time Old Man Reaper reappeared, I was already numb.

By twelve I was already aloof, a cold fish, an unfeeling person, a vulgar iceberg.

I was a fat kid, at least forty pounds overweight, so that added to my angst.

Food had been my friend. My mother was tall and slim.

Old Man Reaper asked, "You knew about what she was doing?"

"Her boyfriend came by time-to-time, had Bible study when he thought I was sleeping. He'd come by and pray, then take her into the bedroom for some more intense Bible study. Her bed creaks and she would start to curse, say 'Jesus Fucking Christ' over and over, and then about five minutes later it would get quiet, and she would walk to my room and check on me, but I would pretend to be asleep."

She was half-crazy. She hated me and blamed me for her being half-crazy. Maybe that was why I felt like I was half-crazy most of the time. My drop-dead-gorgeous mother hated me because Old Man Reaper accused her of cheating and left. My egg donor hated me and in return I hated her, cursed her every chance I got. Giving me lashes didn't

51

matter. She would beat me. I wouldn't shed a tear. Would look at her and scowl. She was dead and I didn't care. And I didn't care that I didn't care.

While we sat in KFC and ate, I asked, "Where are you going to dump me?"

"Nowhere for you to go except for foster care, so they called me to come to get you."

"You got here that fast from California? In a car. I've seen it on a map. That's a long way."

"I'm here. That's all that matters."

"Touch me anywhere near my private parts or ask me to do what this other girl in my class does for her stepdad I will scream and cut your throat with a butcher knife while you sleep."

"Jesus. Did somebody do something to you?"

"No."

"Somebody tried?"

I shifted in my seat. "What's your name?"

"Reaper."

"You have a first name?"

"You can call me Daddy. Or Poppa. Up to you."

"So, you show up out of nowhere and expect me to call you Daddy and I've never heard of you before."

"Well, if you haven't heard of me it's because your momma didn't want you to."

"Momma's dead."

"You want to cry?"

"Where are you taking me?"

"Well, we have to claim her body, pay for them to send the body back to her home so they can bury her there, pack up your things, and either fly or drive to where I am staying in California."

"California?"

"I'm not that far from Disneyland."

"So, what kind of work do you do?"

"I work for a company called Retail Consumer Services, Incorporated."

"What do you do there?"

"I work in collections."

"What does that mean?"

"It means I encourage people who are delinquent to pay their bills."

"What does that mean?"

"It means I'm the last motherfucker you want knocking at your door."

"What were you doing that had you so close to Memphis today?"

"Collecting. I was out collecting."

"Can I have another piece of chicken?"

Two years later we were still living in a two-bedroom at the Californian Fountain Apartments in Huntington Beach off Warner Avenue. It wasn't far from the cold Pacific Ocean and had almost nine miles of sandy beach, palm trees lining the streets. I had been forced to trade Beale Street, Overton Square, and the Pink Palace for a chance to drive from our crummy apartment and see Venice Beach, Santa Monica, and Beverly Hills. Before Memphis, I had only seen palm trees on television. Within a month after I landed on the West Coast, Old Man Reaper would stock the fridge with healthy food, leave me a few hundred dollars, then vanish for two or three days at a time, sometimes for a week — always had to go on a business trip for the company called RCSI. The weeks he was home, he made me breakfast, dropped me at school if I asked, but every evening he picked me up, did homework with me, then took me to a gymnasium. Made me work out between two and three hours every day he was home.

Daddy barked, "Last time telling you, start your kicks with your left side."

"I'm right-handed. I don't kick with my left leg."

"That's why we start with your left. I always start with my right side. That is why I do twice as much with my right side. That's why I am able to switch sides. We always start with the weak side. We will always do more with our weak side. That's how you become stronger. That is how you will damn near have equal power on both sides. You don't get stronger by working your strong side while your weak side rests. You ever see a man push weights with just one arm? He uses both. You don't make yourself better than the rest of the world by doing what you can already do. You will be able to push out three kicks in one second. You will be able to use your legs like you use your hands, throwing the equivalent of hooks and jabs by using sidekicks, roundhouse kicks, front kicks, spinning back kicks, crescent kicks —"

"Blah, blah, blah, blah, blah, blah, blah."

"Twenty push-ups and twenty burpees for that."

"Can we just get started with this bullshit before you talk me to death."

"Now it's forty and forty."

"Why not make it fifty and fifty?"

"Now it's sixty each."

He sat down, frowned, shook his head, and looked at me.

I dropped to my knees.

"Get off your knees. We don't train like that. Push-ups like a man."

"You're still an ass."

"Seventy and seventy."

"I hate you. Really hate you."

"Eighty and eighty."

"Are you fucking mad?"

"One hundred and one hundred."

"I'm a girl."

"When I'm finished with you, you will be a woman who fears no man."

"Still an ass."

Then he added speed drills. Left-leg side-kick down the black stripe to the end. Turn around. Right-side sidekick on the return. While I was exhausted, panting, he made me keep going. I refused to let him break me. More roundhouse kicks. More hook kicks. Soon it was same leg down and back, then change legs, down and back, doubling the number of kicks, and while I was exhausted from his regimen, I had to do two hundred front kicks into a heavy bag, one hundred with each leg, each striking with the ball of my foot, each time trying to make the bag fold in half. Training went on for hours. Spinning back kicks. Crescent kicks. Jumping double kicks. Reverse punches. Jabbing punches. Lunge punches. Punches in a series of three. And there were katas to enforce my stance and blocks and form and fluidity. Upper rising blocks. Middle-level blocks. Down blocks. Foot sweeps. Block after block after block. Elbow strikes. Spear hands. Upper-elbow strikes. After all of that we did kata after kata after goddamn kata.

I yelled, "I hate katas. They are bullshit."

"You need katas, need form, grace, and repetition."

"Do I look like I want to be Ip Man?"

While normal girls were taking ballet and losing their virginity, while they were talking about giving boys blow jobs, while they were kissing and being fingered by boys, this was

56

what I was doing.

Soon he came in with bō, staves, kamas, shinai, sais, nunchaku, swords, and tonfa. There was a hatchet, sling blade, and a baseball bat on top of all of that. I was kicking around the gym, at that point able to do that on my own, and when I finished I stood in front of him, my T-shirt soaked in sweat.

I asked, "What's this?"

"Weapons training."

"What do you do for a living, Daddy?"

"I told you to never ask me that."

"I'm going to ask every day until I get an answer. You can make me do push-ups all day and night and I'm still going to ask. I'm your daughter and I have the right to know what you do."

"I hurt people."

"What, do you call them names and hurt their feelings, or something else?"

"I freelance for powerful individuals who want to operate outside of what's legal."

"Freelance?"

"Sometimes I do more than hurt them."

"What's more than hurt?"

"Gear on now, or one hundred and ninety-nine push-ups."

"I still want to know what you do for a living, Old Man Reaper."

"I'm thirty-four."

"I'm fourteen. To me that's old."

He paused. "You want to know what I do, who I work for, after we're done, I'll tell you."

FOUR

Five years later. Two years ago.

I was a new hire being indoctrinated in the company's philosophy.

It was midnight when Old Man Reaper pulled up outside of a dive bar on the outskirts of Dallas. He wore a gray suit and tie. I wore slacks and low heels. I wore a top that had no sleeves, no jewelry, hair slicked back, black leggings, flat shoes. He drove us to a club in a building that looked like it had been a church, a bowling alley, and a strip club over the years. Loud music. Large crowd. I smelled the ganja in the parking lot. If cocaine had a stench, I was sure that it was in the air too.

Daddy parked near the club, made a call, hung up, then said, "The target is inside."

"Who is he?"

"It's a woman. About your age. She's three inches taller and about two weight classes up from you. Wearing a Bob Marley top, tight jeans, heels, hair dyed bright red. Looks like a clown."

"She's carrying a weapon?"

"No idea."

"What do you need me to do?"

"Show no mercy."

"Mind if I ask what this is about?"

"Never ask what it's about. Down the line, that's the way it will be. If you come on board and they want you to know, you'll know. Even then don't be eager to find out. Listen if they tell, but never ask."

"Okay. But I am a girl and I guess that we tend to be inquisitive about things."

"Lose that habit."

"Sure. Whatever."

"Follow your orders. Beat her ass. Give her a message."

"Just give her an old-fashioned ass whooping?"

"Tell her that nobody fucks with Reaper and gets away with it. Nobody. Reaper will always come after you, no matter how long it takes. Tell the target that, hit her ten more times, then walk away."

Old Man went in with me, stood near the door, pointed out the target.

The girl was standing at the bar. Dressed as described. High heels supporting a round, plump, meaty, circular ass. Laughing like she owned the world. Her girls were at her side. I pulled off my motorcycle gloves, gloves that had rock-hard protective plastic across each knuckle, gloves that could be used as brass knuckles or have the impact of a sap. Old Man Reaper nodded. I pushed my way through the crowd and went straight to her. She looked my way and without pause I threw a hard punch into the center of her nose. Her drink fell and she wobbled in her shoes. Blood gushed. On the heels of the first blow I dug in and threw a right hook to her solar plexus. Her hands dropped from her bloodied face to grab her new pain. One of her girls ran over to save her and was met with a spinning back kick that hit her gut and lifted her in the air before she dropped in agony. A second girl came and two punches left her on the ground in dreamland. A guy came. I looked toward Old Man Reaper. He was gone. The guy cursed me, charged at me, but I dropped, made him trip and fall. By the time he was getting up, I was putting a bottle to the side of his face. Then my right hand came down on his face until he begged me to stop hitting him. He was done. I grunted, looked at the crowd, then went back to the girl I had been sent to give a message to, went to the terrified woman and threw another hook that landed on her blood-damp chin. As she was falling I hit her three more times.

I looked at the crowd. Nobody wanted to fuck with me, nobody wanted to tug on my cape.

As they watched, I grabbed the girl's hair,

gave no mercy, beat her from pretty to ugly to atrocious, and as she suffered, I gave her the message. Her eyes had widened in surprise.

I repeated, "Nobody fucks with Reaper and gets away with it."

She moaned, "Reaper."

My fist was a hammer.

Ten. Nine. Eight. Seven. Six. Five. Four. Three. Two. One.

She had been unconscious since eight, maybe since nine, but I had hit her anyway.

When I got back to the car, Old Man Reaper was inside.

I slid in and he pulled away from the curb slow and easy. I was sweating and breathing hard. He was listening to Luther Vandross sing that a chair was not a chair with no one sitting there.

I raised my fist and showed him my bloodied glove as proof of the mission accomplished.

"I gave her the message from you."

"The message was from you."

"Why would the message be from me?"

"When you were a fat little girl in Memphis, that bitch used to bully you. She beat you up on the playground. She called you names. Called you fat. Talked about your mother. Stole your lunch money. She stole your confidence. She had almost destroyed you in your youth."

"That was Alberta Simmons from when I was in Memphis?"

"That was that little bitch."

"She got fat. And now she's ugly."

"The day I had picked you up, she had beat you up on the playground."

"That happened a long time ago."

"No matter how long it takes, always pay a motherfucker back. Whatever they did to you, you take them double. You make them not forget to never fuck with you again. You make them piss when they hear your name. You make them turn the other way and start running when they see you coming."

"How did you find out about her bullying me?"

"Your elementary school counselor told me."

"Miss Smith?"

Old Man Reaper said, "Yeah, Miss Smith."

"When?"

"The night I left you at my hotel, I went over on Blair Hunt Drive and went to see her."

"Why?"

"She extended an invitation. Southern hospitality. Didn't want to be rude. I wanted to know why you were bruised when I picked you up. Wanted to know why you had a black eye. Your momma had just died and I didn't want to ask you if she had been physically abusing you. So I asked her."

"Then you ended up having Bible study."

"Without the Bible."

"Gross."

"She's well versed with the Song of Solomon. And she cooked a good chicken."

"Much people picked on me."

"She said you were made fun of a lot, pushed around, called much names."

"Do I get to go after them all? Can I go after the teachers who made fucked-up jokes too?"

"If you want to."

My nostrils flared with the memories. "Now what?"

"We go to work, get to the real reason we drove two days to get here from California."

"Collections."

He nodded. "This debt might be beyond collections."

Hours later, as the sun was about to rise on a Sunday, we were in an office near downtown.

The building was empty, Dallas a place where people went to church.

My dad told the man, "You're nine hundred thousand in the red with the Barbarians."

He raised his broken fingers, wiped his bloodied mouth, and looked at my old man though his swollen eyes. "Reaper, I took out a five-hundred-thousand-dollar loan to make things right."

"The money didn't get to the Barbarians,

not within the last ten minutes."

"Because the moment the money was transferred to my account, the goddamn shitty-ass fucking IRS seized my funds. They froze my account and they took it all to pay my damn back taxes. To top it off I have a tax lien in the state of New Jersey, and that one has fifty-one thousand in interest due."

"That's a shame."

"Tell me about it, Reaper. Tell me about it. I have helped them launder so much money through churches, and now they are coming down on me. What's that expression?"

"Well, the Barbarians told me to tell you that that nine-hundred-thousand-dollar debt, with penalties and interest of course, is now at two point two million dollars."

"Jesus. Are you fucking serious?"

"I'm not a comedian. You know what I do. I collect for the Barbarians."

"Look, after I get to court and get my child support payment reduced — I mean, I am paying damn near a million dollars a year for my four boys — and after I settle up this thing with the government and the courts, when I can sign off on this next deal, I'll have access to around five million."

"Five million. That's much money."

"That will be my cut. It will be in cash, I kid you not."

"The man behind the double red doors wants his money, that's all."

65

"Tell the Barbarians that I will get them every last dime. Tell the man behind the double red doors that I'm good for it, that I just need the time. That's all I need. Look, man. Me and my second wife . . . she's pregnant . . . just found out . . . so this will be my fifth child . . . aren't you going to congratulate me?"

"Benny, you have ten million in an offshore account."

"Shit."

"They already know that. You had a mansion built. Six bedrooms, twenty-thousand-square-foot lot. They know about the next wife you have tucked away with the house in her name. They know about the new identity and the new passport. The man behind the double red doors told me to tell you that."

"Reaper, don't trust that sonofabitch hiding behind those red doors. Never trust that mother —"

Rorschach.

My father's hand was inside of his dark jacket. So was his gun. He fired one shot and blew a hole in his jacket pocket. It hit the lying man in the center of his forehead. A Rorschach made of blood and brains painted the white wall. The conversation was over. My father's job was done.

He picked up the phone, dialed a number.

He gave them his designation and said, "Tell him that it's done."

He looked at me. I nodded. I was okay.

He said, "My daughter has done well each time. I can vouch for her. She's here now."

A minute passed, a minute with him listening and nodding, then he hung up the phone.

He said, "Once the man behind the red doors makes his decision, if he wants you to come in as a collection agent, one of the reps will want to talk to you at some point."

"Whenever they are ready to call, I'm ready to answer."

"Be sure you want into this business. It's not one made for women, not one for girls."

"I want in. Get me an introduction and I will take it from there. Won't need you anymore."

"I need you to understand what you'll be doing. You'll get your fingerprints removed, they'll need to know your whereabouts around the clock. When they call, you answer and go where they say to go."

"Why did you get in?"

"Same reason many of my ancestors went to work the Panama Canal. Not much options where I came from. People on the islands have limited opportunities. We have to go to Canada, England, or come here to America to make the kind of money we want to make. Back home you either work in tourism, at a bank, drive a taxi, or sell coconut water on the side of the road."

"You're an assassin."

"This wasn't what I came here to North America to do, but it's what I ended up doing."

"What did you come here to do?"

"I was going to be a soca singer."

"Soca? Is that like reggae?"

"Not reggae. Thought I was going to change America into the United Soca of America."

"You sing?"

"Did when I was younger. Switched over when I came here, saw that I'd go broke here trying to sing. Regrouped. Used my fighting skills to be a bouncer, then ended up in collections."

"Why?"

"The money. It was fast money. It was quick money. It was easy money."

"How old were you when you came here?"

"Same age you are now."

"You're not rich."

"In America the rich man's objective never will be to make the poor man rich."

"Never heard you sing."

"Life stole my voice a long time ago. Nothing left to sing about."

He looked at me. I leaned against the door, arms folded across my chest.

He said, "This is serious. Once they call, once you're in, there is no getting out."

"You get to travel and see the world, right?"

"I've left Little England, left my island and

seen more places than I ever thought I would."

"You go to the Bahamas a lot."

"Unfinished business there and a few other places."

"Women and Bible study? Spreading the word while they spread the legs?"

"Unfinished business, that's all."

"I have wanderlust, need to see more than Thugland, California, and the muddy Mississippi River."

"Lust?"

"Wanderlust."

"Okay."

"I might start dating soon too."

"Not yet."

"I can date if I want. You have no say in the matter."

"Not while you're under my roof."

"You treat me like I'm a boy, but I'm a girl."

"You're not dating. You're not ready."

"I won't be under your roof much longer. I'll start making my own money."

"Who is the boy?"

"Were you ashamed of me when I was born?"

"What?"

"Were you ashamed of me?"

"It was complicated. When you were born, it surprised everybody."

"Are you still ashamed of me?"

"I've never been ashamed of you."

I paused. "Just a guy. He's just a guy who thinks I'm cute."

"Black or white or what?"

"Black guy. He asked me out."

"You tell him about me, about your mother?"

"Not yet. Haven't decided if I'll go out with him."

"He wants sex."

"I might want sex too. I'm old enough to want sex, right?"

"Have you been having sex?"

"Not that it's any of your business, but not yet. Not yet. Would be my first time."

"As long as he's not Mexican. I don't want your first time to be with a Mexican. I don't want you to end up having a baby with a Mexican, not in America. America treats blacks bad, Mexicans worse."

"You don't get to choose."

"I want better for you."

"I've been treated worse than any Mexican has ever been treated. By you and my mother."

"I've never mistreated you."

"You walked out on me before they cut the umbilical cord."

"I came back."

"Twelve years later. Like you had a fucking choice."

"I've apologized to you a thousand times, Goldie."

"You don't get to choose. You lost that right when you walked out."

"I'm still your father and I want what's best for you."

"You walked out the day I was born. That's the story my mother told me every fuckin' day."

"Let's not do this again."

"The moment I was born."

"Goldie."

"What?"

"You haven't asked about your mother since we left Memphis."

"So what?"

"Haven't said her name."

"She never liked me either. That's why she gave me this stupid name."

"You never miss her?"

"No need worrying about someone who didn't like me."

"She was angry at me, not you."

"Whatever. What-the-fuck-ever."

I went toward the wall, stared at the Rorschach.

He asked, "What are you doing?"

"Relaxing."

"By looking at that mess?"

"It's like art."

"What?"

"It's like art."

"What are you talking about?"

I said, "Dora the Explorer smoking a joint

71

with Jesus."

He stood next to me, tilted his head, and stared at the art he had created.

He said, "John Lennon riding a Jet Ski in the snow."

"Who rides a Jet Ski in the snow?"

The other guy groaned. He was the bodyguard. Old Man Reaper had sent me in first and I had gone toe-to-toe with that guy, had done a spinning back kick that hit him in the gut and before he could recover I had beaten him into dreamland with my knuckledusters. The guy tried to crawl to the door so he could escape. Old Man Reaper handed me his gun. I shot the man in the back of the head.

A Rorschach appeared on the beige carpet.

I said, "Now, *that* looks like John Lennon riding a Jet Ski in the snow."

He shook his head. "Dora the Explorer smoking a joint with Jesus."

I asked, "Are we done here in Dallas?"

"We're done here in Dallas."

"Any more jobs?"

"Nothing pending."

"I think it's time for us to part ways."

A long moment went by before he said, "Sure about that?"

"I'm sure. I still feel a raw anger. I should leave. I could turn on you one day."

"Hate you feel that way."

"I can work for the Barbarians and feed

myself, get my own place, buy my own clothes."

"Okay. You're an adult."

"Maybe this time I'll be the one who vanishes for twelve years."

"If that's what you want."

"You can go on with your life."

"Before you take that call from RCSI, just be sure."

"I want to be a Barbarian."

"Why?"

"Because I've never been anything but picked on, ridiculed, and bullied."

"You could go to Hollywood and do voiceovers, be an actress, become a doctor."

"People have been mean to me all of my fuckin' life. I've never belonged to anything."

"Why become a Barbarian?"

"To make money. To get away. To find where I belong in the world."

He asked, "Are you okay?"

I didn't answer.

He said, "You really want to hurt my feelings."

"No more than you wanted to hurt my mother's feelings."

"Don't do this, Goldie."

"You hurt mine first. You hurt mine first."

"Before we part ways, I need to train you for another sixty days."

"What have we been doing?"

73

"Compared to what you will need to know to work for the Barbarians, that was bullshit."

FIVE

Memphis, California, and Dallas fell away from my mind, as did Old Man Reaper.

Had to focus. Air conditioner hummed in the bedroom of the safe house. Rain had just stopped falling in the north of Trinidad, but the streets were clear down in the Port of Spain and in Cascade.

It was getting close to show time. Like a fighter, I slipped into my ritual. I stretched for forty minutes. Did push-ups. Threw a hundred kicks. Then for the umpteenth time I went over the plans for the Carlton Savannah. I drove from the southern part of the island, from the safe house that was past the lighthouse, went back into Port of Spain, rode the world's largest traffic circle, exited that roundabout and found my way to the Carlton, to the small car park next to the pool, left my ride staged one wall away from where the late-night party would be. I left a wig, a change of clothing. Since I had no driver I left the doors unlocked, keys in the ignition. I staged weapons as well. Then I saw it was after eight p.m. Rain was falling. I walked back up the road that led to the Hilton, checked in as Samantha Greymouth, went to the room, showered, changed, checked myself in the mirror, then I turned the AC up and waited.

Minutes before eleven the phone in my room rang. King Killer was in the lobby. When I exited the elevator I saw that he had arrived in a limo, a murderous Prince Charming to collect his deadly Cinderella.

King Killer set the pace for the night, kissed me on my neck right away.

Penetration would be required to pull off this job.

I'd take one for the team, let them know I was committed to the cause. The target was a good-looking man. I could think of worse chores. Maybe I'd finally take one for me too, take one and be able to forget about Johnny Parker. Take one from a handsome gunta and be able to put Florida behind me.

King Killer put his soft lips on my neck and a chill ran up and down and up and down my spine and settled between my thighs. I trembled, then pulled his face to mine, gave him my tongue, played cat and mouse with our tongues, heated up the lobby. Not since Johnny Parker had I felt a tingle like that.

King Killer admired my lips, hair, cleavage,

said, "Had no idea you would look so stunning."

We French kissed. We kissed again. Then we tongue-kissed a third time.

I said, "We better leave before the growler gets too moist."

His driver drove us around the world's largest roundabout. King Killer rubbed my thighs as he pointed out the notable "Magnificent Seven" landmarks set around Queen's Park Savannah, ran his finger across my vagina as we passed Queen's Royal College, leaned over and kissed me as we passed a fairy-tale-looking Stollmeyer's Castle. He moved my dress from my shoulder, pointed out German Renaissance architecture as he rolled my nipple between his finger and thumb, pointed out French architecture and leaned in, licked my nipple, the president's house, White Hall, Roman Catholic archbishop's house just words he mumbled as he sucked my nipple like a baby. He stopped feeding long enough to tell his driver to make another trip around the Savannah, and drive slower.

He put his face between my legs. I closed my eyes and my fingers dug into the seat.

He ate my pussy. He ate my pussy well.

Like Johnny Parker had done thirty nights in a row.

Then King Killer sat back, drank wine, and smiled.

I adjusted my dress, grinned, returned the

same wicked expression.

Minutes later the limo driver was letting us out in the tight driveway at the posh and contemporary Carlton Savannah, a hotel like the W in the States. Town Cars were in a line to let their passengers out. The Laventille Killers had booked every room. Drug money gave many the opportunities of a lifetime, something going to college for four years rarely did. The LKs owned Trinidad. They had so much control that the newspapers and television stations never mentioned them for fear of them doing a blackout, killing them and all the members of their family. I looked up in the air, my attention drawn by the bright lights and the hard beat from soca at the top of the chic five-star hotel. The main party was on the roof. From where I stood I could tell no one was downstairs at Waterbaby Bar by the pool. No one was at the two bars or the two restaurants, Relish and Casa. Fuck. The self-important men had shut down everything except for the top level of the hotel, had everything locked down like they were the Secret Service guarding the president. That had not been in the intel. They had flowcharts on the walls of the safe house, had delivered me a doorstopper, and this was not the plan. The instant we entered the hotel, security was searching every man who wasn't an LK, and they searched all the women, first with a metal detector, then a pat-down that felt like molestation, more foreplay than I'd had in the last month.

We made it to the elevator and I was searched again.

My intel had said that the party was going to be on the main level, poolside. I had staged my exit based on that information. I could have done the hit and if anything went south, could've been over the wall in two blinks of an eye. My escape vehicle was still there, tinted windows, keys in ignition, had seen it as we pulled up in our limo. Evidently some-one had changed the plans and the gathering wasn't right off the lobby. It was too late to turn back. When we got on the elevator, the attendant pushed the button for the top. With no workable plan, I'd have to effect a hit twelve stories high. I cursed.

King Killer asked, "Are you okay?"

"Lifts make this Kiwi a wee bit nervous. Bit claustrophobic."

When the elevator door opened on the 2,400-square-foot rooftop, soca ruled the air and I stepped into the party of all parties. It looked like people who were Roman Cath-olic, Anglican, Seventh-day Adventists, Pres-byterians, Methodists, Jehovah's Witnesses, Spiritual Baptists, and Orisha by day all had the heart of lust and wanted to wine at night. It was as colorful and extravagant as Carnival in Rio. Most of the women had on sexy, easy-to-take-off dresses, but walking in the crowd were dozens of women in high heels, feathers, beads, and Carnival costumes, only most of the women were topless. Beautiful women were dancing with suited men, smoking ganja, drinking hard liquor and wine, partying, wining to soca.

Some women were giving men oral in the open, but no one seemed to notice.

I said, "Wow. Looks like I've stepped into real-life Internet porn."

"You wanted to have a night in Trinidad that you will never forget."

The moment I exited the elevator I was stopped, then I was searched again. A shapely woman searched me. She was more percipient than she appeared to be. She held her hands over my vagina and anus and asked me to cough. She was serious. I thought that this humiliation was the end, but she wasn't done. It took a woman to notice my hair sticks, Swarovski and rhinestone chopsticks, plum flower in an antique brass finish. With a kind smile she asked me to remove both. I did and let my long mane fall.

She looked the hair sticks over. If she had found the release buttons she would have been surprised. One had a removable tip that would expose two inches of steel sharp as a scalpel.

The second had its tip dipped in the deadliest of poisons.

She said, "I have to keep them."

"Those are priceless family heirlooms from my long-dead nana in New Zealand."

The bitch ignored me, handed me a claim check number in her next breath.

King Killer touched my shoulder. "She is only following procedure."

"Those are priceless."

"They will be returned."

Behind the rude girl with the fuck-you-foreign-tall-and-elitist-bitch attitude were dozens of French combs and hair chopsticks. She pointed to items taken from other women, none as extravagant as mine. Again she inspected my hair pins but never found the release button, was über-fascinated by the detail, their beauty. She regarded me with envy and disdain. The outsider in her West Indian world.

I let that go, focused, walked like a model, slow steps, hips moving in a tick-tock motion, breasts firm yet with a subtle bounce, and took in the fete. "This is wild. I thought this was a Christian island."

"Old Testament tonight. My organization, we prefer to follow the Old Testament."

"An eye for an eye."

"We do what needs to be done. Turning a cheek has never helped a man advance in this world."

"So, you rich and handsome blokes are fans of the vicious God who had fits and destroyed all. A God who didn't hesitate to destroy every man, woman, and infant, cattle, sheep, camels, and donkeys."

He asked, "Are you against revenge?"

"I am a pacifist. I don't hold the bleak belief that vengeance offers the only recourse in a mad, violent world. Revenge turns people into the shadow of the enemies they despise."

"All that aside, is this type of celebration too much for you?"

"It's perfect. I'd never be able to do anything like this with my husband."

"Let me show my stunning date off to a few people."

He introduced his Kiwi catch to a handful of politicians, men who were in a conversation with lawyers and men from South American drug cartels, men who'd done kidnappings and beheadings then gone to eat ice cream with their children, men who insisted on touching my body, regarded me as a comfort woman. One of the men thought that I was one of many women who had been trafficked from Europe, and offered to buy me. When King Killer told him I wasn't a slave, the man laughed and offered to buy me for the night, told me how stunning I was. With a grin, I told him I considered his offer a compliment, then turned down the payday. Other men told me that they wished they had met me first.

King Killer said, "This Circassian beauty, for now, is my personal lover. Respect her."

"She is beautiful, spirited, and elegant and desirable."

I led him away, led him to the edge of the building, gave him kiss after kiss, feigned like I was in awe of the view of Cascade, the Savannah, and the grounds of the prime minister's residence, did that so I could see if there was a way to do the hit, then escape from being thirteen levels above the ground. Twelve stories plus the entrance floor was too high to jump, but not high enough to use a parachute.

King Killer caressed me, ran his hand up and down my bare back and settled on two handfuls of buttocks, pushed his erection into my thigh and tried to grind and wine on the Y.

He said, "Tonight, when we are done with this part of the night, I will take you to the WOW Suite, will fuck you where Queen Elizabeth II stayed, where Nicki Minaj stayed, will fuck you in the same bed."

"I can hardly wait for this part of the night to end so I can wallow where others have wallowed."

"I will show you sunrise from here. The most beautiful sunrise on the island is right here."

He did a line of premium cocaine, insisted that I do the same, frowned when I declined the nose candy. I told him that my job required random drug testing so I had to avoid the white horse. Then he was hyped, showed me off to everyone. Members from the Senate and the House of Representatives. Wanted me to be seen by men and women who laundered money and supplied arms, thugs who stood in a group showing one another their prized firearms. Men who were in a debate with the People's National Movement and the United National Congress. Politicians whose support fell across ethnic lines. People chatting in English, Trinidadian and Tobagonian Creole, Spanish, French, and Bhojpuri.

Many people looked me in my eyes. Too many glossed-over eyes saw this Kiwi face up close.

War Machine arrived, stepped off the elevator like he was the king of the king of kings.

Right away King Killer held my hand and took me to the LKs' CEO and leader.

War Machine shook his head, looked me up and down, jaw tight, and he greeted me with unkindness. His jacket was open, his holstered gun unhidden. He was a handsome man, a well-groomed and suited man whose face had beauty marks earned from living in the slums as a child.

War Machine said, "Who the fuck are you?"

Six

King Killer said, "Relax, cousin. This is Samantha Greymouth. She was a last-minute addition."

"She wasn't vetted."

Strong shoulders. Accent almost British. Very proper. Very educated. Very rude.

I said, " 'Vetted'? I came to party, to lime as you say, not to apply for a job with your organization."

"We don't let strangers into our fold. Everyone has been vetted, a background check has been run on everyone who stepped onto that lift but you. My cousin seems to have forgotten protocol."

King Killer said, "I vouch for her. I vouch for this beautiful Kiwi one hundred percent."

"Should that be good enough?"

"If not for me, we would not be as powerful as we are. We would not be. Have you forgotten?"

"Cousin, please. I was there. I know the truth. Let's not let revised history derail us."

"Let's not argue. Don't embarrass me. Mrs. Greymouth is already here."

"We have rules, cousin. We are as strong as we are because of our standards."

King Killer said, "Ask the others. That is how we resolve this matter quickly."

War Machine snapped, "I am the final word in all matters. I resolve all matters."

"Karleen is final word. Without my sister, the power that comes from the people vanishes."

"I am final word. I will always be final word. Never forget that."

"Cousin, let's not fight over this simple issue. We are and always have been more like brothers."

"We are brothers. In my heart we are brothers, but our cause is greater than blood."

"This one time, ask. If the other leaders feel the same, then I will remove her, as you see fit."

That was a threat on my life: *As you see fit.* I pretended to remain confused.

War Machine paused, nodded, then motioned like he was the Obama of Trinidad.

This was not the plan, but in the business of killing, nothing ever went as planned.

Other men came over and I was overwhelmed. War Machine called over the gunta they called Appaloosa, Appaloosa being a man who stood close to seven feet tall. He had fingers like erect penises. The print on his pants told me that his penis was a concealed weapon. The ultimate Alpha male.

Another gunta named Guerrero was called over. His name meant warrior. He was tipsy, came over with two women, both topless, and they waited on him as he came to see what the issue was.

Then came the gunta who used the name Kandinsky. He looked like Wentworth Miller.

King Killer. War Machine. Appaloosa. Guerrero. Kandinsky.

The top five men of this group stood facing me, evaluating me with militaristic eyes.

Five men who carried at least ten guns on their person had me surrounded.

War Machine repeated, "Security violation. She wasn't vetted, but was allowed past security."

Again King Killer repeated, "I vouch for her. Mrs. Greymouth is from New Zealand. She wants to have a good time with us before she leaves. I brought her to give her an unforgettable night."

"This isn't a tourist destination. This is a private gathering. You should be more concerned with the guest of honor being late to arrive than sullying this occasion with some strange red legs."

Appaloosa looked me up and down, reached out, touched my chin with his penis-like fingers.

He said, "Wait. Wait. Physically she is amazing, that is without a doubt. She has a body like the French dancer Aya. Hardly any fat, at least none that I can see. This one is exceptional."

Again War Machine reiterated, "But there is protocol, even for Mrs. Greymouth."

I said, "No need to be a bloody yahoo. No need to be rude and act like you're a flower-pot because you've got a hole in your bum. I'm not from Eketahuna or Timbuktu or Waikikamukau and I'm not a fuckwit and I'll never be able to haunt a ten-room house. Let me translate: I'm a good-looking bitch. I have options. If I'm not wanted at this over-the-top shindig and cock-sucking coke festival, I care two-thirds of five-eighths of fuck-all. I will be more than happy to get my A into G and find another cock for my laughing gear to please before it's time for my morning tea. Now, gentlemen, pardon my candor, but I'm not one to piss around, and I don't appreci-ate being treated like I'm one sammy short of a picnic, so be kind enough to escort me back to the bloody lift, allow me to claim my fam-ily heirlooms from the rude wench who all but finger-fucked me, and I can arrange a taxi from the lobby. Beautiful women up here, but I bet if their brains were barbed wire they couldn't fence a dunny. My work colleagues are at a lounge on Ariapita Avenue, so I can just buzz them and go there and lime and have my drinks, get well mounted, can still enjoy myself before I leave here and return home to the land of the long white cloud."

The men stared at me, savage expressions, tense necks, killer glares, and one by one the men who had been born the lowest of the low, men who had been murderers most of their lives, they grinned.

West Indian men being talked to that way by an irritated foreign woman, not a good thing.

I had interrupted them. I had gone hard, spoken up, and refused to be invisible.

War Machine and the rest of the intellectual savages watched me, death in their eyes.

A soca jam by Machel Montano played, the roof exploded, and the revelers jumped up like it was Carnival, fists pumping, red, white, and black flags waving, but the men facing me didn't jump, didn't pump fists, didn't wave the flag of Trinidad. They glowered at me; it felt like I was about to be beheaded.

Appaloosa's massive hand squeezed my ass over and over, like an anxious heartbeat, said, "He vouches for the sexy Kiwi. She is his responsibility. Do we all stand in agreement?"

Tense seconds passed before War Machine nodded. Then one by one, the rest nodded as well.

With a kind gesture, I removed Appaloosa's hand and penis-like fingers from my ass.

War Machine smiled and said, "By the end

of the night, maybe she'll learn to be polite. One must have certain etiquette when they step into someone else's country, especially when done so uninvited."

I said, "It was not my intention to offend. There has been a misunderstanding. I could just leave."

"You're here now. My cousin has used his influence and brought you through many levels of security. Enjoy the night, Mrs. Greymouth. Enjoy the night."

King Killer led me to a tented section reserved for the top members. We stepped inside, then around a girl giving a tall and lean gunta head as a muscular gunta pounded her from the rear.

The rooftop lounge was filled with women, their high-priced designer clothing recklessly thrown across the colorful sofas. Girls sipped martinis, sucked golden cocks, laughed like this was their normal way of living. I pulled off my little black dress, but kept on my luxury lingerie. King Killer smiled, led me to his area, to his sofa, sat me down, got on his knees in front of me, pulled my panties to the side, French kissed my sex. His tongue shocked my system like I had been injected with coke, smack, meth, made me wonder if he had put coke on his tongue before he went to feast. I held his head, made soft moans, and spied the people on the rooftop, looked for the target to appear.

I had to make King Killer stop tongue-fucking me like a maniac.

He said, "What's wrong, Sam?"

"Let me make you come, Neziah. All day I've dreamed of making you come."

I unzipped his pants. Spat in my hands, then stroked what felt like concrete.

One of the guntas came over, brought him a Stag beer, brought me a martini.

I said, "I prefer a beer. Bring me one in a can. Unopened. Thanks."

King Killer shook his head, held the martini to my closed lips, encouraged me to open my mouth, smiled and held my face until half of the drink was gone. Then he sat back and sipped his beer.

He reached into his pocket, handed me a condom.

I said, "Not here, Neziah."

"You wanted excitement, Sam."

"I do."

"So here, Mrs. Greymouth. Here and now is where it starts."

The top guntas watched me, all but Appaloosa. He had moved away, distracted by someone who had just arrived. Second- and third-tier thugs did the same, studied me and their killer of kings.

Using my teeth, I tore open the condom, started rolling it over King Killer's crooked cock, a long and narrow cock that was shaped like a scythe. The rooftop shifted. I blinked a few times. Light-headed.

A second surge of light-headedness. Then a chill, the night air raising the hair on my neck.

I asked, "What was in that drink?".

He kissed me again, kissed me and put my hand on his stiff cock, encouraged me to masturbate him, then pulled me to his lap, rubbed his length against me, tried to work his way inside of me.

He said, "When you have gone back to New Zealand, you will remember this night."

As I raised my hips and prepared to let him inside, everything bad went deeper into hell.

SEVEN

Minutes before, when I was being confronted by hard-faced War Machine, another politician had arrived, another minister of something considered important on the island of Trinidad, another politico on the LKs' payroll, still not the target.

The politico's tender mistress was on his right arm. She was the issue. She was a glamorous Punjabi in a sexy sari. She was a teenager with a face made for Bollywood and a body made for porn. Her untouchable beauty created the uproar.

The politician was more than twice the girl's age. Old sperm and young eggs. Young eggs deserved young sperm to make a strong baby. Inebriated Appaloosa found that an insult.

While I had been taken away by King Killer, when I had begun masturbating him, at that moment the hulking Appaloosa had gone to the politician, told him his mistress was too fucking beautiful for his old ass, demanded that he hand over his Desi bitch to a younger man without hesitation.

Appaloosa was serious. His suit coat was open, his gun on display but holstered.

The argument had become heated, louder than the music, stole everyone's attention.

Now as I hovered over an erection, hell arrived and broke loose of its chains. Before skin was broken, King Killer pushed me to the side. I fell to the floor and knocked over a table of drinks. Not concerned with me, he jumped up, then he grabbed his pants and headed toward Appaloosa.

The politician fumed, made fists, told Appaloosa, "Back the fuck off. Fucking respect me."

The small man stood tall and told the oversize gunta who had fallen off of a beanstalk that the woman had chosen him. To respect that. The hulk-size gunta knocked the politician down, stomped him. As the man rolled in pain, Appaloosa faced the beautiful woman, grabbed her arm, pulled her to him, pulled away her clothing, and took her to the floor. She was horrified. When the dazed politician was able to sit up, he saw Appaloosa was between the open legs of his mistress, viciously fucking her as soca played, as everyone wined and watched. Her expression said she wanted him to fuck and get it over with and have the nightmare end. She cried and bit her bottom lip, trembled and looked at the older man she had been with, the weak man who had failed to protect her. The politician rose up and attacked the gunta. He kicked Appaloosa in the head, caused the gunta to stop and roll away from the mistress.

The LKs attacked the politician, became rabid pit bulls. War Machine led the charge, and King Killer tucked his condom-covered erection inside of his pants, joined in, and showed me how disgusting he really was, became an evil motherfucker in a $2,000 suit, following the rage of War Machine, Guerrero, Kandinsky, a dozen others, all howling like wild animals. Appaloosa joined in, gave the man his rage, gave him the ultimate rage. They attacked the man the way ruthless gangs in L.A. attacked their unarmed prey, the way San Salvadorians attacked their enemy. Naked ingenues cheered like they were in a coliseum, like they were watching lions attack Christians. The LKs left the politician battered and broken, all but unrecognizable, left his defiled mistress abused, distressed, and cowering in horror. The LKs surrounded the older man. The inebriated and drugged crowd cheered.

Handsome and suited guntas took out their cocks and pissed on the injured man.

The vetted people roared like they were at a European football match and a goal had been scored.

The mistress screamed. She scampered away only to bump into more young guntas. One grabbed her by the neck and pulled her with him, took her to the ground as if she wasn't done.

Beaten, battered, the politico refused to admit defeat. As he lay bleeding he snapped, "I will go to the *Trinidad Express,* will show my wounds to *Newsday,* will send photos to the *Guardian,* will take to Twitter and Facebook and tell the world the truth. Savages. You're nothing better than savages. There will be no New Trinidad. Motherfuckers, I will expose the five husbands and Diamond Dust."

Diamond Dust. That was the handle given to Mrs. Ramjit, War Machine's wife.

War Machine said, "You threaten my wife? You fucking come here and threaten all we have built?"

War Machine motioned, raised three fingers, then pointed to the edge of the rooftop.

Guntas cheered. They roared like savages and did some sort of battle cry.

Six different muscle-strong guntas picked the politico up, grabbing him by his legs and arms, then rushed him through the cheering crowd and raced toward the edge of the five-star hotel. Without hesitation they threw the piss-stained politico into the night, sent him on a twelve-floor swan dive.

The middle-aged man's death scream came

to an abrupt stop, as did his fall.

Model-esque women from a dozen nations grabbed their garments and heels, stopped giving blow jobs, licked the corners of their lips; women in Carnival costumes took a final hit of cocaine, picked up their drinks, and scurried toward the elevator, some wining to soca, Bunji Garlin singing that he was ready for the road. I had to make a decision. The job wasn't done, but the target wasn't there. Stress choked me. My intel had been bad. I recovered my little black dress and hurried with chipping feet, re-dressed on the crowded elevator as international women continued to laugh and dance and party and drink. Skyscraper-high stilettos clip-clopped across floors and moved through Trinidad's dream hotel.

While I decamped into the night with a crowd of drunken vixens, many of them laughed and danced, said that they had had the best night of their lives, planned to go over to the Avenue and find another party. Legs turned weak. Balance tried to fail me. Surrounded by the inebriated, by women on ecstasy and cocaine, I wasn't alone. I cursed a thousand times. Once off the lift, the crowd hurried past the restaurant, moved like it was the running of the bulls, pulled me in their arrogant current. By the time I made it to the reception desk, I blinked over and over, saw him through the double glass doors that led to Cascade. The target had arrived, flanked by two bodyguards, both men with their weapons drawn.

The target. The target. The target. Those words echoed in my head.

The man they wanted dead before he gave a wicked speech.

I had to kill him. I had to kill him. I had to kill him. I had to kill him now.

I reached into my hair. No chopsticks. The rude girl upstairs. The bitch had taken them.

They were twelve stories above where I stood, and it was impossible to go back for them.

The target and I made eye contact as I passed, were shuffled close enough to touch. He looked into my faux hazel eyes, grinned, then frowned like some alarm had gone off inside his head.

His guard pulled him upstream as the crowd forced me downstream.

The target stared at me, never moved his eyes away, then he disappeared.

Everything was blurry for a moment, maybe only for a second, then my feet were being stepped on and I was crushed in the malicious crowd. Everyone had stopped chipping. Many had stopped to stare at the landing spot of the dead politician. He was a broken doll, his body in an impossible position, an expired contortionist. He had landed on his head. He had landed on his damn head.

Dora the Explorer sitting next to Lassie on a Yellow Submarine.

A few women laughed while men saw the brain matter and threw up.

Others took photos, made videos, were Instagramming and BBMing the world.

I blinked a dozen times, the world out of focus, the stars over my head too close to Earth.

I wasn't done. This contract wasn't completed. I always did my fuckin' job.

I rushed down the driveway, broke to the right, to the car park one wall away from the swimming area, retrieved the bag that I had staged, hopped inside of the vehicle I had left staged, started the engine, threw away my heels, and was about to drive away, but that would be failure.

I called the Barbarians. "MX . . . MX . . . MX-401. Code red. Code red."

"Line secure. What's the problem?"

Head spinning, words starting to slur and stick together, I told the Barbarians what had happened. This had gone to hell and I needed to be extracted right away, to have passage on the next flight out of Piarco International Airport and I didn't care where the plane was headed on the globe.

I said, "The location . . . was changed from the intel . . . you supplied . . . moved to the roof. They did full body search . . . took the chopsticks . . . I had ordered. Felt like . . .

everything went wrong."

They told me that I had to stay. This contract was a done deal. The man behind the red doors told the go-between to direct me to stay and see the job through; there was no other option.

I said, "You said that this night would be the only opportunity to effect this hit."

"You left the event?"

"Everyone vacated the event when it became a murder party. Politicians, clergy, drug dealers, they all left before the spinning blue lights could get here. Then the target walked in as I passed the lobby."

"You were in. All you had to do was stay where you were, wait for the target to arrive."

"They beat and murdered a man, raped a woman in front of a hundred people."

"That changes nothing. Our contract is still on, still has a deadline, Reaper."

"That changed everything. I create crime scenes, but I will not work on top of one."

"We will be forced to make it happen tomorrow."

"There are no events tomorrow night, none that were outlined in the intel."

"Daytime. He has a bank drop tomorrow afternoon, a last-minute photo op before he goes to make the speech. It was added to his agenda just before he arrived in Trinidad. It will have to do."

"You have someone on the inside?"

"We have new intel."

"Has that been verified, or is it as fucked-up as the info you had regarding the party that was supposed to be on the fucking ground level at the pool, then ended up on the roof-fucking-top?"

"It has been verified. He made an appointment at Scotiabank in Port of Spain."

"You expect me to do a hit at a bank during the day? During high-traffic hours?"

"We need it done before nightfall tomorrow. It will be the last chance to make it happen."

"When did you forget about his bad idea and pull that worse idea out of your ass?"

"It's only been on the table for the last two hours as backup. We had hoped you would have succeeded tonight, but you have let us down. Get to the safe house. We will send you the updates."

"This is bullshit."

I told them about the way the target had looked at me as he was being rushed inside. It made me anxious. The main guntas had seen me up close. I was disguised, but they had seen me up close. I had been compromised. It was a gut instinct.

I said, "There will be no tomorrow, not after they killed a man tonight."

"Don't be paranoid, MX-401."

"I'm not fuckin' paranoid. I just watched them rape a young girl and throw a man from a fuckin' roof. There were a hundred people up there and she was raped for sport, raped while the man she was with was beaten half to death and pissed on, then the monsters threw the man from the roof."

"Calm down, MX-401."

"Look, bitch, go behind the red doors, pick up the phone, and let me talk to the man at the top."

"Get to your safe house. Stay there until instructed otherwise."

"No."

"No? What does 'no' mean?"

"Until the man behind the double red doors calls, I'm sticking to the plan."

"Listen, you arrogant bitch. Get to the northeast of the island to the safe house."

"I'm not a fuck-up. I will see this bullshit plan through. I'm going back in, weapon-heavy. I can get in before the police show up. If not, I can walk right by them. I'll go floor to floor and find the target's suite. Guards will be outside of his room, that will be the tell. I'll get by them and do the fuckin' job."

"We will make it so you can do this tomorrow. Those are your new orders."

"No way am I going to walk into a bank to kill a man."

"And those orders have been double verified."

"I will do this my way, not according to that plan, and it will be done tonight."

"That's the main issue. We're an organization that has a structure. We have a pecking order. You're unpredictable. Random. You take the simplest task and make it as fucking complicated as possible. We sent you on this job and you were to stay until it was complete, and you failed."

"I will finish this tonight. There is nothing complicated about that."

On fire, I killed the call and dropped the phone on the floor.

They called and called and I ignored the ringing of the phone.

I pulled on combat boots but didn't change the rest of my clothes, didn't pull on a vest, didn't change into dark clothing. A flush of heat attacked me. Dizzy. I grabbed at my backpack, trying to hurry, taking deep breath after deep breath. I slapped my face over and over, tried to shake off whatever had been put in my drink, now afraid, drowsy, and angry as fuck. I could do this tonight. I was strong. Could get my breath, shake off the poison. Had to. Needed to hurry back to the hotel, had to find where the guards had taken the target, could threaten whoever was at the front desk and get the information. As I sat in the vehicle, I started digging inside my bag, pulling out a .9mm, pulling out M84 stun grenades. Hard. I would have to go in hard, flash and bang, shooting off rounds, shooting guntas.

I looked at the end of my wrist and saw six hands, each hand holding a gun. Each finger weighed a thousand pounds, my tongue a ton of red meat. Soon I was barely blinking. Soon I was almost paralyzed. I fought it. Opened and closed my hands in slow motion. Lifted my arms.

As people rushed to cars to leave the area, as a dozen sirens zoomed toward the Carlton Savannah, I grabbed my hair, accidentally removed my wig, dropped it in my lap, cursing soft curses as my world started spinning, as the world went black, that heavy gun in hand, the world went away.

I died.

EIGHT

I saw my mother. That meant I had gone to hell.

I saw her standing outside the car, six feet tall, slender, her brown skin so beautiful.

She hated me. I hated her because she hated me.

When I closed my eyes and opened them again, she was gone, now replaced with many men in Italian suits. King Killer, War Machine, Appaloosa, and the rest of the savages were outside my car window.

They reached for their holstered weapons.

I reached for my gun. It wasn't there. It wasn't on the floor of the car.

Rapid gunfire attacked me.

Hard taps on the tinted window woke me, taps that were like rapid gunfire. I jerked awake, head pounding, dress stuck to my skin, one breast exposed, sweat running down my face and back.

TTPS. Trinidad and Tobago Police Service

were outside my driver-side window.

Fighting to regain consciousness, I adjusted my clothing, tried to remember what had happened.

The sun had come up. Police cars were in the lot with mine. The gun was at my foot. My flash and bang were on the floor. I let the window down. Raised my hand to my eyes to block the sun.

The officer had seen me through the front windshield.

He asked, "Are you okay?"

"I'm fine."

"We thought you had overdosed."

"Wow. All these police cars. What's going on?"

"Were you at the Carlton Savannah?"

"I was on Ariapita Avenue, then had to drive back to my hotel, got lost, then felt sick and pulled over here, closed my eyes. I think someone at the bar put something in my drink. I passed out."

"You're American."

Once again a Hitchcock blonde, I nodded, said, "From Brooklyn. Down here on vacation. Broke up with my boyfriend. Got into it with his ex-wife. Long story short, I came here to drink and get away."

"We're glad that you're okay, but did you notice the woman in the next car?"

In the same parking lot, in the car next to where I was parked, a woman had been found dead. She was still in her car, body not covered. It was the girl who'd admired my hair sticks. She had stolen them. She had worked off the cap to the stick that housed the poison and that poison had touched her flesh.

She had been paralyzed, then each organ had shut down.

It had taken her two minutes to die, which had to have felt like an eternity.

That method of closing this account was no longer an option.

The officer asked, "Was her car here last night when you parked?"

"Didn't pay attention. It was dark. I was drunk. Lot of cars were here."

They had just found her dead, headlights on, engine still running. She had vomited, shat herself, and died, my beautiful hair sticks in her lap. A picture of her child was on the dashboard.

Grunting, I rubbed my eyes, hand combed my wavy, boy-short hair, asked, "What time is it?"

"Quarter past noon."

"Noon?"

"How long have you been parked here sleeping?"

"Eleven, almost twelve hours."

"Still drunk?"

"Head hurts. I have to pee. Other than that, I'm okay."

"Lucky you didn't get robbed. Be advised, we have a murder almost every day here."

I assured the officer from TTPS that I was fine, just parched, then asked for directions to the Hyatt in Port of Spain. I rubbed my eyes again and sped away, zoomed back toward the safe house.

The safe house was far away, at least three hours, northeast in Toco, past the ancient Chacachacare Lighthouse. At high noon there was high traffic. Woozy, I stopped thirty minutes into the drive. I had to face reality. With these congested roads, with construction, there was no time to go to the safe house, no time to get a new wig, no time to create a new persona. No time to sleep off the drugs. I checked the online pages for TV6 and the *Trinidad Express*. I checked the Internet, Facebook, and Twitter feeds as well. It was as if last night had been a dream. Hours ago when the police arrived at the Carlton Savannah, they found the dead politician, his tribute to Dora the Explorer untouched, but no one had seen anything, nor had anyone heard a scream. The woman who had been raped, she had vanished.

I had expected to see her on the front page, screaming to the world that she had been wronged.

She wasn't my concern.

A rude girl had stolen what didn't belong to her and died from curiosity.

A thief gets what a thief gets. I despised thieves. She wasn't my concern either.

Sun high, clouds forming, sweating profusely, I still had a racist politician to kill.

I was awake, but I remained in a slow-moving cloud, sweating down Bad Dream Boulevard.

I called the Barbarians, got my rep, and asked, "Which bank, where, and at what fuckin' time?"

"You have thirty minutes."

"I'm at least forty minutes from that part of the island."

"Thirty minutes."

NINE

Mouth dry, coughing, squinting, blowing my horn over and over, cursing, speeding, and running people and cars off the clogged roads, I searched for Scotiabank in the city of Port of Spain, modern and cosmopolitan alongside the traditional and the derelict, skyscrapers huddled next to old zinc structures. Downtown was now and then. When I hit the narrow roads into town, too much fucking traffic. The square ran down both sides of an island that was as wide as a street and filled with vendors, shoppers, and loiterers. Looked at my watch. Kicked on the windshield wipers. Turned music up louder to keep me alert: Burning Flames. Passed Gillette's Building Supplies. Nelson Street. Catholic cathedral. George Street. Express Newspapers. Abercromby Street. It was somewhere, right fuckin' here in Independence Square. It was here in Port of Spain. Was like being in Times Square for the first time. I had no plan. Hadn't checked out the location. Was flying blind. There was no time to change identities, so I pulled on the red wig, the hair now wild and unkempt, and returned to being the Kiwi, maybe a homeless version of the same diva from the night before, my makeup smeared from being in a date-rape coma all night, drugs in my system battling with the adrenaline rush in my system. No time to stage a secondary vehicle. No time to plot three escape routes.

No scanner to know the position of law enforcement.

No time to remove my barely-there dress from last night, a dress that when accosted by the sunlight would show my body as if I were walking in the nude; no time to take off the combat boots I had on. I didn't remember putting them on, but they were on my feet, so they would stay on my feet for now.

On foreign soil I would have to go inside a bank I had never seen before.

Had no idea what type of security would be present, didn't know what barriers existed.

All the new intel said was that the target was there to close the loan on a commercial building that was being financed with dirty money. He had come out of his hiding place and was the most hated man in Trinidad to press flesh, take photos, kiss babies, hug men, and kiss sexy women on their cheeks.

Something else went wrong. Ever since I had landed on this boot-shaped rock, something was always going wrong. I parked my vehicle, left the engine running, and spotted the Town Car that was being used to transport the target. The car was double-parked, lights flashing, traffic backed up and going around their arrogance. The two guntas assigned to guard the politician had stayed inside the car.

Walking by unsuspecting people, oversize purse over my shoulder, I pulled out my gun and screwed on the suppressor as people saw me coming across Independence Square and hurried to get out of my way. Just as I came up on the Town Car, as droves of people moved in both directions on the sidewalk, both guntas looked in my direction. The one nearest me saw the gun in my hand, down at my side.

He saw the eyes of the messenger of death, of a mechanic, of an assassin.

They saw a street preacher ready to write her sermon in lead to the condemned.

They saw MX-401. They saw Reaper.

I raised my weapon, a stranger in their town, and shot first, shot second, shot third, shot fourth, and prayed they didn't have God on their side. They didn't. Old Man Reaper had said no one did.

Then I spat into the rain, adjusted my bodacious wig, and put my gun inside my purse but kept my finger on the trigger, moved through skies that had darkened, walked into the bank.

A member of the clergy was inside the bank. The clergyman was in the same business as the politician. The LKs owned him. He had been on the rooftop of the Carlton Savannah the night before. I had met him before he was sent away to engage in coitus with two young girls. His being here now, it was a coincidence. The clergyman had seen the politician photo op and rushed over to say hello to his friend, had patted him on his shoulder, called for his attention as I walked through the glass doors.

The target was there. All that mattered was that the target was still there.

The damp soles of my boots squeaked, but I didn't hear the noise.

I moved in the target's direction, my right hand easing my gun from my oversize purse.

The target turned around, then stood to shake hands with the priest, and at that moment he saw me walking his way. An alarm went off inside of his head, as if he knew. I saw it in his eyes.

Then came the Spanish Inquisition. No one ever expected the Spanish Inquisition.

The politico pulled a gun from a black briefcase that was open on the desk in front of him, and in a crowded bank he started firing at me. He panicked. Without pause, suddenly on the defensive, jaw tight, teeth clenched, my hand trapped inside of my purse, I pulled the trigger over and over, blew holes in the bag, was shooting, shooting, no longer the mechanic, no longer the messenger of death, no longer the assassin, and now he was the one shooting first while I prayed that I lived, now I had become the condemned shooting to stay alive. The drugs in my system. I felt the drugs reignite in my system.

The first bullet I fired hit the clergyman. I was off due to the drugs, the shot a bad shot.

My lead created pink mist, opened the head of the clergyman, who stood between the target and me, a man of the cloth who ran to the right and stepped into a chunk of lead being sent from my projectile emitter. My second bullet caught the target in the leg. He screamed, lost his balance, and as he fell and fired at me, I fired at him. My next shot hit his chest and was caught by his bulletproof vest.

I pulled the gun from my bag, let the bag fall to the floor, and fired like I had been trained by Old Man Reaper after that job in Dallas, when he had taken my training to another level, when he had tortured me for sixty days, made me stronger, made me a warrior. The target's head caught the next projectile. Dora and Kermit the Frog eating a ham sandwich. Then I stood over him, frowned at his gun, at his vest, added two more shots to his head. For trying to kill me.

I didn't like it when someone tried to kill me.

Not until then did my hearing return, not until then did I hear the screams. Every wild shot from the target's gun had hit a customer. He was not a gunman, yet like every amateur in America he had a gun.

A security guard raised his weapon, but I beat him to the draw. He took a shot in the shoulder, and the pain took him to the ground. My next shot left him in the waiting room to see Jesus's daddy.

Then I looked at the rest of the people in the bank, the young, the old, children, men, women, they were all down on the ground, all shaking, shivering, afraid for their lives.

I grabbed an umbrella that a customer had dropped in the panic, hurried out of the bank with my gun at my side, and expected to see a hundred LKs waiting on me. People had congregated where the bodyguards had been killed. Traffic had come to a stop. The malicious were in the mix.

Cell phones were out. Facebook. BBM. Instagram. Twitter.

Someone opened the passenger-side car door, and the body fell out into the street.

Four people dead. Maybe a dozen wounded.

Dead bodyguards. Dead bank guard. Dead politician.

Collateral damage inside that bank, bleeding out.

Blood flowed in two directions, the Nile reaching for the Mississippi.

The living becoming the dead, waiting to chat with Jesus's daddy.

Dora the Explorer many times over.

I let the umbrella open and strolled into the rain, walked by that crowd like I was leaving the Trincity Mall. A woman had dropped her shopping bag, horrified at the sight of the dead men. I picked up her bag and kept moving. The shootout inside the bank had taken twenty seconds at most. Twenty seconds that had felt like twenty-hundred years. Two weapon-heavy LKs were dead on the side of the road.

If those guntas hadn't been dead, after that shootout my exit would have been impossible.

I would've ended up in a second shootout with those minions, maybe dead in the street.

As I left collateral damage behind me, the echo of sirens came from all directions.

Police. Ambulances. The news station was in the area, would be there within moments.

Even then what struck me as odd was that I had walked into the bank armed.

No alarm had sounded when I walked inside with my gun, but a teller had pushed the button.

I made it to the car, dropped the umbrella, pulled into traffic, sped down side roads, hit a one-way street going the opposite direction,

but took that road to the next street and ran
with the flow of traffic.

   Sirens. Sirens. Sirens.

TEN

Beautiful architecture and slums went by in a blur. Colonial firehouse, National Association for the Performing Arts, Knowsley, St. Philip's Anglican Church, Our Lady of Montserrat Roman Catholic Church, the pink Dattatreya Temple. I wasn't sure how much of that was real, how much I had seen on the drive to and from the safe house when I had first arrived, which images I had seen when I googled locations on the island, but what was real was I woke up in the back of my vehicle drenched in sweat. Woke up feeling stiff, dehydrated, and hungover. Could hardly breathe. Had to let the windows down to catch fresh air. It was dark. Middle of the night. Gun in hand, I left the vehicle, walked to get my bearings. I was north of downtown Port of Spain, on a hill overlooking the city. Looked around. Stone walls. Cannons. Bars on windows made from rifle barrels. Victorian-style signal house. Signage told me that I was on the grounds of Fort George.

No police. Not a person in sight. I stumbled across the grass like I was leaving a bad dream. I went back to the car, picked up my cellular, and walked past cannons to the edge, looked out at city lights and Caroni Swamp, second largest mangrove wetland in Trinidad and Tobago. Gulf of Paria was out there in the darkness. Westmoorings, Carenage, and Pointe Gourde were out there too.

There was no bathroom available, only the bathroom that had been installed by nature.

I pulled napkins from the glove box, went into the bushes, and relieved myself.

When I was done, I staggered around the grounds, rubbed my temples, and called the Barbarians.

"MX-401?"

My voice was raw, coarse, like I had a cold. "Yeah. MX-401."

"Where the hell are you?"

"Trinidad."

"Where in Trinidad?"

"Not sure. I'm sort of lost at the moment."

"Did you return to the safe house?"

"What's the issue?"

"What the fuck happened? You went off grid again, were off grid for hours."

I told them that I had closed the contract and needed to be extracted.

"What happened at the bank?"

"I killed the target, as I was instructed to do."

I got down on my haunches, coughed a few times, felt where mosquitoes had bitten me while I was unconscious, scratched myself, and then told them about the shootout.

"Did you go back to the safe house and lay down incendiary devices?"

"I haven't been back to that part of the island. You gave me a safe house so far away it's like driving from Atlanta past Birmingham to get there. Was too much traffic. Had to improvise."

"Your photo has been broadcast."

"Shit."

"Red hair. Half naked in a black dress. Boots. They have video of you inside the bank."

"I killed the target."

"You killed a priest."

"Then I killed the target."

"You killed a bank guard."

"After I killed the target."

"You killed two members of the Laventille Killers."

"I killed the target."

"You killed two fucking members of that group and that was not the job."

"I impro-fuckin'-vised."

"You fucked up, Reaper."

"I did what I was assigned to do."

"You're a wanted woman. You're too hot to handle. You're a risk."

"Calm down. All this screaming is giving

me a headache."

"Outside of the footage from the bank, that and photos that will be on the front page of every paper this morning, you killed two LKs on the busiest street on that island and it's already gone viral."

"You make it sound like I assassinated Archduke Franz Ferdinand and his wife, Sophie."

"You might as well have. It was a simple job and you killed everyone to do it."

"I did what I had to do to get the job done."

"You arrogant, belligerent bitch, that was not the assignment."

"Now what? What do I do now?"

"This situation is beyond fucked-up."

"What's the plan for getting me out of here?"

"The man behind the double red doors is outraged."

"What's the plan?"

"Get back to the safe house."

"For the last time, I'm three hours from there."

"Get back in one hour."

"Fuck you. You should be congratulating me. How about asking if I'm injured?"

"Safe house. One hour."

"Three."

I hung up, took steps back toward the vehicle.

My phone rang again. The Barbarians again.

"MX-401, don't return to the safe house. Someone has traced you there."

"Impossible."

"A new plan is being constructed. I will text you a location to meet."

"Don't set me up. I'm a Reaper. Remember that. I'm a goddamned Reaper."

"No more contact until you hear from me or another rep from the Barbarians."

"I get it. Don't call you, you'll call me, if you call me at all."

"You fucked up."

"I'm alive. The target is dead. That's all that fuckin' matters, bitch."

The call ended.

ELEVEN

By sunrise I was where the Caribbean Sea met the Atlantic Ocean, in Toco at a Roman Catholic church. The doors were wide open. Only two other cars were in the parking lot. I stepped out, gun in hand, eyes looking for a sniper, knowing the Barbarians were about to put me down. I walked inside and a man in a black suit was there, waiting for me. Tall. Older. I'd never seen the man before in my life.

He showed me his empty hands, then raised his suit coat, let me see that he was unarmed.

That done, he lowered his hands and said, "Designation."

I didn't lower my gun as I responded, "MX-401."

"So, you're the one who earned an *M* and an *X.*"

"Your designation?"

"Since we're in a church, just call me Preacher."

He motioned toward a green duffel. An

envelope rested its weight on top.

I opened the envelope. Three passports were inside, numbered 1, 2, and 3.

I said, "There is no money."

"MX-401, I just deliver what I am told to deliver. It's been delivered. I'm done."

I opened the bag. There was clothing. Dresses. Flats. Wigs. Other items.

Still no money.

Preacher reached into his pocket, tossed car keys at my feet.

He said, "Your vehicle is hot. Take the Kia. Three days from now, leave it at the airport."

Then he started to walk away.

I said, "You tell me that I have to lay low for three days. I have no money."

"Not my issue."

"I was supposed to be paid. They didn't send me one coin."

"After yesterday in Port of Spain, you're lucky to be alive."

"Maybe I was blessed and highly favored."

"No, you were fucking lucky."

"Maybe God has other plans for me."

"On this island, the LKs own God. You were fucking lucky."

He stopped walking. He opened his wallet, took out a thousand dollars in the local currency, which was less than $160 in US dollars. He set it on a pew.

Without looking back he said, "Eat doubles. They're cheap. Drink tap water."

"Three days. Fuckin' seriously?"

"Let me tell you something, and listen without complaining. I grew up in Southern Africa and I once went six days with no real food. Six days. I won't describe to you the shit I ate to stay alive, to get protein. You do what you have to do when you want to stay alive."

"All that to say? . . ."

"You are lucky to have three more days to hide. Be thankful their god took a nap."

I nodded.

He said, "Stay out of Port of Spain. They've dropped a net over everything from the airport to cruise ships, all hotels have been notified. Car is full of gas, so you won't need to go to a gas station. If you sleep, sleep in the car and don't get out of it unless you have to. Drinking water is on the front seat."

"I have no desire to go anywhere near Port of Spain."

"If I were you I'd lay low this way, north in Cumana Village, L'Anse Noire, Mission Village, or Monte Video Village. Maybe park down on Salybia Bay, but keep away from the Olorisa."

He moved on. Hard shoes moved across gravel. A car started before he got in on the passenger side. Then he was gone. I pulled a can of gas from the trunk of the first vehicle I had been in, set the car on fire, left it burning in the church parking lot. I had no fingerprints, so what I had touched at the safe house was of no consequence, but I had left the diagrams on the walls. I had left the blueprint to this mission.

As I drove the Kia over rugged road, I switched wigs, put on Jackie O shades, and inserted false teeth to make it look like I needed mild dental work and plaque removal. I became British. Hours later I sat in the car, parked off the main road, hidden in bushes, engine off, heat practically unbearable, afraid to step out, and waited. I had been left out here alone. Contact had been cut off.

I pulled out the passports, looked at the travel sequence.

None of the places on the itinerary was anyplace I'd been before.

Neither of the three was anyplace I wanted to go.

I stayed parked in the bushes, turned overgrown grass into my closet.

TWELVE

The first day I used makeup, gave myself freckles, a different hairline, shaved away my eyebrows and drew in arches, and made sure I had a tan so dark and sunburnt that I looked nothing like the Kiwi on the news. I found a spot and sat by myself at Maracas Bay. I was so unattractive that little children avoided me and clung to their mothers. On the second day I took a razor, shaved my head bald, applied makeup so that I would look sickly, wrapped a scarf around my bald head, created a walk that said I was a woman low on energy. I went back to Maracas Bay again, sat in the sun all day.

Alone. Not a word spoken to anyone, not even when I bought bake and shark.

I sipped bottled water and slept in the Kia each night.

The third day, still not a word from the Barbarians, I went to Piarco International. I grabbed the duffel bag, mixed with the crowd, and headed toward the terminal.

Police were all over. I passed by much security and many police, walked by many from the military. I passed undercover cops as well. I passed by men and women who glanced at me, then dismissed my tanned ugliness and searched for the red-haired Kiwi.

People carried the morning papers, my image as a murderous Kiwi on every front page.

On each television was a news report, again my image as a Kiwi the lead story.

They showed the images of the dead politico. The dead guard. The wounded.

They showed interviews from people who had been inside and on the street.

They did interviews in the hospital. A dozen injured and all wanted stage time.

Mrs. Ramjit's face was in an interview, outraged that this had happened to her island.

She said, "And from what we understand, the assassin was present at the Carlton Savannah. She was seen with or near our other beloved politician before he fell from the roof. We believe that she was involved. We believe that he had exposed her, then she attacked him and threw him from the roof. We have had more deaths in two days than one can bear. More murders in two days than I will tolerate. I love my island. I love my country and this breaks my heart. We want her found. We will stop at nothing. We have been attacked. There is a conspiracy, and all involved will have a day with justice."

As I sat in Piarco, sixteen miles away from where I'd had the shootout in Port of Spain, after I had glanced at flights to the United States, Canada, Central America, South America, and Europe, after I had glanced at destinations that weren't mine, I looked out at the runway just as a sleek private plane arrived. War Machine stepped off the plane. He was angered; it showed. He was just coming back from somewhere and it looked like he wasn't happy about having to deal with some issue.

Moments later Appaloosa, King Killer, Kandinsky, and Guerrero walked into the terminal.

War Machine entered. Went to his men. They passed by without looking at the crowd.

Three days had passed. My guess was they figured the Kiwi was long gone.

My palms were a river. Throat was a desert. Heart a drum. Belly growled from not eating.

My cellular rang. It was the Barbarians. After three.

Leaving me out here alone had been psychological torture, had been Guantánamo.

I said, "MX-401."

"Things have changed. We have a new plan. We need you back in the saddle."

I was being force-fed another assignment. I needed to be sequestered at the North Pole, but they wanted to shove me back into the field. My jaw tightened in protest. I felt my brain swell.

My pointer finger moved over and over as I grunted and asked, "Here?"

"Not there. We're done there. The man behind the double red doors is not happy."

"Well, I'm not exactly down here throwing a party."

War Machine and his men were marching out of the airport. Mrs. Ramjit was being played again in the news cycle. She wore diamonds, her German-made wedding ring stunning, unique. They all wore rings by the same jeweler. Thinking back, the priest and both politicos had worn the same style ring as well.

I was a nobody and I had the equivalent of $15 left in my pockets.

Across from me, another passenger read the paper, the image of the Kiwi staring at me.

The image of the red-haired Kiwi was all around me.

I would do anything they asked to get off of this boot-shaped rock. To get away, I would do anything to make it right.

THIRTEEN

I fled Trinidad by Caribair, made my way to Grenada, stayed a night. Then the Barbarians secured my passage on Liat to the Grenadines. They shuffled me around and soon I was dropped in Barbados. I was greeted by a storm when my flight landed at Grantley Adams International Airport. I walked through customs a tanned Paris Hilton blonde with sea-blue eyes and braces over false teeth, teeth that made me have an overbite like a rabbit. Backpack in hand, I looked like a teenager in a Princeton T-shirt, right arm covered in henna to make it look like I was a tat freak using a British passport.

I left customs, sat inside of Chefette, and exhaled. Lost. Nervous. Isolated.

A political killing in Trinidad wouldn't be front-page news on the island country of Barbados. The news here was on local concerns; the ATM at the airport had been robbed. Gun play at a children's party in an area called Brittons Hill. Guys were rolling around in a car robbing people at gunpoint. People were going to events with guns in their waistbands. There was even an article about violent crimes up north in the Bahamas, police working twelve-hour shifts with no overtime compensation. Most of the islands looked like paradise built on sand and decorated with palm trees, but the local papers made them sound like South Central. Made it to the last page. Nothing regarding Trinidad. Nothing about an APB for a Kiwi. Using my cellular, I went online, found a website, played the unfiltered video from the bank, looked at myself, focused on me. Saw myself soaking wet, passing through metal detectors and rushing into the bank. I was off. As I marched by the guard, I could tell I was off. Drugs had left me loopy. I remembered that horrible feeling. I watched myself approach the area where the target was, my hand in my bag.

Saw the politico freak out, pull his weapon from his open briefcase, and open fire.

I saw myself snap out of the trance and fire, my stance perfect, my movements becoming crisp.

Saw the priest run into the patch of my first shot, catch one in the center of his thinker.

He collapsed. Instant dead, just add lead, and customers dropped to the floor, terrified.

The politico lost it, backed away, fired shot after shot, missed me and hit customers.

I kept moving toward him, toward his shots, pulled the gun from my bag.

I screamed. There was no sound, but my mouth opened to scream.

I saw myself shooting to survive, shooting until the politico went down.

On the way out I shot the bank guard before he could lose his panic and shoot me.

I stepped over the dead, wounded, and dying and casually left the bank.

The marker showed that I was inside the bank for fifteen seconds, less than I thought.

It was the worst job I'd ever done. The worst fuckin' job ever.

My cellular buzzed. Text message. A coded message from Old Man Reaper.

An hour later I was at a KFC in Black Rock, a shopworn area near Eagle Hall farmers' market. From the airport I had taken a taxi down to that area, a section of the island above Deacons Farm Housing and below UWI Cave Hill. The next text message from Old Man Reaper came in while I devoured a chicken sandwich. After the message came I stepped into the bathroom and destroyed the phone. I finished my meal, left KFC, and went to the left, on foot, the rain falling hard. No umbrella. It didn't matter. Wash Day Laundromat was across from the two-shades-of-blue, two level Wing Kwong Plaza. It was in one long building next to an auto-repair shop. The laundry shared a wall with a bootleg video store and the bootleggers shared a wall with a Chinese restaurant and the Chinese restaurant shared a wall with Chicken Galore. A Kia Cerato was parked at the end of the strip in front of South Garden Chinese Restaurant. Headlights flashed as a signal. I swallowed, then I walked through the storm, approached the car. I was a drenched zombie, my hair now the darkest of black, my makeup smoky, my fingernails and toenails dark, I saw the windows had limo tint. I tapped on the driver-side window knowing that I could be shot right there, that whoever was inside could drive off in the storm, let me die in this barren car park. That was how the Barbarians would eliminate a problem. I had done that for them a dozen times. The window rolled down, just enough space for a loaded gun to send lead my way. Everything changed. I saw an assassin, and everything changed.

I had expected a man to be waiting on me, but a woman was inside. She looked like a teenage girl, but she was a woman. She was alone. She was younger, might not have been in her twenties, her hair tied up in a black scarf. Right off, despite her kind face, she had the hard eyes of a killer.

In an Italian accent I said, "I believe you have something for me."

"What's your designation?"

"MX-401. What's yours?"

"I have a question."

"Ask your question."

"The man named Reaper, is he your father?"

"Yeah. What's it to you?"

"I've met him. We lived together for a while."

"You're his girlfriend or something?"

"Reaper is my sperm donor too. He's my father."

We stared at each other, searched for some resemblance, her more than me, found none.

For me no resemblance meant no trust.

I asked, "What's your designation?"

"I'm a GDI, not a Barbarian."

"Never heard of you."

She sucked her teeth, shook her head, then retired her gun to the small of her back.

I took my finger away from the trigger of the one I had concealed.

Her supposed kinship meant nothing to me. It didn't make me drop my guard.

I asked, "Why does this feel like a setup for a roadside hit?"

"Get in the car or catch a bus to Six Roads. You'll have to go to Bridgetown, change buses, or catch a minivan, and that will have you in the rain another three or four hours. Up to you."

"You're a GDI. Barbarians don't freelance."

135

"If I had come to off you, you would've been dead while you were over at KFC eating your chicken sandwich. Would've used a high-powered rifle. From that house across the road."

I had sized her up from the start, told myself I could pull off my itchy wig and kill her in hand-to-hand.

I asked, "How would you have done it?"

She said, "One shot to your cranium. I wouldn't chat with you. I don't chat with targets. At least, not a pointless conversation. So, I repeat, it's up to you. You can crawl to the safe house for all I care."

Soaked, I walked to the left side of the car and slid into the passenger seat, my soaking-wet frame transferring water to the seat and floor. Once I was inside, she handed me a new phone and told me that the Barbarians were pissed off and would call me when they wanted to talk. She handed me a map that had been downloaded from Google, directions highlighted in yellow, the safe house circled in red, the description saying it had a blue gallery.

She said, "Check the glove compartment."

I looked in the glove compartment. There were three handguns. All loaded.

I asked, "Mine?"

"I cleaned and loaded them myself."

"Thanks."

"Just did what Old Man Reaper told me to

do. Thank him when you talk to him."

I looked at where we were, at this strip mall that was practically empty.

The rain ended here, but the sky told me it was still raining elsewhere. She left the parking lot. I was tense. She made the left and took the damp road. Within a half mile three zooming trail bikes shot up from behind us, overtook a half dozen cars, then cut in front of us, each rider almost clipping the front end of her car. A fourth biker appeared and whipped around us, only this one took off her side-view mirror.

She snapped, "Muddasik."

She sped up to catch them, kept them in sight as she sped past a block-long psychiatric hospital, a place that looked more like a prison for those flying over the cuckoo's nest.

The reckless bikers were caught at the light at Eagle Hall Market, in the left lane. She plowed into them going the full fifty kilometers per hour and knocked all but one of the rude asses into the intersection. She jumped out of the car. I did the same, stepped out of the car and left the door wide open. She popped the trunk and took out two crowbars, tossed me one. It was sticky. Already bloody. I beat the first one I reached, broke his legs, struck his knees, back, and elbows, and when he rolled over, I chopped him over and over across his helmet, made the headgear split. One made it to his feet, saw me beating his compadre, and came at me. I dropped to one knee and swept his feet from under him, made him fly up high and land real hard on his back, the wind knocked out of his body. My wig came off, exposed my bald head. I remained focused on the guy. I introduced him to the crowbar and a few broken bones. It would be months before he would be able to handle a motorcycle again. The first one my irate driver had attacked with the car, the last one in the line and the first to get hit, he was on the ground, on the rugged and uneven pavement, in severe pain. Old Man Reaper's other child gave that dude hell. She was stomping him like he was a roach. She raised her foot up and brought her heel down into his gut over and over and over.

She lost it. "Cutting me off like that was dead wrong. Bey, why did you do that?"

"Wha de rasshole? You is a cunt?"

"You hear what this mango-skin fool said to me? The fool must be on rat bat."

"Yeah, they're high. This one smells like Bacardi."

Again she raised her foot and brought it down on his gut.

The fourth guy, the drunk bastard was angry, came running at me, fists doubled.

My spinning back kick caught him dead in his gut, took him off his feet. He hit the ground doubled over. He stayed down, pulled himself into the fetal position, ribs broken.

The last guy picked up his bike, hopped on. Fight or flight had led him to choose flight.

A city bus entered the intersection and knocked him through the intersection and toward the R.A. Mapps rum shop. Everybody stopped eating rotisserie chicken and drinking Banks beer, watched the accident.

Old Man Reaper's Bahamian daughter said, "That's what you get. God don't like ugly."

He lay on the ground, his arms moving, legs broken and twisted, calling out in agony. I picked up my wig, wiped away water, put it back on, then surveyed the area.

I said, "That blue building across from Downes Funeral Home. We're twenty yards from the front door to the local police station. They'd arrest us for the fight."

"The fight is nothing. They would hang me for what's rotting in the trunk."

She wiped rain from her face and walked back to the car. I told her to get in on the passenger side. She took her time. I drove away at a bank robber's pace, the scent of rotisserie chicken, gas from Rubis, and the aroma from Legendary Fish Cakes filling my nostrils.

Her cellular rang.

She answered talking: "It's done. Got what he deserved. Busy now. Pay me tomorrow."

Then she hung up and threw the cellular out the window.

She directed me toward Government Hill. From there I turned left at the J.T.C. Ramsay Roundabout, took to the ABC Highway, made two left turns, and ended up at the Sheraton Mall.

On the second level of the car park, we went to the trunk and she opened it up.

An elderly man was in the trunk, his body resting on top of thick, industrial, leak-proof plastic. The man had a close-cut gray beard, was bald, had deep brown skin, a green shirt, casual pants. His body wasn't cold yet. Duct tape over his hands, ankles, mouth, and eyes. Plastic bag over his head. His throat had been cut, a strong clean cut, the trunk a lake of blood.

I said, "I caught you in the middle of working."

"Finished right before I picked you up."

"It looks like you broke every bone in the old man's body."

"He raped his own grandchild at least two times. Made the little girl give him oral. How do you molest your twelve-year-old granddaughter and walk the streets like it was nothing? How are you almost seventy and you molested your daughter years ago, now you violate her daughter too? He did it to at least three other girls. His reign of terror started back in the eighties. He's done. At least. What the fuck is wrong with people? He could have gone up by the Garrison or Nelson Street or some fucking place and paid for a blow job. Girls would have been happy to service his old ass for next to nothing. His disgusting ass could've had a girl and been done with it."

She slammed the trunk.

She said, "This girl was lucky. Another preteen was raped, killed, and thrown in a gully like a dog. That one was raped by her grandfather too. He's been remanded. Lucky for him."

I didn't care. I'd been on the run, needed sleep, and didn't care.

Any other day, just not that day.

She said, "Was going to arrange it so his body washed up on Welches Beach. In case you need to know, that's the best way to get rid of a body around here, feed it to the sea. She spits it out and vomits it back on the land bloated after the fish have had a meal. Much bodies wash up on the beaches in the islands. The sea kills all evidence. Too late to feed the fish now."

"Much bodies."

"Yeah. Much bodies."

"Okay. Much bodies."

We dumped the hot ride. I dumped the black wig, put a scarf around my bald head. While she distracted security I stole a blue Kia. I pulled away and picked her up as I exited the car park. She settled in. I put on Wayfarers and took to the uneven road that went through Vauxhall and passed the entrance to the Globe Drive-In.

The volatile woman next to me said, "Forgot to ask. Need anything special?"

"A new wig."

"Besides that."

"Roads are narrow here. People stop to chat and hold up traffic and block the streets."

"Highways are smoother."

"No emergency lanes. No bike lanes. Barely room for two cars to pass. A traffic accident could shut a road down. Might be impossible to get away if I were in a chase."

"You plan on being in a chase?"

"I didn't plan on being here. I need a motorcycle for a few days. Would prefer to be in a muscle car, but looking at this infrastructure, my best bet will be moving on two wheels."

"You want one of those numbers I just ran off the road?"

I said, "A real motorcycle. Something that can outrun how you drive."

We kept it moving past sugarcane fields, eventually came up on Foursquare Rum Distillery, Emerald City coming up fast, then the last roundabout before the safe house.

Her phone pinged. I cringed. Took a deep breath through clenched teeth.

I was tense. Having to go to a new place, on a different island, alone, a place I'd never seen before in my life, a landmass too close to Trinidad, it had me tense, anxious, in a bad mood. Barbados could have been Beverly Hills and it still would have been the worst place on the fuckin' planet.

Before the roundabout at Six Roads, she asked, "Want to have some more fun?"

"Not really into having fun, but okay. Sure. Need to make the time pass."

"Turn around. I'm not ready to go home and put my husband to bed."

"Kind of early for that."

"Never too early. Never the wrong time for that."

I cruised down a narrow strip of gravel road situated between two rows of sugarcane, kicked up dust and rock for about nine hundred meters until we came upon the area for archery and skeet shooting, the starting point of a country club nestled in over seventy acres, a club that was a restored World War II building. Had no idea where I was, only that she said she was taking me to Kendal Sporting in Carrington, parish of St. Philip, up the road from the safe house. It looked like the perfect place to kill. I turned off the main road onto what a sign said was Kendal Road, an area that used to be a plantation but now was a lime spot, a place for business meetings, corporate functions, retreats, and weddings.

Only a couple of people were at the bar, only three people in the pool. It was like we had gone to another island. A well-to-do island. She took me on a tour. Clubhouse, swimming pool, table tennis, billiards, darts, archery, and, most important, the gun ranges. Pistol. Shotgun.

She asked, "Any good with a bow and arrow?"

"I've trained with Old Man Reaper, but bullets move faster and reloading is quicker."

"I used one on a job. Used a compound. Hit the target from forty yards."

"Center of mass?"

"Neck."

"Lucky shot."

"I was aiming for his neck. Went straight through his esophagus."

"Why not a gun with a silencer?"

"Muzzle fire gives away your position."

"Big contract?"

"Small to the world, big to the island. Issues down in the Deacons Farm Housing area."

"Farmers?"

"Not farmers. It's the projects."

"What was that all about?"

"Politics. Money for votes."

"They buy votes down here under the table?"

"They buy votes in public. Some Bajans stand in line and wait to get paid before they vote, then take photos of their ballots to prove they earned their bribe. One hundred people at a time were waiting on money right outside of Deacons Primary School at the voting place."

"Bold. How much were they paying?"

"Three hundred Bajan bucks a vote."

"A Bajan buck is worth fifty cents in the US. Not much to sell out."

"Some don't make that much a week. People showed up in droves, in packed minibuses. Guy on the other side who ran a clean campaign and lost, well, he's not so clean anymore."

"Sounds like someone is out for revenge."

"It was ugly. Other things happened. Personal things. Just waiting on the call."

"Call from?"

"Same people I worked for earlier today. The government."

"What, are you some West Indian version of the CIA?"

"Not the government, but someone in the government who makes things happen to keep the island looking good. People who want to make sure the island thrives by any means necessary. If someone damages their image or hurts tourism, they call. If a politician needs a favor, I handle it."

While adjusting the scarf on my bald head, I said, "Worst-case scenario, since my money is low, can I get work down here?"

"Oh, there is an open contract in Trinidad."

"Not interested in anything to do with Trinidad."

"It's an easy one. Girl was murdered, a brutal murder down on some place called Incinerator Road. Old guy beat her, burned her with cigarettes. Guy cut her fingers off. Damn near cut her head off."

"Anywhere but Trinidad. Can't travel. I don't have a good passport."

"How did you get here?"

"People I work for pulled it, told me that it's not any good from here on out."

"Why in the hell would they do that?"

"Don't know."

"Are they sending you a new one?"

"I hope to get one soon. If you can get me local action, I'd be grateful."

"Will see what I can do. Might be small local jobs."

"All money adds up. A dollar is made of pennies, nickels, and dimes."

"Anything else?"

"Antsy. Wish I had a local boyfriend to bide the time and get the edge off."

"Could make it happen tonight. Give me two hours. What are you into?"

"Thanks for the offer, but I'm not that kind of girl."

We went to the indoor pistol range, loaded up, then we fired off six hundred rounds.

I said, "You're a GDI."

"My handle is Nemesis Adrasteia."

"Definitely the name of a vigilante."

"In Greek mythology, Nemesis was the spirit of divine retribution against those who succumb to arrogance before the gods. 'Adrasteia' means 'the inescapable.' 'Nemesis' means 'to give what is due.' Nemesis Adrasteia. I give what is due. What is due is inescapable. What should I call you?"

"Reaper."

"That's it?"

"Just call me Reaper."

"My sperm donor calls himself Reaper too." I told her my real name.

I asked, "Should I call you Nemesis?"

"Petrichor is my real name. Haven't said that name in forever."

I paused. "Wow."

"What?"

"My mother had said that Petrichor would've been my name. If Old Man Reaper had stayed long enough to sign the birth certificate, that was what he would've named me."

"So, you're telling me that I have your name?"

"I was going to be named Petrichor. Old Man Reaper took one look at me, made accusations, and left, so the last thing my mother was going to do was give me the name he had picked out."

"Why did your mother pick your name, if one had been chosen?"

147

"My mother named me what Old Man Reaper said I looked like when I was pulled from between her legs. She did that to spite him. She named me Goldilocks to spite him."

"Petrichor is my true name, sorry about that."

"Nothing to be sorry about. It's just a name. Everybody has one."

"Here my name is Christine Braithwaite."

"Christine. It means 'follower of Christ.' "

"Your mom named you Goldilocks because she was pissed at my sperm donor?"

"Sure did, Petrichor. Sure did. She named me after a chick who did a B&E and stole porridge. I was destined to be a bad girl. My name means 'person with golden hair who steals.' "

"You steal?"

"Never have, but when I find three bears with porridge and beds, it's on."

"Goldilocks."

"Well, I'm Baldy-no-locks now."

"Funny."

"It grows back fast."

"You look cute. You can pull off bald."

"Thanks."

After that we went for the bow and arrow. She was amazing. Old Man Reaper had trained me with a bow and arrow, but I hadn't used one in a while, hadn't been needed.

When we were done, she waited for a

minibus at the end of the gravel road.

She was going to ride a bus back to town, have her husband pick her up there.

We sat in the stolen car, chatting about the only thing we had in common.

Old Man Reaper. We made light of his many serious and redundant conversations.

She said, "You know he's Bajan right? He was born here, from the Pines."

"I know. He told me story after story about how rough he had it. Told me I should feel lucky that I had cable because they only had one TV channel, was lucky to know someone who had a VCR, and he used some kind of oil stoves, so I should be thankful we had an electric stove."

"You had an electric stove?"

"Yeah."

"Must be nice."

"Well, we were in America. We lived in Huntington Beach, California, for a while."

"California. Must be nice. I've seen the beaches on television."

"Yeah, well, day and night he went on and on about how his parents didn't have TV at all, only radio, and not everybody had a radio. Something called radio fusion or something."

She corrected me, "Rediffusion. It was called Rediffusion."

"And how his granddad went on a one-way trip and worked on the Panama Canal."

"God, he always ranted about how Bajans

went to the Panama Canal way back when."

"He told me. 'Tens of thousands of black Bajans took jobs no other man would take.' "

" 'On the canal, there were five thousand dead for every mile.' "

"Inhumane conditions. Jim Crow. Dysentery. Unimaginable diseases. A new kind of slavery."

She said, "Yeah, my sperm donor told me how rough people had it back in the day."

"He would go on and on, then make me work out, make me fight like a man."

"How was he? How was he to you? How was his personality with you?"

"He was like the Bible. Incredibly wise one moment, then extremely barbaric the next."

She nodded. "Same here."

I coughed, paused, looked into the distance.

She said, "Something is on fire. Bad times for anyone with asthma."

"A fire was down by the airport when I landed. The rain put it out."

"Strange. Out of season. Four or five big cane fires a day. Big fires all over."

I was glad when the bus came. Was glad to say good-bye. We shook hands.

I said, "Don't hurt anybody else before you get home."

"Will do my best."

"I probably won't see you again."

"I know."

She hopped on the blue-and-gold transport

bus heading toward Bridgetown.

I left the stolen car where it was and waited for a bus on the opposite side of the road.

The rain came again and I stood there without any shelter.

A yellow minibus came, filled to the brim, people practically falling out of its windows. As lewd lyrics about female body parts blasted, I asked if it went as far as Six Roads. The conductor said something in dialect, saw I was confused, than he nodded and I climbed on board, took my soaking-wet frame and backpack and squeezed in. I ended up next to an old woman transporting a large bushel of okra, potatoes, and squash.

I exited the crowded bus at Six Roads, an unfamiliar world. For a moment, I stood lost between RBC Bank and Williams Equipment, got my bearings and headed away from the roundabout, toward a shopworn red rum shop. Men and boys who thought they were men speckled the street, sat on the concrete benches at the empty bus stops, owned the curbs on both sides of the road. Stranger. Outsider. Foreigner. Woman walking alone. I had all of their eyes. Bandanas wrapped around their heads and faces. My gun was at my side. I walked with confidence and kept moving by an open field, and at the end of the block, saw the pink, purple, and beige wood-frame homes under coconut trees, those being landmarks I had memorized. I saw the sign that said I had arrived at the Ministry of Transport and Works, Six Roads Depot, looked to my left and cut between cinder-block homes facing some sort of rowdy marketplace, that being an area filled with beer-drinking, laughing patrons. Music boomed, assaulted my nerves like it was party central.

The two-bedroom safe house was under a thousand square feet in size. A rich man's closet. Two bedrooms probably big enough to hold all of Diamond Dust's shoes. Like a flat in London. Hot. Stuffy. Didn't want to open the windows or turn on lights. Curtains were thin. Found a fan. Turned it on. It rattled like it was on its last legs, looked like it hadn't been cleaned since mud was invented, but it circulated the staleness. The music across the road grew louder with each passing minute. There were kinder renditions. Took my first cold shower, had no toiletries and was forced to use the Axe soap that was left there. Windows vibrated as I went to the dirty kitchen dripping wet, naked, carrying two guns, and searched the unfinished wooden cabinets for something to eat. Fuh Real Jerk Seasoning. Mauby syrup. Carib beer. Hairoun beer. The only place to eat around here was Chefette. Saw it when I had exited the bus.

Soon I heard an engine outside. It was the engine of a big truck, like a Ford F-250.

It roared over the calypso from across the road. The truck roared like the LKs had tracked and found me, and this was the showdown, the music across the road a perfect cover for gunfire.

The safe house became a tomb. I panicked, grabbed my weapons, took to the floor, crawled across the room, got near a window, prepared to shoot whoever I saw first.

I waited. Listened the best I could over the roar from across the road. There was a break in the music and I heard noise out front. Men talking, Bajan dialect, conversation indecipherable. Not the LKs, but that didn't mean they weren't still a threat. Music kicked back on. I waited some more. The vehicle rumbled, the horn blew three times, then it pulled away. I spied out of the small window over the kitchen sink. A motorcycle was out front. Matte black Superbike 848. The truck was easing by secondhand cars parked on the willowy road. I cracked the door, gun leading the way. A box was on the porch. I pulled the box inside and pulled back the flaps. Gloves. Helmet. Extra bullets and clips.

And five top-shelf wigs, various hues and styles.

When the rain stopped, I looked out the twelve-pane window, the next home being only three car lengths away. I went to the walls, clicked light switches on and off six times, eight times, ten times. Nothing happened. Soon I sat on the bed, saw the neighbors, but they didn't see me. Married couple. Her hair was wrapped up. His hair was short.

I understood why the binoculars had been left behind on the dresser. The last hired gun had sat here on this spot, taking in the carnal festivities.

With a fully loaded burner in my lap and two clips at my side, binoculars up to my azure eyes, like I was in the movie *Rear Window,* soca and dub and calypso the soundtrack of the moment, I watched the love show. The music made it impossible to rest, even if I could rest. This was as close as I would get to positive human contact for a while. After I downed two more beers, I lay in darkness and touched myself. I pushed two fingers inside of me, up to my knuckles, imagined Johnny Parker being inside me.

■ ■ ■ ■

ICHIROUGANAIM

■ ■ ■ ■

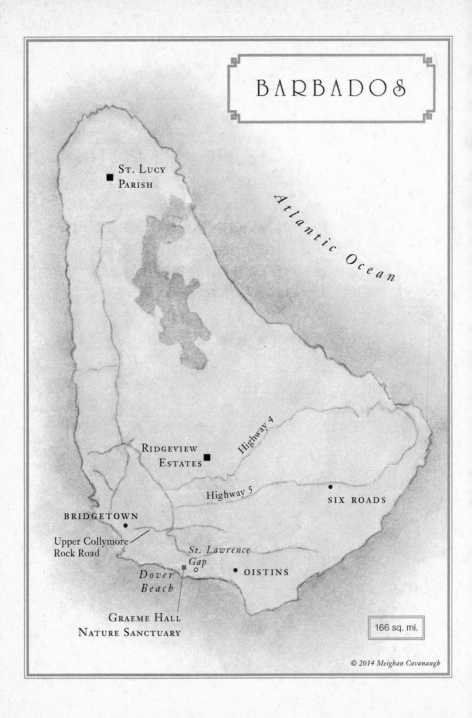

BARBADOS

Sᴛ. Lᴜᴄʏ
Pᴀʀɪsʜ

Atlantic Ocean

Highway 4

Rɪᴅɢᴇᴠɪᴇᴡ
Esᴛᴀᴛᴇs

Highway 5

SIX ROADS

BRIDGETOWN

Upper Collymore
Rock Road

*St. Lawrence
Gap*

*Dover
Beach*

OISTINS

Gʀᴀᴇᴍᴇ Hᴀʟʟ
Nᴀᴛᴜʀᴇ Sᴀɴᴄᴛᴜᴀʀʏ

166 sq. mi.

© 2014 Meighan Cavanaugh

FOURTEEN

Forty days after the Trinidad debacle.

I remained on the island country of Barbados.

It was another night of guns and roses without the roses.

The Barbarians had yanked my chain four hours ago, after the sun had been swallowed by the Caribbean Sea. The last-minute assignment was to end in St. James Parish, near Fitts Village.

Around midnight I followed a stolen BICO truck from the northeast side of the island, from the bush and cane fields in St. Lucy, from the country to the more cosmopolitan side of the island to Fitts Village. Two vehicles followed the ice-cream truck, two cars with darkened windows. From a distance, with night binoculars, I had watched them load up. All three vehicles had men and women who were heavily armed. The Barbarians wanted them stopped before they made it to the ships waiting at the sea.

Those were the orders from the man behind the double red doors.

Again it was a job made for three or four people, and I had been sent alone.

When the drug mules were in Fitts Village, I pulled out from behind the three vehicles on my motorcycle, sped in front of them, came to a hard stop, then hopped from my bike and drew my weapons.

I gunned down the driver of the ice-cream truck as his bright lights came straight at me. When he veered left and crashed, as his cohorts exited, I fired on them. I used a spray-and-pray, popped each multiple times, popped anyone who came from the second vehicle as they exited shooting, hit them in their legs, stomach, popped the targets so fast that the people stuck in traffic had no idea what was going on.

The third car following them came at me, came head-on, gun out of the window, but instead of running away, I charged the car returning fire, jumped onto the hood and flipped, a maneuver that Old Man Reaper had taught me years ago, landed on my feet. They ran off the road, dropped into a drainage ditch, crashed. Before anyone could exit the vehicle, I ran behind the driver and put two in his head.

Then Death let me know that it showed no favoritism.

A bullet hit my helmet, the impact jarring me.

Wearing a motorcycle helmet to hide my face had left blind spots.

At first I thought it had been a bull's-eye, that I was a dead woman.

I turned and saw the terrified shooter facing me. A woman. She thought that her one shot had killed me. Was confused why I was still standing. She raised her gun again, had her gun aimed at me and mine wasn't ready to reciprocate. Before I could put her at the bad end of a gun, pink mist came from her head. I hadn't raised my weapon, but pink mist came from her head.

A bullet had entered her head from my right, left a watermelon-size hole to the left.

The drug runner's body crumpled to the ground. I was still off, slow from lack of sleep, forty days without decent rest, had never raised my gun at her, but a sniper's bullet had found her and killed her.

Petrichor.

The urgent assignment was to disrupt the drug shipment, to kill all the workers.

Then ghost. Back to my prison. Back to solitary confinement.

I ran back to my motorcycle, took in the surroundings for half a second, looked for hostiles.

Bajans had seen the shootout from their kitchen windows, then ducked when bullets shattered the glass. People who had come outside to investigate ran with their babies on their hips.

Many lay dead as I sped off into the night, two thousand pounds of marijuana left behind.

Again, I had almost been killed. That night, gunfire sounded like cannons.

In the morning paper the Police Marine Unit and the Barbados Coast Guard would be photographed next to taped polyurethane bags. They would take all the credit for the bust.

Without a doubt they would take the credit for millions of dollars of product left on the street.

That would disrupt one level of the local economy. It was a street hustler's bread and butter.

I sped off into the night, zoomed away from populated areas, through cut-rock road, through one of the many cane fields that had been on fire earlier in the day. I was used to the stench, the smoke.

A handful of cane fields had burned every day since I had arrived.

When I made it back to the safe house, another assignment was waiting.

I wanted to kick chairs and turn over tables, but there were no tables and chairs to kick over.

FIFTEEN

Six Roads, Parish of St. Philip
Forty-one days after Trinidad.

With a grunt, I jerked awake, woke with a lurch, eyes wide, anxiety burgeoning, heart pounding, a cold .9mm in my hot right hand, a Kahr P380 in my left, both trained on the abrupt sound that had shocked me from my recurring nightmare. Disoriented, sleep-deprived, and stressed, the world a blur, I sprang to my feet like I'd never been asleep, in a rush, moved corner to corner, from room to room in the safe house, guns aimed, fingers on triggers. No one was here to kill me. The panic dismissed itself one breath at a time. I had exploded. Panting, I lowered my weapons. For now, I was safe.

I dragged my fingers over my short mane, whispered, "Trinidad. Get out of my damn head."

Since Trinidad, I'd had intense nightmares night after night, like a soldier fresh back from Afghanistan. I sat on the worn bed and inhaled, coughed a dry cough that went on forever.

The room was stuffy, dull beige tiles underneath my feet as cold as the stale air that surrounded me. Seconds passed before I frowned at the map I had left on the floor. A map of a Hilton hotel, its entrances and exits. I gazed up at the dingy off-white walls of the safe house. My head cleared.

I remained trapped in St. Philip Parish, thirty minutes from Bridgetown, Barbados.

A forty-minute flight from Port of Spain, where I remained their number-one enemy.

Again I whispered, "Get out of my head and let me rest one night."

Another chill ran through me, God giving me the middle finger.

I rubbed my eyes, shook off the residue from that nightmare and refocused, looked down and saw forty-one black markers, all dry, then my eyes walked across the walls, across graffiti, across my journal.

Forty-plus days of black graffiti gave life to the dull walls.

A girl screamed for her life. Gun in hand, I jogged to the front room, spied outside. A woman was under the streetlights, beating her preteen daughter with a plank. In a strong Bajan accent, one I could barely understand, the mother yelled that the girl had been caught bringing a boy into the house. Her third time being caught. Neighbors recorded the corporal punishment with their phones. I mimicked the woman, mimicked her every word, made myself sound like her. Then I mimicked the daughter, copied her high-pitched voice, mocked her pleas as I went back to the bedroom, picked up the package, opened the envelope, and slid out the photos of a disgraced cricketer destined to die tonight. As the madness outside continued, I studied the photo of the target. Then I dropped it back on the floor.

Angry, I kicked the package to the side.

A photo of another man was taped to the closet. Portly. As attractive as a roach in heat. That one wasn't a contract from the Barbarians. They hadn't paid me, and I was doing what I had to do to garner enough money to survive. If the money had been here, I would've handled that business days ago.

I was breaking the rules. The rule I was breaking carried the penalty of death.

Fuck the Barbarians.

The Barbarians hadn't paid me and I needed money, so I would do a side job, if needed.

More noise erupted, only the sounds came from the house next door, fifteen steps away.

Inside a darkened two-bedroom made of concrete blocks, fan blowing in my face, I sat in the window, dark curtains barely parted, night-vision binoculars in hand. The neighbor was just out of the shower, a towel wrapped around her body. Her husband came into their bedroom and pushed her down on the bed. He was naked. Their nightly routine. Work. Home. Dinner. Shower. Fuck.

My cellular buzzed with a text message: Get to location. Wait on verification.

I put the binoculars away and replied: How long will I be trapped on this fuckin island?

No response.

I typed in all caps, YOU SENT ME OUT IN THE OPEN TO TAKE OUT FUCKIN DRUG RUNNERS THAT HAD HIGH-POWERED WEAPONS AND YOU'RE GOING TO SEND ME BACK OUT AGAIN LESS THAN TWENTY-FOUR HOURS LATER ON ANOTHER JOB? I'M DONE IN BIMSHIRE. GET ME OFF THIS DAMN ISLAND BEFORE I END UP BEING HUNG BY THE LAW.

I picked up my phone, looked at the online paper for *Barbados Today*. The front page was about the shootout in St. James, one of the most pristine tourist areas on the island. A baker's dozen of drug smugglers had been gunned down. A day ago everyone complained about the economy; the day before, there was the heated issue about pornographic stills from a video of school kids having sex in a classroom being posted in one of the island's newspaper; but today it was all about the shootout and funerals. I had topped conversations for the management of the resources of the country island and kiddie porn.

I was trying to put the pieces together and figure out the drug hit.

I scowled at my damaged motorcycle helmet. The helmet was the equivalent of an Aston Martin DB5. Now it was worthless. It wasn't bulletproof. A bullet from a high-caliber weapon had blown open its side. Three inches to the left and I would have been a dead Jane Doe cooling in the morgue right now.

Flexing my toes, I glowered at the phone, waited for a text response. Then I gave up, flipped the pages on the digital paper, went to the next page. A Rastafarian family had squatted on prime real estate on the island and the megabank that owned the property was doing all that it could to get them removed. They had squatted for twenty years, long enough to have thirteen children.

Thirteen rounds of natural childbirth, not a cesarean in sight.

Sounded like the woman had been squatting over stiffness and reproducing without pause.

That article meant nothing to me and I forgot about it the moment I glanced it over.

Pissed off, I sent another message: I need a safe house with a better location. Where I am, there are houses, many families, men pissing on the mango tree outside my window, women outside beating their kids for kicks, and the local rum shop is outside my window and it's always too damn crowded. There are too many people living down here. I stand out and you know I stand out. I did a job last night. What if someone recognizes me? Just get me away from down here where I don't fit in.

Ten minutes passed.

They replied. Get to location. Wait on verification. Until then, STFU.

Me: What are these West Indian jobs about? Are these random hits or is there a big picture?

No response. I had asked the same question yesterday.

I typed, The LKs. The authorities in Trinidad. I need an update. Now.

Still nothing.

I haven't been paid since before the Trinidad job. You're not honoring your end of our contract. So for the umpteenth time, send my money. Another passport. Credit cards. Get me off of this rock.

The Barbarians: Last time, MX-401. Get on location. Last time. STFU.

I rubbed my temples, asked my aching head to give me some reprieve.

My aching head gave me the middle finger.

I looked inside of my backpack, counted the few bills I had, cursed.

Across the road, thunderous music kicked on.

I screamed, begged for the torture to end.

■ ■ ■ ■

I changed SIM cards, took a deep breath, and did another sweep to make sure there were no listening devices within these walls before I used a disposable phone and sent a text message.

MR. BJ. NO MONEY, WON'T BE ABLE TO FIX ISSUE. PARTS AND LABOR IN ADVANCE.

MS. R, $ FOR P&L WILL BE DELIVERED AS PROMISED. JOB SITE IS CLEAN.

MR. BJ, I CAN'T FIX ANYTHING BEFORE I HAVE $ IN HAND TO PAY FOR LABOR.

"BJ" stood for Black Jack, the handle for a nickel-and-dime West Indian broker in Barbados.
I needed that side job, but I wasn't going to work without being paid up front.
Desperation.

MR. BJ. THE HUMMINGBIRD STOPPED SINGING. I NEED TO KNOW IF THERE IS A NEW SONG.

MS. R, WILL DO WHAT I CAN RE-

GARDING THE HUMMINGBIRD AND ITS SONG.

Trinidad was the land of the hummingbird.

I typed: WILL NEED VARIOUS FIRE-WORKS FOR THE 4TH OF JULY. AMERICANS LOVE TO CELEBRATE.

He replied: WORKING ON THAT TOO.

Fireworks meant things that go boom and blow up everything nearby.

A thousand flaming, riled-up scorpions lived inside of my brain. Head ached. I was on edge. Intel coming from the Barbarians, anything regarding Trinidad had died off two weeks ago. The Barbarians had all but shut me down, had unofficially made me an unpaid outcast. Still I had read the Trini news online. I didn't know what the LKs knew, where they were searching. I only knew their home base was less than an hour away by plane. If the wind blew while they pissed on their beaten and battered enemies, the slosh could dampen my face. I knew what they did to men, what they did to women as well.

The Barbarians weren't giving me updates, so I had to do what I had to do.

Backpack loaded and on, damaged black helmet on with chinstrap tight and face shield up, dressed in black jeans, black jacket, and masculine black boots, tugging on my black gloves, I climbed out of the bedroom window, dropped to the ground unseen, then closed the window.

I stepped on a frog the size of a New York rat. Slugs were there too, those on steroids as well.

The clamor of soca, dub, reggae, and a karaoke setup that kicked out R&B and country-western songs overlapped. It was this way almost every night until two a.m. With this headache, with this anxiety, it was too much to bear. The ruckus came from an obnoxious fete on the grounds of the Six Roads Public Market, a fenced section that was right off Farm Road. Composed of dozens of small, shoulder-to-shoulder low-end rum shops. Pubs without glitz and glamour and where four beers cost five American dollars. Alcohol was cheaper than chewing gum. Women arrived dressed in outfits that would make red-light workers blush. Men were out, beer in hand, wearing wife-beaters and T-shirts, pants sagging below the rounds of their asses, some barefoot and lounging on the curbs, yelling profane and blatantly sexual things as sexy women passed, eyes on bubble butts like they were all professional ass inspectors. The safe house was located in the heart of this communal madness. Every Sunday evening, a dime-store preacher and his congregation stood on the corner and gave a louder-than-loud sermon and did some bad singing until close to midnight. That was another level of punishment. Another reason to loathe my employer.

I kicked my Ducati into first gear and rolled it from its hiding place beneath a coconut tree. I zoomed away from my jailhouse and out of this section of government-built housing.

The bright lights from Chefette and the family homes in Emerald City East were behind me as I sped down Highway 6, whipping around slow-moving cars until I hit a roundabout at Nature Care, a plant nursery. I kept straight and rode a worn section, a strip of neglected roadway that led to PLAE in Balls, Christ Church. PLAE was twelve acres and stood for Play, Lounge, Advertising, and Entertainment. I drove between shelves of cut-rock road, headlights leading me into the mouth of total blackness, across road that was like three miles of severe acne, the kind that Proactiv couldn't help. The rough ride ended when I made it to the Tom Adams Roundabout, a well-paved highway that was the "A" part of the ABC Highway chain. I sped to the next roundabout at Kendal Hill, parked on the left edge of the road, across from a Rubis gas station. I put my bike in neutral, put down the kickstand, pulled a small plastic bag from my backpack, snacked on a conkie, sipped coconut water, and nibbled on Purity great cake, the Cockspur rum strong.

A Corvette 427 zoomed my way. Arctic-white exterior. Blue diamond leather wrapped interior. Racing stripes in pearl-silver-blue ran the length of the car. Sixtieth Anniversary design package. The beast moved like it was on the track at Bushy Park. The driver, reckless. Arrogant. Moneyed.

I dropped the last of my snack, kicked into gear, peeled out, shot through the round-about, and matched the Corvette's speed in a matter of seconds, trailed that speed-limit-breaking Bajan down ABC Highway. I rode as I had ridden last night when I had put many lawless men into the ground.

As I had done ever since I had been banished here, I rode with Trinidad on my mind.

SIXTEEN

Less than two hundred nautical miles from Barbados, on the country island of Trinidad

More than a month had passed since the public assassination. The controversial politician's body had been displayed in his family home, taken to Mosquito Creek and his remains placed on blocks of wood, his body then wrapped in flammable materials. A match was struck, the crackling began, and the politician was cremated as many stood around and had a celebration that was like a picnic.

His ashes were scattered on the island of Tobago.

The country vowed to find whoever had killed their political brother.

Two members of the LKs had been eulogized, the funeral private, for members of their corporation, of their family, and their legitimate children only. Both young men were cremated, ashes scattered. The priest had been buried. The same had happened for the bank's guard. He had been destitute, a hardworking man who in the end had left his wife and children with nothing but tears and debt.

The LKs had paid for his funeral and promised to set up a college fund for the children.

Trinidad remained restless.

The country was restless because the LKs were angered and restless, but they had to move forward at the same time. There was a big picture, a larger plan.

The search for the Kiwi continued.

Other news, other crimes, other political issues, other deaths had become the news du jour. There were other street killings in the slums that had the ear of the people.

But there were still people who whispered about how the invincible Laventille Killers had been killed so effortlessly by a female. The female assassin was unintentionally being given praise. Someone had taken photos of their dead brothers and those horrific images had been posted on the front pages of the Trinidadian papers.

The images were online, were still being circulated in cyberspace.

Social-media experts had been used for redaction, as they were always used, and all negative content regarding their organization was expunged from the Internet, negative videos instantly removed from all sites, and any Twitter account that had too many followers who were their enemy vanished, or was hacked and repurposed. When the name of their organization was dropped into a Google search or put into Bing, the results were all positive. The spin that the LKs wanted was all that would be found.

From the roof of the Carlton Savannah, guntas in Italian suits behaved like well-educated men; the bluestocking wives were classy ladies. They held a benefit for the Express Children's Fund. The day before, they had one at the Hyatt for the Cancer Society. Events were held almost every day, positive press used as a way to direct attention away from the deaths, away from the questions regarding the politico being assassinated on their watch. As photos were taken, guntas entertained children, held hands with their wives — women they had been assigned to marry, those selected for breeding.

Despite the attempts to quell talk of the murders, one fact kept grabbing the imagination of the populace: a woman had done it, had killed two of the baddest of the bad men in Trinidad.

A woman.

Some called the red-haired Kiwi a one-woman army. Someone had drawn her as a comic-book character with wild and luxurious red hair, one with Angelina Jolie lips painted red, a small waist, and exaggerated breasts popping out of her cleavage as she gunned down five men at once. They had put her in a wet see-through dress, high heels, and a thong, made the killing of the LKs a pornographic event.

The LKs had been lampooned by an unknown artist.

And that had inspired dozens, if not hundreds, of Bitstrips.

Fucking Bitstrips.

The shame had become global.

Many thought the LKs had become vulnerable. None said so directly. It was implied. What gave War Machine the most pang was when the wives of the dead LKs begged for answers, when they demanded justice with their kids at their side or newborn babies on their hips.

When War Machine fell silent, his wife, Mrs. Ramjit, the beauty known as Diamond Dust, stepped forward, took her husband's hand, squeezed his palm twice as a signal to let her handle this matter.

To the poor she was Karleen; to the rest she was Mrs. Ramjit.

She spoke emphatically. "The Kiwi will be found and brought back here to Trinidad, and she will look into the eyes of the wives she has made widows, and we will be the ultimate law in this matter. We will not involve the police, so we will punish her as we see fit, as long as we see fit, and when we are done, dispose of her as we see fit. No matter the cost. That is my commitment to you."

War Machine listened to his stunning wife make a promise that would not be easy to fulfill.

Another woman asked, "How did she walk into the bank with a gun in her purse and no one noticed? Why was the alarm at the bank turned off? The alarm should have alerted the security guard."

War Machine said, "The Kiwi had to have had it arranged that way."

Someone chimed in, "Then someone at the bank had to be her accomplice."

Diamond Dust said, "All were checked. All were clean. All were just as traumatized."

War Machine looked around at the others, at the self-important people who flocked to them, to those who were attracted to power, to money — the same people who never helped a gunta when he was living in the slums. Now they were begging for donations and an audience with the king.

Like a politician, his wife continued to make promises he would have to live up to.

He'd had words with her about that before.

He would have to have words with her again.

War Machine kissed his wife, hugged his children, left the rooftop festivities, took the guarded elevator down to a floor reserved for his men, and entered.

He paused long enough to switch SIM cards and make a phone call.

War Machine snapped, "That was the third incident in a month."

"You double-crossed me. There was no payment."

"No, your end of the bargain fell through."

"Your end failed."

"The terms were not satisfied."

"Then we have nothing else to talk about."

"Tread lightly."

"You do the same."

He hung up and destroyed the SIM card.

War Machine entered the private suite and found Appaloosa waiting, cognac in hand.

Appaloosa asked, "How much did we lose on the shipment?"

"Not enough to stop our momentum." He poured himself a drink. "Nothing will stop us."

"Jamaicans? Sounds like it was the Seven Jamaicans, but I doubt it. Money was taken, but no drugs were stolen. Jamaicans would not leave the drug shipment. They wouldn't take the money then leave a million-dollar shipment. They would have taken it all."

War Machine nodded. "I know how they work."

"In the last month we have been hit in Miami. In New York. In Barbados."

"Unprecedented. We'd become comfortable with our operations."

"What is lost is lost, until we find who robbed us, then recover what was taken."

"Appaloosa, what's the concern? Are you here on behalf of the rest of the men?"

"First the Kiwi, and now someone has declared war on that aspect of our organization. Now the deaths here. The men are concerned, want to be reassured our other investments remain solid."

"The company remains solid, but the wives are restless, a stirred hornet's nest."

"Should we continue to search for the Kiwi while so much is going on?"

"The wives care less about the other issues than the deaths of their spouses."

Appaloosa nodded. "Then let's find the Kiwi bitch so we can get to the real war. Let's hunt her."

Guerrero and Kandinsky entered the suite, both in Italian suits, sovereigns of their hamlet.

Kandinsky said, "Our intel thinks the Kiwi is still hiding in the West Indies."

"What intel?"

"Diamond Dust hired a new firm to track the Kiwi."

"Who authorized a new firm to be hired?"

"She did."

War Machine nodded. His wife had gone behind his back.

He said, "My cousin was fooled by the Kiwi. If not for him, this would not have happened."

Guerrero said, "The Kiwi was good. I had been fooled as well."

Kandinsky said, "I had stood close enough to fuck her and had no clue that her perfume had stink like death. Bamboozled. Brothers, King Killer brought her here, allowed us to be bamboozled."

They looked across the room at War Machine's low-born cousin. They stared at King Killer. He stood with other men, drinking, smoking a Cuban cigar.

War Machine stared at his cousin the longest.

They had played together as boys, had committed the best of sins together.

Kandinsky said, "This calls for disciplinary actions, War Machine."

"It will be done."

Guerrero said, "It should have been done immediately."

"Are you questioning my leadership? My judgment?"

"Of course not. Just recognizing the unfortunate position we are all in."

Kandinsky said, "At some point it will be done. Our men were ambushed. The only way the Kiwi could have known where the minister was going to be, she had inside information. Our men had no idea where they were driving the minister until early that morning."

War Machine glowered at his cousin, nodded in agreement. "Someone did."

Guerrero said, "Diamond Dust is right. We have to find that Kiwi bitch."

War Machine said, "We will find the Kiwi, kill the Kiwi, then kill whoever sent the Kiwi and punish their wives and daughters. We will take their children and make them our bed wenches and manservants. For now, while I wait on this other set of information, let my cousin enjoy himself."

Like Diamond Dust, under pressure, asserting leadership, he made hard promises.

For War Machine, this situation was his Syria.

Diamond Dust entered the suite, came and stood at his side.

She said, "Motherfuckers are driving me insane."

She ranted, vented. Each day, she received dozens of calls, hundreds of texts, and just as many e-mails from all the other wives.

No one knew what was going on, only that no one wanted to be the next widow.

No one wanted to lose her standing in the organization, because a widow would be treated like an ex-footballer's wife, would no longer be on the guest list, would no longer be a celebrity by marriage. Widows would have to be moved from their million-dollar condos, downsized and sent away, treated like outgoing presidents were treated, sent to again be normal citizens, knowing that if one secret was shared, they wouldn't live to see the next sunrise. The other wives had protested that policy, this being a different situation. These weren't natural deaths. They happened while the men were working.

Diamond Dust would find a way to handle the internal politics gone awry.

Diamond Dust stood tall.

Kandinsky said, "This will not be tolerated."

"No matter the cost. We will find the Kiwi. Bring her back. Burn her on the Savannah." She nodded. "We have to do what needs to be done."

That said, she looked at King Killer, looked at her twin brother, looked at him in disgust, as if she wanted to cross the room and stab him in the throat with a poniard.

Then she again looked at her husband, smiled, and softly said, "We have rules."

She walked away, a soft-legged sovereign who ruled the hardhearted monarch.

SEVENTEEN

Parish of Christ Church, Barbados
The Corvette jammed a hit by Chris Brown
as it turned left and entered St. Lawrence
Gap and passed Café Sol. I signaled, made
the same left turn. The Gap was the Sunset
Strip of Barbados.

I rumbled through the din, a shadow on a
black motorcycle heading toward the stretch
of million-dollar condos that looked like they
had been regurgitated by Crayola, overpriced
condos that stood next to a rainbow of low-
budget hotels that had been regurgitated by
the same company. I paused in front of the
dullness of an Anglican church, sacred
ground in a cove of sinners. As a soul train of
cars passed by, each set of headlights revealing my position, I killed my engine. Waited.
Patience was not one of my strong points.

After the Corvette parked in the ten-dollar
pay lot, its driver emerged. Six-foot-three.
White shirt, short-sleeved with trendy stitch-
ing. Black pants, slim legs, sag to comple-

ment his swag. He passed by smoking a joint, talking on his cellular, shouting, angry as hell about a deal gone bad, but it was all rapid and in dialect. He ended his call, and finished his smoke, spat, then paused to flirt with a European woman in a translucent skirt. The way she stood when the lights hit her, every man could see Buff Bay.

He lost the dialect and I was able to read his lips: "I'm a famous cricketer."

"What's your name?"

"Scott Pinkerton."

"Never heard of you."

"Let me show you photos of my new house and my new car."

After he showed her the photos, she grinned, they exchanged numbers, and she left, impressed.

He wore matte and shiny sterling silver bracelets; around his neck was a gray titanium cross pendant on a black cable. His watch was worth at least four grand. West Indian baller. Well-manicured. Metrosexual. There were at least thirty restaurants, bars, and clubs for him to choose from. He passed up Reggae Lounge, paused at Hal's Car Park Bar, took in the loud music and horrible karaoke that could be heard from two miles away, but he only paused long enough to buy a Red Stripe beer and flirt with a few British women, then moved on, walked into the next car park, the one for Sugar Ultra Lounge.

I should have chatted him up then, but I needed double verification.

Anyone seeing a biker chick with him, that would have been too easy to remember.

I stood out. I needed to create a wassy walk and blend in with the rest of the midnight hoochies.

I was on the other side of the road, helmet on, trailing him, stopping in front of a plethora of roadside vendors selling baked chicken, fish, and macaroni pie. Again my belly growled to distraction. I waited and made sure that he went inside the club, then checked my watch.

My body felt heavy. I removed my matte-black helmet but left the black stocking cap on my head, and then I reached into my backpack and pulled out a Red Bull. Drank it. Pulled out a second one. Drank it.

I took out a disposable Samsung phone and did what I shouldn't have done. I put in one of the many SIM cards I had purchased around the globe, gritted my teeth, and dialed a number in Florida.

On the third ring, as I was about to hang up, he answered. "Hello?"

I didn't say anything. The call was international, his voice clear.

He asked, "Jennifer, is this you again? Area code 672? What area code is this?"

In a soft Brooklyn accent I whispered, "Johnny."

"Jennifer."

"Hey, Johnny. How have you been?"

In a frustrated, sad, and angry voice he said, "You broke my kid's heart."

"Johnny Parker. I miss you."

"For the last time, don't call again. Don't keep stalking me."

"I'm the victim here, Johnny."

"My child is in therapy. Did you hear what I said? My child is in therapy."

I listened to him inhale and exhale, counted to five, and killed the call.

Then I became MX-401 again and went to one of the Cable & Wireless pay phones across from Hal's Car Park Bar. Bad karaoke, misogynistic soca, super-loud old-school reggae, and R&B from two decades ago had numbed my senses while I used my cellular to make a call.

"MX-401. Calling for double verification."

"The project for tonight has been sanctioned."

"I did a job yesterday and you're throwing me back out here to work again tonight? Once a-fuckin'-gain, I am a Reaper and you need to show respect. You put me at risk over and over."

"Grow up, kid. Grow the fuck up and manage your personality disorder."

"Doing a hit on an island is like doing a kill in a small town, then going to the only IHOP in town to eat. You don't have a shootout and stick around for a Rooty Tooty Fresh 'N Fruity."

"Right now we are trying to keep a war between us and the LKs from breaking out."

"Why would a war break out?"

"Look in the mirror and see the answer. Things didn't go as scheduled. You didn't burn the safe house. You killed two LKs. Do I really need to cover that major fuck-up point by point?"

"Look, if I stay on this island, I need supplies. Call Tradespan, send two barrels of supplies."

"Make do with what you have. Need cash, you can always try to sell what you sit on."

"Respect me. You expect me to work and work and work and show up every damn day and not get paid a damn dime? Who do you think I am, a schoolteacher in Antigua? I demand my money."

"The man behind the double red doors will send someone from the Barbarians to meet you."

"I know how this goes. All problems are redundant and redundancy is eliminated."

"Unless notified otherwise, the meet with the representatives will happen in two days."

"Get me credit cards and a clean passport. This is my last time asking nicely."

"Just be prepared for the meeting with the team members they have organized."

" 'Members.' Plural. Who is coming down here to this ham-shaped rock?"

"The team has been prepped. They will come to the Six Roads safe house."

"No. Not my safe house. If we meet, we meet in a public setting."

"You don't control this, Reaper."

"My way, or there will not be a fuckin' meeting."

There was a long pause. He put me on hold. Forced me to listen to elevator music.

He came back on and said, "Don't fuck it up like you fucked up in Trinidad."

"Fuck you. Pick up a newspaper from down here and read how I handled last night, you prick."

"No more calls or texts to Pembroke Pines, Florida. You've made at least one call to Florida a day. We were hoping you would put that behind you, but you continue to put this organization at risk."

"You've tapped his phone."

"The man behind the double red doors sent a message, one for me to read you."

"I'm listening."

" 'Johnny Parker. He's a nobody, but it could get ugly for him and his child. Nobody likes to go to a double funeral for a father and his kid. So let's avoid making that accident happen.' "

My Ducati was fine where it was parked. I

stood where I was until a young woman in a black sequined dress parked her Toyota Allex on the side of the road, then went toward Sugar Ultra. When no one was watching, I went through the gate that led to the Anglican church. Went in dressed in black jeans and a dark hoodie, and emerged as a vixen with gray eyes, mid-back-length bleach-blond hair with sandy brown lowlights. The basics were important. People recalled hair and eyes. Most of all, they remembered accents. My guns had been left inside of my backpack, and my backpack had been hidden on church grounds. Soon I strolled by a crowd of aggressive taxi drivers. One potbellied man walked out to the road and up on me, told me that I looked thirsty and offered me a beer.

With a raspy, Cockney accent, a female Michael Caine, I said, "Is the lager complimentary?"

He quirked his lips and in a hard Bajan dialect he said, "Englishwoman, meat gaw pull?"

Meat gaw pull. The old man had asked me to fuck him for a can of beer.

He stood there wearing a red T-shirt, TIME'S UP FREUNDEL in bold letters on the front.

I dropped the Cockney, sounded as Bajan as flying fish, and snapped, "Fuh fakkin Banks? Go suck a shitty rasshole you old ass nasty son-of-a-fucking bitch. Old ass acting

188

like a hard-ears saga boy wid nuh brought-upsy. Open your nasty mouth again and you get catspraddled in a bassa-bassa wid me. I will fuck yuh up, boi."

If we hadn't been on a main road, a crowd passing, I would've kicked his ass, Chicago-style.

I showed him two middle fingers, turned around, shook off the urge to bash his face in, became a lady again. Irritated. Last night I was gunning down drug runners. Tonight my target was a cricketer.

In my mind, as I walked like the child of Tyra and Beyoncé, I tried to connect the dots.

First I tried to understand why the hell I had been sentenced to this prison for so long.

Then I wondered how many people I would have to damage to close this next contract.

EIGHTEEN

Diamond Dust entered the private suite at the Carlton again, head high, this time excited.

War Machine rose from his seat, went to his wife. "Was there a new problem?"

"No. Good news just arrived. I need all of my top men to hear this announcement."

Appaloosa, Guerrero, King Killer, and Kandinsky came to her, stood in front of their queen, their Princess Di of Trinidad. War Machine stood in front of his men, their leader, their one true king.

Diamond Dust said, "The workers we hired to go above and beyond what the authorities here are capable of doing have found something. They have spent every moment studying bank footage and have pulled images from all cameras in the area. We have information the police will never access."

War Machine said, "What do we have? Get on with it."

"We have a solid image we can use to track

her using facial recognition software. The Kiwi is cunning. Quick. Daring. So we have to remain vigilant, not let another moment pass. Believe it or not, after all of this time, the bitch might still be in the West Indies. She might be on our island."

Kandinsky sipped his liquor, asked, "What good will the photo do?"

"No matter what deception the killer used, the workers said the distance between the eyes is all we need to try to run an image through databases. The alarm had been off, but the camera was active."

King Killer put his hand on his sister's shoulder and asked, "And there is a clear shot?"

"Yes, my brother. They have gone frame by frame and found a shot."

Appaloosa said, "Finally. We can run that through databases at the airport and see if she left on a plane. Same for the ships. It's a long shot, but it's better than nothing."

Diamond Dust said, "It is a shot we should have had forty days ago."

War Machine said, "Until that leads us somewhere, we can only wait, so we are done."

"No. We are not done."

War Machine asked his wife, "Is there more?"

"There is more. I have hired others to track the Kiwi."

"When was this done?"

"I hired a group out of South America."

"I was not aware of this project."

"Not important, husband. They came here, reviewed what had been left behind, and have found the safe house she used. It's northeast. I had expected it to be in Port of Spain, but it's northeast."

War Machine asked, "Why wasn't I informed? Why weren't my men informed?"

She paused. "I am informing you now. I am informing all of you, everyone on this team. The police haven't found the safe house, aren't aware that it exists, so we are ahead of everyone on this."

"I will say this for all to hear, and I will only say this once," War Machine said, and tightened his jaw. "*I* am the strategist."

"I see things that you fail to see."

"Karleen, my ambitious wife, don't overstep."

"Don't talk to me that way in front of my men."

"And don't ever make me look weak in front of my soldiers. Don't ever try."

She paused, smiled, raised her hand, touched War Machine's face, and in a soft voice said, "Apologies. I had forgotten how fragile an ego can be. Forgive me for that oversight. Two of our brothers were killed. Good news arrived and I was excited. I didn't think that anything I was doing would lead to anything substantial, but it has. I have sent men there to secure the safe house until we can arrive."

"You sent men? How in the fuck are you going to send *my* men without notifying me?"

"I did what needed to be done. If it had turned out to be nothing, then no one would have . . . I wasn't sure if it was the location, so I sent three men there to stake it out, see if she returned."

"Under whose authority?"

"Under my authority. Be glad I did. They broke in and it was more than we expected."

"And I wasn't notified? None of the top five were notified?"

"There wasn't time."

"We sleep in the same bed, woman."

"Can we move forward?"

"Move forward."

"The men texted me photos of what was on the walls. She was there. I don't know how many were there with her, who were her accomplices, but that small house in the north was where this was plotted. Blueprints, plans, everything is there, intact. The assassination was planned, and I am sure that it was part of the conspiracy to discredit our organization and cause us to lose favor with the people."

"You don't give military commands. You don't use my men without my authority. Sending men up there without proper backup, they could've all been slaughtered, and whose fault would that have been?"

"But they weren't."

"You're missing the point."

"There is a conspiracy in play. We have been attacked in Miami, New York, and Barbados. Do you think all of that is a coincidence? The island knows we have faltered. The world knows."

"Other organizations know as well."

"Exactly. Now men and women who need protection are going to other groups, and will do so until this is resolved. Our brand is damaged. We have a reputation to maintain and we will not cease our hunt until we have someone in the ground. We will do what we have to do to fix our sullied reputation."

The men said nothing, just shifted, looked to War Machine, waited for him to make a call. Warriors would always follow the word of the king. But War Machine knew that his wife had ensured an emotional connection between her and all the top men. She had been cunning, smart, forward-thinking.

She said, "We will make the widows feel the satisfaction that comes with revenge. We will make the rest of our organization know that we are solid, and make the outside world know that we remain competent."

War Machine looked at his wife, displeased. Her words, her voice, her speeches were always as powerful as his gun, his sword, his sharpened knife. She had an undeniable gift. If he damaged her, then all would be lost. He loved her. He hated her. He couldn't destroy her without destroying himself.

He had to let this play out. This course of action had momentum and resistance was futile.

She said, "I sense the tension between us all. Soon we can all meet at Passy Bay. It has been a while since I have conferred with all five. It has been a long while since we have bonded."

War Machine nodded. "Men. Finish your drinks. Let's prepare to move to the northeast."

King Killer took his sister's hands, kissed her cheeks, her lips, then looked in her eyes.

He said, "As usual, you have done an excellent job. We will find her."

She nodded. "We will find the truth. Neziah, my brother, the killer of kings; we will find the truth."

Nineteen

St. Lawrence Gap, Parish of Christ Church
Biggie Smalls. Tupac. Dr. Dre. Snoop Lion
when he was Snoop Dogg. American music
bumped hard. I had spent my teen years in
Southern Cali and the music was taking me
back.

Men were in their own line, being searched
by security at the door. Women were in a
separate row. I stepped to the rear of the
queue, felt the music, and my body started
moving, wining. Bajans were in line, many
Bajans talking fast, dramatic, humorous,
expressive. Nothing like the dialect in Trinidad, but the European ear couldn't distin-
guish the two songs any more than they could
differentiate between soca, calypso, and reggae. I listened, mimicked the dialect, repeated
idioms and words like mobaton, ovadayso,
obzocky, pancart, suck salt, wunna, jipsey,
chossel, spranksious, peenie, cafuffle, cut eye,
do-flicky, cumma, barrifle, rangate, salt bred,
long talk, onneat, duppy, cheese on bread,

bruggadung, lemme, muddah, caniption, ig-
rant, bullcow, bassa-bassa, collyfox, wulloss,
too sweet, onliest, and nuff.

"Much people here tonight."

"Too much people."

Most Bajans used the word "much" instead
of the word "many."

I had picked up that habit from Old Man
Reaper years ago.

A bouncer inspected the women in short
dresses and high heels, most dressed like they
wanted to be featured on Bajantube, and I
was called to the front.

The big Bajan bouncer spoke to my breasts
and said, "Like, whoa. Sexy body, Englishwoman."

With a shy smile, I nodded. Anyone who
wasn't brown was assumed to be a foreigner.

"All that swag and niceness. You too sweet
to be in a line. Come on in, you lovely thing."

With a broader grin, I winked and thanked
him for being a bigot.

They searched inside of the women's
purses, did a visual inspection, nothing as
intense as they did in the clubs in L.A. and
New York and South Beach, nothing like the
violation in Trinidad. I opened my foot-long
clutch and the bouncer saw a tampon, a condom, lip gloss, and two hundred dollars in
the local currency. The security guy at the
door put on his best smile, winked.

In a rapid Bajan dialect he told me, "Sexy

Body, if your body don't need the tampon, I'll be more than happy to help you fill out the condom to the last digit on the serial numbers."

"For true?"

"For true, Englishwoman. Gimme your BBM."

"I'll check for you later. Nice wedding ring, by the way."

I walked in right after a tall, brown-skinned woman wearing high heels and a black sequined skirt. Her backside shimmered in the light. Men flirted with her in droves, stared at her butt without shame.

A well-dressed man-boy came over to her and said, "Hey, sexy."

She said, "When a man calls me sexy, he's acknowledging what I already know."

"How ya bumper get so nice? Dress make it shine bright like a diamond."

"Leff me alone now."

Her accent was Haitian, highly educated, very irritated. An Amazon who stood tall enough to be a model, but had an attitude that said she wasn't a toy, that she was more interested in Ultimate Frisbee and rugby. I bumped into her, her frame feminine but solid, then she frowned at me, at my powerful shoulders and strong arms, at my core. I sized her up, and without apology, I moved on.

The man who drove the Corvette finally

saw me. He grinned and licked his lips and took his attention away from the girl he was chatting up. He pushed away from the girl, and he wagged his fingers, told me to come to him.

I shook my head and went the other way. He abandoned his VIP area, pushed through the crowd, touched me to get my attention. He touched me like he was entitled to any woman he desired.

He said, "Hope Solo, are you walking away from me?"

"I am not Hope Solo, nor Han Solo, just walking solo."

"You sexy like US football player Hope Solo, legs and body, only better."

He was Bajan as well, but his accent sounded close to English West Country, Bristol, Gloucester, Devon, that kind of area. A Bajan accent was nothing like the rest of the Caribbean, nothing like Trinidad.

If the job had required chopsticks, I could've touched him right then and disappeared.

He said, "Come to VIP. Come celebrate. I paid two thousand for everything. Drinks free."

"You walk over and expect me to pop around the Jack so you can rabbit on until the dickory hits twelve."

"What?"

"Sorry. We talk in a rhyming slang back

home, so I need to adjust my tongue. I asked if you expected me to go to the bar with you."

"Come with me."

"No thanks. Get your Tommy Tank from your China plates. Lot of Khyber Pass in your party, most in Irish pigs, all wearing too much tomfoolery, but that's your kind of struggle and grunt."

"What?"

"You have a lot of sexy women in your area. Nice asses and wigs, and most are draped in a lot of jewelry. That's your type. Go back to them."

"No? Did you just tell me no?"

"I did. Same answer when I'm Oliver Twist."

"Oliver Twist?"

"Drunk."

"Obviously you don't know who I am."

"Everybody caters to you. You must be bloody famous and all bees and honey. Are you the prime minister?"

"I'm more important than the prime minister. I am a cricketer, true, but I'm also a businessman. I create jobs while the government is taking away jobs. I do more for the island than anyone on the prime minister's payroll. I am going to bring big changes here. I am going to change Barbados."

"What kind of business do you have?"

"A very successful one. Import and export. Everything on the island is imported. Every car. Every refrigerator. Clothes. Look around this room. From the lights to the prettiest of the pretty women, almost everything comes from Japan, China, London, or the States."

"What do the people manufacture here?"

"Babies." He laughed at his own rude joke. "Now look at my photos."

"Don't you have cobbler's awls?"

"What dem?"

"Balls. You have balls."

He took out his BlackBerry and showed me photos of his million-dollar home in the Prior Park section of St. James, his the most expensive in the exclusive and gated Palm Court community.

I said, "Wicked bed. That's a high bed. Looks sturdy and unbreakable."

"Made in Italy and imported from Italy. Only two in the West Indies. Big man has the other one."

"Good Lord. Must be a Cadbury's Flake."

"What?"

"This must be a mistake, showing me this. You have at least a hundred naked women trapped inside of your phone."

"They love my bed. Why are you making a nasty face like that?"

"Is that an Irish pig between her legs or a misplaced Afro? A woman should get a Brazilian before she takes photos like that."

"She *is* Brazilian."

"That makes it worse."

King Bubba & Lil Rick screamed that they wanted drinks and the room demanded the same as they danced. The target wined up on me. I danced with him, grinned, shook a finger, and told him not so close. He grabbed my hand and dance-walked me to the bar anyway. Ordered drinks. After I finished a chocolate martini, he ordered shots. I ended up standing practically hip to hip next to the tall woman who wore the black sequined skirt. Tall and toned. Her hair was long, the perfect weave. She had been watching the cricketer too. She was so close I inhaled the scent of her perfume. Lola by Marc Jacobs.

I motioned at the sexy Amazon in the sequined skirt and asked, "She one of your fans?"

"I ain't know she. Probably one of my many fans."

Two shots and a Mudslide later, after he'd had six Banks, shots, and something made with dark liquor, he pulled me to the dance floor. Tipsy, I danced how they danced, did Up Deh, logo logo, Willie Bounce, killed the Swag Dance, and when Soca Cartel commanded the women to grab their ankles, I did a quick-and-dirty six thirty and brought it back up into a respectable tick-tock.

The cricketer said, "Cock-back. Baby, you cock-back real nice."

Lost in the groove, I leaned in to him and asked, "What was that?"

"You pooch back real good like a back way you love. Your ass move like that on top?"

I ran my hand over my hair. "It's hot. Meet me outside in five minutes. In front of Hal's."

"Then what?"

"We'll see if I move my arse like this when I'm on top. Where can we go to be alone? Would love to introduce you to my north and south."

"North and south?"

"Mouth. Would love for you to meet my mouth — my north and south."

"The beach. A parking lot. Something by the water."

"I saw a better place, near the Joe Baxis."

"Joe Baxis?"

"Taxis."

"That not far."

"You have condoms?"

"Dem make me itch."

"I'm not half-a-idiot. I don't want to Posh 'n' Becks and get breed and have watermelon in my belly. Would be a total Lionel Blair. A nightmare. Of epic proportion. I have a pot and pan waiting at my room, but he's sterile. So, if you give me a dustbin lid, you'd have to make me your trouble and strife, Adam and Eve me when I say that."

"What?"

"No condom, no sex. I don't want to end up pregnant."

"I pull out faster than Bolt can run."

"Just don't fuck that fast. That would be a Lionel Blair, too."

"I go long time with you, Hope Solo. Go real long time. My dick big and go long."

While the crowd sang along to the music he leaned in to French kiss me. When he did that a girl who had just arrived stormed over, grabbed his arm as we were kissing, and made him turn and face her.

She snapped, "What de fuck? Wha de fuck going on?"

"Cheese on bread. I don't know she."

"Don't rub shit in my mouth and tell me that it's pudding."

The girl made threats, cursed him hard, said she was no fool, then walked away.

Too many eyes were on the foolishness. I turned to leave too.

He grabbed my arm. "Where you think you going?"

"It's time to Christian Slater."

"What?"

"Time to say see-you-later."

"Where you going?"

"Down the jack to my hotel. Going back to my boyfriend now."

"We're not done."

"That was embarrassing. I want to get some air."

"Where this botsie go, I go."

"You love April in Paris a little too much."

I pushed his hand away. "Could you stop

squeezing my arse like it's some Uncle Fred?"

"She gone. Tell your boyfriend this sweet ass belong to me tonight. All the other girls have a botsie big and soft like rotten fruit, but yours is round and firm, hard like green mango on the tree."

He followed me through the crowd, outside into the coolness of the Caribbean air. Not until then did he give me some space. A Honduran girl confronted him; this one just happened to be passing by with a group of girls and saw him walking out of the club holding my backside, and she wanted to have harsh words with him. I kept going, waited across the street. I wanted this bullshit off the books. Didn't want the Barbarians giving me more shit. He left the girl, hurried and caught up. I let my hair loose, strolled behind a crowd of Canadians. Then the cricketer was behind me, had broken free from all other women, squeezing my ass and telling me how good he was going to make me feel.

He said, "You walk so wassy."

"Enough of the Chitty Chitty Bang Bang."

"What?"

"Let's get off the road before another one of your women shows up with her hot grumble and grunt and a slice of Sexton. Let's go here."

I led him toward the black-and-white sign in front of the Anglican church: THE CHURCH OF ST. LAWRENCE. We went through the wrought-iron gate, vanished from the world of sinners. He kissed me and groped me until we were in the rear of the monument to the glory of God, its architecture not on the level of the Neoclassical, Gothic, and Baroque elements that were at St. Paul's Cathedral, but it still looked like a throwback to the 1800s when the area was, I think, just known as Bath Village.

He said, "Why you pouting?"

"What if I want to change my mind about this?"

"I don't like being teased. Don't dance with me half the night and let me buy you drinks and make me turn down other beautiful girls and get hard and think you can leave me with blue balls. I don't change my mind so you can't change your mind. I have made your mind up for you. Understand?"

"Okay. I don't want you mad. You'd think me a slag, a dumb slapper, a bint, who was a cock teaser, a cow too afraid to get some Harry Monk on the north and south."

"You have sexy breasts. Real sexy breasts."

"Might even take off my top and get some on my Eartha Kitts."

"You have a beautiful mouth and I want you to leave red lipstick all over my dick."

I led him to a shadowed spot at the end of the car park, an area that stood facing the jagged rocks on the calm beach. He pulled me to him, held my face with his dank hands, and licked my lips.

He said, "Your kiss real sweet, like cane sugar."

I opened my clutch, released its hidden compartment, took out what gave my clutch its weight. I took out a BC-41, one of the deadliest combat knives ever made, one that could chop the branch off a tree, its handle with a grip that could be used like brass knuckles, its blade surgical-sharp. The knife was nine inches long, the knuckle guard being almost five of those inches. His eager hands came up, grabbed my breasts, pulled one from its bra, and sucked the nipple. I slid my fingers into the knife's grip, held his head, and closed my eyes. He pushed my straps from my shoulders, was busy sucking my left nipple — too much suction, yet the pain was sweet. It felt good. Felt so good for a moment.

I whispered, "You're a fucking Richard the Third."

"I'm a king?"

"No. You're a turd."

The first two blows were hard and wicked thrusts, strikes that inserted the BC-41 inside of his body up to the knuckle guard, fast like a boxer putting jabs to his lungs, the full length of the blade digging in deep. That was the worst place to be stabbed. It created a sucking chest wound. The moment I pulled the blade out of its new home, he couldn't breathe. Right away he grabbed my hair and my wig came off, gripped in his hand as he coughed up blood. He went down on his knees. Eyes open wide. He was in shock. His lips trembled and he had a "what de shite" expression on his face.

In my true voice I said, "Do you have any idea how fuckin' annoying you are? Jesus. I wanted to scream. You're pushy. You're a fuckin' bully. I hate bullies. But you. You have to be the most arrogant, irritating, annoying son-of-a-bitch in the Caribbean. You talk too much. You go on and on and on and just love to talk so you can hear the sound of your own irritating voice, and all of these women like you?"

If only Trinidad had gone this way. That was all that I could think at that moment. If only the target and no one else had been put down. If I hadn't been drugged, it would have happened differently.

I forced him on his back, cut away his belt, felt a lump in his front pocket, thought it might be a weapon, pulled it out, saw that it was a big wad of money, all hundred-dollar bills in American currency. It paused me. It was like a starving man finding a fresh loaf of bread, warm, still wrapped up.

I put the wad to the side and sat on his thighs, pulled out his penis. I castrated him, held his offering in my hand, ready to force it down his throat. Those were the instructions.

Then there was a gap in the music. There was abrupt silence.

A momentary loss of power in the village had left me vulnerable.

Bracelets jingled behind me. High heels tapped the concrete. The wind brought me her scent, her familiar scent. The woman was tall. Wore a black sequined skirt that shimmied in the broken light. She was a dark silhouette, an unmistakably shaped silhouette, and I knew that as she stood in silence, as I had done a shocking thing on sacred grounds, her eyes were on mine.

With each breath I inhaled the scent of Lola by Marc Jacobs. It was the same girl from the club, the one who had been eyeing the cricketer all evening. She had been on my heels since I had arrived.

As the sea licked the sand she saw the blood dripping from my once-shiny blade.

My adrenaline was high. I was on fire. Couldn't stop sweating.

She stood in the shadows, underneath the shadows of the symbol of an imported religion.

Blade in hand, I went toward her the way I dreamed the LKs had come after me.

I went toward black sequins as they shimmered on Caribbean-brown skin.

She stood in the shadows holding a Beretta. An assassin's gun.

"Hurry up, Reaper," Petrichor said.

"Give me a moment."

"I'm late and need to get home to my husband."

"Let me do my fucking job, will you? Just let me do my fucking job."

I went back to the cricketer, flipped him over, and with my blade I cut the back of his neck.

TWENTY

Six Roads, safe house

The Caribbean sun pulled itself from the ocean at around five in the morning.

Unable to sleep with the sun shining on my face through the thin curtains, I sat up, pulled myself from two hours of fitful sleep, head aching, much on my mind. Looked at my hands, expected to see blood. My hands had been scrubbed clean. Dressed in a wrinkled blue T-shirt, red shorts, and black biker boots, I opened the bedroom window, smelled the smoke from cane fields that had burned half of the night. The air had owned a stench since I had arrived, another reason to keep the windows shut. I crawled out of the window, stepped around frogs, and went to the corrugated fence. Snails. Centipedes. Ants. Flies. Everything attacked me or was squished. The neighbor on the next road had a giant lime tree, its branches hanging over the shoddy, thrown-together barrier. I pulled four small limes from a low-hanging branch. The neighbor in the house near the main road was outside. Thin woman. Maybe thirty. Brown. Short hair. Five-foot-two in flip-flops, shorts, tank top. She saw me, went back to hanging laundry.

Area was quiet. Local dope man and his ashy-foot flunkies weren't up yet.

I climbed back inside the window, washed my hands, put on hand sanitizer, then scrubbed a can of sardines to kill all the germs, opened the can, deboned the fish, mashed it with a fork. I added lime juice along with chopped-up onions. After I sprinkled on a little pepper, I chopped up a tomato and added that, too. I grabbed a box of rice crackers, stared at the food, but put all of it to the side.

Tired, shopworn, and feeling five times my age, I brought the floor fan into the front room, put it on high. Stretched for thirty minutes. Down on my haunches, I put my laptop on the floor, popped in an Insanity DVD, did a plyometric cardio circuit as a warm-up then dug in deep and did max cardio conditioning and cardio abs. I shadowboxed, cursed my invisible opponent, then did katas.

I looked up at the walls and whispered, "Fuck you, Johnny Parker."

Two hours later the workout ended, the floor below my feet a puddle of sweat.

I mopped the dull tile, and since I had

earned my meal, I ate, chewed smashed sardines and crackers as I paced back and forth in my cell, unable to cool off, stormed from room to room, ended up in the stuffy bedroom. The previous day's newspapers were scattered on the worn-out, unmade twin bed, a bed that hadn't been made up since I arrived and wouldn't be, not by these hands. The sheets were twisted from my angst and insomnia, a dark vibrator unconscious on the sheets due to me trying to give myself therapy so I could get a decent night of sleep. I pushed the *Barbados Advocate* and *Nation* to the floor. The headlines for both papers were almost the same: FORMER WEST INDIES CRICKETER FOUND KILLED IN ST. LAWRENCE GAP WHILE OUT ON RAPE CHARGE. ACCUSED RAPIST MURDERED IN CHRIST CHURCH.

They remembered the cricketer dancing with a bashy English girl then arguing with his fiancée and almost getting into a bassa-bassa on the dance floor. "Bashy" wasn't a compliment. It meant I was wild 'n out, and their brown eyes saw me as a slut. "Bassa-bassa" meant fight.

I showered in cold water, same as I had done for the last forty days. After the quick cooldown, I checked my phone again. Nothing from the Barbarians. Nothing at fuckin' all. Had to live my life.

I packed my backpack with extra clothes and just-in-case tools. Crawled out the back window again. The same curious neighbor peeped from her window when I started the Ducati.

I hit the Wynter Crawford Roundabout and attacked Highway 5. I outran the stench from the slaughterhouse and took the main highway toward Haggatt Hall and Government Hill, my destination the heart of Bridgetown. I drove tired, with the blood from a cricketer washed away from my hands.

Ten minutes later I was beyond Sky Mall, passing the prime minister's home, maybe three kilometers shy of Bridgetown. Had to find the Chefette near the top of Broad Street.

An Amalgamated Security Armoured Division truck passed by and I wondered how hard it would be to hijack them, too. Rumor was no one had ever nicked a money truck in Barbados. I could dress in the habiliments of a student at Princess Margaret, put on a wig that had ponytails, my backpack loaded with the guns I needed, catch them at a pickup, gun them down, be gone in sixty.

Over the past two weeks, I had given that boldness, that foolishness, serious thought.

Thinking along those lines told me how frustrated and desperate I had become.

I would have to find a way to make money and use that money to make my own plans.

I would have to find a way to escape from Alcatraz.

TWENTY-ONE

Bridgetown, Parish of St. Michael.
Visited by the Spanish and Portuguese and left unclaimed until the English showed up and claimed it for King James I and turned paradise into an island of slaves harvesting sugarcane. Two-hundred and fifty miles northeast of my nightmare, Trinidad and Tobago.

Guyanese. White Bajans who were the offspring of Scottish indentured servants and Irish who were "barbadosed" to the island. The offspring of enslaved Africans. Chinese Bajans. Lebanese and Syrians. Jewish. Muslim-Indian. Some 80,000 people lived in Bridgetown and it looked like more than half were driving the roads and walking. It wasn't as diverse as New Year's Eve in Times Square or a Sunday afternoon on Santa Monica Pier; most owned darker hues than the people had in Trinidad, but I would fit in. I parked the Ducati illegally on Flower Alley, a slender and empty passageway across from an Ameri-

215

can Airlines and FedEx outpost situated in another powder-blue building that looked to be around five decades old. I left my bike on the side of Access Point Cafe. A couple of lead pipes were in the alley. This passageway didn't stink of urine, not like the serpentine alleys behind Cave Shepherd and on Swan Street. I picked up one of the lead pipes. Had a habit of collecting anything that could be a weapon, a habit I had picked up from Old Man Reaper. Solid pipes. A good swing could open a head. Both were the right size for stick fighting, or could be modified and turned into a pair of nunchaku.

I added both to the wicked things I carried in my backpack.

All I smelled was the scent of jerk chicken, oxtail, and snapper. Stomach growled. I put on a wig. Black pixie cut. Put a purple bandana on top of the wig. Darkened my eyes, became punk. I took off my boots, put on flats. The rain was tolerable by the time I made it to Broad Street. Thousands were in town.

Damaged motorcycle helmet in hand, sliding my backpack down my right arm, I went inside Chefette, inhaled the scent of curried meat and broasted chicken as I scanned the place. Didn't see the broker. I waited in a long line, ordered a vegetarian burger, fries, and a Mauby to wash it down. An unsmiling woman took my order and another with the same expression handed it to me.

I found the last empty table facing Broad Street. A few feet away a woman with long dreadlocks, hair soaked from the rain, begged for handouts from people as they left the ATMs in the area, three infants at her side. People with overloaded shopping bags passed her by, kept on trucking.

The broker had six minutes to be in the seat facing me. Might give him five.

I pulled two newspapers from my georgie bundle. Sat one paper next to me, an American newspaper, used that to cover my anxious .380. I picked up the other, a local newspaper, saw an article about the dead cricketer staring at my face. I started reading. The first girl who went off on him at Sugar Ultra Lounge was Sherry-Ann Willoughby. Said they were engaged. She attended Queen's College, a model, a Miss Barbados World delegate last year. Vexed, she had left Sugar Ultra Lounge, gone to Storey Gap, and taken her anger to an off-road entertainment joint, thrown back drinks like they were tap water, hooked up with an ex-boyfriend, and spent the night at his mother's home riding his stiffness.

A jealous girlfriend was also a vindictive girlfriend. Betrayal was her alibi.

But having an alibi didn't mean that you had nothing to do with the crime.

I put the newspaper down, left it faceup,

one article about the local TGIF shutting its doors, another about telecommunications company LIME sending home more than two hundred people, others about construction workers being let go, page after page of black-and-white misery looking up at my frown.

I checked the time on my phone. Black Jack had two minutes.

I scanned more of the newspaper. The cricketer was twenty-seven. His name was Scott Pinkerton. I had read his lips, had seen him tell another woman this, but he never told me. He had never asked me mine. Unlike the doorstopper I had received in Trinidad, the intel that had come from the Barbarians on the cricketer had been very thin.

If I had done the job and been sent away, curiosity would've died on the plane, but I was here and I wanted to know who he was. Ten kids in five countries, all less than ten years old. I saw no reason to put the man into the ground. No reason to kill him the way he had been killed. The paper printed that his father had had twenty-six children by almost as many women. They printed that like it was a good thing. Maybe for the man, not for the women. The cricketer had grown up in St. Michael.

Then came the writeup about the cricketer being accused of rape. He had paid the alleged rape victim off. She said that she had met him at Priva six months ago. He bought her shots, beer, and Ciroc, had left the club and stood in front of Limegrove and burned a tree with her, had gone back to Priva and danced with her, then offered her a ride in his shiny car. She accepted. He hit on her, demanded ass for gas, weed, and liquor. She tried to get away. He grabbed her as he had grabbed me, only she was five-feet-three inches tall, didn't weigh more than ninety pounds. She said that he had overpowered her and battered her and raped her, then left her in the dirt, drunk, throwing up, come-soaked, and in tears.

After an hour with the cricketer, I chose to believe her.

I put the newspaper down, started packing my bag, eased my .380 from underneath the paper into the small of my back. Just then a horn blew outside the window. It sounded a half dozen times. The driver held up traffic, let his tinted window down and waved frantically. It was a man wearing tattoos from shoulders to wrists, an art form that was called sleeves in the tattoo world. He was in a twelve-year-old black BMW X5 that had left-side steering, a rarity on this floating rock. The first letter on his license plate was the letter *G*. St. George Parish. The ID on the vehicle matched the car number that had come in the text before sunrise. I sat back down. He parked illegally where the taxi drivers were herded, said a few words to the marginalized men in that group that yelled and complained, threw his hands up and snapped back at them, then crossed traffic on Broad Street, cut off cars, and came inside through the main entrance, hurried across damp floors and by noisy children and impatient teenagers and exhausted parents. He came toward me shaking his head like he was pissed off, then sat down without saying hello, as if we'd been talking for the last four hours and he'd walked away to use the john and come back. I pushed my food to the side, but held on to my Mauby. He made himself comfortable in his seat. Black Jack was a slim man, toned and decent-looking, clothes simple, unremarkable, his T-shirt claiming, in red bold letters, that he was a SINNER BY BIRTH, SAVED BY THE GRACE OF GOD, EPHE-SIANS 2:8.

I read his shirt and said, "Seriously? Trying to get struck by lightning?"

"Good morning to you too, Reaper. Good fucking morning to you too."

He was Bajan by birth and that couldn't be hidden by his accent, but he wasn't black. Nor was his name Jack. He looked like Anderson Cooper with a goatee and dirty-blond-turning-white hair below his shoulders, yet something was very Brad Pitt in *World War Z* about him.

He said, "I'm upset that this contract I extended to you sub rosa is still open."

"The money hasn't been delivered."

"The word that I received was that the money was sent two days ago."

"They lied."

"Incompetent fucks."

"Don't curse. Kids are around."

"Some of the parents here are cursing in front of their kids now, just in dialect."

"Look, I agreed to work for you on the side, provided that everything went smoothly. Black Jack, this is straight bullshit. I've waited for a week for something that should have taken half a day."

"It's the island. Things move slower here."

"Time on all the clocks here move at the same rate as the time on my watch."

"I'll find out who dropped the ball."

"If it's not in my pocket by the time the sun drowns itself, then I'm done dealing with you."

He asked, "You gonna eat that burger or let it grow mold?"

I slid the veggie burger his way. I'd bought it so I didn't stand out.

He thanked me with a nod, then took a bite that devoured half the sandwich.

I said, "Just remember, I don't do Bajan time. I do on-time. Be glad it started raining."

"Can I eat first?"

"Eat. Not like I have anywhere to go. Still, I'm not one hundred percent comfortable."

I reached into my backpack, pulled out a Red Bull, opened it, and took a few sips before I said, "Now, swallow your burger and move on to our business. Let's start with the fireworks I need."

"I've checked on obtaining the artillery you wanted. Even with me contacting South America, going on the black market, and going face-to-face with the local dealers from Peru, obtaining all you want is still tough. You order hardware like that and people think you're planning a terrorist attack."

"Second item on my agenda. I need to know what Trinidad is up to. The LKs, need to know their location, especially if you can track War Machine and Appaloosa. Same for War Machine's wife."

"Diamond Dust. Mrs. Karleen Ramjit."

"You said that like you have the hots for her."

"I wouldn't kick her out of bed on a rainy day."

"Whatever." I rubbed my eyes with the palms of my hands. "I need the top men tracked."

"War Machine. Appaloosa. Guerrero. Kandinsky."

"Plus King Killer. The five top dogs. One of them would be the team leader."

"And the wife as well."

"The wife. The way you said that, what does that mean?"

"People say she is a regular Rajo Verma. A modern-day Draupadi."

"Is that true? In the videos they had posted online, in all the newspaper articles about that organization, she comes across as being family oriented, dedicated to only her husband, War Machine."

"Rumor is all the main men are eating in one house, so to speak. Not all at once. She has a lot of Princess Di in her blood, and Princess Di was a wild one, a freak who made infidelity look chic. They say that Mrs. Karleen Ramjit is the same way, and many women secretly applaud her supposed lifestyle."

"Rumors. I need facts."

"Lots has been said over the years, but nothing proven."

"Give me a fact."

"The men have studied the killing style of Dole Chadee. You know about Chadee?"

"Some, not a lot."

"Chadee was a Trini, the notorious leader of a ruthless gang of men who were heavily involved in the drug trade. Suspects in more than a few unsolved murders. The LKs are like him, never seen in public other than immaculately dressed in well-fitting suits, hair slicked down, sometimes wearing dark shades, accompanied by armed bodyguards."

"That sounds like War Machine and his crew."

"One girl spoke out against the LKs, made claims about Diamond Dust's lifestyle, about her having multiple husbands, and she was found burning on a cross in a park over there. Burning alive. When they went to notify the girl's family, they opened the door to the house and found her ten family members had been executed. Take the LKs out of the equation and I'll bet the murder rate in Trinidad drops significantly."

"Chadee is dead, right?"

"Rumor is, and yes this is another rumor, when Chadee and eight of his top men were executed —"

"How was he put to sleep? How do they do it down here?"

"Old-school. They used a rope and hanged them until their feet stopped kicking."

"Nine hangings."

"Not all at once. They hanged them all over a weekend — three on Friday, three on Saturday, and three the following Monday. They say that on Tuesday, Karleen De Lewis — aka Mrs. Ramjit, aka Diamond Dust — was born, and the morning she was born she inhaled her first breath and took in the wandering spirit of Chadee. She took a breath and the spirit of the Laventille Killers was born. Some say she is Chadee reincarnated, which I think is bullshit, but a good urban legend. But I know this: with Chadee out of the way, two decades later Diamond

224

Dust and War Machine were able to move in, to start their revolution, to pick up the drug business left behind by Chadee, a business that never ends. Only, they were smarter."

"They hang murderers in Trinidad. That's crude."

"That would be kinder than what the LKs would do if they found you first. They'd make you beg to be hanged. The girl they burned alive, she was sixteen, and she was pregnant for one of the guntas."

I sipped the last of my Red Bull, looked outside; then my eyes came back to Black Jack.

I commanded him, "Find out where the LKs are. I need to know. My trail should be cold. Should be frozen. Maybe that's the reason the Barbarians have stopped supplying intel."

"But you need to be sure. Hacker is trying to crack into their systems and pull intel."

"Obviously Hacker is an amateur."

"She's the best hacker up at UWI, and that's every UWI in the islands."

"Black Jack, the intel is important. If that's the best that Hacker can do, find someone else. If Trinidad comes this way, be it LK or law enforcement, I need to know long before they arrive and put a toe in this sand. I'm an hour away from a country that wants me dead. They could ride a Jet Ski over here."

"You're all wound up for a fight. When was

the last time you slept?"

"I haven't had good sleep since before Trinidad. Not much since Florida."

"What happened in Florida?"

"Not your concern."

It started to rain again. Umbrellas went up. Not many. Few sought shelter. It was one of those days when it rained for ten minutes, then stopped for ten, would do that into the night. People were used to this. Many kept walking like it was a sunny day, puddles be damned. Something else was different. Women didn't freak out about their hair getting wet. If this had been Atlanta, if a drop of water had touched their hair, real or over-the-counter, Southern women would have been screaming like the Wicked Witch of the West when she had been hit with a bucket of water, that or running like they were on fire.

I said, "Can you help me escape? Passports. Traveling documents. You look old enough. You could pretend to be my dad and we could exit this rock like we're going to a family retreat."

"Can't. I'll help you while you're here, but I can't afford to put myself or any contact I know in jeopardy by doing something that would have the Barbarians doing a blackout. But if you made it north and landed on Providence Island I could get you on a mail boat and tuck you away at one of the safe spots at Mangrove Cay, Fresh Creek Andros, or Great Harbour Cay. No one would find you there."

I tapped my fingers on the table, stopped, and said, "Keep me posted on Trinidad."

"Can I ask you something?"

"You can ask whatever you want, but don't expect an answer."

He said, "How many were on your team for the assassination at the bank?"

"Three."

"Three?"

"Me, myself, and I."

"Team of one. They sent you over there to do that job by yourself."

"When you're schizophrenic, you're never alone."

"A politician with a gun in a bank. My mind can't process that."

"It didn't start out that way. Won't say what, but there was another plan from the night before that fell through. Things went bad and the bank was the only moment left to make it happen."

"I have an issue with the bank deal. A politician walked into a crowded bank with a gun."

I said, "A murder happens in Trini every seventeen hours. That island is the go-between for drugs leaving South America for Europe and North America. The smugglers bring the guns, then when the drugs are on their way, they leave the heavy artillery behind and return home. The man knew how it was inside his country. He was afraid and was armed. Maybe he wanted to act like he was an LK."

"I saw the video. He fired on you before you fired on him."

"Was off my game. I had been drugged."

"He still fired on you before you fired on him."

"I just do what I am told to do. I go by the game plan laid out before me."

"Okay, question about this urban legend. Is there really a man behind red doors?"

"I can't comment on that. Not supposed to comment on Barbarian business, Black Jack."

"They left you in need of money. They're a big corporation. Makes no sense."

"Change the theme of this conversation."

"Keep a woman broke, keep her under control. Give her just enough to get by. She won't starve to death, but she'll never be able to afford to leave. That's from the handbook on how to be a pimp."

"Sounds like it's from the handbook on how to be an effective husband."

"Same handbook that has been handed down from generation to generation."

I asked, "Anything else? Or are you going to eat my food and find more ways to call me stupid?"

"The politician had two men guarding him. They had been with him every step of the way, day and night. Why didn't his armed men come inside, or at least stand outside the door and wait?"

"Hard to ask a dead man why he dropped his guard and did something stupid. I assumed he wanted all the publicity for himself, didn't want to be seen on camera with the LKs, same for the priest."

"That's dumb. They didn't get to the level they're on that fast by being stupid."

I let a moment pass before I said, "Give me all of your thoughts, your conclusion."

"Thought you wanted me to change the subject."

"Actually, I wanted you to shut up, then you called me stupid and dumb."

"Far from. I respect you and think you have balls and are good at what you do. Especially after that bank thing in Trini. Any other hired gun would have been on the bank floor dead."

"Barely remember any of it. Told you, I had been drugged."

"How?"

"Not important. But I had been drugged the night before."

"I would have been fucking dead. In this area, I'm a house painter sitting down with Picasso."

"Okay. Thanks. I'm not Picasso, but thanks for considering me competent."

He took a deep breath. "I'm going to be late for my next meeting."

"Money by the time the sun drowns itself, otherwise lose my contact information."

He took out his phone and showed me a picture of a young boy.

I asked, "That's him?"

He nodded, then showed me another photo, that one of a young girl.

I asked, "Her too?"

He nodded. "Both of them. She first. Then he."

I sat back. Wanted no part of this, but I needed the cash.

He asked, "You have the stomach for it?"

"Worry about the funds. By the time the sun drowns in the ocean is your deadline."

He looked at his cellular, had a perplexed expression.

I asked, "What's the problem?"

"Do dead people have access to Facebook?"

"I doubt it. Why?"

"Why do people write messages to dead people on Facebook?"

"Whatever makes them feel better. I'm sure the dead cricketer has a thousand posts from people chatting with him like he can still see them and chat back or poke them at some point."

"Scott Pinkerton was never that good at cricket. He wasn't even mediocre."

"Sure about that?"

"Sure as baby shit stinks. Other cricketers here are still living with their mothers. If he has a big house and a luxury car, he had another revenue stream, and my guess is that he's had it for a long time."

"I had no intel on him. Order came and a few hours later I was stalking him, doing my thing."

"That revenue stream is what got him killed."

"So, you don't think being an accused rapist had him put in the ground?"

"Not the rape charge. Hate to say it, but I have to be honest; nobody . . . well, not many . . . not many down here would pay to have someone killed for rape. Not many women report it. Somebody might get a cutlass and wait for the man, maybe try to cut his throat while he sleeps, but from what I read, they just get raped and keep moving, not many bother calling the police, or pressing charges because they end up with their photo in the local papers. Small island. Women don't want that shame, that stigma. Only a few watering holes here. They would have to pass the man who raped them on the road or end up in the same minibus with him. Or at the same church. That's from what I hear. I can't see a poor woman like that taking the payoff money she got and spending most of it to have someone killed, then go back to being the working poor. Then again, I'm not a woman, just speculating. What do I know?"

"You're right."

"That a woman wouldn't spend her last dime to hire a professional to solve her problem?"

"No, that you're not a woman. A woman would spend her last dime."

"An American woman. A British woman. I love my island, but it's still a destination for women from the Dominican Republic, Guyana, and Jamaica. The same for St. Lucia, the Netherlands Antilles, and Suriname. Sexual exploitation is big business in the islands. Not only the women get bad treatment. Men from China, India, and Guyana are trafficked for slave labor, are exploited in construction and other sectors. It's not as extreme as it is on other islands; we pretend it's not a big deal, but it exists. Those are our Mexicans, to put it in terms an American can understand. Women from here in Barbados are trafficked to other islands and to England as well, for the same reasons: sex and domestic servitude. So, in my opinion, if she was raped, and if she was paid, she would take the money and leave Barbados."

"You're right. I don't know shit about this island. I'm a dumb and stupid American woman."

"I better leave while I'm ahead."

"Yeah, do that. While I sit here and realize I've been exploited as well, you do that."

Black Jack left Chefette, stopped by the

beggar with the triplets and gave her some coins, then skipped puddles and headed across Broad Street, climbed into his ride, and left Bridgetown.

Bad luck was all I had had since I came to the bottom of the West Indies.

I made it back to my motorcycle just in time to catch two hooligans trying to hurry and push its weight up on the back of a Toyota pickup truck. The wheels were locked, so they had to use much manpower. They saw me, damaged motorcycle helmet in hand. No one walked the alley with me. They jumped off the truck, came toward me, and without a hello or introducing themselves or asking me how my day was going, they barked and demanded my helmet and my backpack.

One in a stupid cowboy hat yelled, "Where the money? Where the money?"

I slid my backpack off, let it fall.

Before it hit the ground I had used my helmet and disarmed my aggressor. I came to life. We danced. There was rain, but there was no singing, no Gene Kelly moves, only knees to their faces, elbows to their eyes, blows to their throats. I was Ip Woman. I was the female version of Tony Jaa. I moved so fast, they couldn't touch me, but so much happened to them.

Each blow that I struck told me that I was

competent.

Again I had proven that I could handle myself and I was competent.

I wasn't dumb. I wasn't stupid.

I said, "Hard-ears saga boys wid nuh brought-upsy, catspraddled in a bassa-bassa."

I spat on the ground, then kicked their cheap silver gun in one direction before throwing the bullets from the gun into the throat of the alley. Straining, I put the key in the ignition of the Ducati, unlocked the wheels, and rolled my heavy bike back off the truck. The driver's-side window of the truck was broken, all sorts of electronics on the floor of the cab. They had been on a robbing spree.

Behind me hooligans were on the ground, broken bones from ankles to arms, two steel pipes on the floor of the alley. Helmet on, gloves on, I mounted my Ducati. As it drizzled, I sat there thinking.

I whispered, "Keep a woman in poverty, keep her under control. She'll never be able to leave."

TWENTY-TWO

Studio lights shone on her pulchritude, on the youthful face of the woman called Diamond Dust. She wore a red-white-and-black outfit by local designer Deron Attzs, stunning and runway ready, was introduced as Mrs. Karleen Ramjit, a woman born in Laventille married to the man who was CEO of both Trinidadian holding companies Hummingbird Limited and Trinity Limited. Those were two of the companies run by the organization known on the streets as the Laventille Killers.

She was in an interview on TV6. She was strengthening their brand.

Mrs. Quash, the interviewer, asked, "Your husband has made a few controversial comments regarding TTFA."

"He spoke the truth. The Trinidad and Tobago Football Association now has to reconcile the twenty-five-million-dollar debt, to rebuild its image away from Jack Warner's shadow and to function as a proper business.

My organization would be capable of bringing success to that arena as well."

"You befriend civilian politicians, yet you tend to portray them as corrupt and ineffective."

"We are neutral and work with all parties, and we give constructive criticism to all. We do what is required, and that is not always pleasant. It's called tough love. We are for Trinidad, not an individual. If you are for the people, as we are, there is no need to be afraid of an honest assessment of your efforts."

"Okay. You were nine when you discovered *The Fountainhead,* and it changed your life."

"Yes. Within two sentences Ayn Rand and her way of thinking, her rationale, changed my life."

"She is probably the most debated philosopher in the world."

"Undoubtedly. If her controversial points weren't valid, she would not be remembered."

"She is your role model."

"I look up to her. I would have loved to have had conversation and dinner with her."

"Ayn Rand promoted a totally irrational, destructive, movement-destroying, freedom-destroying . . . the Russian woman came across as an intellectual thug, and to top that off she believed that believing in God was a cop-out and destroyed man's ability to reason, and argued that going with emotions and not reason went against reality. So far as morality, she led a polyandrous lifestyle, a lifestyle that you and your members are rumored to have as well. I have read . . . oh . . . Mrs. Ramjit? Mrs. Ramjit?"

Trinidadian viewers saw a cold stare rooted in the hills of Laventille, a telling glare that was more than an ultimatum, it was a deadly promise. In the interviewer's eyes lived fear, on her brow sprouted sweat like she was in the pouring rain. An unpalatable fear that the viewers felt left her frozen.

Mrs. Quash swallowed, shifted, in a trembling voice said, "I . . . I apologize, Mrs. Ramjit."

"I take offense to that horrid characterization. As would my husband. As would my children. You say things as if I am not a mother, as if my children would not hear these lies. Mrs. Quash, simply by raising such preposterous questions you're sinking to a new low, a new low even for a second-rate journalist like yourself, and you're doing nothing more than spreading hearsay and malicious rumors."

"I . . . I . . . I had hoped that we could dispel many of the rumors regarding your group."

"We are a family. Educated. Professionals. Proud Trinidadians. That is what we are."

"Shall we continue with the interview?"

Diamond Dust sat still, silent, nostrils

flared, looked at Mrs. Quash like she would cut open her chest and shit inside her heart. Diamond Dust removed her microphone, stood, and exited.

Five minutes later. Backseat of her limo. Moving through traffic in Port of Spain.

Every day was a day to make a new friend. Or discover a new enemy.

Diamond Dust poured herself a glass of Henri Jayer Richebourg Grand Cru, wine from Côte de Nuits, France, the most expensive on the planet, the wine she drank daily, her only bad habit.

Before this travesty, before the Kiwi, none would have dared challenge her.

No one would have dared to blindside her, and never on live television.

She felt vulnerable. She did not like feeling vulnerable.

This was the fault of her brother. King Killer's actions had weakened them in ways she had not realized. They were losing respect, and without respect there would be no power.

She had worked hard. She deserved the best. Only the best.

Her cellular rang. She looked at the number. It was her oldest child.

She answered, smiling, "Hey, baby. You saw mum on TV? Mum will be home soon. *Croods?* We can watch *The Croods* again. No junk food, baby. Eat fruit. Mum wants you healthy and strong. Another Barbie? Sweetheart, boo bear, you already have over one hundred. We'll see. Love you too."

She ended the call, frowned. Her children had seen her be weak.

Her children had seen her be vulnerable.

She screamed.

Fucking Kiwi.

Her brother had brought the red-haired Kiwi bitch into their fold.

Her brother, the first boy she knew, the man she loved most.

The man she had given her secrets and had trusted first more than she had trusted any lover.

She whispered, "Neziah, what have you done? What have you done to my dream?"

Her brother was with the others. With War Machine, Appaloosa, Guerrero, Kandinsky, and whoever they had taken, all at the warehouse, as they had been for days. She would go visit him now.

When you had issues, you looked the other person in the eyes.

You did that no matter how difficult it might be.

She would look in her brother's eyes.

She would tell him how fucking disappointed she was with the choices he had made.

She would tell him that his dick-led decision had brought insurmountable shame on what she had worked to build. His one bad move was fucking up what she had sacrificed and killed to create.

She would tell her twin brother her grievances.

She would tell him to his face, as he died.

TWENTY-THREE

Back at Six Roads, I questioned everything about the Barbarians, every job I had been given. In the front room I collapsed on the sofa. The brick structure and its metal roof turned the inside of the safe house into a convection oven. I sat in the stuffy room and sweated as I continued to read about the dead cricketer. Curiosity was strong. Soon I turned the fan on high, stripped down to my panties, rubbed ice across my breasts and neck and read to distract myself.

The cricketer hit that I had effected, just like the island's hotel rape case in Sandy Lane, there had been a payoff, the amount undisclosed. It was the money that had my attention, the money that kept me reading. Always follow the money. Especially when you had none.

I took out the roll of bills I had taken from the cricketer, the bloody greenbacks. I put the wad on the bed, stared at the cash, tried to own it, but it didn't feel like it was rightfully mine.

I had those kinds of hypocritical issues, raised to kill, but not to steal from another human.

I made men widowers, women widows, children orphans, made grandparents have to take care of their dead children's babies, made children have to bury their parents. I wondered what Johnny Parker would think if he had seen my true résumé, the one written in blood. Wasn't like Parker knew that I was a hit woman. Wondered what he would have thought of me if he had seen me on the roof of the Carlton Savannah, or if he had walked into Sugar Ultra and seen me dirty dancing with the cricketer.

Parker knew Jennifer, but had no idea who I really was.

I wasn't Jennifer.

He had no idea what I had been through, had no idea what I was capable of doing sans remorse.

Parker's ex-wife knew. That psychotic bitch knew.

Johnny Parker had left his wife two years before we shared a bed, but when she found out about us, she began harassing me, used a friend who worked at Verizon, obtained the number I used under my bogus identity, and then blew up my BlackBerry. When I didn't reply, she made my BlackBerry ping-ping-

ping all night long, then made it ping-ping-ping into the next morning, ping-ping-ping into the afternoon, and ping-ping-ping again into the next night. Johnny was over and we were in bed. I was giving him head and the damn phone started to ping-ping-ping. I jumped up and told Johnny to end it. I told him that if he didn't, I would. The ping-ping-ping never stopped. Then she came by my place looking for him. Now she had obtained my address, probably from the same friend at Verizon. She ping-ping-pinged me all day and then she had the nerve to ring-ring-ring my doorbell at three in the morning, and when I opened the door wearing a T-shirt and boy shorts, she called me a bitch, whore, slut, whatever she could think of. I stared at her. I had a coveted middle-class existence. I lived from job to job, was barely making my ends meet, but like my neighbors, I held on to the façade of being richer than I was. It was a normal existence in a capitalistic world. I didn't live in a neighborhood of violence. So when Parker's ex-wife had come to my door, I had to maintain my identity, one of a kind and peaceful neighbor who gave smiles to everyone she passed, so I had to pretend and respond accordingly. She went to her car and right away my phone started to ping-ping-ping. I did all I could not to scream. She ping-ping-pinged my phone while she drove away.

She had bullied me. I loved Johnny Parker, so I had allowed her to bully me.

I lived in a cul-de-sac and she had to turn right, exit a slow-opening unmanned security gate, then make another right again to get to the main road. The main road was to the left of my townhome. By the time she had exited my swanky complex, I had sprinted across the perfectly manicured grass, had passed by a new unit under construction, had picked up a brick, jumped over a six-foot wall, and stood to the side. Just as she came up on me, speeding of course, the brick went flying like a tree dove, crashed into the center of the windshield. Her Lexus swerved and crashed into the wall. I went to the driver's side and opened the door. She was stunned from the impact, beaten by the airbag, but not beaten enough. I pulled her out by her blouse, ripped the material, and then gave her a strong head-butt. Her nose exploded and blood gushed from her face. I pimp-slapped her. I bitch-slapped her. Followed by another pimp slap. She cried out in terror and tried to stop me from slapping her around, but the dance had started. I grabbed her left hand and bent her fingers until the one she had flipped me off with broke like a dried twig. She needed to be accountable for her actions, regret her choices.

I said, "It's three in the fucking morning, and you want to play games? Stupid, arrogant beeyatch, Parker left you. Get over it and move on. This is how this will go from here. Don't make my BlackBerry ping-ping-ping. Next time you ping-ping-ping, you will wake up on a boat and your hands and ankles will be bound and I will drop you in the ocean. Do we have an understanding? Do you understand?"

She nodded ten thousand times, had been nodding through my entire diatribe.

I needed her to see and remember the seriousness in my eyes.

I said, "Do not make my BlackBerry ping. That's not polite. It's rude. Don't be rude."

I picked up the brick. She freaked out, scampered back over the oil and dirt on the asphalt. I wanted to do it. Wanted to smash her head in. Was going to smash her head in. Then I heard the child crying. Parker's six-year-old daughter screamed. She was in the backseat. Strapped in, no child seat.

Jarred, I snapped, "You brought Parker's daughter on a fool's run? Without a child seat?"

The kid cried like she was a newborn. She called for her mother and looked at me like I was a monster in the night. Two days before I had played with the kid, had combed her hair. Now she hated me like I was the devil. I shook my head. The kid would be traumatized. I couldn't undo that.

I said, "You disgust me. You don't deserve

to be a mother. I'd be a better mother."

She cried. Her daughter screamed hard enough to burst a lung, and she cried.

Her hand was fucked-up. Her face was fucked-up.

I said, "Let me get my car. I'll take you to emergency. You can blame it on your air bag."

Adrenaline high, I jogged across the road. There was no sidewalk on this stretch. I pulled myself up and jumped over the wall, recrossed the neighbor's back lawn as a shortcut, and gently put the brick where I had found it. I would never steal from a neighbor, not even a stray rock.

The kid was still screaming. Parker's daughter had seen the bogeyman.

I heard an engine revving, tires burning rubber, screeching, and frantic driving.

Johnny Parker called me from the emergency room. His wife had called then ping-ping-pinged him. He had panicked and run to the mother of his child, had run to her like she was still his freakin' wife. He was pissed, yelled at me, but had called to warn me, to tell me that she said I had tried to run her off the road and kill their child. She had called the police, said that I had attacked her and her child unprovoked. She said that I had made terrorist threats, again unprovoked.

As she was on a gurney, an IV in her arm, she had given them my name and address. I had twenty minutes before sirens showed up on my porch. If they arrested me, I would be fingerprinted. Then they would realize I had no fingerprints. They had been burned away by plastic surgery down in Rio. Acid took away prints, but skin grew and the prints would come back. Skin had growth memory. No prints would raise all sorts of flags, most of all with national security. My escape bag was always prepacked; I was prepared to leave without warning. Maintaining a relationship had been a challenge, especially since it had been built on a lie, on a monumental omission, on a deception. He didn't know about Reaper. I was just another girl people called Jen, a woman with generic red hair and unimpressive brown eyes.

I had to call the Barbarians and tell them I had a situation.

I needed them to get me out of Florida.

At three in the morning, after being dormant, I slapped on an unattractive black pixie wig, broke out a stack of bogus IDs, implemented the walk of a nerdy gimp, put on makeup and new contacts that made my eyes hazel. I put on horrible teeth, made myself dog ugly, grabbed my georgie bundle, put on a brand-new Boston accent, and moved the fuck on.

Ping. Ping. Motherfuckin' ping.

TWENTY-FOUR

Stopped thinking about Johnny Parker long before I made it to the Parish of St. Michael.

Now I was in the southwestern portion of Barbados. One of the original six parishes.

The suite faced the Caribbean Sea, the lights from Bridgetown not far away. The king-size bed was filled with the target's belongings, books and CDs in basic Portuguese, clothing, suitcases, duffel bag, and DVDs. He was prepacking to leave, a map and boarding passes on the bed showing that his next stop was going to be an overnight layover in Port of Spain, then on to a hideaway in Tobago the next morning. From there he would be on the edge of South America, a short plane ride to the final destination of many criminals. I went into the bathroom, looked at myself in the mirror. Tonight I was a man. I peeled away the mustache and beard, put on a different wig. I removed the baggy Dickies work pants and work boots I had worn, took off the two-inch dildo that had made it look like I was soft and hanging to the right, and traded that gear for black jeggings, black tee, and trainers. I washed my face, put on lipstick, regarded myself again. While I sat at the desk waiting in the dark, a card key was put inside the door.

I stood up. The door opened. I was MX-401. I was Reaper.

He turned the light on, saw me, and jumped. I smiled. He relaxed. The fat man smiled.

He asked, "Who are you and what are you doing in my room?"

"Please, have a seat, Mr. Carlson."

"Should I know who you are?"

"May I call you Fred?"

Without answering, he sat on the bed, the mattress bending underneath his weight.

He took a deep breath. I recrossed my legs. Checked the phone. Saw the time.

I said, "Tell me the most horrific thing you have ever done to another human being."

His voice cracked. "You know, don't you?"

"Tell me."

"I have an issue with porn and desiring sex with those who are not of the age of consent."

I looked at my phone again. Nothing. I looked at the time and stood.

He asked, "What are you doing?"

"Leaving."

"Don't go. I need to talk to someone."

I sat back down.

I said, "The girl. She was a thirteen-year-old virgin."

"She brought the alcohol from her parents' pantry. She wasn't a virgin. That was a lie."

"You fed her cocaine like it was cotton candy."

"She . . . all the celebrities she admired did it and she wanted to be like them."

"You're taking an experimental drug called Truvada."

"How did you know that?"

"That's a drug for AIDS."

"No. It's a pill that reduces a man's chance of being infected. Not an AIDS drug. It will protect sex workers, needle sharers, wives of infected men, gay men, prison inmates, everyone."

"Adults are supposed to protect children."

"I don't do anything different from what thousands of people go to do in Thailand and the Philippines. They go there for sex with girls who haven't begun to menstruate. They go there to have sex with boys who sell themselves to support their families. I am better than them. I am better. They have sex with children who are six years old, or younger. Many go there to have sex with the flamboyant lady-boys. I have never understood men who adored lady-boys. Compared to them, I am a normal man."

I asked, "How old are you?"

"I'm forty-seven on Facebook."

"You're fifty-six in the real world. Facebook is not the real world. Fifty-six minus thirteen. That's basic math, right, teacher? Work that out in your brain. You were old enough to be a young grandparent when she was born. You were forty-three years old when she was born."

"I know. I'm disturbed. I know better than to go online and seek out children who . . . who want adults to . . . to . . . it's wrong. If only you could see inside my heart and my head."

I checked the phone again. Nothing.

I said, "Tell me about the boy."

"I thought that this was about the girl."

"Not about Natalie. I am here because of Timothy. Was just making conversation."

He shook his head. "That situation was different."

"What made the boy different?"

"The boy . . . he was tall . . . wide hips . . . and his smile . . . his smile was so beautiful . . . so damn beautiful . . . his hair long, silky, and golden . . . he is . . . was . . . he was feminine. Like you. He was sexy like you. If you looked at his lips, if you looked into his blue eyes, you would know what I mean."

"You posted a sexual photo of him online."

"He threatened to tell everyone and destroy me. I was angry."

"He hanged himself."

"When I am angry, when I am afraid, logic

leaves me and emotions take over."

"He hanged himself."

"I loved him so much."

"The girl?"

"She was just a girl."

My cellular buzzed. It was a text message: MONEY AT THE DROP POINT.

I nodded, put the phone away, and said, "You were saying?"

"I am a United States citizen. I demand to be taken to the embassy. I have rights."

I didn't respond.

He repeated, "I am a United States citizen. I have rights."

"Not here."

"I have rights."

"I'm not with law enforcement, so there will not be a trip to Wildey. Sorry."

"If not a police officer or some sort of law enforcer from the States, what are you?"

Eyes on my target, I leaned to my left and picked up my backpack, reached inside, and took out my gun. Then I put the backpack down on the floor next to the chair.

His eyes went to the gun, processing this moment, coming to one conclusion.

I took out the suppressor and screwed it on the weapon's business end.

He shook his head, his expression saying that this couldn't be happening.

I nodded.

It was happening.

People walked the hallway, laughing loudly. The accents told me that it was a group of intoxicated Americans. His eyes told me that if he could hear them, then they would be able to hear him. He opened his mouth to scream. His scream wasn't aborted, but it arrived stillborn. The wall behind him was suddenly decorated in red and gray brain matter. Ear-piercing laughter moved down the hallway as his body collapsed back in the bed, bounced on the covers, then slid from the soft mattress.

I stepped back, looked at him. His body shifted and he toppled over, his head making a dull thud when it crashed into the carpet. He was dead, but I shot him three more times.

I said, "She was just a girl."

I shot him two more times.

"I'm a girl too, motherfucker."

TWENTY-FIVE

I rubbed my temples, wiped the gun down, and tossed the hot .22 on the bed, made it land and bounce on the comforter. Then I looked at the wall. Dora the Explorer drinking tea with Hemingway and Faulkner. With that done, I slipped on a pair of climbing gloves and grabbed my gear. When I opened his sliding patio door, climbing rope hung from above and reached to the ground below.

If a camera had seen me enter the room, as a man with my head down, they wouldn't witness my departure. Within seconds, I had made it to the ground level of the hotel unseen.

Once on ground level, I tugged twice.

Nothing happened.

I tugged twice again.

The rope retracted, disappeared with rapid yet uneven pulls.

Without looking back I put on an auburn pixie wig, tied a colorful scarf around my neck, kept my head down, and took a slow stroll in the cool night air, went across the parking lot and through a fence, headed to a stretch of darkness where a Yamaha Jet Ski was waiting in the sea. Black Jack was there. He had on shorts, sandals, and a long-sleeved T-shirt. He saw me, stood up, and grabbed a backpack that was on the ground. He handed me the cheap backpack, black, empty except for five grand in American money. I took the payoff from his backpack and stuffed the currency into mine, then tossed him his empty bag.

He said, "I put everything else on hold and spent all day trying to get you sorted out."

"Hope you did more than try. I need a win."

"The LKs have a wicked computer person. Hard to get into their systems."

"You need someone on a higher level to do your dirty work."

"We got in."

"Why didn't you say that from the start?"

"We were in ten minutes, downloading as fast as we could, before we were shut down."

"Get anything good?"

"You're referred to as the Kiwi. The Woman of a Thousand Faces."

"An exaggeration, but flattering. I only have nine hundred and ninety-nine faces."

"The safe house you used there, they found it. Seems like you left much information behind. They have upped their game and assigned a team to find you and they have been working nonstop."

"Who is on their team?"

"The big guns. Guerrero. Kandinsky. Appaloosa. War Machine."

"I've met them all. There should be another one called King Killer."

"King Killer wasn't on the intel."

"They threw the politician from the roof of a hotel when I was in Trinidad. Appaloosa beat the politician, pissed on him, raped the politician's coolie date in front of everybody."

"That's old-school war. During battle the men would beat the enemy, and after each battle all the women would be raped. You killed the man, pissed on him as an act of dehumanization, and left the sperm of his enemy deep inside of his woman. That drove the enemy mad, made him reject his wife. You allowed all men to rape her until they could rape no more. That was how you destroyed your enemy."

"Sounds like the LKs' strategy. Never saw any man like them. They're like the Salvadorian gangs, MS-13, the ones that don't mind dying, don't care about anything, are unafraid of everything."

"What they are doing, searching for you, that takes money."

"They have the money. They have South American drug money, maybe unlimited capital."

He nodded. "At least one would assume."

I whispered, "They're not giving up. I'll need to move soon, very soon."

"This island never should have even been a layover for you."

"I know. I moved next door to the enemy."

"If you can escape to Nassau, I can put you up, hide you for a while."

I heard voices and jumped. Silhouettes. Laughter. People were coming out to the beach. So was a security guard. My hand was in my backpack, gun inside aimed at shadows.

Black Jack stepped away and said, "We should part ways."

I saw no threat, then slid my backpack on one shoulder, became über-girly, giggled, sashayed toward him, fingers extended, and commanded, "Hold my hand, Black Jack."

"Wow. You just shifted and became someone else from head to toe. How do you do that?"

"Leaving abruptly could raise a flag. Security comes, you leave in a hurry, basically you run away, then a dead body found later, they remember a man acting suspicious, a Bajan man with tribal markings on his arms. If the guard passes by a couple being romantic, when the shit hits the fan, we're the last people he will remember because in his mind, he will be trying to remember anything odd. Don't be odd. They'll never look for me. They will walk by women all day. A bad boy like you will always be a suspect."

"This is why you've never been caught."

"This is why I was able to walk out of the front door of Trinidad."

He moved closer, swallowed, did what I asked. His hand was sweaty and it continued to shake. Touching me terrified him. He didn't know if I was luring him in close so I could gut him with a blade. Killing him would ensure the Barbarians never knew about this transaction. He was nervous. I hummed. Cargo ships lit up in the distance, the lights from Bridgetown so beautiful.

He asked, "Hungry?"

"I need to eat a decent meal."

"Stop by my place and eat."

"Where do you live?"

"Near Coral Ridge Cemetery. Ridgeview Estates."

"You already have food at home, or would I have to come by and cook?"

"Ackee and saltfish. Might be leftover stew fish in the house too. I think I have some mash-up. Fruit. Yellow rice. Jonnycakes. Junkanoo juice. A few Oh Henry chocolate bars."

"Who made all of that?"

"I cook. I made everything except for the Oh Henry."

"Wine?"

"I have some. Probably have five different types."

"No roommate down here?"

"No steady girlfriend, no one who would

pop over unannounced, if that's what you mean."

"Neighbors?"

"Expats. Professionals. Brits. Groundskeepers and housekeepers are gone by six in the evening. Most catch the bus at the end of the road. The residents keep to themselves."

"I need a comfortable place to rest. The cheap mattress down there is killing my back."

"I have a private gallery in the back that looks out on a sward that goes on as far as the eye can see, and the closest neighbor can't see jack. There is a plunge pool you can relax in."

"You have air-conditioning?"

"In all the bedrooms and downstairs, so the whole place is at a comfortable temperature."

"Air-conditioning at night. Sleeping without sweating. I think the heat keeps me up. The inability to breathe fresh air makes me wake up suffocating. What you have sounds like heaven."

"You could have upstairs to yourself and I could sleep downstairs."

"Are you attracted to me?"

"Yes. I am."

"Does that mean that you want to have sex with me?"

"It crossed my mind two or three hundred times when we were at Chefette."

"I'm on the run from the LKs and you're thinking about getting your dick wet?"

"From a medicinal perspective, might help you get the edge off so you can sleep."

"How old are you?"

"Fortysomething."

"Even without the 'something,' you're old enough to be my father."

"Experienced men make the best lovers."

"They should. They've been at it longer. You were in the arena before I was born."

"Hot water. Bed with a brand-new pillow-top mattress. Plunge pool."

"You had me at 'hot water.' "

"I can tell you how to get to that part of Christ Church Parish from here in St. Michael."

"Thanks for the offer. I'll pass. I might be too dangerous."

"In bed?"

"I meant with the LKs hunting me. Would hate for them to find me naked with my ass up and face in a pillow bumping back into your stiffness and moaning to Jesus and his daddy."

"Did you have to say that?"

"Was keeping it real."

"Not going to happen?"

"No. You were older than I am now when I was born. I was in Pampers when you were in condoms. I was shitting on myself and you were fucking the shit out of some woman."

"Anything else you need me to do?"

"Stay focused on my professional needs. Get Hacker to learn how to be a better hacker. She got in once, have her break in again. If she is in this business, she has to outsmart them."

I let his hand go, gradually, not all at once. Didn't really want to let go. I hadn't touched anyone with kindness in more than a month. Hadn't felt human since Parker. Needed human contact.

Under starlit skies, music coming from the Hilton, Black Jack headed toward the Jet Ski.

I said, "Wait."

"What?"

"We're supposed to be a couple. Hug me and pretend you're saying good-bye."

I put my arms around his waist and pulled him closer. We squeezed each other.

"Reaper, you can let go now."

"Women always hug longer."

"Considering something is not ever going to happen, you're holding me damn close."

"Please ask your dick to stop growing."

"Sorry about that, but it rarely listens to what I say."

Someone passed us. A tall brown-skinned woman. The Amazon trekked back to the parking lot, put a suitcase inside of the trunk of her car, climbed into the small four-door, a gray Allex, and pulled away from the parking lot. I studied her, smelled her perfume.

She never looked my way twice.

I kissed Black Jack on the lips. He tried to give me his tongue.

I let him.

When that was done, he took a step back.

I said, "By ten in the morning, that perv upstairs, he'll be found by housekeeping, cops will be called, the body taken down the service elevator and loaded up in the back so tourism won't shift its business to another resort. Gun was left in his room. No fingerprints. Nothing left behind. You okay?"

"You are young and wild. Bubble gum filled with razor blades. Pressed your breasts against me and right away you set me on fire in a way I haven't been set on fire in a long time. Now I'll have a mean sleep. Hate to say it but, damn, I'd like you in my bed, Reaper. It would be an honor to be with you."

"Go home, masturbate, get over it, then get to working on what I need, Black Jack."

"We'll connect tomorrow."

"We're not going to connect."

"You know what I meant."

"Why do they call you Black Jack anyway?"

"Because I don't like anything over twenty-one."

"I don't like anything under twenty-one."

"You like older men."

"Mature men. Just not as ripe as you."

"It's your call, Reaper."

"Good night."

"Ridgeview Estates, if you change your mind."

He climbed on the Jet Ski and took to the sea, cut across waves, vanished in the darkness. I tingled. Aroused. Wet. Was tempted to kiss him for real, kiss him and jack him off, make him come for kicks. I was good at that, masturbating men, making them feel so good they came so fast, a way to avoid fucking them. It was a necessary skill in my line of work. I wouldn't have fake-fucked him.

Tonight I would've gone for the real thing. Tonight I needed the real thing.

I strolled across the congested car park to my Ducati.

My cellular rang. Felt it vibrating in my jacket pocket.

I answered, "MX-401."

"Where are you?"

"Why are you calling at this hour? Miss me? Hemorrhoids flaring up?"

"It's not because you're in our good graces."

"You're not in mine. Got my passport and money by any chance?"

"We only call for one reason."

"Don't do this to me. Please." I took a hard breath. "I can't go back out on another job."

"You are needed, MX-401. When you are needed, you will go to work."

"Anywhere but here. Job after fuckin' job. I

263

need to be in motion. Get me off of this island."

"You don't get to choose where you work. You go where you are assigned to go."

"I am willing to work, but I will not work here. Never again."

"Are you running RCSI? Are you a CEO?"

"I have earned an *M* and an *X*. Not many men have done that."

"So the fuck what?" Are you a five-star general of the Barbarians?"

"Get me to high ground. I heard the LKs have a group assigned to finding me."

"How would you hear that?"

"They find me, then they find the Barbarians."

"Are you threatening the organization?"

"Get me off of this island. North Pole. South Pole. Get me out of LK range."

"Are you not still employed by the Barbarians?"

"I quit."

"You really want to do that? Say it again and I will make it happen."

I paused.

He said, "Say it. I will walk to the double red doors and repeat, then it will be official."

His tone was dark, it was brutal, a promise, a threat to cut my throat, maybe pull the plug and leave me in Barbados on my own, maybe direct the LKs toward me if I remained disobedient.

He barked, "Say it, MX-401."

I felt the veins trying to explode in my neck. I imagined my blade easing into his rib cage.

He said, "Say it for the record. Say you want out. Quit. This call is being recorded."

He dared me. In the tone of an unreachable bully, he dared me to jump. Eyes wide, anger so hard, so monstrous that not being able to set it free left me unable to blink, and not blinking had my eyes tearing, I looked out at the dark waters, then scowled toward Trinidad.

Breathing heavily, talking through my teeth I said, "Let's do this."

"Are we okay?"

"Send the fucking package. You want me to kill everyone in Barbados, fine."

"Yes or no. This call is being recorded for your convenience."

"Yes."

"Repeat response for verification."

"Send the fuckin' next assignment."

"It's on the gallery at the safe house. It's been there for five hours."

"Who encroached on my space without notification?"

"If you had been there, if you had followed your instructions, then you would know."

"If I had been there, they would have ended up dead. Be glad that I wasn't."

"Where are you?"

"None of your fuckin' business."

265

"Who are you with?"

"I'm alone. It's hot. I went for a drive to cool off."

"A five-hour drive?"

"I got lost."

"How big is that island again?"

"I was bored and hot. I rode up the highway to a place called Casa Grande. Went bowling, played video games, shot basketball, rode the bumper cars, then drove mini race cars on the track."

"That wasn't authorized. You are not there to interact with anyone. Understand that."

I looked at my helmet, frowned at the hole from the bullet, from my almost-death.

He said, "From now on, don't vanish any longer than it takes you to take a shit."

"I get constipated, so that takes a very long time."

"Know when to shut the fuck up, Reaper. Know when to shut it down."

"The drug bust. The cricketer. Now another one. Why are there so many missions here?"

"Just do what you are told when you are told and how you are instructed."

"If someone from the group left a package, then I'm not in Barbados alone."

"Do not leave the island."

"Why would someone else from RCSI be here in Barbados?"

"From now until the end, stay at the safe house as ordered."

"Is someone watching me? I will fuckin' shoot first and ask questions later."

I was talking to myself.

The Barbarians had yanked my chain, riled me, then killed the call while I ranted.

TWENTY-SIX

Stilettos clicking across concrete, Diamond Dust dropped a stack of photos, images of the Kiwi, let them fall. Then she looked at everything that had been taken from the Kiwi's safe house, information on all of them. Someone on the inside had given the Kiwi much information. Diamond Dust felt that this confirmed her worst fear. She stormed out of the room, left the warehouse, jaw tight, eyes watering, angered. His voice echoed when her brother called her name. He called her name as loud as he could.

She had told him good-bye. With a soft kiss to his swollen face, she had told her twin brother good-bye. She had wiped blood from his brow and said that she would see him on the other side.

Until then she would remember him as a little boy, as Neziah De Lewis.

Neziah hadn't had any sleep for days.

Appaloosa and a crew of guntas had dragged him out of his bed at three in the morning, had raped his wife as he watched, and then had put a bullet in his wife's head, made him watch her die, then beat him unconscious, put a black bag over his head, threw him in a van, left their newborn baby crying in an adjacent room, then transported him shackled and naked to the NIPDEC Warehousing Complex.

They were at First Avenue and Western Main Road, Chaguaramas, an area situated on 2.7 hectares. That was 6.7 acres of land. From there, screaming was futile.

War Machine had given the order.

King Killer was kept naked, bound, and hung upside down, Saint Peter without the cross.

He had been used as a two-hundred-pound boxing bag, had been kicked and beaten beyond recognition, had pissed and shat on himself until he couldn't piss and shit anymore.

Appaloosa told him that they had his baby in the next room.

Unless he told the truth, they would kill the baby in front of him.

He was a dead man.

It was just a matter of how much he loved his seed.

Most of his teeth now gone, one eye swollen shut, the other gouged out, and he cried in a barely audible voice, a tone of extreme exhaustion, cried and told them once again that he didn't know anything, that he had met her, that she was a Kiwi, a businesswoman from New Zealand, a married woman in Trinidad on a short business trip, that he had met Samantha Greymouth at Rituals that morning and later that evening he had picked her up from the Hilton and taken her to the gathering.

He said, "She told me to call her Sam, as all of her friends did."

Enraged guntas screamed in his face, said the New Zealand company that she had used as a front employed a woman named Samantha Greymouth, but she had never left New Zealand, and the bitch was in her thirties, fat like a cow, and nine months' pregnant. Without alerting the rest of the men, Diamond Dust had sent someone to New Zealand only to find out it wasn't the right woman.

War Machine said, "Cousin, it pains me to do this."

"Let me talk to . . . to Diamond Dust one more time."

"The Kiwi sandbagged us and you were the one to bring her into the fold. Because of you, because of your incompetence, she was able to conceal, to misrepresent her true position, mask her potential, shadow her intent, and take advantage of us and make us look like fools. Because of you, she was able to hide the truth about herself and gain an advantage over our organization."

"Please . . . cousin . . . Jeren . . . please."

"Don't call me by that name. Jeren stopped existing when I became War Machine."

"Please. I beg you."

War Machine looked down at the blood beneath his battered cousin, then raised his head and looked at his cousin's unrecognizable face and said, "We do to you as you have stood by my side and done to others. If I had been weak, you would have stood next to the guntas and done the same to me."

Guntas took out the swords, large daggers like those used by ancient Illyrians, Thracians, and Dacians. Thirty inches long and made of hardened steel. They rested their sica arena swords on open flames. One by one they laid the burning blade on his flesh. On his shriveled cock. On his shriveled balls.

For the thousandth time, War Machine's cousin choked on his blood and saliva.

War Machine said, "She killed two brothers. Someone has to pay. It starts with you."

Neziah De Lewis, King Killer, wished that he had never fuckin' met a goddamn Kiwi.

All the men told him that they wished that they had never been dishonored by a member of their own family. War Machine nodded at his guntas and then he left the bloody room.

He went to another part of the warehouse, to an empty office.

He cursed, screamed, kicked walls, knocked

over anything in sight, made agony echo.

He had proven his loyalty to the LKs at a new level. He had killed his own blood, had killed a lieutenant and his wife to show his love for the LKs. That pain would give him energy. He would kill to avenge his bereaved family as well. His wife had demonstrated her level of commitment to the organization. She had sanctioned the death of her brother. She had kissed him, told him good-bye.

War Machine wept, pounded the cinder-block walls with his fists.

He should have been in that other room.

Not King Killer. Not his cousin. Not his brother.

But this was the way it had to be.

He stood tall, straightened his suit, washed his face.

He returned to his men. To his warriors. To his cousin.

He drew his weapon and put a bullet in King Killer's brain.

The man was already dead six times over.

He shot his cousin anyway, the gunfire the echo of his frustration.

He shot the man who had been closer than a brother.

TWENTY-SEVEN

Between three and four in the morning in Bridgetown, Bidechaina Charles, a Haitian woman, fell to her death from the roof of Carlisle House. An hour later, two teenage ruffians who had robbed three British tourists of their gold and money were shot and killed on Gitten Road. Two more boys were dead inside of the home. A fifth boy was gunned down as he fled the assassin that was on his trail. As he ran up a section of cut-rock road back toward Haggart Hall, pink mist filled the air. A sixth boy had run across Government Road and bolted across an open field that led toward the projects. When he was halfway across the field, a Bone Crusher Carbon Arrow landed in the ground right in front of him.

He changed course, ran harder. Twenty yards later, he felt the abrupt pain in his back.

He looked down and saw six inches of arrow sticking out of his chest, protruding between the white numbers 2 and 4 on his purple-and-gold L.A. Lakers jersey. He fell over, died with his eyes open.

I had nothing to do with any of that.

That was the work of Nemesis Adrasteia.

Tonight, Petrichor had become Nemesis Adrasteia.

The spirit of divine retribution. The inescapable. Tonight she gave what was due.

Old Man Reaper's Bahamian daughter was busy.

I was dealing with RCSI and their bullshit. Again the Barbarians had tugged my chain and sent me on another assignment, again at the last minute, again alone, an encore with no backup.

TWENTY-EIGHT

Upper end of Collymore Rock Road

I parked in a small, twenty-space car park in front of the shopworn edifice in Gertz Plaza. I waited in front of Fresh 'n Clean Laundromat. A black BMW pulled up. I knew his stats before I saw him. Six-two. Three hundred on the scale. He dragged himself out of his fancy car and headed up the concrete stairs that ran up the side of the building from down near Andy Ann's Restaurant, stairs that weren't visible from the main road. Nothing was upstairs there except for Mag's Barber and Beauty Salon and Harry's Heel Bar, both closed at this ungodly hour. I had already walked the area looking for witnesses. Mane Attraction, Pearson's Pharmacy, Channel's Supermarket, KFC, Shell gas station, everything was dark. I took catlike steps, and followed Big Guy up the stairs. He wore an NY baseball cap, black suit coat over an orange polo, brown sandals, had rings on four fingers, plus a silver earring. He looked like a

pimp who needed to work mornings at Starbucks and then be a greeter at Walmart in
the afternoon to make ends meet.

He unlocked the heavy-duty iron floor-to-
ceiling burglar gate that led to the offices
upstairs.

I said, "Richard Barrow."

Startled, he turned and saw me. I was
dressed in all black. I wasn't in the best of
moods.

"Who you?"

I peeled away my fake mustache. He was
surprised, shifted when he realized that I was
not the wearer of testicles. My breasts had
been wrapped down so I looked flat-chested.

I said, "Big Guy, doesn't matter who I am."

My dusky look, Scottish accent, and rough
tongue jarred him. Seeing he had a surplus
of nose hair, a baby Afro growing from each
nostril, that both jarred and disgusted me.

He said, "You're with them. The man
behind the red doors sent you to deal with
me."

"Let's take this inside, Big Guy. To your office."

We went into the hallway. I had him put
the heavy padlock back on the wrought-iron
gate. That gate spoke of high crimes. The Pine
was right behind here with its own reputation.

I took out a sap and slugged Big Guy across
the back of his neck. The pain took him down

to his knees. The floor was made of hard tile, and that added more pain, made him roll over, one hand holding his head, the other grabbing at his knees. I hummed as I put on my biker gloves, straddled him. Blackened his eyes. Broke his nose. Hit him over and over. Hard blows. Pretended I was beating the fucker from the Barbarians who always ruffled my feathers. Pretended I was beating the LKs. Was beating Parker's ex-wife. Bruised, bloodied, and humbled; when I stepped away and stood up ready to take this to the next level, he tried to get up, but collapsed back against the cinder-block wall.

He pulled out a handkerchief, pressed it against his fresh injury, absorbed blood.

I took out a phone, snapped a photo of his bloody mug, e-mailed it to my people.

He asked, "What else they tell you to do?"

"That depends on you. The money."

"I don't have it."

"Find it. It needs to be transferred within the next ten minutes."

"I don't have it."

"In that case I will need a finger."

"You have to break a finger too?"

I opened my bag and pulled out a pruning saw.

His eyes went wide. "Shite, shite, shite, shite, bloody shite."

I asked, "Which finger can you live without?"

"I guess . . . I guess that I could get by with one pinky. The one on the left hand."

"What's the issue with the money? Why are you delinquent?"

"I have the same problems that they have."

"What problem is that?"

"Everything is at a standstill. You don't know about the squatters?"

"Is that a singing group from the fifties?"

He struggled to get up. I reached out and helped the big man to his feet.

He said, "You hit hard. Damn, you hit like a man."

"I hit harder than most men. I pulled my punch."

"Thanks for not knocking me into the middle of next week."

"I tried to knock you back into last month, but don't mention it."

"I'm a contractor now. I'm doing some work for your people, but the thieves are raiding my construction site. I just left there. I have to stay there half the night to make sure they aren't stealing everything. I'm losing money left and right. It's the squatters. Thieves. They are breaking into my containers and stealing windows, copper, air-conditioning, and raw materials."

"Okay."

"I know that it's the same family of squatters that they are having issue with."

"I don't know anything about an issue with

squatters. It's above my pay grade."

"I lost sixty thousand dollars in windows alone. Just as much in doors."

"Hire security for five Bajan bucks an hour."

"I did, but the damage has been done. I had to replace the damn windows and doors out of pocket so I can work the project. My credit is bad and I had to pay cash, cash that I needed to pay your boys, so my money is tied up in windows and damn doors. I'm working on mansions. Do you have any idea how much it costs to import top-shelf windows and doors?"

My cellular buzzed. Without looking at the ID, I handed the phone to Big Guy.

I said, "Answer it. It's regarding your imprest."

"My what?"

"Your loan, asshole. You owe the company six figures and they are not happy."

He looked terrified, shook his head a hundred times.

I went to his new coffeemaker and made myself a cup of coffee. A *Daily Nation* was on the counter. I turned to a page showing a twenty-year-old pregnant Jamaican being led from the District B Court after pleading guilty to transporting seventeen packages of Mary Jane in her stomach. I looked at photos on Big Guy's walls. Vanity from floor to ceiling. He had more than a few kids. He used to be a soca singer. Won competitions. Sweet Soca Monarch. Party Monarch. Calypso Monarch. Road March Champion. He was solo and the front man in some local group twenty years ago. I guessed that once that business moved from vinyl to bootleg CDs, thievery did him in and forced him to consider other revenue streams. Other plaques on the wall said that he was also in the import business. That covered a variety of illegal activities.

He told them, "I know it's them. They steal my raw materials and are building a bloody new parish up there. Said they have a claim. By Bajan law. I don't make the law. Not yelling. Sorry. Maybe you can reason with them using money. I'm doing the best I can do. If we get this resolved, then all will fall in place. My nose. Yeah. Broken. She fucked up my left eye, too. Yeah, she kicked my ass good."

I said, "I've done better."

He paused. I sensed some change and looked at him, a poker-face stare.

He said, "This Ecky Becky Red Annie Grey Goose is Reaper's daughter?"

Jaw tight, I nodded. Despite the string of Caribbean insults, I nodded.

He told me, "I have known your dad ever since."

"Ever since when?"

He said, "When we were kids, we were both at the Tercentenary Ward down on Jemmotts

Lane at the same time. Both of us were getting tonsillectomies. Back then our lights was always getting cut off and our gas bottle was always running out and we had to sleep on the floor."

" 'Gas bottle'?"

"Propane gas. Everyone has to buy their own propane gas. Anyway. Plumrose hot dogs, dolphin, and fried flying fish. He only had one uniform and had to wash it every night."

"Focus on your phone call."

Tense, he went back to the call and said, "Yeah, she is evil like her old man. Ruder and more arrogant than some of the personnel at Grantley Adams. Airport. It's an airport. Okay. Back to our issue. You have to make the squatters a better offer. They said no, but everybody has a price. Money is money. They have been offered more than that. Sweeten the pot. Give the Rastas another chance."

He paused again.

He said, "Cash money. They wouldn't have a bank account. I'm not joking. Not everybody down here trusts a bank. Well, the sooner you get that resolved, the faster I can recover what was stolen from my construction site and do what I need to do to earn and pay you. My other business? Oh, that business. It went to hell. Ganja raid on his property. But look, and I serious, I have a

281

huge shipment of Remy hair about to come in. Weave. It's hair. Women. Well, I have a huge shipment coming in and that hair sells for over two thousand for each customer. Weave. Hair. No, it's not the same as a wig. They can glue it in and wash it and go to the beach and take a sea bath and wash it and blow-dry it and fool themselves into thinking they grew the hair themselves. Human hair. From Asia and Brazil."

I shook my head. "Jesus. Do those dumb fucks know anything?"

He went on, "Yeah, in that case, I guess there are much bald-headed women in Asia and Brazil. Yeah, much. They robbed women in Venezuela, held them down and cut their hair off. They steal hair in Maracaibo. No, I don't understand it either. They don't do that in Barbados. Not yet, anyway."

"It's before sunrise and I've been up all night, so can you get back on point?"

He shrugged, pointed at the phone. "No, it doesn't snow down here. Yeah, we have television. Internet, too. No grass skirts. Dress the same as the people up there. English and dialect. We have schools. Made out of brick. A very classic education, international and commonwealth sporting events."

I muttered, "Fuckin' seriously? Can you kill the travelogue and wrap that shit up?"

He took a breath, trembled, and slid the phone back to me.

He was irritated, pissed off, hated the stereotypical ignorance on the other end.

I picked the phone up. Took a deep breath.

I asked, "Is this the man behind the red doors?"

"Of course not, MX-401."

"You again."

"Me again."

I asked my contact what the next move was.

"Give him another week."

"Will I be here that long?"

They hung up. Then I hung up and slid the phone back across the desk.

Big Guy asked, "What they say?"

"Your coffee is horrible."

"Is it that bad?"

"Tastes worse than beer from St. Vincent."

Hands trembling, he did a jerky motion and opened his desk drawer.

I drew my gun and moved to his head so fast he almost shat his pants.

He pulled out a small black package. At first I thought it was a condom, but it was Organo Gold, gourmet black coffee, 100 percent ganoderma extract. Whatever that meant. I went to his small counter, found a coffee cup that looked clean, poured in cold water, sat the cup in the microwave and three minutes later I added the coffee, stirred it, sipped, sighed.

He asked, "What did those well-educated gentlemen have to say?"

"Don't worry about it."

"Dumb fucks. How did America get to be a superpower with so many dumb fucks?"

"Bombs. Those things that go boom. We won the big-dick contest."

"I don't care how many bombs they have, they are dumb fucks. Highest incarceration in the world. Most fat people. Highest divorce rate. Outrageous student loans. Everybody on antidepressants up there in that watch-pornography-all-day, godless country, where people don't speak to their neighbors and spend all day and night eating fast food poisoned with hormones and antibiotics."

"Don't push it. No matter what country you hate, somebody lives there and loves it."

"Just plain dumb as a coconut. That's what happens when you live where they will spend three hundred dollars on a pair of jeans but won't spend twenty dollars to buy a book. I watch CNN. America has homeless people on every corner, is a food-stamp and section-8 country, and they talk down to us."

"We talk down to everybody, so don't feel special. We're those kind of Christians."

"Dumb fucks. I mean, how insular can a narcissistic, drone-sending country be?"

I asked, "What do you do for the people I work for?"

He rubbed where I had hit him. "Whatever Retail Consumer Services, Incorporated needs."

"Passports?"

"I can get top-of-the-line passports. Would have been easier out the office I used to have in Super Centre Warrens. I am not happy with the way I was forced out. My business was there for a decade. Anyway . . . But I know a guy who knows a guy who knows a girl who can get it done."

"You can get me a clean passport?"

"Maybe. Depends on the Jamaican guy that knows the Guyanese guy that knows the Puerto Rican girl that has the hookup in St. Lucia, if the guy hasn't gone back to Brixton in England."

"How long will it take?"

"Let me find out."

"Do that."

"You can watch *Django* while I make the call."

"I don't watch movies with black people depicted as slaves, maids, or butlers."

"Dem good. Why not?"

"Old Man Reaper said it's the reinforcement of the way the majority want us to see ourselves. Most are made or financed by white people. He said white people look at slave movies the way children look at movies about Lassie. Even if the white man never appears on-screen, the black man didn't free himself in the same forceful manner that he was taken, so white people are comfortable with that."

"Damn. I just asked if you wanted to watch a movie, not start a revolution."

"Start dialing or start losing fingers."

He made the call. I listened from the first word until he sighed in pain and hung up.

He looked at me and said, "Two weeks."

"Price?"

"They cost about ten grand each. High cost, but technology has changed the game and unless you want one from someplace like Zanzibar or Yugoslavia, it's top-dollar."

"I can get one in a few hours in the States and it won't cost ten grand a pop."

"You want it at that rate, go up there and get what you need. This contact supplied fake Canadian passports to much Algerians. He hooked up a terrorist network and was able to send sleeper agents anywhere in the world. He probably sent more than a few terrorists to America."

I shook my head. "Ten grand each."

"It will be worth it, trust me. The color, the paper, everything is top-shelf."

"I need it in a week. After that, it might be too late."

"A week. A rush job. That would be top priority and would cost more money."

"Can you for sure make it happen?"

"The Barbarians didn't tell me to. They use the same contact."

"Fuck the Barbarians. I could take a pinky, thumb, and ring finger and you'd walk around all day poking people in the eyes like you're one of the Three Stooges. What, you don't think that's funny?"

He looked at his hand, imagined what it would be like to send text messages with nine fingers, maybe wondering if he would then be entitled to 10 percent off his next manicure.

Nose broken and bloodied, he limped across the tiny office and made a cup of coffee. He was so shaky he dropped the cup and broke it. He kicked the cup to the side. It took him a moment, but he managed to make his coffee, then drank it down and made another cup.

He said, "Rastafarian squatters fucking it up for everybody. First lawless people were stealing my metal and taking it to B's Recycling, stealing from me and going up there and selling and making a profit, and now this squatter thing. Hard to be halfway honest in an all-the-way-wicked world."

I opened my backpack and took out four thousand Bajan dollars.

I said, "I will need six passports."

He touched his head, his eye, then counted the money and shook his head like he had the upper hand in the transaction. "Six top-shelf passports will cost a lot more than that."

"When they come in and they are clean, I will pay whatever you charge."

"Mind driving me to the hospital?"

I shook my head. "I'm not a chauffeur. Work that shit out yourself."

He nodded and blinked his good eye, tears draining from the other.

"Stay focused. I need a half-dozen passports. Hook it up. This is between your ears and the ears of Jesus's daddy. Repeat one word and I'll come back and next time I will not be this nice."

"I'll end up losing my pinky."

"No, you'll end up with a bullet hole in each hand, one hole in the head, and your wanker cut off and shoved down your throat. Mag will open her shop and find you in the hallway."

He nodded again. "The cricketer."

"You know the island. You know what's not in the newspapers. What do you know about the cricketer they found dead the other day?"

"Same shit happened to another guy not long ago. Rumor was that he had stolen drug money. Was stealing from a drug lord. That was the word that spread around the island."

I asked, "Cricketer was involved in the same dealings?"

"Only the drug lord, his spine wasn't removed."

"Was the cricketer involved in the same dealings as the drug lord?"

"Not at liberty to say."

"Was he?"

"Yes, but you didn't hear it from me. I

heard that he gave up cricket and took over that aspect of the drug business when the last drug lord was taken out two or three years ago."

"What was his connection to the Barbarians?"

"I have no idea. If he was on the Barbarians' payroll, nobody told me."

I nodded, focused on my needs. "Six passports. Get me as far north as Nassau."

"To make that miracle happen, I will need the balance of the money very soon."

"Ten grand US a pop. You're gouging me."

"The government gouges everybody for everything, so as a businessman I have to pass on the cost to my customers. Tourists get tax breaks, but the citizens pay full price for everything."

He unlocked the gate.

I said, "Double-cross me and earn a Chelsea smile. Do you understand me, Big Guy?"

"Understood. I don't want to look like the Joker."

"I don't want to come back and act like the Joker."

"You are definitely his daughter. You're crazy just like him."

I thought about Sabina. Then the beautiful West Indian woman who had birthed me.

I said, "Not like him. Like my mother. Mean like my father; half-crazy like my mother."

"Half-crazy?"

"Don't push it."

TWENTY-NINE

Six Roads

Sleep-deprived since Florida. Antsy since Trinidad. Troubled since birth.

It was a little after ten in the morning. Outside held heat that rivaled the center of the sun, but it was ten degrees cooler than the inside of the safe house. I was too far inland to feel an ocean breeze.

I decided to do the geek shuffle, small steps, pigeon-toed, drooping shoulders, send the message that I was insecure, disorganized. That decided, I headed between homes on the edge of the main road, Farm Road, walked underneath a mango tree, inhaled the scent of grass and dead animals from the slaughterhouse. One of the neighbors was on his porch using his electric razor to shave; another was hanging laundry. The close-knit community woke up like rural Arkansas. First roosters crowed, dogs barked, then the roar and fumes of cars and transport buses dancing with the heat of the sun.

I came up on the red-hued rum shop a block over. A dread, wearing a hard hat, strutted over to a younger boy. The kid checked the streets before he strutted toward the short tree in front of the shopworn pub. The dope boys worked there day and night, and hid their drugs in the trees and bushes until a customer arrived. I'd seen many transactions as children sat at the bus stop at the foot of the rum shop. Their boss was a low-level drug lord who lived on the road next to the rum shop, and the rum shop was on the back side of Princess Margaret Secondary. If a man ran a drug business by a school, he would always have new customers. The laborer wearing the hard hat did a hand exchange, money for drugs, then crossed the road, took long strides into the heat, and went back to work at the Ministry of Transport.

Dope boys looked at me.

"Looking real sexy."

I responded, "Cheese on bread."

"Lemme part ya walls."

"You taking six for nine. Leff me alone now."

The Six Roads Library was my destination, a three-minute walk from the safe house. Nonstop traffic came through the island's unique six-point roundabout to get to Highway 4 and Highway 5. Hundreds of brick homes with tin roofs stretched into the distance, cane fields facing those communities. This area used to be an old village, now sectioned off and sold to create retail and housing. Many waited on buses, minivans, and Zed-Rs heading toward Bushy Park, the Crane, Bayfield, Oistins, Culpepper Island, wherever they went in the heat. Many walked, some with rags in hand to wipe away sweat, some underneath umbrellas to hide from the Caribbean sun. They hid from the sun the way I was hiding from the rest of the world. Today I was on foot. I mixed with people heading toward Knight's Pharmacy, Emerald City Supermarket, Shell, Barbados National Bank, Chickmont Food Store, and Chefette.

The public library sat back off the road, was hidden in plain sight, sandwiched between the entry to Princess Margaret Secondary School and a small building for the Southeastern Farmers' Cooperative, that property having grass at least a foot high.

On edge, the shootout from the bank in Trinidad still playing in my head frame by frame, I scanned the area one more time. My eyes went to the building that housed the co-op. The building was one level, thirty feet away from the library. The metal roof was flat, not an A-frame. Perfect for a sniper. Princess Margaret Secondary was behind the library, the two lots separated by a metal fence. Much noise was going on over there. I walked to the fence and saw that students were out being recorded, doing their version of the Harlem Shake. I hadn't expected them to be outside.

That was not good.

I gritted my teeth, looked at my watch. I had thirty minutes before the killing started.

I hoped the kids would be done and back inside by then.

I went into the small library, a library about the same size as the two-bedroom safe house I had been forced to live in. Walls were made of cinder blocks, hurricane-proof, bullet-proof. Fans blew and the inside was cool enough, but my adrenaline made me an oven. Six older Dell computers faced the main road and the plaza at Emerald City. Hadn't anticipated much traffic at the library. Connected to the Internet. Went online. Found a website and played the wretched video from the shootout in Trinidad.

Horns blew as an SUV turned left, pulled into the unpaved car park, and negotiated the uneven terrain, taking to its mild incline. I glanced at the time. If that was them, they were thirty-seven minutes early. The first letter on the license plate was an *H*. That meant it was a car for hire, a rental.

I took the safety off of my .380, placed it in the small of my back, then went to the cubbyhole where I had left my backpack, reached inside, and took the safety off my other two weapons, and then I picked up my backpack, put it on, the straps adjusted to cause the bag to hang and cover my gun.

Maybe I had been lucky in Trinidad.

Maybe my luck was close to its end.

This might be my final moment in the sun.

I passed the weather-beaten railing, held my backpack in my left hand, went down the steps. Would be easier to draw my gun now. Music kicked up louder. Beyond the fence, kids jumped around and recorded their version of the Harlem Shake. Bad fucking timing to make a video. I was concerned with stray bullets hitting an innocent child, as innocents had been shot in the bank in Trinidad.

I didn't know how aggressive to be, but I knew one fact.

In this business, he who shot last died first.

Today she who fired last would be the first to die.

The Toyota RAV4 parked. Three doors opened at the same moment, like they were on the synchronized door-opening team for the Special Olympics. Three pairs of expensive shoes touched the gravel and grass at the same instant, then three men closed three doors at the same moment.

The first man wore high-end rags by Dormeuil. He was tall, at least six-foot-four, and sported a dated George Carlin ponytail. In his thirties. Something Jason Statham–esque about him, the cocky walk, the square chin, the excessive forehead, the nose that had been broken and reset and broken and reset, the way he looked like he longed for a good fight. He was an ugly handsome, had a face that some women might like after a few hard drinks but would never want to see on their daughters.

No one else had anything in their hands, but he carried a black briefcase. That stood out. It was big enough to hold guns and ammo, maybe blocks of C4, if that was their intention.

The second man wore clothes by Zenga. Big like a linebacker. Barely looked twenty-one. Neck big, like a thigh. Daniel Craig expression, one that said he was the badass who killed the badasses and pissed on their graves, his hairline receding like the banks of the Mississippi during a severe drought.

The third man was average height for a man, around five-nine in his shoes, so that meant that he was really about five-eight. He was slender, wore rags by Loro Piana, a suit with a great lapel, inner linings of a silver hue. He was the only black one in the lot, the only one who could remove his overpriced suit, throw on cargo pants, sandals, and an I BAJAN T-shirt and blend in with the West Indies.

All overdressed men were either pallbearer or casket-ready, depending on how this went.

The man in the Dormeuil suit made it to

where I stood, his walk square-shouldered, led with his nose. He scanned the urban area, not impressed. This side of the island was nothing like he'd seen in the travel brochures. I don't think it was even in the brochures. He probably thought the entire island would look like the five-star resorts where the Brits spent their winters to avoid having to put on a winter coat.

Dormeuil evaluated me and spoke first. "Black parents give birth to white baby."

Ice water replaced my blood.

Zenga said, "Your old man is as black as a day-old cup of coffee and your momma was so dark if you poured coffee on her it looked like sweat, and you came out looking like Barbie?"

The boys in fancy suits looked at me like I had a cleft lip, then laughed the same laughs that schoolyard bullies had. My stern expression let them know that I hated them just that fast.

Zenga said, "If you're Goldilocks, I guess that makes us the three fucking bears."

Then they all laughed, three tenors enjoying an insult, one that could be their last.

Zenga raised his hand and I saw five dots tattooed in his flesh. Four of the dots were the corners of a square and the fifth was in the center. The four dots represented the walls of a prison, the one in the center was the prisoner. No tattoo tears, the sign of a murderer, were on his face, but those could have been removed, the same as, for now, my fingerprints were gone.

I said, "Before we go any further, I need to hear your designations."

Dormeuil told me his first, then Zenga, then the handsome black guy spoke up.

Zenga and Dormeuil had burners underneath their jackets. Small guns in holsters created a bulge, same as it had done for the LKs. I could beat them to the draw. No. I could beat one of them to the draw. Then the shootout. Dormeuil sounded like Brooklyn. Zenga was Chicago, the side near the now-defunct Sears Tower. The black man, his accent was West, Texas, from the Bible Belt.

Dormeuil said, "You're the infamous MX-401. You're Reaper."

I asked, "Why did they send Manny, Mo, and Jack to purgatory to chat with me?"

"To collect debts and solve problems and keep pallbearers and ministers busy."

"Am I the problem?"

"You are *a* problem, have been a problem since you fucked up in Trinidad, but there is a larger issue. We took care of one thing in Miami and now we've been assigned to end this lingering problem."

"I have no idea what's going on. The new problem is here in Barbados?"

"The problem here isn't new."

"So it's connected to a problem in Miami?"

"Not connected to Miami or New York."

"What happened in New York?"

"There was a bad debt. We shut it all down, and we'll shut this down."

"Okay. One more time. Some sort of problem exists and it's here."

"It's new to you, but not new to RCSI. The shit has hit the fan."

"The man behind the double red doors sent you here, and the problem here isn't new."

"This problem? It's been going for months."

"Is that why I've been detained?"

"You're one big headache, but on this day, the other problem has garnered priority."

"Who is the client?"

"We are."

"You three trying to pass for a Vegas Rat Pack are clients for the Barbarians?"

"You could say that RCSI has hired the Barbarians to look out for the interests of RCSI."

"I'm in the dark. We have hired ourselves to do what, exactly? Against whom?"

"Someone who is costing the organization millions due to an oversight. Big investment, the largest RSCI has had to date, and there is a clog in the wheels that has brought business to a standstill."

"Is that the holdup with my paycheck? Are you telling me RSCI is bankrupt?"

"No one has seen a paycheck or cash payout for two months. Don't feel special."

"This has to do with the drug hit and the cricketer?"

"I don't know anything about that. And if I did, I would say I don't know anything about that."

"Tell me the details on what you do know, starting with Miami and New York and whatever the reason is no one has been paid by RCSI in the last two months. What the fuck is going on?"

"Not your concern, MX-401. If you need to ask anything, all you need to do is ask how high to jump and when you can come down and where on this planet you have permission to land."

"I've been doing bird like I'm O. J. Simpson. You need to tell me something."

"I can tell you this, the Barbarians have big, big money invested here, and that money has been tied up. People down here have chosen to rob the wrong company. We don't know how they do it down here, but RCSI is willing to burn this crummy island down to make a point."

I looked at the smoke in the distance. "The Barbarians started the fires."

He nodded. "Doesn't take much to start a fire."

The black guy grinned and said, "When land is dry like this, not much at all. Easier than killing. Not as much fun, but much easier. All you have to do is catch a few mongoose, set their tails on fire, and watch them run through the cane fields and ignite it from end to end."

"You guys . . . we're . . . we're . . . RCSI . . . the Barbarians are burning the island?"

Dormeuil said, "That particular team has been here for the last two weeks."

I looked at the black guy. "You were on that team."

He didn't confirm, but he didn't deny.

I said, "You set mongoose tails on fire and made them run through the cane fields?"

He shrugged. "Cruel, but it works. Very effective. Very effective."

"Why didn't anyone tell me I wasn't on this ham-shaped rock alone?"

Dormeuil said, "They were deciding what to do with you."

"What the fuck does that mean?"

"Trinidad is still an issue, the LKs are hunting you, the bank is hunting you, your photo was posted internationally, rewards have been issued. If you're caught, that could hit RCSI and the Barbarians in ways you can't imagine, so, MX-401, congratulations you fuck-up, you're a big issue."

"Between cane fields, cow lick, and businesses, there have been over twenty fires a day."

He nodded. "This place is a pyromaniac's playground."

The black guy said, "I used to work for the

fire department in Hope, Arkansas."

I said, "So, you are the expert fire starter."

"I just enjoy my job, that's all. Fire is a beautiful thing. It's alive. It has life. Nothing like watching a beautiful fire dance and cleanse a place of sin. I used to go to Detroit and burn the vacant houses. So many houses to burn. Was relaxing. It takes away stress. When you set someone on fire, watching the fire wash the skin off the bone, it's arousing, better than sex."

"You make it sound like you set fires and masturbate."

"I am not ashamed to admit what arouses me."

I asked, "Why the fires? Burning down the island makes no sense to me, none at all."

Dormeuil said, "You will know when you need to know, if you ever need to know."

"Why the secrecy? I mean, we are a band of brothers here."

"You're not one of us. Two dead LKs. That botched Trinidad job should have had us here putting you in the ground, preferably after we ran your disarticulated body parts through a tree shredder."

"That's not a nice thing to say to a young female assassin. Not nice at all."

"They have gone back and forth on what to do to you every damn day. Every damn day I have had to hear your name, Reaper. You were done. Good thing someone up top liked the way you handled things over in the Grenadines, and they said something about the job two days ago, so you impressed someone who needed to be impressed. You were lucky and closed those accounts expeditiously."

" 'Expeditiously.' Great adverb."

"I have a ton of 'em — adverbs of purpose and frequency and adverbs of place and adverbs of time and adverbs of completeness, and many don't end in -ly. Impressed?"

"Nope."

"I'm not awed with you, either."

"Don't like me? Have a seat with the rest of the bitches waiting for me to give a fuck."

"You went off the rails and killed two lieutenants and the LKs are in war mode. You've been here since you fucked up that simple assignment in Trinidad, wherever the fuck that is."

"It's that way, a few breaststrokes before South America."

"Like I give a rat's ass."

"If New York and Miami are all you guys know, you really should buy a globe or a world map or get a few more stamps in your illegal passport. All of these places you don't fuckin' know are on maps."

"You're mocking me?"

"I'm mocking your stupid Brooklyn accent."

"Stop mocking me."

"Stop mocking me."

"Stop it."

"A man who doesn't have sense enough to buy a map deserves to be mocked."

"Don't fuck with me. All the trouble it took to get here, getting lost, driving on the wrong side of the road, don't fuck with me, MX-401, or Reaper, or whatever the fuck they call you. I am from America and I use fucking GPS. We don't need no goddamn maps on paper. We ain't used a Thomas Guide or a fuckin' road map in over a goddamn decade. Have you heard how people give directions here? We stopped and asked some shoeless Bob Marley on the side of the road how to get from being lost to being un-lost and direct us here. 'Make a left at the coconut tree after the roundabout and don't go past the brown cow and don't turn at the road with the green fence.' What the fuck? There are no fuckin' legible street signs and nobody knows where any-fuckin'-thing is. All they seem to know is where they live and how to get to work, and most don't know the name of the road they live on. I saw a dead monkey in the middle of the road. A dead fuckin' monkey. To top it off, my goddamn Siri don't fuckin' work down here. What kind of malarkey is that shit? Who in the fuck lives on the planet without GPS and Siri?"

"You can use Google Maps."

"They told us the goddamn safe house that

we had been assigned was gray and unpainted and next to a yellow-and-peach gallery and we drove on the wrong side of the goddamn road all morning looking for a goddamned art gallery. It's called a goddamn *porch*. I fuckin' hate being anyplace they drive on the wrong side of the road and use the wrong words to describe shit. Who does that? Nobody stocked the damn place with any water or food I recognize. Ain't no McDonalds. No 7-Eleven."

"There's a Burger King."

"Fuck Burger King. Why would they have a Burger King and not a McDonald's? Who does that? The Miami Beach here is nothing like the Miami Beach in the real Miami, and that pisses me the fuck off as well, and we have been from store to store and no one sells stool softener on this damn island."

He took a harsh breath, straightened his collar, anger leaving his pores like rain.

He asked me, "How the fuck can you stand this damn heat?"

"Sorry to hear about the problem with stool softener. Try soft bananas. Eat them. Don't use them as a suppository. Unless that's what you're into. If you are, start with a green banana."

"I'm jet-lagged and need coffee."

"Ah, the reason you're going off the rails."

"I need Starbucks."

"It's the invisible building next to the Mc-

Donald's that they haven't built yet."

"Is there at least the equivalent of a Barnes & Noble here?"

"You're standing in front of it."

"Fuck. I'm dying for a goddamn grande iced half-caf triple mocha latte macchiato."

Zenga said, "Tell me a-fuckin'-bout it. I'm dying too. I need a fuckin' quad venti half-caf breve no foam, with whip, two Splenda, stirred, skinny ten-pump peppermint mocha."

The black guy wiped sweat from his nose. "I'm partial to an iced half-caf quad venti nonfat six-Splenda, with whip, extra-ice, extra-caramel, upside-down caramel macchiato."

In a silly Valley Girl accent I said, "Like, oh my God. I prefer one java-chip frappuccino in a trenta cup, sixteen shots of espresso, a shot of soy milk, caramel flavoring, banana puree, strawberry puree, vanilla beans, Matcha powder, protein powder, and a drizzle of caramel and mocha. For sure."

All three well-suited men grimaced at me as the heat assaulted them.

Zenga stared at me. Stared at me too long. Fucked me with his eyes.

I said, "What's the problem, Hercules?"

"There an issue, Goldilocks?"

"Did you lose something in my cleavage?"

"Was trying to read the message."

"It's a Jessica Lee T-shirt. Elements from the periodic table. Stop moving your lips while you read and let me pronounce them for you so you don't make yourself look bad. Fluorine, uranium, carbon, potassium, bismuth, technetium, helium, sulfur, germanium, thulium, oxygen, neon, yttrium. I doubt if you have the IQ that would enable you to comprehend its meaning and decipher the message."

Zenga kept ogling my chest and he grinned. "Black parents, white baby."

"Get over it. Eyes off my breasts, asshole. Take a picture and go kick rocks."

"You sure wear those pants short and tight on your little round ass."

"Seriously? Can you be professional? This is a meeting, right?"

Dormeuil asked, "So where's a coffee shop that compares to Starbucks?"

"I'm not your tour guide. Get a map. Work it out."

Dormeuil frowned, nodded, and took a breath. "Maybe we got off on the wrong foot."

"You think?"

Zenga said, "There are three of us."

"If there were two more of you, then the odds would almost be even."

"You'd get cut down."

"Just try me. I'll rip your fuckin' spine out and wear it like a necklace."

Zenga said, "Somebody is hot under the collar."

I said, "First you disrespected me, then you

insulted me. Yeah, I'm hot under the collar."

"Thought niggas liked calling themselves niggas. I mean niggas say and sing and rap the word 'nigga' so much. Look at that white nigga bitch, looking like a nigga with an attitude."

I grinned. "Sure you want to push me until I explode? Sure you want to do that? Want to keep acting like you're in preschool or high school until I snap and blow your fuckin' brains out?"

Zenga said, "Jesus. Will you look at this shit coming this way?"

A woman crossed the road in front of the library. Tall and in a blue uniform, like one the girls wore at the banks in the area and in town. She carried a black umbrella, and her slow and deliberate high-heeled walk was hotter than high noon. Her attractiveness had created silence, but her walk created awe. She had a West Indian tittup, an exaggerated prancing, a sashay that made everything bounce.

As she passed by us, in a strong Jamaican accent she said, "Good afternoon."

When she vanished inside, the men looked at one another.

Zenga said, "That fine-ass bitch looked like child support waiting to happen."

Dormeuil said, "On another note, where can my boys rent a few women?"

Zenga said, "How much for a clean, white

nigga bitch?"

I took a deep breath, calmed myself, and asked, "Are. We. Done. Here?"

Dormeuil said, "Not quite. We're going to need a large refrigerated truck. Big enough for sixty cows. While we are handling other aspects of this assignment, I need you to make that happen."

"I need passports, cash, and my fuckin' pay. Get me what I'm due, then get back to me."

Zenga said, "White nigga bitch needs to be bent over and brought down a few notches."

I grinned and said, "Sweetie, call me out of my name, say one more word to me, I'll kill you."

The men looked at one another again. The pyromaniac stepped to the side, body language saying he didn't agree with Zenga. He was the weak link, not a hand-to-hand man.

I said, "The people up top, have them arrange your damn truck. Tell them I said that I work on your level. I don't take orders from you. I'm not a fuckin' Miss Moneypenny at a desk. I'm guns and roses without the roses. If you have a problem with that, pass it up the chain of command and have them call me. Tell them, before they make that call, to have my money and passports waiting at the front door."

Zenga stepped forward. I put my hand at the small of my back, on my weapon.

Dormeuil stopped Zenga from whatever he

was about to say to test my last threat.

Dormeuil motioned at the briefcase and said, "MX-401, this is your package."

"I didn't order a package."

Zenga kicked the briefcase toward me.

Dormeuil drew my attention and said, "Squatters."

"The singing group from the fifties. Second time hearing them mentioned."

"You know the laws down here?"

"Never studied law. Would hate to find out that what I've been doing is illegal."

"Looking at that Chefette place. They refrigerate their goods. Maybe we can appropriate one of their trucks and pull this off. Sixty cows. We'll need one that can hold about sixty cows."

"Are we doing collection on a farm? Will somebody man up and tell me what is going on?"

He looked toward the fires. "Don't open the package until instructed."

I said, "This wasn't confirmed. They didn't tell me about a package."

Dormeuil said, "Follow my orders. I'm the leader down here."

"You're not *my* leader. Again, no one told me I'd receive a package."

Zenga said, "Must have been none of your fucking business, then."

"Bet you make the same face when you're giving a blow job."

"What the hell did you say to me?"

"You heard me, bitch."

Dormeuil grabbed his shoulder. My hand was already at my back, on my gun.

They turned around and started walking.

I said, "Hey."

They turned around.

I said, "Easy-on-the-pocket hookers are near town. Ask for the Garrison. Just remember that you get the diseases you pay for, and the ones you get are the ones that men like you left behind. Don't blame the Garrison Girls if you wake up the next day and your dick has a bad cold and looks like a foot with infected toenails. Like every car on the island, the STDs were imported, only they arrived duty-free."

Dormeuil asked, "So where's a coffee shop that compares to Starbucks?"

"A few Italias are here and there. Coffee Beans are all over. Stables Coffee Shop is near the Garrison. Overall, I'd recommend Novel Teas Teahouse in Hastings. Small shop. Quiet."

"What's near here?"

"Nothing."

"Where are those places you rattled off so fast?"

"I'm not your tour guide. Ask at the Shell gas station. Maps are free. Work it out."

"Stool softener?"

"Knights Pharmacy. Plaza, other side of

roundabout."

" 'Roundabout?' "

"The traffic circle."

"Why don't they just put up fucking red lights like normal people?"

"Revenge at Americans for breaking away from the queen."

They turned around again and moved on, expensive shoes crunching gravel.

Zenga looked back at me twice. Both times he caught two middle fingers.

When they made it to their ride, they had forgotten that it was right-side drive. Zenga was driving and went to the wrong side, as did the other guys. They crossed each other again, shaking their heads and sweating. The Starbucks-deprived driver hesitated at the driveway. His windshield wipers came on. The controls were reversed on the car as well. He got the wipers turned off and the signal light came on.

They took to the rugged two-lane road and followed the crowd, headed toward the Wynter Crawford Roundabout, followed traffic flow, went to the left, and vanished up Highway 5.

Then the three unwise men were gone.

I took a nervous breath and picked up the briefcase.

It was heavy. Could be rigged. Could have a detonator, and when they were a half mile away they could push a red button and make my world go boom. Then I looked behind me. I had left my back wide open. The library's window was a few feet away. There was no glass, just concrete, board, and bars. The woman who had just entered was standing there. She stared at me from behind iron bars.

She held a Beretta 92FS, an assassin's gun, the business end pointing out the window.

THIRTY

Petrichor exited Six Roads Library, sweat on the tip of her nose, stood next to me, almost shoulder to shoulder, her Beretta no longer in sight, tucked away in her purse, and patted her weave over and over.

I took the .380 away from the small of my back, put the safety on, then dropped it inside of my backpack. I pulled out a purple LIME bandana, dabbed sweat from my face and neck, then tucked it in my back pocket. The hired gun next to me opened her umbrella again, gave us shade, but I could feel the heat emanating from her brown skin, polyester making her a furnace.

She said, "I don't see how women wear these polyester uniforms all day."

I snapped, "You were fuckin' late."

"Muddasik, Reaper. Can't you at least tell me good morning or good afternoon?"

She had lost the spot-on Jamaican accent and spoke in her natural Bahamian brogue.

I said, "Fuckin' seriously? You should have

been in position, on top of the Farmers' Co-operative with your rifle. I had hoped that you were and I couldn't see you. Minutes later you came walking up, walking and doing a wukkup like you were Mother Sally and you worked for Rachel Pringle. What the fuck?"

"You're angry and looking like ya bound."

"I set this up, had them all out in the open. You should've been there. If I made it here before you, if they arrived first, then you were late. This is inexcusable. Fuckin' inexcusable."

"Noted. It rained on my side of the island. Then I came down Spring Garden Highway and it was jam up because the students at UWI were in the road having some sort of impromptu Mas party. They were chipping and wining, grinding on top of each other and their trucks that blocked the road. DJs were yelling and doing some sort of crazy celebration down by Brandon's Beach. I was stuck in traffic."

"Inexcusable. Don't you dare give me that muddasik face again."

"Do we have to do this in the sun?"

"What kind of backup are you? You're supposed to be a professional sniper."

"Reaper, I had your back at the Hilton. Gimme some damn credit. I was on time, waiting in the room one floor up, and I dropped the rope down on time, pulled it

315

back up when you made it to the ground. You walked in the room looking like a guy, then you vanished. I helped you do that."

"That was then. I needed you to have my back this morning. This was crucial."

"Do. We. Have. To. Do. This. In. The. Sun?"

We stepped up the stairs and stood in the shade. It was better, but it was too late to cool down. Anger made me sweat. I handed her the envelope that I had stuffed with Bajan money.

It was her delayed payment for watching my back at St. Lawrence Church and the cricketer job.

I said, "Your wicked ass threw a Haitian woman off a building."

"The government wanted her out of their pockets and out of the news."

"Anyway. You put down four guys in one night."

"Five. No, wait. It was six. No, seven. Lost count. But I think it was seven in total."

"You put an arrow through a guy's chest down by Government Hill?"

"Through his back. He was running across the field, trying to get into the projects, to his guns."

"Why so many jobs in one night?"

She yawned. "Last two guys had seen my face. Had to handle that."

"You didn't wear a mask?"

"Didn't want to mess my hair up."

I said, "Don't get caught. You live here. I haven't reached out to you unless I had to because of that, but when I do my back is against the wall and I have no other options and I do it so you never have to be seen. I protect you. This is serious and I've kept away from you because I don't want you at risk, and you're shitting where you eat? That's not good. Why do you do that, work where you live?"

"Saves on gas."

I said, "Next time, if I'm here, let me handle that for you. You won't have to lie to your husband."

"Sounds like you care about me a little bit."

"It's just a professional courtesy, nothing more, nothing less."

She said, "What about the other thing?"

"What other thing?"

"The watch."

"Oh. Right. I washed the blood away and cleaned it."

I handed her the faux Rolex and jewelry that I had worn when I had met with the cricketer. She liked it all. I liked things, but I'd never been attached to material things.

She dropped it inside her purse and smiled.

I said, "Forgetting something?"

"Oh. Right."

She opened her bag and gave me the black sequined skirt she had worn at the Gap.

She said, "Don't be mad. I'm sorry. Forgive

me for being late."

We shook hands like men at the end of a business arrangement.

She said, "You're going to hell for cutting the man's dick off in a church parking lot."

"I did more than that. What I did was trademark for an assassin on my level."

"Wicked as shite. Bloody and brilliant. You really need to show me how to do that."

"Forgot to tell you. Been preoccupied. He had ten grand US on him."

"Damn. Who walks around in the Gap with twenty thousand in Bajan?"

"You want that, too?"

"Nah. You paid me. The fake watch and costume jewelry are enough."

"Maybe I'll get the money back to his legion of kids."

"Why? Finders keepers."

"Kids need to eat."

"Twenty thousand divided by twenty kids won't be much for each kid."

"Twenty kids?"

"From what I hear the number is still rising. Not including whoever is pregnant."

"Not including who else he breed. No matter how it divides, better than nothing."

"All his baby-mommas will do is run to Limegrove and buy bags and shoes."

I said, "He must have been dating American women."

"Most probably watch the Kardashians.

They learn from the best."

"Right or wrong, responsible or irresponsible, even if the kids have much more coming, even if they have nothing coming but hard times, that money should be for them to divide."

"That bey was kinda hot. You should have got some before you detached the goods."

"I prefer to have a boyfriend for certain things. Not a one-off kinda girl."

"Met anybody since you've been here?"

"The broker for the Hilton job hit on me. Black Jack came on strong."

"Bey was sexy enough. Bey was fit. W'happen?"

"He offered me his bed. His hot shower. His plunge pool."

"He'd let you plunge in his pool if you let him plunge in yours."

"Passed on it."

"You need a bedroom bully. I bet that he would have been a good one."

"The older guy?"

"No, the cricketer. He was all muscles and swag. Bet he was damn good in bed."

"Anybody but that alcoholic, weed-smoking, baby-making slut. I'm not on the pill and he would have refused to wear a condom. Last thing I would need to do is end up with watermelon belly."

"You would've had to flush it."

"I'm not a flusher."

"Would be bad if you breed for a dead whore who has twenty kids already."

"Not funny. Dead rapist-whore at that. So it's not funny. Half the girls who have had his baby were probably raped on the side of the road and are too ashamed to say they have a rape baby."

"Sorry, it tickled me until you put things into perspective."

"You said he was up to at least twenty kids on the books?"

"He fascinated you."

"He disgusted me."

"I stand corrected."

"The wad of cash piqued my interest."

"That wad of cash piqued the interest of many women."

"Wondered how he had so much money. He owned everything but a condom."

She said, "He might even have babies by the same mother and daughter, too."

"That's two more child-maintenance checks sent to one address."

"Twenty-plus kids. Hope they know each other before they end up dating each other."

I said, "He should've been broke, on the city bus, not rocking a brand-new Corvette."

"The laws here, if they put him in court, they'd be lucky to get fifty Bajan dollars a month."

"That wouldn't cover the bare necessities.

Not even a decent pair of shoes from Pay-less."

"This ain't the US or England. In the UK they pay fifteen percent of their pay for one child, twenty percent for two, and twenty-five percent for three. But in the US, getting pregnant by a baller is a sport that can pay better than having an education, a job, and a sponsor. That's the lottery. Charlie Sheen pays over one hundred thousand Bajan a month. Nas pays almost the same. Russell Simmons pays eighty-thousand Bajan. Martin Brodeur pays over a quarter million Bajan dollars a year. Britney Spears pays the fat loser she married and bred for forty thousand Bajan a month. Tax-free money."

"Turn off the idiot box. You're minding other people's business too much."

"Most women don't bother putting the man in court because it's a joke. A rich man pays very little here. Man can be rich here, nice house, rocking Mercedes, and his child living like he or she homeless."

"I'm surprised they haven't killed the men for insurance."

"Most are uninsured. But at the same time, much men down here are paying for children they have no idea is not theirs. So there are more than a few reasons why some women don't take a man to court. On another note, since we're on that page, a big-time soca man down here has at least six illegitimate kids, not as bad as the cricketer, but he's out of control."

"Uh-huh. What's the point of this conversation? What's the business?"

"A contract is coming on him. If they want him handled in L.A., New York, Toronto, Atlanta, or Miami, I will shop the job over to you. If he's here, I can handle it, sniper-style."

I asked, "You have a kid and issues? That's why you know so much about maintenance issues?"

"No kid. Not pregnant. I have neighbors. Miserable, chatty, malicious women who have maintenance-support issues. They come over from time to time. That's all they complain about."

"How can so many women have babies by so many men who already have so many babies, babies they do nothing for? Women ignore history. Always think it will be different for them."

"It will be different for me. I'm married. We're in love."

"He has kids?"

"He takes care of them."

"Don't assume he will take care of yours."

"He's not like that."

"Don't assume he will take care of yours."

"He's not like that."

"Don't assume —"

"Stop it."

"Just don't assume he will take care of yours."

For a moment I wondered what would have happened if I had become pregnant by Parker. Maybe it was good we had split before it had become that complicated.

She said, "You're stressed. Every time I see you, you look so damn tense."

"Always stressed. Always have a headache. The incessant heat is torturous."

"Up to you if you want me to make that call and get you some relief."

"Is that what you do, call in an order and have it delivered?"

"I'm married now. I just stroke it, roll over, suck it if I want, and ride it."

"Whatever. You're faking a marriage."

"You faked a relationship."

"I didn't fake a marriage. That's a different level. Don't forget that."

"Reaper, I'm faking a marriage and doing it well. Well, I'm married, but I'm not really legally married, but my husband and the court system down here think we are, and I really feel like I am."

"He's Bajan?"

"Yeah. He worked hard, went to UWI, and now he owns an insurance company and has a window-tinting business up in St. Michael. I did my due diligence and ran a background check."

"I did the same with Johnny Parker."

"My husband is the best. While I clean, he washes my Toyota by hand every Saturday morning. When he's done, he comes and helps me finish cleaning. He goes to church. I don't go. He doesn't make it an issue. I stay home and cook dinner. I'm traditional. I cook almost every day of the week, unless we go to Chicken Barn or Bubba's or Just Grillin' or TGI Friday."

"You mention him and don't stop smiling. Miss hardcore, you really love that guy."

"I have never been like this with any other man, and there have been more than a few. We love being together. Sometimes we get up early and play road tennis before we go to work in the morning. Road tennis is like a playing a combination of Ping-Pong and tennis on asphalt."

"You've made yourself over and turned into a true Bajan."

"But this is what gets me."

"What?"

"Sometimes, the way he looks at me, I always feel like my husband knows something."

"I know that look. I would be doing something, in Jennifer mode, and catch Parker looking at me and I would wonder if he knew, if he had found out, if he gone through my e-mails, or if the Barbarians had contacted him, if I had fucked up and used the wrong accent. I know that look. Know it well."

"This morning, it was like he was trying to sort something out in his mind."

"They know something is wrong. We're not normal. Women like us aren't normal."

At the same moment we both looked down at the briefcase that had been left behind, a reminder of what we were. She was curious, but she didn't ask. We were in the business of not asking. She raised her black umbrella. Not until then did I notice that it was branded ARSENAL.

She said, "We've never talked that long, Reaper. Never had a real conversation."

I shrugged. "Sorry for being vexed. You've had my back. Thanks for the Hilton, too."

"You're welcome. So, that was Black Jack who was all over you."

"It wasn't like that."

"Looked like that. I'm not judging you."

"Wasn't like that."

Again I looked toward the smoke rising in the distance.

The skies here reminded me of the smog over Los Angeles.

Petrichor said, "Sent you a goodie box to your holding cell."

"What did you send?"

"No more questions. Let me know if you need me for anything."

"Okay. Thanks in advance."

"And I love the T-shirt you have on."

"Understand the message?"

"I love chemistry."

"The message the elements spell?"

"I already put them together."

"Profound message."

" 'Fuck bitches, get money.' Brilliant, using the elements' abbreviations to spell that."

"Yup. If I had followed Jessica Lee's favorite rule, I would've been better off."

"That's why I'm a GDI."

"You really like this tee?"

"I want that T-shirt."

"It's yours. Will hand-wash it."

"I want to wear it to church one Sunday."

"You don't go to church."

"I will if I can wear that tee."

"You'll get struck by lightning."

"I believe in the Almighty, but I wouldn't call myself a Christian. I'm churchgoing if I have to — weddings, funerals. Well, funerals if I didn't have anything to do with the sad occasion."

"I'm sure that FBGM is already a Bible verse."

"Probably covered under 'do unto others.' "

"Probably is."

"Yup. Fuck bitches. Get money. FBGM. Amen."

"Amen."

"Jessica Lee is a genius. A fuckin' genius."

Again Petrichor's slow and deliberate high-heeled wukkup-walk brought heat to the day.

THIRTY-ONE

Back at the safe house, I went around the back way, climbed in through the rear window again. Once inside, I checked every room, each closet, my loaded gun leading the way.

I went to the front door. Moved the sofa I had put up as a barricade, opened the front door, the breeze feeling good on my skin. The package Petrichor had sent was there.

Neighbors were outside in the blaze playing road tennis. A woman was walking with her little girl. Boys were home from school, riding bikes like Evel Knievel. They saw me. They stared.

I pulled the box inside, closed the door, put the barricade back in place.

It was a box of Agent Provocateur goodies, the Regina Baptiste collection. Four sets of panties and bras. Petrichor's note said that everything was brand new and had been washed.

The box was heavy for what was inside. I pulled back the false bottom.

Underneath the lingerie was the true gift. Two pistol-grip Pepper-blasters. Four blades, two like I had used on the philandering cricketer down in the Gap. Two more handguns, another supply of ammo, plus concealment clothing, all black; a tank top that would allow my .38 to rest underneath my left arm, Spanx that would accommodate a Glock on my right hip, a crew neck that would accommodate another gun on my right side, a belt-clip holder for a .380 or a Ruger. I could travel five handguns deep, and a blade could be fit on each calf and thigh. Five guns, four blades. Still wouldn't be enough.

She was looking out for me. Had been since I'd landed. I didn't know how to take that.

Never had anybody looking out for me before.

Drenched in sweat, I showered again, cold water and the rattling fan from my air-conditioning.

I'd never had Agent Provocateur panties and bras before. All I had were the two-dollar panties and bras that they sold on the side of the road here, the kind you wash, wear, and toss.

The panties and bras made it feel like my birthday.

The guns and the gear made it feel like Christmas.

I couldn't wait to try all of it on, especially the holsters.

I wanted to be ready for Barbarians or LKs. Might need to be ready for Black Jack.

I took out a pink razor, made sure no one could tell the carpet didn't match the drapes. Shaved my armpits last. Washed my hair and removed the blackness from my mane. Sat in front of the fan and gave myself a manicure, pedicure, painted my nails with clear polish. All the while my mind was on dead drug dealers, a dickless cricketer, and now a black briefcase, this special delivery that had weight.

All of this shit had to be connected.

Whatever was the reason behind this suitcase was the reason no one had been paid.

The briefcase slept quietly at my feet. It was my child to watch.

I hated children the same way my mother had hated me.

If a man looked at our child and walked away because of its looks, I'd kill him. That was one of my biggest fears.

I pulled on my new undies, colorful skyscraper heels, put on a holster and guns, slicked my hair back, painted my lips red, looked at myself in the mirror, struck a dozen poses.

Sexy. Was tempted to take photos of myself.

Would love for a man to be on a bed naked, waiting for me, then to dress like this and walk into the room. Killer sex. I'd only been with a couple of men, but I had been with each many times.

The first guy had been the guy before Johnny. I had been with Johnny Parker the most. We'd had sex more times in a month than most people have in two years. He had set the standard.

My body was craving. Wanted to sip a brew, be randy and get some relief, be a woman, be facedown, ass up, moaning for Jesus and his daddy. I had no male friends. No potential lover. My options for sexual healing were few. I thought of a plunge pool, air-conditioning, and Black Jack. The kiss I had put on his lips was gratuitous; hugging him was my own curiosity. I had felt him and been aroused too.

I whispered, "Roll over, stroke it, suck it, ride it. Lucky. So fuckin' lucky."

No time for old regrets, not when new regrets were the soup of the day.

I had to deal with RCSI and Barbarians. I had to deal with the LKs and Trinidad.

I called Big Guy and asked, "You making progress on the passports?"

"I'll need photos."

He told me where to go and I hung up without saying good-bye.

THIRTY-TWO

Diamond Dust was onstage, like Tim Cook at Apple introducing a new product.

The wives were assembled. She explained their roles in the creation of their kingdom.

She spoke on the importance of family, the importance of motherhood, said that they were all citizens of heaven, and their heaven would be here on Earth, on their island.

Their kingdom would grow.

She spoke to the women, no one over the age of twenty-five, the majority with college degrees, some with their master's, and they listened to her as if she were their savior.

Diamond Dust looked out at the women.

Wives wore Wellendorff wedding rings, all sparkling under the lights in the room, stars on the finger of commitment. Three hundred thousand Trinidad dollars sparkled on each wife's finger.

The rings represented the marriage to the group, to the cause, not to the men.

The men wore 18-karat gold rings by the

same designer as well.

Diamond Dust said, "We are strong. We are those who refuse to give up. We have all had to endure too much. Which brings me to the next order of business. The Kiwi. Finally, after days of searching, after nights of crying and mourning, we have found something of importance. I cannot say what, but we have found her trail. This I assure you, we are close to victory."

The lights dimmed. Big-screen televisions came on.

A montage of photos went by. All looked like a different woman.

Diamond Dust said, "This is her. All photos are of the same woman. A woman of many faces. An assassin who could be anyone, anywhere. The Woman of a Thousand Faces. This is the cold-blooded bitch someone sent into our organization and brought an unfathomable shame to our family. We will reverse-engineer this, find her and her organization, and put the motherfuckers in the ground."

The Laventille Killers knew that the Kiwi had fled Trinidad. Two days ago they had found the fake passport the Kiwi had used to exit the island, knew her destination, and now they were on the island of Grenada. The Kiwi had landed there a dark-haired gimp. They knew that when the Kiwi left there she had fled to the Grenadines a redhead wearing braces, white Levi's, and a blue South Carolina T-shirt. She had arrived in Bequia dressed in a colorful sundress and wearing long braids, her hair Bo Derek–style, her nationality Swiss. Each time her eyebrows were a different color, a different shape, her makeup had changed the shape of her face, other makeup had changed her hairline, her breast size different each time, her nationality different. Her height only varied by inches, her stated weight varied by twenty pounds in either direction, reasonable ranges. They didn't know if the Kiwi was still on that smaller island or had fled to Balliceaux, Canouan, Mayreau, Mustique, Isle à Quatre, Petit Saint Vincent, or Union Island. Diamond Dust ordered the LKs to send a small group to catch a flight to Saint Vincent and arrive in the Grenadines in a few hours.

Appaloosa wanted to be in charge, said that War Machine should be like the president, should stay out of harm's way, should stay in Trinidad and be the face of the company.

War Machine refused, insisted that he lead his men.

He said, "I am a warrior. Not an armchair warrior. I carry my own sword into battle."

When the Kiwi was caught, when this exploded, he planned to be there.

Two hours after her speech, with War Machine being unavailable, Diamond Dust oversaw the delivery of cocaine being transported from Catia La Mar, Venezuela, through Trinidad. She kept some for her group, for her members. Recreational use was permitted, as long as it was only recreational. Suitcases of cash were handed to her. Containers of cocaine were transferred to her buyers. South America had never failed. Only one shipment out of the last one hundred had been dumped as the suppliers evaded the law, that cocaine in the Caribbean waters being called "white lobster."

It had been a bad season. New York. Miami. Barbados.

Today was a day to celebrate. Today things were back on course.

Each victory was cause for celebration. Women came in, women she had brought along, and they entertained the drug runners. Men from South America paused for an hour and celebrated on their vacation paradise, land of sandy shores and crystal-clear waters, where the Africans, Creoles, Chinese, Indians, Spanish, and French had all left their mark. They prayed to their absentee gods, broke bread, ate the indigenous food of the islands Trinidad and Tobago: iguana curry; flower dumplings; conch and the penis of the conch, the penis being the part Diamond Dust enjoyed eating the most; breadfruit; sweet potatoes; plantains; sea grapes; lobster; pig's feet souse; chicken's feet souse; cow-skin soup; chicken, beef, goat, and liver rotis; doubles, cow-heel soup; callaloo; pig's tail; Richard's Bake & Shark; and kingfish heart.

The women were there for the pleasure of the men.

Diamond Dust knew how to do business, how to keep customers happy.

Then came the true entertainment.

One of her men against one of their men.

She always brought a boy, a soon-to-be man who wanted to become a gunta.

Her counterpart always brought a man who wanted to be part of their organization.

Before them all, as they sat in silence, the men fought to the death.

Men were willing to die, end their hell, as a chance to get into someone's false heaven.

After that she was in her private plane, drinking the most expensive wine in production, Shipwrecked 1907 Heidsieck, $275,000 a bottle, doing a line of the best of the best cocaine, her Brazilian mistress going down on her as the plane took them into the sky. Her mistress made her come and weep as she escaped the world and flew above the islands for two hours, took her away from the world. Her life had been hard. Had been so fucking hard. Every day so intense. Her phone rang. She answered.

"Husband?"

"Catch you at a bad time?"

"No. What's the issue?'

In the Grenadines, the image of the Kiwi had been matched against that of a woman leaving Saint Vincent with a ticket set to arrive in Barbados a little more than forty days ago.

She told War Machine, "Get to Barbados. See where that leads us."

"The men are tired. Two hours of sleep over the last two days. I'm working while they recuperate. She will be gone. I want to find where she went after Barbados, if it is possible. It's been more than a month. The way she moved, she never stayed in one spot more than two days."

"But she never left the islands. There has to be a reason for that."

"The men need some downtime to remain highly motivated."

She understood. She needed to get away as well, so she understood.

After a night of women and wine, after a night that rivaled the orgy they had given on the roof of the Carlton Savannah, the Laventille Killers would rest, then rise and travel in the darkness.

She looked down at her Brazilian lover, whispered, "Love you."

War Machine responded, "Love you too."

Caressing her lover's cheek she said, "I want this resolved."

She hung up, ran her trembling fingers

through her lover's luxurious hair.

She wanted everything to be perfect, for her, for all involved.

Which was why she worked hard now. It was hard to evoke change.

One had to embrace corruption, master that art, to make change.

Kindness never won a war. The kind filled many graves.

THIRTY-THREE

Sheraton Mall, Parish of Christ Church
The photography studio was near the KFC entrance to the contemporary food court, near Nature's Discount Nutrition Centre. I entered the establishment dressed in a green business suit, long strawberry-blond hair in a workday ponytail, lips dark, my face in makeup, but not too much. Using a Russian accent I asked for Nigel, then I stepped to the side and pretended to read the morning newspaper. Nigel appeared. Made eye contact. I nodded. He motioned for me to follow him.

He was nervous. Sweating. Reputation preceded me.

In a back room, I became six people from various countries. Combinations and permutations. I created six new names. Once the photos were taken and printed, I made sure they were deleted from the camera and the computer, then instructed Nigel to pass the prints on to the big guy who had sent me.

I went to the ladies' room, locked myself inside of a stall. By the time I made it to the three-level parking structure, I was in Levi's, boots, and a wrinkled UWI Cave Hill T-shirt over one of the black tees I had been given to conceal a .380, my hair red with blue streaks, my walk quick and impatient as I devoured a slice of pizza. When I finished my meal, I called Big Guy's cellular number. I called five times before he answered. The moment he mumbled hello, I blasted him with curse words. He hadn't answered right away, and that had left me swimming in paranoia. In a voice that made the message clear, I told him the clock was ticking, and his clock was ticking a helluva lot louder than mine. I had calmed enough to hear his drugged-up voice as he explained. He had been rushed to the hospital. The head injury. Dizzy. Vomiting. Hadn't been right since he'd met me. I didn't give a fuck. He could talk. He was conscious. He could answer a phone. Hospital was better than the morgue. In a tone that left no room for ambiguity, I instructed him to get a bucket of strong coffee and wake up and get up off his ass. I told him to contact Nigel right away and get out of that damn hospital bed and go collect the package that I had left behind within the next hour, and to send a message to this number to confirm it had been collected. He said he needed more money for the friend of the friend of the friend who did the passports. I told him I would get him more fuckin' cash. If I had to rob every Butterfield and First Caribbean and RBC and Scotia and Republic and CIBC bank, if I had to become Bonnie without a Clyde and stick up every Texaco, Rubis, Shell, Esso, and Sol gas station on the island, I would get the fuckin' money. Was losing it. I snapped, barked, told him to remember the cricketer, told him to read about that death, imagine the pain, to realize that missing fingers, and I'd take ten, wouldn't be a problem for a dead man. Then I killed the call, rubbed my temples, screamed, the echo scaring every child and gentle bird on the island.

Hated needing people. Hated being dependent.

Felt like I was begging everyone to lend a hand.

There was no answer at Black Jack's number and his message box was full.

I sent him a text.

Waited ten minutes.

No response.

I cursed him.

The Laventille Killers. The Barbarians. The island shrank with my every breath. The island was hot and they had me on lock, had to keep my weapon loaded, had to keep moving.

Always had to keep moving.
Only the dead remained still.

THIRTY-FOUR

Oistins, Parish of Christ Church
I pulled into the parking lot at the Brenda Cox Fish Market. Dozens of chattel-house vendors were grilling or preparing to grill fish. Fishermen trapping small fish to use as bait to capture larger fish. Sea turtles bobbed up in the clear blue waters. At the end of the dock, I took out my binoculars.

I wasn't close enough.

I found the concrete bathroom and changed into a pink bikini, stuffed my riding clothes into my backpack, covered myself with a green wrap, and then headed down to the beach and chatted up a dread. Lean, toned, wore slim ragged jeans cut off above the knee, was shirtless.

I said, "Jet Ski. How much, handsome man?"

He scratched under his hairless chin and grinned. "Sixty US for half hour."

"You charge the Bajans thirty Bajan, and that is fifteen dollars US."

"That for Bajan."

"Does the Jet Ski somehow run better for tourists and worse for a Bajan?"

"It run the same for everybody."

"Exactly. Don't gouge me. I know the economy is fucked and times are hard, but don't disrespect me like that. You know what? I'll take my money to someone else. Have a nice day."

"Okay, pretty legs. T'irty Bajan, t'irty minutes. That Bajan price."

"Okay, thirty minutes."

I pulled on a giant red, yellow, black, and green crocheted brimmed hat, a novelty item that had fake dreadlocks hanging from all around its brim down my back. I rode the waves, struck them, porpoised the waters until I was on the backside of the Barbarians' other safe house. I rode by several times, made loops before I stopped and took out my binoculars. The Toyota RAV4 was there.

Zenga was upstairs. He had on red biker shorts and nothing else. There was a gym up there. He was doing speed sets. Pull-ups. Bodyweight squats. Chair dips. Calf raises. Inverted row. Lunges. Decline push-ups. Leg deadlifts. Chin-ups. Jumping rope at a boxer's pace.

Dormeuil was downstairs at a table poring over what looked like a map.

The black pyromaniac from Texas was outside walking the perimeter.

343

Soon two more SUVs pulled up in the front. Not many homes on the island had garages. Only a small percentage had carports. This one had a garage and the SUVs pulled inside.

The pyromaniac looked out to the ocean and saw me sitting there, rising and falling on the waves, the sea trying to push me back toward the island's sandy and rocky shores. The pyromaniac lit a match, lit a cigarette, and stared. I was a dot on a water vehicle. I took my bikini top off, sat in the sun topless, breasts bouncing. He waved for me to ride his way. I wanted to be sure he was looking at me and not off into the distance. I put my bra back on, adjusted the sorority sisters, then took off on the Jet Ski.

I went toward the east, vanished for five minutes, then doubled back.

By then they were closing the curtains and shutters in the house.

Before they had shut me out, I saw who had been in the SUVs. It was two SUVs loaded with women in short dresses. So they had found themselves a few Garrison girls. Drinks were poured. Tops came off. The women started to dance, to wine, to spread the eagle. They would be occupied for a while.

Prior Park section of St. James Parish. The newspaper had practically printed directions to the dead cricketer's front door. I found his townhome behind Redman's gas station, in a new development tucked away in a cul-de-sac. Looked like a fete. Many people were parked, all heading to his home. Many people. I wasn't the only one who had gotten directions from the newspaper.

My face was without makeup. My shoes were steel-toed, and my jeans were worn, carried a day's worth of dirt, and were loose-fitting. My top was a purple polo with the logo for Simmons Electrical.

There were dozens of other vehicles there, the first letter of the cars', SUVs', and trucks' tags telling me they had come from all parishes. Many men were there. It looked like every woman he had ever slept with had showed up to collect the panties and earrings they had left behind. When I limped up, bad skin, unattractive, they turned their heads away, went back to talking as if I were invisible.

"What de shite? His dick and spine was removed? How the shite do you remove a man's spine? Do you pull his dick so hard his damn spine comes out? How sick would you have to be to do that?"

"That's not funny."

"I serious. How do you do that? Only the devil would do something like that."

"They said that the back of his neck had

345

been cut, his spine taken out; that's all I know."

"I'm not surprised."

"I knew it would get him one day. Just didn't know it would be so soon."

"Hush. She coming."

The pregnant girlfriend was found and directed toward me. She had been engaged in a heated conversation with one of the cricketer's brothers, a man who felt he was entitled to his dead brother's car. The dead man's mother was there to investigate as well, wanted to find out what would happen to the house. Exasperated, about to explode, the luxuriously dressed pregnant girl saw me waiting and brought me a brand-new frown, asked me if I was another one of the cricketer's girlfriends. I told her "N-n-no."

She asked if he and I'd had a baby together. I told her n-n-no.

I was here on b-b-business, an appointment that he had scheduled last week with the homeowner. Backpack in hand, I told her that I was an electrician who had come by to do an emergency follow-up in-in-inspection on all electrical work that had been done by S-S-Simmons Electrical. Two homes had caught on fire and we wanted everyone to be safe and not endanger their homes and the lives of family. I told her I could come back another time, in a couple of weeks, a-a-after the funeral.

She put her hand on her belly and it looked like she imagined a middle-of-the-night fire, and said that she wanted me to inspect her home. She'd had enough bad luck to last a lifetime.

I was left to walk the upstairs portion of the home alone, clipboard in hand. The smallest of three bedrooms had been converted into a shrine to his weak career as a cricketer, and the entire home was a museum that honored his love of his British-born sport. I was in a home that didn't have the photos of any of his bastard children on its walls. A photo of the pregnant girlfriend was in a frame that was easy to move and hide when he brought other women here to be facedown, ass up, grabbing sheets and screaming his name, if they knew his name. They probably did. I doubt if he knew theirs.

His bed was Italian and on a raised platform — a throne, raised up higher than the average bed, a place to perform and look down on the peasants. The only things missing were chairs for an audience.

It was the star in the room of luxury.

It was made of the best ebony, sapele, and curly maple, smooth lines. The bed also had iPad holders and charging stations, all that and a pop-up swiveling television and computer monitors.

The walk-in closet that he had shared with his pregnant mistress was the size of my safe house. He had clothes like he was a movie star, but she also had a very impressive wardrobe.

She had a plethora of expensive shoes. She'd done a lot of shopping in New York and London.

Then I saw his computer. He owned a 24-karat-gold-plated MacBook Pro with a diamond-encrusted Apple logo, 24-four-karat-gold gilding over the entire MacBook Pro case.

I looked at the wad of money that I had taken from a dying man.

When I was coming here, part of my intention was to return it, leave it sitting in a dresser, or maybe inside her lingerie drawer, but seeing I was in some sort of Fort Knox, I reconsidered.

Next to a row of high-end watches, a book-size jewelry box made of toffee birdseye maple and cherry was on the dresser. The simplest thing in the room. I walked across beautiful rugs, flipped the box open.

It was loaded with his bracelets and necklaces, but the rings were what made my heart race.

He had owned three Wellendorff rings.

He owned the same style ring the LKs wore.

I didn't believe in coincidences. I had stumbled into the enemy's den.

Someone was behind me. I sensed them before I heard them breathing.

I turned around and faced the pregnant woman of the house.

THIRTY-FIVE

She asked, "Are you almost done?"

"A-a-a-almost done. T-t-ten m-m-m—"

"Ten minutes. How does everything look so far?"

"F-f-f-fine."

"I'll be downstairs when you're done."

"The man who d-d-died?"

"My husband."

I noticed her ring. It was a 2.4-carat blue diamond set in platinum between two diamond baguettes. She wore the same ring that Diamond Dust wore. She was the wife, not the wifey, not the girlfriend.

"Didn't know your h-h-husband play-play-play —"

"Played cricket?"

"Yeah."

"Neither did I. It seems he did a whole set of things that I had no idea he was doing. Bitches and babies. That's all Barbados is BBMing about. His bitches and those babies. I'm too angry to be sad right now. I am the laughingstock of Barbados this morning. He horned me good."

Kids ran up the stairs with their mothers on their heels. That distraction pulled the cricketer's wife back into the hallway. She took the hands of two overactive kids, had words with their mothers about controlling them in her home, and headed back down the stairs. I pretended that I was busy working, looking at an outlet. The door to another bedroom was open. One of the dead man's baby-mommas was in there, heard her talking bad about the dead cricketer, said she should steal everything she could carry. A man was in there with her. He talked bad about the cricketer too. It was one of the dead man's half-brothers. Both had drinks in hand. A kid ran into that bedroom, called the woman Mommy, and she snapped and told the kid to go play with her brothers and sisters while Mommy talked to her uncle in private. The kid ran back out of the bedroom, almost fell down the stairs. Her mommy touched her baby-daddy's half brother with her fingertips. She put her glass down on the expensive bedside table. He ran his hand across the side of her face, then closed the bedroom door.

I headed back toward the golden MacBook Pro.

Ten minutes later I headed down the stairs,

passed all the people.

I asked the overwhelmed pregnant woman to sign off on the inspection.

I told her t-t-thank you, that all l-l-looked okay, and said that I was sorry for her l-l-loss.

She had no patience for an unattractive pair of red legs with a speech impediment.

Just as I was leaving, the woman the cricketer had argued with at Sugar Ultra Lounge hurried toward the house. Slacks, low heels, top with the Going Places Travel logo. She stormed right by me, entered what she'd assumed would one day become her castle, then came to a halt when she saw the collection of women and the gaggle of hyperactive kids, all resembling her dead lover, playing together.

She shouted at the top of her lungs and told the world that she felt like a fuckin' fool.

Warrens, Parish of St. Michael

When I made it to the bottom of the hill at Warrens, I hit the roundabout and drove to the car park on the backside of Super Centre, the one that held Chicken Barn. Petrichor was there. This time she was early. I pulled up and she stopped texting someone. I handed her the hard drive that I had just stolen from the golden MacBook Pro. That last ten minutes I'd been left alone was all I had needed to change occupations. I told Petrichor about all the high-end shit I had seen inside the dead man's house.

"A gold-plated MacBook Pro? What the shite kind of operating system would that use?"

"The rings. That tells me that the cricketer had association with the LKs."

"Shite. I thought the Barbarians were trying to keep you away from the LKs."

"They put me deeper into LK territory. An annex for the shit they're doing in Trinidad."

"I'm confused."

"That drug shipment I attacked probably had something to do with the LKs as well."

"Where was the cricketer that night?"

"Had to be at the end, waiting at the docks. Bet we hit them before they made it to him. He probably was far enough away to see the shootout, but had no interest in participating."

"He might've been in his fancy car getting a blow job."

"Maybe. Otherwise, he would've died the first night. He didn't die, so they sent me the next night to wrap up loose ends. That's the way I see it. Cricketer thought he was clear. He had planned to celebrate that deal, but we fucked it up. Then he went to the Gap, was arrogant enough to go party anyway, got himself killed at church."

"Some people love to fete too much."

"You think?"

"Someone dies, people fete. People lose a job, they fete. Lose a drug shipment, throw yourself a fete. Nothing ever stopped a fete. Not in the islands. People in Trinidad, they hear a hurricane is coming, they have hurricane fetes all over the island. They had a state of emergency over there, so instead of going home to beat the curfew, they would leave work and go to the clubs and fete all night, then go to work the next morning and sleep. People being killed at a drug bust stops nothing."

"I'm learning. I'm sure the LKs will throw a big fete if they ever catch me. A real big one."

Petrichor said, "Now I'm feeling malicious and want to know what the hell has been going on."

"Malicious?"

"Nosy. We call nosy people malicious."

"Why?"

"Because they are malicious and thrive on maliciousness."

"I need someone to be malicious and bring some maliciousness and check that hard drive for hidden files. Know anybody?"

"I know somebody who knows somebody. What are you looking for?"

"Anything on the LKs. He probably has nothing but porn on his hard drive, but look anyway."

"Wait. Why would the Barbarians stop a

drug shipment by the LKs?"

"Had to be business. Maybe somebody larger than the LKs had to pay them to step on toes."

"Crossing the LKs like that, first in Trinidad, then here, that could start an island war. They already fight over flying fish, have soca battles, but this would take it to a new level."

"I'm in the middle of something that I don't understand. I'll figure this shite out on my own."

She asked, "Need me tomorrow? My husband will be on the East Coast all day."

"I'm good. I did a whole set of jobs like this when I started."

"This one paying much?"

"Not much. I need every dime I can get. Forced to work this way at the moment."

"You look so stressed."

"I am. Body is off. Can't sleep."

"You need a massage."

"Need more than a massage."

"If you have downtime, I can set up that other thing for tonight."

"Mrs. Child Support Waiting to Happen. Go home to your fake marriage and have fun."

"Don't hate."

"Not hating."

"Well, take a break, give Black Jack a shot at plunging in that American-born pool."

"I don't know him like that and I don't

want to know him like that."

"It can be a one-off."

"Don't be rude. He's not the guy I want to be naked and share my scars with."

"Let me set this other thing up then."

"No."

"Let me."

"Focus, Petrichor."

"Please?"

"I just need you to handle that little mission."

She shook her head. "The Barbarians had you attack the LKs' drug shipment here in Bim."

"Then I'll bet I killed the man the LKs used to move product through Barbados."

"He wasn't killed over being a rapist."

"We'll find out for sure."

"So their Barbados operation has been shut down, or at least suspended."

"That means they might come here to investigate."

"They might already fuckin' be here."

THIRTY-SIX

Trinidad

Diamond Dust and a dozen wives walked the lively roads in St. James Market.

As they weaved through the crowded market and patronized vendors, her cellular rang.

She answered, "Speak."

She was informed that someone had hacked into the company's computer system.

She asked, "Was it shut down?"

"Yes. It happened here in the Caribbean."

"Find them. Terminate with extreme prejudice."

"Should I contact War Machine?"

"No. My order is the only order you will ever need. Once we leave here, we're going to the Tunapuna Market. Keep me posted."

Smiling, she hung up the phone without asking where the violation had originated, hung up because she was surrounded. She faced the world and smiled, a few people stopping her as she passed, asking her to pose for photos to post on Facebook, Instagram, and Twitter, others too timid to ask and sneaking photos of her, in awe, intimidated, in the place Diamond Dust was born.

To them she was more valuable than any entertainer.

The top entertainers begged to perform for her.

Begged.

It made her feel like she was Eva Perón.

She made things, incredible things, happen.

She turned slum girls into intelligent Cinderellas.

Even now she was working, thinking forward, recruiting.

She went to those women, and if they were young enough, without children, had a profound love for Trinidad and Tobago, were interested in being educated, she took their names, numbers.

Women who were poorly dressed, women who had poor social skills, women with low self-esteem, she spoke to them as well, encouraged them to be more, to become an asset to the nation.

It was about tough love.

She was the radiation that would kill the cancer. Radiation killed before it cured.

Some good had to be removed to destroy what was bad.

Some would have to die.

From long before the creation of the Bible, long before the Seth Rebellion during the reign of the pharaoh Seth-Peribsen of the second dynasty of Egypt, to long after the Libyan Civil War, there has been blood spilled in the name of change, in the name of a revolution. In every revolution, there was chaos, death, then control, acceptance, then calm. It took many deaths to get to that period of calmness.

Death was never easy.

Necessary.

But never easy.

So many had died on the streets where she was born.

Death had touched every family, some many times over.

An idea came.

She would organize the women, the grieving mothers, and march the streets of Laventille protesting the deaths of their slain children, holding their photos high, as the mothers in Argentina marched and protested the 30,000 gone missing there at the hands of the military junta.

Every mother would be asked to join in.

The mothers of her slain men would stand up front.

She would form the Mothers of Trinidad.

Every leader needed a movement that defined him.

Every leader needed a movement that helped unite the people.

Death would work in her favor.

She looked around. Two generations away from perfection.

THIRTY-SEVEN

At four thirty in the morning, less than an hour before sunrise, I passed by scorched cane fields that led to Coral Ridge Memorial Gardens. Less than a mile up the road from where the dead were sent to rest until Gabriel sounded his trumpet, just before Frere Pilgrim and Edey Village in the parish of Christ Church, I found the small mouth that led to Ridgeview Estates. That was where Black Jack lived in comfort.

It was a private community between here and there, situated between rural and urban, between working poor and the mansions of the seem-to-be rich in the prestigious St. Georges Valley. Black Jack's hideaway was on eight acres of landscaped grounds, reminded me of town houses in Florida and L.A. I downshifted to first gear and drove from rugged road to the smooth paved tongue that led from the main road into that enclave. The smoothness of the road spoke of a different standard of living. I drove in first gear, rumbled by a playground, then passed by a gray garbage truck that was leaving the community.

They gave me lights as a hello. I waved, hoped they wouldn't remember me.

In the section facing the clubhouse and swimming pool, I searched for Black Jack's BMW.

The neighborhood wasn't enormous, only had fifty-two town houses, and all parking was uncovered. Within five minutes, I found his dirty German ride parked in front of a set of units that faced the clubhouse and its swimming pool. A black Toyota was parked next to his ride. Every townhome had two spaces outside its front door. I looked up at the windows on the bedroom level. No lights were on at the front side of the townhome. Shutters closed. He might be between legs right now. The Toyota. I touched its hood. Warm like an engine turned off a few hours ago, the right time for a midnight booty call. He could go back to fucking after we had a short meeting. I knocked softly. No one answered. I called his number. No answer. I rang the doorbell. Rang again. Knocked on the door six times.

A neighbor appeared two units down. The chubby blonde came out and walked in my direction. Female in a tennis skirt, sandals, wife-beater. She had two little dogs on a leash. She was overfed and the dogs looked malnourished. All three paused when they saw me standing at the door, my helmet still on. I waved. She returned the greeting, then stood tall, the dogs yapping as she studied me a moment, then she went back to the little rats on the leash, both tugging at her, both aching to get to their favorite tree and shitting spot. I looked up again. No lights had come on. I touched the hood on Black Jack's ride. It was cold. I was about to walk around the units and find Black Jack's back entrance, tap on his patio door, but I left, my eyes on my mirror as I pulled away, looking to see if Black Jack appeared I left his sweet community. As I rode, I dug inside of my jacket pocket, removed three Durex condoms, tossed them to the road.

I took my energy to Garfield Sobers Gymnasium, stretched, hit the heavy bag, gave my anger to circuit training, tempo runs, walking lunges, grunted and ran around the complex six times without pause, ran all-out the seventh time. I showered and pulled on white shorts, threw on my backpack, and called Black Jack again, ready to blister him the moment he answered. No fucking answer. That was bullshit. Frustrated, I was tempted to return to his townhome. The overnight and morning Bible study should be done by now and the day started, but I was on a tight schedule. It was time to continue being defiant.

Back at Oistins, I changed my attire and haggled with the same flirty man-boy and leased a Jet Ski at the Bajan rate, then rode toward Miami Beach, spied on the safe house. Naked women were all over the place, lounging and watching television. World's oldest profession. Pussy would never go out of style. Even when it became old, somebody would buy it at fire-sale prices. I wasn't mad at those girls.

I rode the waves to a beach across from Graeme Hall Sanctuary, a calm stretch of land filled with Brits and Canadians who owned so many shops and condos that it seemed like I was in a separate country. They had carved out their own world here. Properties and hotels were hidden off of the main road, so I could drive through Christ Church all day and night and never see this area.

When I stepped on that pristine sand, hardly a brown face could be found, except for the servers and the renters of dinghies and Jet Skis. I wore a punk-rock purple wig with an asymmetrical cut, a bright-yellow bikini, and bootleg Wayfarers the hue of honey. I had the only purple hair in the area.

Soon a woman came to me. Porcelain skin. Louboutins and a bikini. She covered herself in a psychedelic wrap, sun lotion on her skin, anger in her bloodshot eyes.

We'd never met face-to-face. Without a hello, she handed me a large bag from Chefette.

I nodded. "Are you all right? You look like you're about to lose it."

"Look at the women on this beach. Look at you. I have two babies. Now look at me. I have stretch marks and cottage cheese. What happens to me? When do I find real love? When do I get to be the one running up and down the beaches having sex with all the handsome men that I can handle?"

"Are you okay?"

"At the age of thirty, I look fifty-four. Imagine what I will look like at fifty-four."

I watched her cry and pour her heart out over a man who had rejected her.

It was pathetic.

If she expected a hug or compassion, she had the wrong chick.

While she blew snot bubbles I checked my phone. No messages. Anger rose.

She asked, "Have you found my husband?"

"I have an alphabetized list of the places the target had been spotted. From Accra Beach Hotel to Wytukai Restaurant. He's been going to a doctor in Belleville to get shots and medication."

She looked concerned. "Why is he going to doctors and getting shots? Is he ill?"

"Since he's been here, he's had two testosterone shots and three doses of steroids as well. Time is doing its thing. Guess he can't get as hard as he used to. Or not as often."

"What kind of women has he been seeing since he came here?"

"Island girls."

"How many women has he been with since he came here?"

"You don't want to know."

Her lips trembled and she wiped tears from her eyes. "You know how I feel sometimes?"

"Listening."

"Like leftovers. I feel like leftovers."

"Leftovers?"

"Leftovers are trashed. Everyone wants a new, hot meal. I used to be the hot meal. We're what has been come inside and left to drip dry. Don't you agree? They come inside of us and leave us to dry."

"I've never been come inside."

"You're a virgin?"

"Always used a condom. So, I'm still a virgin to bareback sex."

"You're missing the best part of sex."

"No. Never had a man come inside of me."

"I've never used a condom."

"Never?"

"Well, never asked a man to use one. Never wanted a man to use one."

"Why not?"

"The risk. Guess that gets me high in some ways."

"You're a daring version of me."

"You're a smarter version of me."

She blew more snot bubbles, then took a tissue from her bag and blew her nose.

I asked, "He has insurance?"

"Double-indemnity." She took a few deep breaths. "I'm really doing this."

"It's done, unless you call it off right now."

"I need it to look like an accident."

"I need you to leave, not look back, forget you ever met me."

She walked away, shoulders down, head down, hands in fists, tears falling in the off-white sand.

I called Black Jack again. Still no response.

I guessed that Bible study was still going on.

They should be halfway through the New Testament by now, deep into the part about avoiding sexual immorality, learning to control one's own body in a way that was holy and honorable, and not falling into the flames of passionate lust like the heathen, the sweet, sweet way I had been in Florida.

It was cool.

My feelings weren't fragile, not the kind made to be hurt.

Black Jack was a man. The pattern of men remained the pattern of men.

I wasn't jealous.

I was too busy trying to stay alive to be jealous.

THIRTY-EIGHT

I rode the Jet Ski to meet my depressed client's husband.

Dover Beach at Johnny Cool's Jazz & Blues Beach Bar. He was on a white beach chair, underneath a humongous umbrella that read STAG: A MAN'S BEER. He wore Speedos and pretended to read a James Patterson novel. I took in the crowd. Many sunbathed with their eyes closed while others read novels on their electronic devices. A scarf covered my faux dreadlocks, these top-shelf, thick locks that hung down to my waist, a few of them pink, a few marine blue, a few Rihanna red. I was a rebellious mulatto, a Jennifer Beals, a Lisa Bonet, which was good enough for him. I pulled up on the Jet Ski and he sat up, leaned forward, wondering if I was the mulatto he had ordered for his afternoon fun.

I waved at him. He waved. I paused to check my phones. Made sure no calls had come in from the Barbarians. There were no messages from Petrichor. Still nothing from

Black Jack, either.

I powered down my phones and headed toward the target with a smile, a slow sexy stroll across the hot sand, my feet bare, my grin wide, like I was trying to win the greeter-of-the-year at Cave Shepherd in Bridgetown. My bikini was a thong. My ass exposed, my vagina barely covered, camel toe galore.

He said, "Shadiquah Yarde-Hyman from Kingston, Jamaica?"

In a soft, pleasant Jamaican accent I responded, "Bob Jones, the American?"

"How old are you? You look like you could be fifteen, but the body says different."

"Island girl, born that way. No worries. I legal. What about you?"

"Fifty-six and no gray hair until yesterday."

I handed Bob my suntan lotion. He rubbed from my back down to my butt. He considered me his already. He touched me where I had shaved earlier, touched me as if he were entitled.

The behavior of men, of people, it fascinated me to no end.

He said, "How long have you been having sex?"

"You pay for an hour, but I free all day if you want to pay for more time."

"No. I mean, how old when you started?"

"Fourteen. I good. Nothing to worry about. I real good. Love to fuck every day."

He traced his thick fingers across the material covering the lips of my vagina.

It aroused me. I was so sensitive that his strange hand aroused me.

He rubbed and rubbed and rubbed like he was wishing the genie from the lamp. I grinned and patted my target's hand. My nipples were erect. What he did felt good. Made my eyes dreamy.

Slow and easy, I licked my lips and said, "Time we two leave the beach to have fun."

"Let me finish my beer. I don't want to rush my time with you."

I retied my top, first a knot, then made a tight bow, did that to keep the waves from ripping my top or bottom away from me and leaving onlookers with too much personal information.

He took out a blue pill. Popped it. Winked at me.

I said, "First ting first, Bob. You pop pill, but we have to take care of something first."

He slid me three hundred American dollars. I put it inside of my swimming top.

I said, "Now, where were we?"

He touched me again and I looked at trash cans. Thought about a garbage truck.

I smiled at my man-of-the-moment and said, "You okay over there?"

"My wife is on the island."

"You see she here now? Should I go?"

"No. We're fine. Me and you, we're fine. My soon-to-be-ex-wife and me, not fine."

"You have chirren with she?"

"She has two children."

"She has chirren but you don't?"

"I had a vasectomy two years before I met her and ended up with fraternal twins."

"Why you have a vasectomy?"

"That's the only birth control for men that works. I have a friend in L.A., guy named Jason Wolf, owns his own limo company, he used to tell me that if you can't afford to get a vasectomy reversed, chances are you can't afford to have a kid. When I was ready to have a kid, I was going to reverse it."

"And before you ready, she horn you and make two babies with another man?"

"She fucked me over."

"You take care of chirren from another man like dey your own chirren, for true?"

"I paid for those ungrateful bastards until I'd had enough."

"You know she here. She know you here. Why she here and you here at same time?"

"She saw where I had booked online, then followed me here to try to reconcile."

"When you see she last?"

"She called my hotel when I was at the Accra."

"Hotel here?"

"Yeah. I was there for two weeks, but I changed hotels when I found out she was there, found out she had checked into the same hotel and was in the lobby waiting for me to walk by."

"She crazy."

"She was on her knees begging. That dramatic liar. It was pathetic. I had to walk her back to her room and try to calm her down. She was all over me, begging me to make love to her."

"You give her wood."

"I finally put the wood in her to make her shut the fuck up and calm down."

I paused. This was why we rarely contacted the target, just sent a bullet to say hello.

Part of me wanted to tell him to beware of his ex, get up, walk the sand to the Jet Ski, and leave.

He said, "Sorry, didn't mean to go on and on about her."

"By the clear day I make you forget about she."

" 'Clear day'?"

"By sunrise. By the new sun."

"Love your accent."

"I love you good all day and make you feel like new."

He looked at the knot between his legs and whispered, "Look at that."

"Later, I suck wood and make you come good and sleep away your stress."

"My wife never did that."

"Never?"

"Fifteen years and she never once did that."

He headed toward the Jet Ski rental, jogging like a former jock, his best days gone by, happier than he had been in a long time, belly bouncing like loose breasts. I had more empathy for him than I did his wife. But she was the client. Business was business. I needed money to handle my business.

Fifteen minutes later, Bob Jones was with Jesus's old man. I had climbed on his Jet Ski, sat behind him like I was about to do a reach around, then hit him across the head with a sap. Compared to what I gave Bob Jones, Big Guy had received a love tap. I made it look like the target had had one drink too many and run into a boardwalk's concrete support, then his body had floated out to sea. The dreadlocks wig was left floating in the waters near his corpse, bobbing and riding the currents.

Within minutes I was back on my motorcycle, heart racing, helmet on, face shield up, riding in a drizzle while wearing biker boots and a bikini, my ass causing traffic jams on every sinewy road. Was in a hurry. Took to the stairs, passed by Mag's Barbershop, and carried the Chefette bag to Big Guy. I changed clothes in his office. He counted the money. It wasn't enough to pay that debt, but it was enough to keep his people working on my passports. He needed more money. I needed more jobs.

■ ■ ■ ■

A swarm of police cars were at Ridgeview Estates. No guns were drawn. Neighbors were standing around, some in tears. Outraged. Afraid. Neighbors who had never met introduced themselves, talked about putting up burglar bars on every unit. Mothers held their children close. Husbands held their pregnant wives. Murders had happened in an area where an unnatural death never should occur. Black Jack's body was found by the gardeners when they had gone to the back for lawn maintenance. He was nude, had been decapitated. The black Toyota belonged to a student at UWI. Akilah Clower. The teenager was nude, decapitated as well. Heads were found in the living room, in a bloody living room, on the counter facing the front door. Both naked, headless bodies had been dragged across the tile, out past the patio, and dropped into the plunge pool, the jets in the plunge pool on high, water bubbling like beet-colored soup.

A garbage truck entered the area, had come to begin trash pickup. I had passed a garbage truck right here at four in the morning. No one collected garbage at four in the morning, and never twice in one day, not on this island. Might have been different in this swank community, but down at Six Roads people were lucky to get their trash picked up once a week. I had passed by their assassins at four in the morning. If I had been here at least an hour earlier, either Black Jack and Hacker would be alive, or I would've been inside and three would have been found dead. I preferred to believe the former but couldn't rule out the latter.

THIRTY-NINE

Highway 5

I sped down the two-lane highway, screaming as I drove at double the posted limit, screamed all the way back to my prison. Screaming did me no good, but I screamed. Black Jack had used Hacker to tap into the LKs' system and within a few hours both were dead. Black Jack was with Jesus's daddy and I had to keep moving. Hated that I had to depend on Petrichor. I needed Big Guy to come through.

I was beyond exhausted, both physically and mentally, my brain sluggish and on fire, and I had to get off my feet. I showered, put on jeans and a tee, tried to sleep a dreamless sleep, but I had twenty-seven dreams, and in all of them I saw the LKs, in all of them I was attacked, in all of them I was near death.

Gasping, sweating inside of my prison, I jerked awake, drowning in darkness. Guns in hand I sat up, disoriented. I heard a sound. I sprang to my feet, both guns trained on the noise. A muffled cry. Echo of a struggle in total darkness. I pulled a corner of the curtain back and spied outside my window. A strange car was parked in the bend of the road. The neighbors might have had company, but that would be out of character. The safe house might be surrounded. The muffled noise, the cry, came again. I spied through the dirty screen and out of the grimy bedroom window. The couple in the home beyond my driveway were on their bed. She was on top, her expression saying she had to orgasm or die from the heat.

My attention went to the strange car. Whoever was in the parked car watched them too.

The car door opened. Someone got out and walked toward my Alcatraz.

It was Zenga, the Barbarian who was big like a linebacker, the arrogant one with a neck that rivaled my thigh. Black Jack had been slaughtered. Now Zenga, the assholes of all assholes, was at my door. I held on to my two guns, the .357 in my right hand and the .380 in my left. When he was a few feet away I turned on a light. He stopped where he was. He grinned and raised both hands, his palms facing me to show that he wasn't carrying, but that didn't mean shit. That didn't mean he was alone. The field in front of the safe house, that patch of land that led to another set of homes in the next gap, that was another perfect spot for a sniper to build a nest.

The doors opened outward, the opposite direction of doors for homes in the States. I used my left hand to crack open the metal door, went down on my haunches to keep my head out of pink-mist range, positioned myself with the big gun displayed in my right hand, business end pointed toward Zenga.

I said, "Why are you on my side of the island?"

"Mind lowering your weapon?"

"How's this?"

"Move it from the family jewels. Put the gun down."

"The gun is at home. You're the one visiting."

"Look, I just came to get to know you."

"Get to know me?"

"Maybe you could get dressed and we could go for a ride and take in the cool night air."

"With you and the boys?"

"No. Just you and me."

"You're confusing me. Why would I do that?"

"I want to kick it with you."

"Kick it with me?"

"Hook up with you."

"Are you fuckin' serious?"

I closed the door so hard the windows shook like I was in a California earthquake.

Zenga walked backward and returned to

the car. He flashed his headlights off and on. I didn't reply. I had no idea what the madness and come-on was about. There was no reason for him to be down at Six Roads. Not alone. We had no dealings authorized by the powers that be.

Zenga flashed his headlights over a dozen more times. Neighbors' lights came on. Faces appeared in windows. They watched. Like people in a small town, they watched and they gossiped. I didn't like what was transpiring. I didn't like feeling the heat from a spotlight on my face.

My cellular buzzed and I cursed. It was an urgent message from the Barbarians.

Didn't know if it was connected to Zenga appearing outside my window at this moment.

OPEN THE PACKAGE NOW.

I looked at the briefcase. It still hadn't exploded.

A second message came: TRAVEL HEAVY. WE RESOLVE PROBLEM TONIGHT.

Something had transpired and now they were sounding the alarms.

Travel heavy meant that I was to take my weapons, and they would be used.

I took it to the living room, spied out of the window at Zenga. He was on his cellular. They had called him. He jumped in the car and came down the narrow road, had to pull into the open field and bush in front of my safe house to turn around, his headlights raking across the window. They had yanked his chain. Him being here hadn't had anything to do with the mission. A third message came: OPEN THE PACKAGE MX-401. They knew that it wasn't opened, knew that I hadn't compromised the package. That meant that it was equipped with sensors. I'd swept my prison countless times, but as far as I knew cameras could be all over this dungeon. They could have watched me shower. Sleep. Cry. Talk to myself. Pace. Scream. Touch myself and moan Johnny Parker's name. OPEN THE FUCKING PACKAGE.

Then I realized that Zenga had sped away, was beyond the range of a bomb going off.

He had been sent here to verify I was in the safe house, then report I was eliminated.

I clicked open the left lock. Took a dozen breaths. Palms sweated like I was in the rain.

I clicked open the right lock. Still no explosion.

I opened the package.

FORTY

The Barbarians' coveted briefcase was opened, its contents revealed.

Money. More money than I had ever seen at one time.

Guns in my hands, I ran back to the front room, spied out the front window.

Zenga was gone.

Another message came. PLANS HAVE CHANGED. DO NOT HEAD TO LOCATION. CLOSE THE PACKAGE UNTIL FURTHER INSTRUCTIONS. MX-401 CONFIRM. CONFIRM. CONFIRM.

I confirmed, closed the briefcase, then asked what to do with the package.

I sent a message. WHAT WAS THAT UNNECESSARY DRAMA ALL ABOUT?

CONFIRM.

MESSAGE TO SIT AND WAIT RECEIVED, ASSHOLES. NOW WHAT THE HELL WAS THAT ALL ABOUT?

WHY DID YOU GIVE ME A CASE OF CASH AND NOT TELL ME WHAT THE FUCK I HAD?

STFU UNTIL WE CONTACT YOU AGAIN. NEW COURSE OF ACTION. SIT ON PACKAGE.

I NEED MORE THAN THAT. AFTER BEING HERE OVER A MONTH, I NEED MORE THAN THAT.

They didn't reply.

Headlights flashed across my window again.

Zenga had come back. He parked where he had been parked before.

I looked at the money. By my calculations, it was a half million, enough to change a poor person's life for the rest of his life, enough to give a rich person so that he could have fun for a week in an exotic land. I had used Black Jack to hack into the LKs' system; maybe I should have had him get into the system for the Barbarians. Made no sense owing me and trusting me with cash.

I should take the money and run away, become a fugitive from both sides of the law.

The amount of money in the briefcase had made my heart race. I could pay for a passport, could buy a boat or lease a small plane, could get to South America and learn to speak passable Spanish.

Closed my eyes. Saw two decapitated heads on a counter, two bodies in a plunge pool, bubbles from jets making it look like soup, red soup. Could've been me. Could've been.

I had to think about Old Man Reaper; the choice I made could put him in danger.

So much money. It was hard to stare at the cash and not want it for myself.

Not for greed, but for freedom.

Each note had made my heart beat with the sound of betrayal.

They sent me another message. STAY WITH PACKAGE 24/7, NO EXCURSIONS.

I replied. I'M NEITHER CONCIERGE NOR BABYSITTER NOR ADMINISTRATIVE ASSISTANT.

Zenga was out there. Stalking. His eyes were fixed on the safe house.

I sent another message. WHY IS ONE OF YOUR BOYS PARKED OUT IN FRONT OF THIS SAFE HOUSE STALKING ME? B-159 IS OUTSIDE. IS THIS AUTHORIZED? IS THIS HIS ASSIGNMENT? ANSWER ME RIGHT AWAY OR I'M ABOUT TO START PEELING CAPS.

Five minutes passed and no reply from the men in charge.

I said, YOU WANT ME TO STFU, THEN I WILL STFU. NOT AVAILABLE UNTIL I AM AVAILABLE AGAIN.

I turned the phone off and threw it on the bed.

I left the front room, but left the light on, a warning that I was awake, and returned to the darkened bedroom, locked and loaded, and spied out the next window. The neighbors were still copulating. Up and down and round and round. Zenga waited inside the darkened car.

I turned the lights off and waited for him, for someone, to make a move.

Then I wasn't sure that he was alone. He would have been a fool to come here solo.

This safe house was a two-bedroom coffin; each day it felt like strong men had come and pushed the walls in another half-inch. I put the briefcase on top of the built-in closet, pushed it to the back.

Then I put a new SIM card in my Samsung and made a call.

I showered again, showered with both guns near me, ears listening for any sound. Ten minutes later I had dressed and left the safe house from the back window, walked to the Ducati.

I started the Italian iron horse and cut across the next-door neighbor's yard. Zenga saw my headlight before I appeared. It was impossible to start a motorcycle without the headlight coming on. It was impossible to start an iron horse without being heard. He revved his engine and burned rubber trailing me, followed me across the same yard, was on my bumper when I passed the congregation of neighborhood drug dealers at their favorite Banks Beer–sponsored rum shop and paused at the roundabout. I looked back, showed him a middle finger. I cursed. The EMPTY light was on so I had to make a detour to the Shell station. The next gas station was miles away. They didn't have four gas stations at an intersection like they did back home. Gas stations on the island were still full-service, so I had to get off the bike, speak to a worker, and allow her to pump the gas.

Zenga pulled into the crowded lot, stopped in front of the cages where they stored bottle gas, then stepped out of his vehicle. Arrogant and entitled. Misinformed by whoever had sent him here. I marched toward him, hands in fists. I didn't see anyone else inside of his car.

He said, "You need to be careful, MX-401."

"I could tell you the same."

"You're not supposed to leave your post."

"Snitch. Report me."

"You already have a reputation as a gold-brick. I could call it in."

"Call the man behind the double red doors. Do what you have to do."

"We could always work it out in a way that benefits us both."

"What does that mean, exactly?"

"You look like a woman with a pussy made of iron, but I bet that it's as soft as a pillow."

"You've been drinking stupid juice."

"Had a few Banks. Enough beer to make me think about you from a new perspective."

"What new perspective?"

"Want to know what it's like to fuck a black woman and a white woman at the same time."

"Follow me and this will not end well."

"What, are you allergic to dick?"

"Not at all, but I am allergic to pricks and cunts."

"You calling me a prick?"

"No, you ignorant prick, I'm calling you a bitch-ass cunt."

"You don't want to talk to me like that."

"You do know what the *M* and *X* mean in my title, don't you? Back off, bitch."

We stared, neither one flinching. He had spent years in prison and I had been incarcerated too long. This was our yard. The stare-down wasn't broken until the attendant called for me to come for my bike.

I said, "Take your tampon out and go fuck a dick."

"Nobody talks to me like that."

"I just did, bitch. I just did."

I went back to my bike, paid the attendant, mounted my iron horse, started the engine. Zenga backed up a step at a time, stared at me the whole way, and slipped back inside of his assigned car. I expected him to drive away first. I was wrong. He didn't. He revved his engine like his car was a two-ton weapon.

The ruckus from the nightly liming at the Shell gas station and in the parking lot at Chefette and whoever was sitting on the brick wall in front of Six Roads Polyclinic was drowned out when I gunned my engine. My Ducati yelled *Fuck You.* Zenga gunned his engine in response. *White Nigga Bitch.* I cursed a thousand times. I zoomed from the lot, shot up by Chefette, made a hard right. From the Wynter Crawford Roundabout I took to Highway 5, Zenga right behind me. A half-mile later I pulled over into the parking lot at Jazzie Cuts, a barbershop in a sloping parking lot next to Tyre Shop.

I pulled into the lot and made my bike stand up on the front tire, then shifted my weight and made her rotate one hundred and eighty degrees. I came down facing the driveway. The businesses were closed. No lights were on. No one was at the bus stop out front. Zenga came down the driveway, not sure if I had gone straight or turned left. I was to his left, near the wall, engine off, no lights on to give away my position. I pulled my .380 and opened fire, took out his headlights, shot his front windshield. His head vanished and he lost control of the car, hit the accelerator and ran into the front of the barbershop. I started my bike, then fired into the window four more times. While that jerk was ducked down, while he pissed steroids and stained his pants, I zoomed up the driveway and took to the road.

At top speed, I dodged potholes in the road, and at Sky Mall, I shifted gears and hit the Bussa Roundabout, circled it four times, then shot into Sky Mall and came out by Burger King, exited, and hit the roundabout two more times, all that to make sure I wasn't being trailed by a second car since I left Six Roads, made sure I wasn't being trailed by whoever had done to Black Jack and Hacker what I wanted to do to them. Then I gunned it and went back toward the Pine, only I turned left, made a hard-leaning left where the turning lane was at a deep angle at Barbados External Telecommunications Limited. My horse roared as I shot up that wicked road, beyond Sobers Gymnasium and the cut-rock road leading into Fort George, past the rugged road after, and into the narrow roads with overgrown brush. I drove hard, and minutes later, I ended up back at Ridgeview Estates, back where Black Jack had been murdered.

His death didn't mean that what I needed was no longer desired. I needed to see the crime scene, find his computer, find what Hacker had used and left behind, needed the information he had found, needed whatever had led a killer to his front door, if that computer hadn't been confiscated.

Too many people were still congregated outside.

Police tape was across the front of the property. Had to be the same on the back. The community had hired extra security, but that group was just as afraid, each walking the grounds and deferring to the big guns. The Royal Barbados Police Force, modeled after SWAT, had left at least four officers behind to make the neighbors feel safe, officers alert and waiting for the Bajan version of the bogeyman to return.

I left the area, blew up ABC Highway, then soon I was on the West Coast, the sea at my left. If I'd had my night-vision binoculars and had looked to the seas, I would have seen them.

FORTY-ONE

A magnificent yacht approached Barbados. Music blasting into the night. It was a superyacht, over two hundred feet long, with a helicopter pad that had a helicopter on that pad, a yacht that was on a higher level than the luxury private yacht owned by Tiger Woods.

Three more helicopters flew overhead.

War Machine listened to his men.

Appaloosa said, "The Kiwi had to be part of the crew that gunned down the Bajans."

Kandinsky said, "There has to be a connection. Her coming to our island, the drug bust."

Guerrero said, "The connection has to be King Killer. We did right."

Appaloosa said, "She is connected to the problems in Miami and New York as well."

Guerrero said, "Has to be."

Kandinsky said, "There will be blood in the sand. Soon there will be blood in the sand."

War Machine added nothing.

On the superyacht, despite the chill of the night, naked women, an international lot, sashayed underneath stars in the night air, nipples hard, drinks in hand, all as high as their heels.

War Machine went down below to a special room and pushed a button that caused three walls to slide open. Each wall was filled with guns. Two hundred weapons were on board. Rocket launchers. Grenades. Everything but a drone. The Laventille Killers were about to arrive.

War Machine said, "This has to play itself to the end. To its conclusion."

Two of their men had just been here, had made an emergency flight to Barbados when a hacker had broken into their systems, and that, too, had been done from Barbados. Men who had been sent by Diamond Dust, again without his authority. He would handle her. When all was said and done, he would handle her. The men who had been sent had assumed that it had something to do with the company losing the drug shipment some days ago. Now all knew that the Kiwi had been here during that time.

The men were excited, felt that their current mission and killing the ones who had hacked into their systems were connected.

War Machine said, "It is all connected. Everything is connected. My wife is smart. That is her blessing. That is her curse."

War Machine stood in front of the armory like he was in a museum of fine arts.

They had weapons that had originated in the United States and vanished in Afghanistan.

On a table were the enlarged images of the elusive Kiwi. They had more information than the Trinidadian police had on the Kiwi regarding the assassination, but they shared nothing, had done all they could to misdirect the authorities, didn't want the assassin incarcerated, just wanted her found. The LKs would be judge, jury, and vicious executioner. War Machine nodded and gave his wife her props. Diamond Dust had hired the best of the best, had rebooted the operation, and all had fallen into place.

They had photos of the Kiwi from the Carlton Savannah, photos taken while the woman, pretending to be Samantha Greymouth, was on the roof, images of her from the fiasco at the bank, more images taken from illegal passports in and out of Trinidad, another from a passport used to get to Grenada, from a passport used to exit Grenada and get to the Grenadines, and the picture from the passport used to get from the Grenadines to Barbados. With those photos, more possibles had been created. The Woman of a Thousand Faces. The face that represented War Machine's deepest regret.

War Machine went back up on deck. A

woman stopped in front of him as he stood next to his guntas. She fell to her knees, offered to suck him, but he pushed her away, sent her to the other men.

Appaloosa came and stood next to him, said, "Lights are beautiful."

War Machine said, "Don't praise that island. Only praise the lights in Trinidad."

As they rode up the coast they passed the lights emanating from Limegrove.

Someone told them that the club Priva was over there. It was the type of swank area where the woman in the photos might hang out. The Kiwi had been a high-end party girl, so that would be her style.

War Machine said, "We'll do a search starting there. Work our way to St. Lawrence Gap."

His cellular rang. He saw his wife's face on the caller ID.

He stepped to the side, answered, "Karleen. I miss you."

"We need to talk."

"Talk. Speak your mind."

"Privately."

"What's the issue?"

"Be alone. I will call you back in a moment."

She ended the call.

The warehouse. He had flashbacks from torturing and killing his cousin. He moved away and looked out at the island. A girl followed, one who had pleased him before, now being rejected, now afraid, trembling, tears in her eyes, afraid that she had done something wrong, something to warrant death.

With controlled words he threatened to throw her off the ship if she followed him.

She wiped the corners of her mouth and hurried away.

War Machine looked at Barbados again. They had lost three brothers. Two had been killed by the Kiwi. One had been killed because of his association with the Kiwi, and that death hurt him the most.

His phone buzzed. His wife sent him a photo of their bed.

The bed was opened wide.

A text message came from his wife. CARE TO EXPLAIN?

She was forcing his hand. She knew she was forcing his hand.

He was her number one. Would always be her number one.

They would be the kingpins.

He had a moment of honesty. Despite his power, his control, there was a truth.

He was doing his best to live up to her standards, as they all were. She had vision. Direction. He would have been nothing without her. He would have been with King Killer, at best, doing two-man crime sprees. He knew that he was nothing without Karleen De Lewis, without Diamond Dust.

He was nothing without the cousin he had fallen in love with and married.

She had accepted his love for her, never ridiculed his feelings or desire for her.

As she had accepted the love and desire of King Killer when he was young.

She had been the first one to make him feel that he could be more than a boy of the slums.

Everyone else in his life had been holding him back.

He looked at the yacht, the suite, the helicopters flying overhead.

He had cast away his old life, the life of who he was as a boy in the slums, had cast it all aside.

Now he was War Machine. The most beautiful woman on the island was his wife.

He whispered, "This will not end. Not over this. This will not end over this."

His phone buzzed again. Diamond Dust again.

She said, "A contact just came through a minute ago."

"What do you have for me?"

"There, in Barbados. A woman of about the right size ordered a set of illegal passports."

"A set?"

"Multiple fake passports. I have copies of the photos here. It's her."

"From whom did she order the photos?"

"We will have that information shortly. Within the hour. We're reverse-engineering the contacts."

"Has she left the island?"

"I will find out soon. I find out everything. Remember that. I find out everything."

"Not everything."

"Everything. Did you receive the photo I sent?"

He paused. Waited for her to mention the bed, its contents.

"I did."

"Explain. Or shall I explain it to you, husband?"

"Let's focus on the Kiwi."

"All I have asked is that you never lie to me."

"The Kiwi is the issue at the moment."

"Let's focus on the reason my brother is dead. Let's focus on the Kiwi."

She played her hand so well. Every day with her, a never-ending game of chess.

It had been that way from the first kiss. Since they had crossed that line, become lovers.

She was the first girl he had slept with. She had been his first.

She already had experience.

Maybe he hadn't seduced her. Maybe she had seduced him, as she seduced all.

War Machine said, "If the Kiwi is gone, we

can't turn around. A tropical storm is coming."

"When I am updated on her whereabouts, the top men will be updated."

"Why not update me first?"

"Trust."

"Update me first. I will give the orders to my men."

There was another pause.

She said, "Not this time. I know. Not this time, because I know."

"What do you know, Karleen?"

"I know what you have done."

He paused. "Who else knows?"

"No denial?"

"Who else knows?"

"No one."

"Okay."

"My brother is dead."

"My cousin is dead."

"His heart stopped beating because of my order."

"It was my order. He was a brother to me as well."

"My twin brother is dead, and now I find out he did nothing wrong."

"What should I do?"

"Motherfucker, you should have been a man and spoken up."

"Should I fall on my sword?"

He heard her crying. A long moment went by.

She said, "No. Once a bad move has been made in chess, there is no going back."

"There was a plan, and that plan had a purpose for New Trinidad. I can explain it to you."

"Not now. When you do, bring the truth. I am your wife to the end. I chose you to be my number one, and if I chose badly, then this is my fault as well. I chose you over Appaloosa. I chose you over Kandinsky. Over Guerrero. I have bonded with you the most. I have procreated with you. Does that not work? Did I somehow fail in thinking that bonding with you and making a family would inspire loyalty? Am I a fool? If the members knew what you had done, what my husband has done . . . we will talk. You fucked up. New York. Miami. Barbados."

"It's all connected."

"Tell me. Tell me why we're at war and no one seems to know why but you. Tell me."

He told her.

He said, "Everything went wrong. They went silent. Attacked us."

"How could you do some shit like that without conferring with the top men in the group?"

"I made a decision."

"Do you need to feel important? Does my part of the leadership threaten your manhood?"

"Watch your tone."

"I have men available. I will send them to North America to attack and kill them all."

"No one goes to North America."

"You have no fucking say in this. You have me in a war and I had no idea we were at war."

War Machine said, "I am in charge. We will not put men on North American soil."

In the softest of threats, she said, "I make one phone call, Number One, and that changes."

"Then Appaloosa becomes your number one. He becomes your next husband."

"No, but he takes your place as leader. What you have done makes him seem more competent than I ever realized. Go against me, the truth rises, and you face the consequences of your actions."

"Okay."

"It will make what you allowed to happen to my brother seem pleasant."

"You have the upper hand. The Kiwi? Need to be sure we are on the same page."

"Nothing changes. She remains the blame. We allow her to be the blame. She is needed now more than ever. She's a symbol of all things wrong. We bring her here, offer her to everyone as sacrifice, we burn her as we do all evil, and that helps all heal. There is no other way. No other fuckin' way."

In a calm voice, she ended the call without a good-bye.

War Machine rubbed his temples, cursed, thought about King Killer.

He whispered, "Never should have gone behind the red doors."

FORTY-TWO

The Caribbean Sea's platinum coast was Gucci, Ralph Lauren, and Tag Heuer. Limegrove Lifestyle Centre was like the Grove in Los Angeles had dated Rodeo Drive and had a West Indian baby.

When I reached the resort, I downshifted, looked for a hidden place to park.

I gazed out at the waters, caught a glimpse of helicopters over the waves, glimpsed a superyacht moving north. I wanted to be on that boat. Tonight I would kill to be on that boat.

I pulled off my damaged helmet and took out my cellular, was about to call Big Guy, tell him to get me on a cruise ship somehow, didn't care what he had to do to make it happen, but his ten fingers and ten toes would be appreciative if he did. But I didn't make that call. Had to realize that this was bigger than me. My gut instinct told me that I couldn't vacate this job without endangering Old Man Reaper.

Johnny Parker and his kid could end up like Black Jack and Hacker.

I couldn't protect anyone from where I was.

Had to focus on protecting myself, and I didn't think I could do that, either.

I rubbed my aching temples. Head throbbed with each heartbeat.

Still I would drink the ocean dry just to be able to walk to another country.

Outside the resort stood the nation's flag. Ultramarine on two sides and gold in the center. A broken trident was on the gold, the trident symbolizing that Barbados was an island of slaves that had broken away from England. Yet they still depended on the tourism from the same hands, which was financial dependence, and financial dependence was slavery with a kinder name.

Even when they set you free, they still owned you in their own way.

I parked, then sent a message: On location.

Seconds later came a reply: Can you handle this mission?

I replied: Is everything in place?

The reply came right away: Green light.

I took a deep breath, they replied: Going silent.

I reached inside my backpack, made sure weapons were locked and loaded, then put two .380s into the small of my back. I walked with the .357 inside the backpack, carried the backpack with my hand on the trigger, my trigger finger itchy, anxious, hungry to spill blood, get revenge for Black Jack.

When I opened the door to the suite, a man was sitting in a fashionable armless chair. He was in his twenties and looked like he should have been on the cover of *Better Health* magazine. He was blindfolded, a prisoner waiting in darkness that was broken by a sliver of moonlight that crept through an open window. Waves crashed outside. The sea, restless. Except for a few scars, he was naked. Behind him, a king-size bed. Straight ahead, a private balcony facing sand and sea. His clothes were folded and had been placed in a different chair. A cup of coffee from Zoola Café was on an end table.

I closed the door, entered the room without a word. Gun aimed at him, I turned on the light in the bathroom. He didn't react. His blindfold was that comprehensive. I put the gun down. Square chin. Dimples. Clean-shaven. He was well manicured and decently endowed, was semi-erect.

I removed his earplugs. Not until then did he react to the sound of the ocean, the sound of my breathing, the echo from tree frogs singing their Caribbean song. He had been in restraints, unable to remove them, blind and deaf, as vulnerable as a man could be.

In my true voice I whispered, "We should get started."

"Pardon me for not standing and shaking your hand."

I held his penis, shook it up and down. "Pleased to meet you."

"You sound tense."

"Sex makes me nervous."

"Relax."

"If I could relax myself, I wouldn't be here."

"We can be romantic."

"I don't do fake."

"If you untie me I can massage you and then please."

"This is crazy. I should leave."

"It's up to you. I am here for you. Whatever you need."

"Stop talking."

I let him go, stood in front him, contemplating.

I took out my device that I used to sweep any room I entered, checked for any recording device. The room was clean. I crept back to him, traced my fingers over his rising stiffness.

He asked, "Is it okay?"

"Stop talking."

I moved away from him and stretched my neck, touched my knees with my forehead, went down into a left side split, a right side split, then a Chinese split, stood and stretched my left leg out into a slow-motion roundhouse kick. That calmed me. Candles were on the dresser. I lit two, let the light grow as

404

the scent rose, and returned to my blinded blind date.

I asked, "You're here alone?"

He nodded.

I removed my gun from my backpack, walked the room, looked in the closets and made sure all were empty, did the same in both bathrooms. I put the gun near me and unzipped my boots, took off the left one, then the right. I sat there a moment, reconsidering, then I pulled off my jeans.

I asked, "You do this a lot?"

"Not a lot. Women get more customers than men."

"Men have more disposable income."

"And more freedom to do things like this."

"I'm your first today?"

"Yes."

Another long moment passed before I removed my dark Agent Provocateur thong, took off my short leather jacket, my black tee, and my dark Agent Provocateur bra. Gun in hand, I stood undressed, folded all of my clothing, placed everything neatly on a different chair, a chair that would not be far from me if I needed my clothes in a hurry. I studied him a moment, pushed many thoughts and fears out of my mind, let go of as much of the mental baggage I carried as I could, and pulled at my natural hair.

In a shaky voice I said, "I'll be with you shortly."

He nodded.

I held my gun and went to the shower, cleansed myself, ran my fingers over my ancient scars again, rubbed those spots where I had been stabbed and shot, touched each spot and remembered.

Warm water. I stood underneath warm water and moaned like I was dying. I also felt the heaviness from my circadian clock being all but destroyed. I could have fallen asleep right there, underneath the spray of warm water, in the humidity of the bathroom.

I took in a mouthful of the shower water, Bajan water having come across limestone and having a unique taste. I gave myself ten minutes, eight minutes longer than the showers I had taken over the last forty-plus days. Had lost count. Could've stayed in the shower forever. I rinsed, soaped, rinsed, soaped, rinsed, then stood there humming, moaning. I didn't want to get out. When I turned the water off, losing that feeling ached. Gun in hand, I returned to my escort with water dripping from my body.

Condoms were on the table, next to a tray of fruit. But I didn't use those. I had brought my own. I took out several brands that I had bought at the supermarket in Emerald City, looked to see which style or size would fit his stiffness, went with a King condom, then ripped it open, stroked him a while, stroked him as I had stroked King Killer, as I had stroked Johnny Parker, as I had stroked many men.

"You're really good at that."

"Stop talking."

He moaned like he was amazed, became hard, and I rolled the prophylactic on him. He licked his lips and a guttural groan rumbled in his throat. I leaned into him and rubbed my breasts against his chest.

His skin felt so good against my skin. I bit my lip and inhaled.

He stirred in his armless chair, his strong hands tied to the chair's legs. He had the arms of a boxer. He had the biceps of a weight lifter. His body was fucking ridiculous.

I put the gun down, made sure it stayed within reach.

I stroked him until his stiffness pulled a torrent of blood from his brain.

He pulled at his restraints when it was too much, but he could do nothing to stop me. That was my rendition. That was my act of torture. His muscles flexed and he pushed into my hand. He was ready. I mounted him. I was anxious and wet from the shower, but dry at my sex.

That dryness embarrassed me.

I worked him until my lips parted, made myself open, cringed and did a slow and sensual booty roll, rolled against his gyrating groin, felt what was stiff become stiffer, sat down on him too hard, too abruptly, and clenched my teeth. My left leg began to quiver. That embarrassed me. Then I took a breath, a deep breath, a ragged breath, counted to ten, and again I was back in control.

He moved. I moved.

It felt good. It felt incredible. I bit my hand to keep from letting him know how good it felt. I rolled on him, shuddered as I moved up and down. Up and down. Up and down. Heard a noise. Stopped moving. Looked at the door. Was ready to disconnect and leap for my weapon.

People passed by.

I sat still, but he kept moving, kept wining, kept making circles, kept stirring my insides.

I bit my hand, made sure no one was breaking in the door.

Then I went back to rolling with him. While I had paused, he hadn't stopped moving his hips, hadn't detected that I had been distracted. He moaned like he enjoyed me. Shit. I moaned. He made me moan. Couldn't stop moaning and moving up and down, couldn't stop massaging that tension.

His moans were in my ear, my moans in his.

I began to spin in blackness and fire.

I became fierce, danced on him, embarrassed for being so primitive with a stranger, but unable to control myself, unable to stop. I choked him. He strained his neck and I choked him harder. I choked him as I rose and slammed down into him. I made so much noise. He cursed. I drooled. He made me drool. I could not stop. Muscle tension. Quaking. Shuddering. Confused. Vibrations that would not end. So turned on. So excited. I could not control myself. The sensation that came in waves, and built and crashed like tsunami after tsunami after tsunami. I died one thousand times.

I slipped away from him, fell to the floor, almost took him and the chair down with me.

Eyes closed tight, I trembled and snapped, "What did you do to me?"

"What do you mean?"

"Shit. You drugged me."

"What are you talking about?"

"What the hell just happened? Legs won't stop shaking. I can barely breathe."

"I can't see, but it sounds like an orgasm."

Legs squeezed together, I let out a long, deep moan.

He wasn't inside of me, but I jerked, trembled, and the shaking happened again.

I whispered, "I had an orgasm. So that's an orgasm."

"You've never had an orgasm?"

A few seconds went by with me on the floor, eyes opened wide.

"The trembling won't stop. I'm not on you and it's still happening."

"Are you okay?"

I said nothing. Couldn't talk.

He asked, "You okay?"

I rolled over to my side, then sat up on the carpet, not quite there.

He asked, "You've never come before?"

I hurried to the shower again. Two minutes of warm water to clear my head, then a minute of cold water to try to calm me down. I dried off. Picked up my folded clothing. Dressed in record time.

Then I went to him and freed one hand.

I said, "Don't remove your blindfold. Count down from one hundred. Untie your other hand. Count up to one hundred, untie one leg. Count down from one hundred, untie the next leg. Count up to one hundred and count down again, then shower and go on with your night."

He said, "You're done?"

I whispered, "Start counting when you hear the door close. Understand?"

I clicked off the light, left him in the dark, condom on his waning stiffness, windows open, a zephyr making the curtains dance, tree frogs singing as the waves crashed into the shores. I felt guilt. On the way down I started to input a text message:

I really miss you. Didn't think I would this much FOR THIS LONG. MONTHS HAVE PASSED AND I STILL FUCKIN

LOVE YOU. Jennifer.

Again I began to tingle and I leaned against a wall. It rolled. I felt pins and needles. Painful. Felt woozy. Heady buzz. Knees became weak. The closer I came to losing control, the better I felt. Bit my hand. Went over the edge. Pulsated. Felt like his stiffness was still inside of me. Shit. I was coming again. Moaned. Bit my hand harder. Another orgasm rolled through my body. Felt madness in my brain. Legs trembled again.

I trembled and whispered, "Fuck. Another orgasm. Stop it. Just stop it."

It hurt so good. Like I was bursting. For another minute it hurt so good. Body was contracting all over. When I calmed, when it died down, while I floated, I wanted more right away.

For a moment I looked at my cellular, deleted the message, typed a new one.

FUCK YOU JOHNNY, FUCKIN FUCK YOU AND THAT CRAZY BITCH. YOU NEVER FUCKIN MADE ME COME YOU FUCKIN LOSER. SOMEBODY ELSE DID IN FIVE MINUTES WHAT YOU NEVER DID IN FIVE MONTHS. WEAK DICK BASTARD, YOU AND THAT BITCH DESERVE EACH OTHER. I'M THE STUPID ONE. NOW I'M THE ONE PING PING

411

PINGING YOU LIKE I'M DAMN PSY-
CHO. NOW I'M ACTING LIKE THAT
CRAZY BITCH AND THAT AIN'T
FUCKIN COOL. MOTHERFUCKER
I'M DONE. THIS IS THE LAST
FUCKIN PING FROM ME.

Barbarians were tracking my phone. I didn't
press SEND. I deleted the message, back-
spaced over my temporary insanity and
destroyed that SIM card. Remorse remained,
had me distracted, had me off my game.

Angry, but still tingling, still sensitive. Years
of not having orgasms had caught up with
me. Sex had felt good, penetration had always
felt good, but it had always ended with a
comma, never with a bold, underscored
exclamation point in a super-size font. Was
tempted to run back to the man I had rented.
Having an orgasm with him, losing control, I
had embarrassed myself. I had embarrassed
myself and left, happy that he had no fucking
idea who I was. This had me distracted, and
that distraction was pissing me the fuck off.
Orgasm had taken my mind away from what
was important. I saw why it had been so easy
to take out targets after I had made them
come, after they had become relaxed, unfo-
cused, and dreamy-eyed. After they had died
a thousand little deaths, giving the big one
was easy.

Orgasm made a strong man defenseless,

took him off his game.

Orgasm did the same for women. Had just done the same for me.

When I made it to where my bike was hidden, an assassin was waiting on my arrival.

FORTY-THREE

She waited, her face illuminated by the Black-
Berry in her hand. Old Man Reaper's Bahamian daughter was in the shadows. She was
leaning against a well-polished BMW K
1300, dressed in all black, a tight bodysuit
that made her look like a Kryptonian warrior.

I pulled my backpack on and asked, "What
are you doing?"

"Sexting my husband."

"When did you last see him?"

"Two hours ago."

"When did you have sex with him last?"

"Three hours ago."

"Grow up. I need you to be focused. Not
out here sending sex messages."

She put her cellular away and said, "Well?
How did it go?"

"It was okay."

"Just okay?"

"Just okay."

The weight from Black Jack and Hacker

being dead came back. The thought of Black Jack and Hacker was a claw that had left me scarred and bleeding without a tourniquet.

They had been slaughtered. I had gone to visit an escort to ease my angst.

I doubted if they would've stopped living if I had become the headless assassin.

She said, "Didn't expect you for another thirty minutes, maybe an hour."

"How much do I owe you?"

"Nothing, I told you."

"How much did it cost?"

"Cost you nothing. My way of apologizing for being late down at Six Roads."

"I don't like handouts."

"That was a dick-in, not a handout."

"Cute. Rude, but cute." I paused. "Let me do something for you."

"Buy me six cupcakes at the Cupcake Corner at Quayside and we're even."

I nodded. "Who tied him up?"

"You know he couldn't do that himself."

"Anything you want to confess?"

"No, I didn't do anything with him."

My head still felt light. The tingles wouldn't die down.

She asked, "You okay?"

I paused. "Black Jack. He was killed. Decapitated."

"That was your guy from the Hilton? The thing on the front page at Ridgeview Estates?"

"Fuck. He hacked into the LKs' system,

tracked the LKs for me. A day later, he's dead."

"Him and the eighteen-year-old from UWI?"

Now she was alert, standing tall, no longer a wife but an assassin. "Are they still here?"

"Only a fool would stick around on an island after doing a hit."

She said, "In other words, you have no idea."

"I need to get away from here."

Passports came to mind yet again. I called Big Guy. He answered. I hung up. He was still alive, his head still attached to his body. He had enough pressure on him, from me and the Barbarians. I would threaten him again and deal with him in a few hours.

I said, "Black Jack asked me about the job in Trinidad, asked why it was set up that way."

"Why face-to-face? That section of Trinidad that holds Independence Square has a lot of tall buildings. They could've used a sniper like me and popped him when he stepped out of his car. I could've done that, disassembled my gun, and been gone to shop on Frederick Street before the screaming had stopped. If they wanted him dead at the bank, that's the way I would've done it."

I exhaled a slow breath, replaying the shoot-out in my mind.

She said, "The Barbarians instructed you to open the briefcase?"

I told her about the gold mine that was inside.

She said, "Are you serious?"

"Yeah."

"Why would they trust you with that much money?"

"That's easy. Because I am loyal and honest to a fault. I'm like the bank teller who works around a ton of money. Her job owes her, yet she waits on her paycheck to come so she can pay her bills."

"That being-honest mentality will do you no good in the end."

"Did me no good with Johnny Parker."

She faced me. "The hard drive."

"That's business."

"Should have something from that soon."

"America soon or West Indies soon?"

"West Indies soon. What do you do now?"

"The Barbarians put me back on hold. I wait on the next set of instructions."

I was about to tell her about Zenga stalking me, but I didn't.

I could handle myself. It would sound like I was asking for more help.

A shock of tingles came and I bent my head, rubbed my nose.

She said, "What's on your mind?"

"You like this island?"

"You're not feeling Barbados?"

"I'm trapped here. You chose to live here. It's small. Claustrophobic."

"I guess that it would feel that way when you're on the run."

"You like it here?"

"This is heaven."

"Why is this heaven?"

"You okay over there?"

"Keep talking. Why does my prison feel like heaven to you?"

"I'm in love."

"No one is after you."

"You're doing better?"

"What?"

"Reaper, are you okay?"

"Keep talking. How is being married?"

"It's great. We do corny couples' stuff. Movies at the Sheraton, flying kites at parks, picnics at Farley Hill, and a lime here and there. Went to see Air Supply. We go to the Plantation for Back in Time and jam to the old-school, or go down to Oistins and go back to the part beyond all the bashment and we two-step and tree-step. We go to most of the cavalcades. Jump with a Zulu. We do Foreday. Even if it's raining, we go to Soca on the Hill or Reggae on the Hill. We party hard start to finish. We do everything we can find to do on this island. We get dressed up and do many other social events, things for adults."

"It's more than sex. You have a real marriage. You have what most people want."

"What did that Parker guy do to make you happy?"

"He was kind. He liked me. He made me feel normal. He made me fall in love."

"I feel that way now."

I shook my head, not wanting to talk about him. "Let's get to work, Petrichor."

"Sure you can do this, Goldilocks?"

"Fetes should be over. Drunks will be tearing up the road soon. Time to work the next gig."

"I want to help you. I'll see if I can pull some information on the LKs."

"Don't fuckin' even try. I feel bad for ever asking Black Jack to help."

"You don't have to scream, Goldilocks. I'm right here, not in China."

"Black Jack was found and executed within twenty-four hours of trying to break into their computer systems. They're bad men. Do anything and I'll kill your ass, resurrect your ass, then kill your ass again."

"You're scared."

Another moment passed.

She asked, "Ready to roll?"

I mounted my crotch rocket and started it up.

The rumble almost reignited the tingles.

She pulled on her backpack and started the BMW.

I yelled over the rumbling motors and said, "Hey."

"Yeah?"

"Let's change partners."

"Sounds kinky."

"Whatever. You have a one-track mind."

She gave me her BMW. More power. More speed. Heavier.

I said, "Feel this power. Love this."

"God, I love the way a Ducati vibrates. Like a three-hundred pound sex toy."

"Been riding rough roads on a bike for over a month."

"It's like opening your legs and sitting on a vibrator with the speed turned down low."

"If you're riding up Highway 6, that three-mile stretch of nasty road by PLAE, riding a crotch rocket on that is like being on a magic vibrator, speed turned up high. Turned up extremely high."

She asked, "Does this qualify as girl talk?"

"It's shallow, so it probably does qualify."

"You're more at ease talking about your friends being decapitated."

"I am."

"He did you good. Guy upstairs did you good."

"No comment."

"Yeah. He did you real good."

"What happened upstairs was an interlude. Back to reality now."

FORTY-FOUR

Parish of St. Michael

Down in Black Rock we parked on the side of a rum shop near Christadelphian Church and switched our crotch rockets for a white van labeled MINT CONDITION INDUSTRIAL SERVICES, LIMITED. Then we moved to Hooligan Road and opened the back, inspected the tools.

For now, my mind was off rude Barbarians and deadly men from Trinidad.

My mind was away from thinking about Black Jack being slaughtered.

In the thick of the night, we took care of two jobs, one dealing with a powerful CEO, a man who had robbed many of their pensions and made himself megarich in the process. We had broken into his mansion up at Fort George Heights.

We delivered him to the Parish of St. Lucy. Then we sped south again.

The next one was a politician. We pulled the second target out of his two-story home in Lowthers Park, Christ Church. Petrichor had killed his air-conditioning system during the day, when the temperature was in the nineties, knowing that would force him to bitch and curse and call for a technician who would find the system unrepairable, causing him to leave his windows open and alarm off for the night. We compromised the windows on the ground floor and stepped across the carpet inside his concrete blockhouse, carpet being a rarity on the island, and while fans blew on high and covered any noise we made walking through his spectacular home, we took him out through his garage. He was a big man, a fat fucker. Too big to knock out and carry. So after we had rendered an ass beating that rivaled all ass beatings, holding a gun to his temple, we encouraged the battered man to walk the green mile with us. Duct tape kept his hands behind his back. A black cloth over his head, a gag in his mouth, and earplugs kept him in the dark. We forced him into the van. Old Man Reaper's Bahamian daughter took his SUV. It would look like he had left home. I followed her. The plan was to dump the SUV on one of the side streets in the next parish. That done, I climbed back in the van and we drove him out to the cane fields in the northeast, an area of chattel houses, outhouses, banana fields, tobacco fields — a section of farmers with a thinner population and dark roads that didn't have much traffic through the night. We went off the main road onto a cart road, an unpaved strip that looked like it was made for a horse and buggy. No streetlights. We were far from city lights. Counting the stars in the sky was like trying to count grains of sand on the beach. Cart roads were where people drove to have sex at night.

Cart roads were also where more than a few dead bodies were found.

The sea and cart roads, top two locations for disposing of the recently killed.

Only the sea would eventually spit what was left of the dead back up on the shores.

We stood to the side wearing oversize clothing and Guy Fawkes masks.

The politico was on his knees, delivered to the man who had paid for the job to be done.

He said, "Kenny Omar Payne, what happened to the promise for a clean campaign?"

"Look, don't do this."

"What happened to the honesty and respect you promised the people of Barbados?"

"Think. Have mercy. For the love of God, I have a wife and children and —"

"You called my wife ignorant. Do you have any idea what that did to our children? To have my kids go to school the next day and deal with your foolishness? My daughter is seven and she cried herself to sleep three nights in a row. My wife graduated from UWI, reads Aristotle, and you stood on a platform and called her ignorant. She's a mother, a wife who feels deeply, a woman who wants to encourage every Bajan to better Barbados by putting his shoulder to the wheel."

"Let me apologize to your wife and children, publicly, in the *Nation*. On radio. On CBC. Let my hands go; give me my phone, and right now I will apologize by BBMing everyone on the island."

"I have lost all respect for you. I will never subscribe to such lowlife and classless behavior, which is the type of behavior that is typical of your party."

"It's politics. It's just politics."

"Comparing my wife to an animal is politics? The women in your constituency should stone you."

"Peter Kellman, for God's sake. We went to primary school together. We went to Coleridge and Parry Secondary and we did sports together. I know your mother. My mother and she go to St. Leonard's Anglican Church together. They used to go to Bridgetown together on Saturday mornings. They eat fishcakes together. You are better than this. You are a man of God and this is not Christlike, my brother."

"You forget that I am a husband, a son, a father."

"I am a loyal husband, an obedient son, and a proud father as well."

"Above all, I am protecting my country."

His speech done, the politician took the hood off of his political adversary.

He was on the edge of an open grave. Inside of that grave was the CEO. His head was barely attached to his body. Kenny Omar Payne saw the dead man, the heavy JCB machinery, mechanical harvesters, and other ground-moving machinery.

He shouted, "Just give me lashes. Give me a thousand lashes. A million lashes."

"We are too old for lashes. Way too old for lashes."

"Think about my mother."

"You should have thought about her when you insulted my wife."

"Think about my wife and children being devastated at my funeral."

"This is your funeral."

Peter Kellman removed a handkerchief from his pocket, wiped tears from his eyes, nodded at us, waved good-bye to his former friend, then walked away, went through the cane field.

His car started and drove into darkness. His headlights lit up the cart road and the sugarcane. Soon the only light we had was from the stars above. Petrichor took out a flashlight, positioned it so it lit up the target. We removed our masks. Kenny Omar Payne begged for his life.

My father's Bahamian daughter handed me

a compound bow and carbon arrows. She took out one too. A wayward politician screamed loud enough to be heard in Bridge-town.

Two arrows took flight. Then there was silence. A cool night breeze washed over us.

I wondered if Black Jack had screamed. If Hacker had screamed.

We stood side by side, the stillness of the countryside accented by stars in the sky.

Petrichor said, "That man loves his wife."

"This is probably the most romantic thing a man could do for a woman."

FORTY-FIVE

My father's Bahamian daughter climbed into the dirt mover and covered the grave. I hopped in a three-ton roller when she was done, came behind her, and began smoothing out the earth.

I saw her sending text messages while I finished flattening the gravesite.

We collected our murder tools, turned, and left, not a word spoken as we loaded the van. Petrichor drove the ominous narrow way, bouncing like we were horseback riding through the Grand Canyon. She popped in a CD, a soca mix that started with D'banj singing "Oliver Twist."

Her BlackBerry pinged. It pinged again. Again. Again.

She said, "That's my husband."

"How do you tolerate the pinging?"

"Send him a message for me, Goldilocks."

"Okay. What?"

"Tell him I'll suck his dick real wicked when I get home. Tell him I might suck that bamboo and swallow that nut and I want to hear him moan like he's my bitch and suck him so good he will cry and beg me to stop sucking his fat dick. Then I want him to pound my fat bread like —"

"Enough, enough. I will text that you will give him a blow job and make love to him later."

"It has to be nasty or he will know it's not me."

While she turned around in pitch-black darkness, I did what she asked, then put her BlackBerry down. It pinged again and she asked me to read the message from her husband.

I said, "Fuckin' seriously? You guys do that to each other?"

"A few times. Did it for the first time on my wedding night."

"Perverted nymphomaniacs."

"When I got married I finally understood why wedding dresses are white."

"To symbolize virginity."

"No, to hide come stains."

"That's gross."

"A good reason to never rent a wedding dress."

"When did you start having sex?"

"Oh, are you back to having girl talk now?"

"You're out of control. How old?"

"Fifteen, more or less. With Nigel Collins. Guy was cute. I grew up in Bain Town on

428

Finlayson. Guys sit around freestyle rapping and smoking spliffs big as Cuban cigars."

"Is that what Nigel was doing, getting high and freestylin'?"

"Nah. I met Nigel Collins over by the big pond on Thompson Boulevard."

"How old?"

"He was twenty-three."

"You met him on the streets by a pond?"

"He was going to the College of the Bahamas."

"You graduated at sixteen. College here is two years. He was twenty-three and still in college?"

"Okay, okay. He had graduated."

"If he had graduated, what was he doing hanging out at college?"

"Okay. He was twenty-six."

"What's the age of consent down there?"

She corrected me, "Up there."

"Up there, what's the age of consent?"

"For opposite-sex sex it's sixteen and for gay sex, it's eighteen."

"That makes no sense."

"I guess they want you to try being Adam and Eve before you embrace the rainbow."

"To be clear, you were how old when you had sex for the first time?"

"I was fifteen."

"Are you sure you were fifteen?"

"It was about eleven or twelve months before I turned fifteen."

"So you were new at being fourteen and he was almost thirty."

"He could've lost his job and gotten seven years at Her Majesty's Prison."

"You could've gotten pregnant and been given eighteen to twenty-one years."

"What, are you my mother?"

"What happened to him?"

"He ended up in Her Majesty's anyway."

"Why was he incarcerated?"

"Was caught smuggling cocaine with his sister. His sister was on the police force."

"You knew he was smuggling?"

"Had no idea. Just picked up the paper one day and he was on the front page, handcuffed, being led into jail, his sister at his side. That was the last I heard of him."

I paused. "I had sex the first time two years ago."

"Wow."

"Only been with two guys."

"Three. You've been with three."

"Three." I sighed. "Tonight is the night that Parker and I have officially broken up."

"Why tonight?"

"I just had sex with someone else. Parker had been my last lover. Well, the last man that had been inside. Masturbated a few, did a fake fuck, but that was work, that was business."

"Never went all the way on a job? Not once?"

"Almost did in Trinidad. Almost had to. Good thing they threw a man from the roof."

A moment passed before she said, "The guy I hired for you tonight . . ."

"What about?"

"He pinged me twice while I was filling the grave. He sent a BBM."

"You paid him, right?"

"I paid him. He really wants to see you again."

"Not gonna happen."

"It was that bad, huh?"

We passed a road sign showing the way to North Stars cricket ground, Animal Flower Cave, Farley Hill National Park, and Morgan Lewis. She drove awhile, looked for the road on which to make the next turn, then stopped when she came up on road signage for Barclays Park, Bathsheba, and Bridgetown. I saw a sign for Joe's River, where six had died in a bus crash a few years ago.

I said, "The island has train tracks, but there are no trains on the island."

"They stopped them a long time ago. Almost a hundred years ago. Ran from Bridgetown to Belleplaine. Didn't last two generations."

"Why? Having a train system would make a lot of sense."

"When you depend on the European man to build the trains, when he gets tired of you riding his trains, then the foreign man with money can close down the tr— shite, shite, shite."

She hit something; slammed into the shady figure hard, but she didn't lose control.

I said, "What the fuck was that? You ran over somebody?"

She stopped and we stepped out of the van. She carried one gun and I carried two.

A black-bellied sheep was on the ground. I walked over to the animal, kicked its backside. It raised its head, frowned at the bright lights from the van, got up and moved like it'd had ten Banks beers too many, and stumbled into the darkness. We got back in the van and continued the rugged ride.

When she made a turn at the rum shop called Just a Fork in the Road, she made her way to signs pointing to Highway 2 for Welchman Hall and Highway D for Hillaby via Shop Hill.

"Tell me about my sperm donor, MX-401. Feel funny asking you that. If that's okay."

"We can talk about Old Man Reaper, but don't expect me to be sweet about it."

"Let's go listen to bad karaoke, drink, and talk."

" 'Bad karaoke.' Is there good karaoke?"

We dumped the stolen van on Hooligan Road and retrieved our motorcycles. We rocked it from bumps and potholes that covered the areas where the hardworking natives and working poor rested their heads, zoomed across the smoother streets in Bridgetown, passed by an outrageous LIME fete at the Carlisle House, DJs playing raunchy music, teenage girls bent over at six thirty and six forty-five, guys behind them pumping and dry fucking them so hard I was surprised the girls didn't fall on their faces. We went down to the South Coast, back into the bright lights, the sea at our side, and made our way into the mouth of the Gap. As we rode I went back to the start, told her about the first time I met Old Man Reaper.

FORTY-SIX

Diamond Dust talked to War Machine and his warriors. She had a wireless headset on, her children playing in the background. Diamond Dust, War Machine, and the top men were on a conference call using Skype. War Machine let her be in control. Let her spin this situation. Let her be Diamond Dust.

Some seated at a conference table, others standing, War Machine and his men watched Diamond Dust from a high-tech television with Internet capabilities, her face on a ninety-inch screen. She looked at them from the same size television screen in the den of her home.

Diamond Dust said, "This is out of hand. First the drug shipment that cost us millions. The last one was in Barbados. Now the Internet violation that has been detected in Barbados. Add that the Kiwi was tracked there — it has to all be connected. We have reviewed the drug bust. There were at least two firing on the runners. One could have been the

Kiwi. There is no proof she ever left Barbados."

War Machine nodded and said, "Agreed."

"The members realize that the key runner we used there, before he was found slaughtered in the prestigious St. Lawrence Gap, he had spent time dancing with a European. That could have been the Kiwi. His death was a message to us all. Another insult to us all. A message from someone to us."

She said that she was dispatching other warriors to Barbados. She didn't ask War Machine for his opinion. He nodded. Her connection had found that the Kiwi had ordered passports but hadn't retrieved them. They only had to find the Kiwi's Bajan contact, the fool supplying her with documents.

Diamond Dust said, "Substations are at Belmont Road, Government Hill, Pine Garden, and by the Garrison. Destroy the sites."

War Machine nodded, didn't cross her strategy, watched his wife exercise her arrogance.

Diamond Dust asked War Machine, "What are your immediate plans?"

"Men have been sent to the clubs in the Limegrove area, restaurants on the West Coast, and to St. Lawrence Gap. She loves to party, so I've sent men she didn't meet, weren't a part of the intel that she left behind at her safe house in Trinidad, men she wouldn't recognize, to those locations. Until we hear from your passport contact, since you're the expert, we'll follow your orders, continue searching."

FORTY-SEVEN

Hal's Car Park Bar, St. Lawrence Gap
Across the cobbled road from where I had killed the cricketer. Tourists and locals all over, street vendors busy selling food, vendors selling trinkets to tourists.

Petrichor laughed over the bad karaoke and said, "Dora the Explorer? That's sick."

Her phone ping-ping-pinged again and I wrestled it from her hands. She laughed. For the past hour I had been sipping Banks and sending filthy sexts to her husband every time he ping-ping-pinged. Petrichor was cracking up at the escalating exchanges between me and her clueless husband.

I said, "Look at the disgusting pornographic message I just sent him. You've got work to do."

"Muddasik. Submarine. Row the boat. Wait. No way. You do that with Jell-O?"

"Hope you enjoy, and try not to get a yeast infection."

My cellular rang. The Barbarians. I took

the call. Karaoke ended. Videos played. People were dancing and sweating. Beers and alcohol on every table. Petrichor walked away, Bailey's in hand, and went to take a peek at Sugar Ultra Lounge. She said that she had seen a group of good-looking men going that way. Men in suits. They had stopped and looked at our motorcycles. I was buzzed and didn't care. Every man or woman who passed by the bikes paused. A couple of women had been rude and sat on one of the bikes to take a photo. Any other time I would have blasted them for doing that. I let Petrichor go alone. She was married, but she was still a flirty girl at heart. By the time she returned, I had my new marching orders from the Barbarians. I sat at the bar, rubbing my temples. If I had inhaled, I would have smelled Trinidad. I would have smelled Laventille Killers. Petrichor came back. Her phone pinged. She was needed at home. We went to our iron horses, shook hands again, and parted ways.

She sped away on the Ducati, went left and toward the West Coast. I went right, cruised down ABC Highway on the BMW, went back to Six Roads and being landlocked in my government cell.

Back at the safe house, I sat on the bed, the music from a fete across the road announcing that their Banks Beer–sponsored party was about to end. The single-pane windows rattled from the beat, soca jamming hard. I wanted to go over there. I should've gone over there and partied until the new sun made me sweat. I didn't. I stripped, pulled off my clothing, let it fall haphazardly on the dusty tile floor, and danced to the beat as I headed to the bathroom, angry the night had ended. Showered, tipsy, guns at my side, stared out the window, binoculars in hand, watched the neighbors have sex, then scattered the money from the briefcase on the bed, all thrown helter-skelter. Should have stolen it, but none of the sinuous cut-rock roads would lead me away. I crawled on top of those packets of freedom.

The Barbarians had asked what I knew about squatters. Big Guy had had an issue with the same squatters. Soon I would know why. I didn't know if all of that had anything to do with the cricketer.

The drug bust here was just a few days ago.

I thought about what the other Barbarians had said.

Since I had been stranded here, they had been to New York and Miami.

If you looked up Miami in the dictionary, you saw drugs.

New York was another destination for the same product.

I bet the men sent here had been up in the States doing the same shit I was doing here.

The music at the fete ended. The neighbors ended the show.

I applauded them, pulled the fan up close, let it blow across my damp skin.

I had had my first orgasm tonight. As the air tickled my skin, that thought came and went.

I was afraid. I was angry. I was alone.

The sexting had excited my mind as well.

Petrichor was probably with her husband doing those wicked things now.

That made me sad. Sad for myself. The life I had was so fuckin' sad.

I wanted to be on South Beach. On the Sunset Strip. In Times Square.

Silence covered my jail.

Tree frogs began singing their nightly song and killed that peace.

I tossed and turned in the heat and stuffiness of my prison until sleep came.

Soon Johnny Parker burgled his way into my dreams, came to me naked, fresh out of the shower, tall and athletic. I waited for him. He came to me with an ice-cold vibrator and warm anal beads in his hands, a bowl of green Jell-O left on the nightstand next to a bowl of ice chips and Altoids.

Tree frogs sang as he fucked me in the sweet, perverted way he used to fuck me.

FORTY-EIGHT

The tail end of the Parish of St. Peter, situated between St. Lucy and St. Andrew

Barbarians sent me behind God's back, to the Atlantic Ocean side of the island to hike deep into the bush to have a tête-à-tête with a family of Rastafarians. They showed their hand this morning, told me just enough to carry out this mission. A bank that the Barbarians did business with had bought a large stretch of land in the ninth parish of eleven parishes — prime real estate that could be as profitable as everything built along the island's platinum coast and Port Saint Charles, and now they were going to build luxury condos, mansions, and a high-end super center, something that would redefine that side of the island, maybe even construct a new church to collect 10 percent from the richest of the rich, only to find out they had inherited around sixty squatters. Three generations of squatters had been living back in the bush for decades. They claimed they had been there forty years, but there was no proof. No paperwork. There was an ongoing fiasco in Fort George with Sagicor about the same thing. A squatter and his family had been hiding out on their land for three decades, and now it was front-page news. Only this was RCSI land and they wanted no publicity. This problem had been lingering for weeks. I had to steal a van, wear jeans and sneakers, a long-sleeve cotton blouse, made sure I showed no flesh, wore only lip gloss, my hair now the lightest of brown, carried the heavy briefcase, then hiked an uneven dirt and rock trail that moved uphill, each step uneven and made for twisting an ankle, the trek being over a mile and taking thirty of the hottest minutes ever made. Soon I smelled food being cooked. I smelled fire. There was no smoke.

A little Rasta boy saw me hiking through the woods. There were more than a dozen kids playing. The little boy saw me first and called out some sort of warning and all the kids took off running, zebras fleeing a lioness. By then I was sweating profusely. The heat. No breeze. I passed a ha-ha and hiked about another quarter mile before encountering a slender, shirtless man who had dreadlocks to his knees, a cutlass in his right hand, waiting on me in the shade of a tree that had to be three hundred years old, if it were that young. Centipedes. Millipedes. Frogs. Lizards. Mongoose. Spiders. Monkeys up in the trees. Ants. I didn't react to anything nature had put in my face or at my feet. Fifty yards behind him, his family had congregated. Men. Women. Dozens of children. Just beyond them was a shantytown made of a dozen homes no bigger than chattel houses, all thrown together, and each looked like it was ready to fall apart.

A gaggle of men and women were out. The women were cooking on an open pit.

He said, "You with the law?"

"I'm here on behalf of the people who own this land."

"They send you a long way to get to a place where you don't need to be."

"They sent me a long way to talk to a man who refuses to leave this hill and talk to them."

"I have nothing to say to them."

"You're an interesting man."

"How I interesting?"

"You're squatting on someone else's property, sitting on their investment, and when they offer you over a million as a settlement, you turn it down. That blows my mind, have to say that."

"Boss man sends a woman to do his dirty work."

"You speak for everyone? You have a committee up here, or are you the dictator?"

"I speak for my people and you speak for

your people."

"Then you are the man I should speak with regarding both the provenance and ownership history of this land. If you need to see the deeds for the land, I have copies."

As we stood on a sloping hill underneath a tree, three fires were going on in the distance, black smoke billowing from the lowlands to the blue skies. Water tankers from C.O. Williams Construction were working overtime with the Barbados Fire Department. This was the middle of nowhere. No road. No way for a water tanker to get up here to bring me a bottle of Zephyrhills, Aquafina, or Dasani.

I said, "They want to know how you would feel if you were living overseas and came back and found someone living on your land. Would you see that as right or as thievery?"

"Tell your people I follow the law."

"They say that you build on the land like you bought it. Take more land as you see fit."

"I follow the law."

"The people I work for just want to follow the same law, even though it doesn't benefit them, even though they will lose millions of dollars, even though you get to make up your own rules and occupy more land than you will need, even though you get to live rent-free while they pay a mortgage. An average home is only around six thousand square feet and you're up here claiming more than nine acres. An acre is about ninety percent of a football field, and you are trying to steal over nine. Don't you find that just a tad bit greedy? Don't you have any dignity?"

"I follow the law."

"They can see you being entitled to the houses, but you're claiming a forest and you've never spent a dime for the land. They have paid for the land and they have the documents and your family just moved on and acted like they discovered it, like Christopher Columbus. It was already here. Someone had worked and paid for it, whether they were using it or not."

"I follow the law."

"They say you live off another man's land without offering one penny for compensation. For four decades you have lived here in secret, have bred and bred and bred, and now that you are discovered have not offered to pay one penny. You're no better than a common thief."

"I follow the law."

I touched my earpiece and waited.

They issued me my next instructions.

I opened the briefcase in front of the Rastafarian.

Inside was half a million in cash, money that had been my mattress last night.

There was no notable reaction from the shoeless Rastafarian.

He asked, "Why dem send you all the way to my property with this?"

I said, "The organization wants you to sign the contract. The contract will give you eight hundred thousand for land, land that does not belong to you, and give you an additional five hundred thousand dollars for housing, so you can build a true house, one with running water and electricity, by the standards of the island, and there is another lump sum of six hundred thousand. Plus for ten years you get an annuity of four hundred and twenty-five thousand dollars."

"The money in the briefcase? They want me to take that and just go away?"

"It's a signing bonus. It's money no one will know about. It can be looked upon as a gift."

"Then it's another half a million that you add on to the other money."

"All they ask is that you keep it out of the papers, don't go to an attorney, and that they are allowed to relocate you quietly. They will buy you furniture, new furniture, from Da Costa or Courts or that furniture store Design Décor at the roundabout by Parkinson Secondary in Pine."

"A bribe."

"No, a business transaction that favors you, a man who has never had a job in his life."

"How does taking your blood money benefit me?"

"You don't work. You live off the land, someone else's land. You have a large family and no income. You cut wood and make sculptures that sell down in the chattel businesses on River Road, but that's chump change. You live in makeshift houses that don't have windows and look like they could fall down during the next hard rain, let alone if a hurricane came here."

"We no complain. Hurricane don't come to Barbados, only pass by. God protect us."

"They say it's a legal contract. You benefit from the deal. You benefit more than people who work twelve hours a day. People are out there picking cotton for a few dollars a day and they are offering to make you a millionaire. Someone else owns this land. They have paid for this land. You're an illegal tenant. Your father brought you here as an illegal tenant. He knew that he was doing wrong when he did that forty years ago. You're just lucky it took them forty years to find out. Your family has had forty years of not having to pay for use of the land, forty years of no rent, has lived here illegally, and they are paying you to move. If anything, you are extorting them."

"Is that what they tell you to tell me?"

"Word for word. They have their hands up my ass and I'm just the puppet."

"We have a legal right to this land."

"They want to know what it will take for you and the bank to work this out. How much?"

"It's not about the money."

"With that in mind, what will it take?"

"What you offer, I want twenty-four acres and five times the money."

"Twenty acres and five times."

"An acre for each of my children, plus a little more for me and my wife."

"They want to build up here. Twenty acres is about ninety-six thousand square yards, about fourteen football fields' worth of land, and that's substantial. That's a small town."

"They can build around me. Build a big wall around my land and build around me."

"I will tell them that."

"The money you bring to bribe me, you can leave that while they think it over."

"Sorry, I can't do that."

"Call the boss man and tell him what I say."

"He can hear you now."

"He can hear me?"

"Every word. He says if you sign, the money stays. Otherwise it goes."

"Then there will be no deal."

"You don't think this is extortion?"

"I am showing you what I think of bribery."

I inspected his shantytown, an ocean view in the distance, a great place for homes, condos, a park for kids, a mall that rivaled Limegrove. Another place for the rich to play, eat, shop, and shit. That was what this was about.

He said, "Tell them again that my family

been here forty years."

"The CEO wants to call you and talk. Do you have a cellular?"

"Yeah."

"Really?"

"We call people too."

"You're way back in the hills. No landline. No water. No electricity."

"I have money on my phone. Reception gone."

"How do you communicate with the rest of the island if there is an emergency? How would you know what was going on in the rest of the world or know if one of those fires was coming this way? How would you call for an ambulance or the police if you had an emergency?"

"Don't need to. We family. Family is more than money, more than numbers on a check. Your boss man is big corporation. He make billions and talks to me about a million like I idiot. This land is worth fifteen million. That was in the newspaper. I read that myself. That money he offer us is nothing to him. He think he God. I show him. We not squatters. We been here forty years. The man in Fort George not going to leave. We not going to leave either."

In the distance, sitting in the shade from trees, outside the front doors of their shanty-town, were a dozen young adults, his children, and the children of his children. Each structure had been built using castaway materials, particleboard, stolen bricks, whatever could be found on the side of the road or on a construction site in the thick of the night.

He said, "I go get attorney real soon. I go to the *Nation* and tell them my story too. I get Sandy Pitt and Cherie Pitt to come here and take photos and put on front of the paper."

"If they give you what you asked for, will you consider relocating then?"

"Leave the money and I will consider it then."

"For you to even consider considering the deal I need to leave consideration?"

He nodded.

I said, "And in your eyes, that's not extortion?"

"You just pay me for the time it will take for me to think about it, that's all."

"A half million dollars to think about a deal that's already close to three million."

"I am a deep thinker."

"Which are you, an anarchist, autonomist, or socialist?"

"I am Rasta, not a stupid man. Squatting is the oldest way of life in the world. We are all squatters. Everyone on this island is a squatter. The white man is the Great Squatter. He was a squatter that had no passport or papers and didn't go through customs, just got off of a boat and made this his land, then he brings his laws and his definition and changes it so the people here can't have a little land. Every time they change the law, the man born here gets less. Less money. Less job. Less land. The government make it so the man from England can get land and the man from Barbados lives on the side of the road. He wants his land and everybody else's land so he can build more hotels and buildings that only white people like him can afford."

"Too bad you couldn't go on *Judge Judy* and resolve this in thirty minutes."

"I don't care about no judge. I don't care about no law that come from England."

"They have instructed me to leave the consideration and hope you reconsider."

I put the briefcase down. He didn't hesitate to pick it up.

Maybe in his mind touching it implied ownership, same as placing his feet on this land.

I said, "Two days. Is that enough time to think?"

"Four days."

"You've taken the money and now you have changed the rules."

"We don't want to fight. We want peace. I bother nobody, but when I walk the streets down there, they treat me like I sell drugs, like I armed robber, like I hijacker and home invader, like I murderer since I don't look and act like them. We poor; we have nothing, but we not walking the streets begging. We not on the road hoping somebody will feel sorry for us and come feed we."

"They said to tell you that I'll be back in ninety-six hours."

"Leave. Get off of my land."

"Okay."

I hiked a few steps before I looked off to my left, just beyond one of the structures. I saw it all. Saw what the Rasta thought he had hidden. It was all congregated in neat piles. Windows. Doors. I saw a stockpile of construction materials that had been stolen and brought up here so that they could continue building illegally. I guess that they had found those, too, had found it all behind a locked door on the construction site of the big man from the Pines who was in business with the Barbarians.

The leader walked to one of the open pits. He opened the briefcase and fed a handful of the money to the flames. He looked at me to make sure I saw, then he fed the flames more money. I refused to be his audience. I refused to give him the reaction he yearned for.

I hiked down the slope, stepped over vines and rocks, moved around banana and mango trees, tamarind, the Atlantic Ocean so close, but the red-white-and-blue civilization I wanted so far away. A moment later, I looked back, looked beyond the self-constructed housing up into the trees. Made of rusted galvanized sheets and old wood on underdeveloped land. No sewage system. A soft breeze confirmed that I was near shitting grounds. Beautiful section of earth rising up into the hills. Dried grass and brittle trees surrounded the family's dwellings, a close-knit family living off of the land, food and herbs. Had figured out the issue. Because of having lived on the land, having been in the woods for four decades, they had certain legal entitlements. They were dealing with the Barbarians, not the gentlemen at Sagicor.

When I made it to the bottom, the team had arrived, was waiting.

I walked across land toward them and said, "Did you hear all of that?"

Dormeuil said, "We heard all of that. The transmission was clear from start to end and the organization heard every word. They gave him one last chance. They gave him the deal of a lifetime and he spat in our faces, spat in the faces of the Barbarians."

"I want my money. If they can drop that much money on that guy, I want mine. Pay the big man but keep the little man begging for food stamps. What, am I working for Walmart? Fuck that shit. I want my money and I want it now."

"You haven't been paid, none of us have been paid, because of this. A hold has been put on everything going out, on every paycheck, until this is cleared up. RCSI is in the red."

"The Barbarians are looking at bankruptcy because of this?"

"Money had been invested and was being laundered through this legitimate enterprise and now it's a dead project. The Rasta is holding our goddamn money hostage."

"They made a bad investment, and I have to suffer for that shit? Now what?"

"He took the money, grabbed the motza that you offered him to vacate the premises."

"Yes, he took it. You heard the transaction. I get it. You kept me out of the loop on this project, maybe to be sure that I was not in contact with the Rasta until this moment, left me in the dark until the curtain went up so you know that I wasn't in cahoots with him and I couldn't double-cross you."

"I'm like you, Reaper. I need to be paid, but I am a team player. I'm pissed too. We're down here hurting and the arrogant fuck just walked away with a half million in cash for doing nothing."

"He's burning the money. Throwing it on the open flames as a sign of protest."

"He must be mentally ill."

"Just a man with deep values."

"Better values than his have been sold for much less than the Barbarians are offering him."

"Now what?"

"Operation Blackout."

"Operation Blackout?"

"Or until we're Winchester, which, with the equipment RCSI sent, is very unlikely."

Winchester was military-speak for *out of ammunition.*

I said, "There are at least forty people up there."

"So, get your guns. Get your ammo. Get your knives. Grab a flame thrower. Climb into the all-terrain. We have been ordered to go into the bush and handle this now. All communication has been cut off. He can't make a call. No one will be able to hear them scream. They want this over with."

"I want no part of it. I've been kept in the dark. I'm walking."

"You'll do what we say and go where we say. Now, get geared up."

I removed my earpiece and threw it at their feet.

Zenga fired his gun, made the dirt and gravel around my feet dance. He fired until his clip was empty, and before the last bullet had hit the ground, he had put in a fresh clip.

I didn't jump. Didn't run. As dust rose around my feet, I turned and stared at him.

He said, "White nigga bitch, you have something to say?"

I lowered my head, took two steps like I was leaving. Zenga laughed.

I turned on my heels and ran at him, charged at him like I was a raging bull.

FORTY-NINE

I was on him, hungry, starving for a knockout punch, but had to settle for a hard blow to his nose. His nose shattered. Blood spattered. I drew first blood.

When he tried to swing at me, I was no longer there, but my left leg's roundhouse kick hit his bloodied nose two rapid times. The ground was gravelly and uneven, lost my balance. He charged swinging, dirt kicking from underneath his boot, a charging bull throwing haymakers. Two blows landed. One hit the side of my head, the other my arm. The head blow dazed me. If he had been a real fighter, he would have had me then. He grabbed me, pulled me chest to chest, and I gave him a head-butt that shocked him, did it again and made sure his nose was broken. He gripped me tighter. A brawler who fought like a bear. He expected me to try to push away, but I did the opposite, moved in, grabbed his hair, pulled his head to my mouth and bit his fucking ear; bit down, gripped the meat, wiggled my head, chewed until I had a corner of his ear in my bloody mouth. The pain jarred him. Then I struggled, got my arms free. Could hardly breathe. Was near passing out. I opened my arms wide and came in hard, slapped both of his ears as hard as I fuckin' could. He dropped me. But I still couldn't breathe. He grabbed my neck and choked me. He tried to come in closer, wanted to head-butt me in return, but I held my knee between us, and when he lost his balance in the gravel I opened my arms wide, came in fast and hard, slapped his ears again, then tried to dig my fingers into his eyeballs. He let me go and danced away in pain. Mouth bloodied, I spat his ear meat to the ground. I was panting. I was in pain. I was pissed off. I took a deep breath and ran after his ass, went after him while my lungs burned. He tried to throw dirt into my eyes, tried to blind me, but I turned my head away, closed my eyes, let my hair catch the debris. I ran and jumped, threw another kick that con-nected, then threw a second kick that missed. I feigned like I had lost my balance. That drew him in and when he was right where I wanted him, my leg shot out and my hook kick snapped, connected with the side of his head, hit his jaw with force, but missed his temple, what I had been aiming for. He backed away. I spat again, stepped toward him. He backed away again. I laughed. That enraged him. I had my wind now. I was ready for the death match. He threw punches and I blocked them all MMA-style, no bobbing and weaving, just stood straight and blocked, or slipped away, and each time I blocked, I threw a counterpunch or a kick that landed in his gut, hit his face, his busted nose. I did misdirection; faked like I was coming at him with my knee and when he moved to block, I went in for a punch, took a big leap and hit him across his face so hard it staggered him. Then I looked him in the eyes, grunted, and let him see that I was about to throw a left hook. When he raised his arms to block, he left his body exposed and I took that hook on a new path, managed a left hook to his right side, hit him in his liver, hit him hard and did my best to dig in behind his muscles; wanted him pissing blood. Hitting him was like hitting a brick wall, but I didn't stop banging on him as hard, fast, and deep as I could. I beat his right side but did my best to make my fist come out his left side. My opponent was right-handed, but when it came to fighting I was ambidextrous. He faltered, was coming apart. I had figured him out. He could only hit with one hand. My weak side was just as powerful as my strong side, kicks with my left leg just as fast and just as powerful and accurate as the kicks with my right. Roundhouse kicks smacked his face like jabs. Hard kicks to his thigh slowed his charge. I kicked his thigh and tried to cripple him. Then a spinning back kick made him double over. Zenga wanted to go for a gun. He wanted to pull his blade from his boot. That would be like admitting I had bested him. He came at me as I went after him. He grabbed my leg on my next kick, another spinning back kick, grabbed my leg and I knew that he was going to try to use his brute strength to spin me and throw me like I was a Frisbee, but I pushed off of the opposite leg before he had his grip, pushed and made my body spin in the air, and I caught him in the temple with the opposite heel. He let go of me and went down into the dirt, scrambled in the gravel, dazed. Then someone was behind me and they caught my spinning back fist. It was the black guy from Texas. He was trying to stop the fight, and that wasn't going to happen. His boy was getting his ass kicked and he wanted to stop the fight. Dormeuil told him to back off. Zenga was getting up. I ran to him and gave his face my right knee, gave it to his chin, hit him hard enough to make him need dental work. Then I grabbed a handful of dirt and threw it into his face, left him blinded and spitting away muck and blood. He went for his blade then. I kicked him in his ribs and he abandoned that course of action. He took another swing, found my leg, and yanked me off of my feet. I landed hard on my back. While I was down he then went for his blade again. As soon as he found the handle of his blade, before he had a good grip, I kicked his blade away from his hand. He came after me and I swept his feet from underneath him, made the big man fly, and when he crash-landed on his back, I was right there, relentless. I jumped up and came down on his gut with my knees, dropped all of my weight on him. He swung and caught my shoulder, knocked me back. I screamed and threw a hard blow into his groin, tried to hit his nuts so hard they would have ended up planted six feet under. He screamed. We fought. We wrestled and he pushed me on my back, was ready to beat my face to a pulp, but I caught him in a Brazilian jiu-jitsu chokehold, had him locked as he used his strength to turn us over and over. I never let him go. I couldn't let him go. My life depended on it. My foot was at ninety degrees. Had him where my thigh obscured his right shoulder and he couldn't use his arm to strike. My body was at an angle and I held his head tight with both of my hands, made his other arm immobile at the same time. He tried to use his strength to stand up, but I knew if he stood up, he would lift me and slam me to the ground, so I used my right arm and underhooked his leg. He was stronger up top than he was below the waist. I had him in the perfect triangle, my right instep underneath my left knee. I squeezed my thighs tight. I yelled and squeezed tighter. I had his ass. The sonofabitch wanted to tap out. He'd had enough. I let him go and he collapsed, unable to breathe. While he suffered, I grabbed the fallen gun, pushed the business end underneath his chin, pushed it deep into his flesh. Face dirtied, nose destroyed, part of his ear missing, he grabbed where his ear chunk used to be and stared up ·at me, stared at my dirtied face, my angry flesh, my scarred flesh, my bloodied and wounded flesh, tried to get a grip on my disheveled clothing, but it was too late. He panted and spat and felt the cold steel underneath his jawbone and knew that I could create pink mist. He scowled at my hardcore face, at the face of a Reaper.

Dormeuil called out in his Brooklyn accent, "MX-401."

I was in the zone, the hurting zone, the killing zone.

He snapped, "Reaper."

Now a wild animal, I snarled at the men, regarded the others. They stood watching like we were Romans battling in an arena. I had downed their Spartacus. David ruled Goliath.

Dormeuil said, "Enough."

"Hope you brought an extra-large body bag."

"Stand down or get shot down. Company orders are to stand down or get shot down."

"Anyone who pulls a gun is next. I'm a class

M with a fuckin' *X*. You know what we have to do to earn a forty, and I did it at goddamn level one. You motherfuckers will respect me."

"Stand down, stand down, stand down."

"You didn't tell this fucker to stand down when he fired on me."

"They are ordering me to shoot you if you don't comply in the next five seconds."

"He *fired* on me. It would be a fair kill."

"He didn't attack you. He fired at your feet. The rest was a fair fight."

"Who is nonpareil?"

"Let the man go."

"Who is nonpareil?"

"You are, Reaper. You are nonpareil."

"Tell this stupid sonofabitch what that means."

"It means you have no equal, Reaper."

"Say that again and say it louder."

"You won, Reaper. You are nonpareil. Now stand down."

"Tell whoever told you to shoot me to man up, get on a plane, get on a boat, ride a pelican, swim, I don't give a fuck, tell them to come down here to Barbados and meet me face-to-face to do their own dirty work. Tell them I said that. Tell them that I dare them to even fuckin' try."

"Reaper. Stand down."

Filthy from head to toe, I stood up over Zenga. While my attention was on the other men, Zenga kicked me backward, tried to kick me down, almost kicked the wind out of me. His blow had landed in my stomach, dead center. He kicked me like he wanted to destroy my ovaries. It hurt, but I didn't grab where I felt that mountain of pain. It hurt so bad I wanted to piss my pants. I ran to him and kicked him three times, once to his gut, then twice to his back when he doubled over. I raised my foot to stomp his head, to try to stomp his brains into the earth, but the pyromaniac grabbed me and pulled me off Zenga. He pulled me and within a half second I had flipped him and put his ass on the ground. He was terrified. I raised my foot to stomp on him, but he rolled away as fast as he could. I let him go. He knew that. I took a few steps back, doubled my fist, and shook it off. Zenga stood up, winded face bloodied, coughing, humiliated, no longer the ultimate Billy Badass.

I said, "How does it feel to have your ass handed to you by a girl?"

"Don't flatter yourself, you fucking lesbian."

"You can't believe a straight woman handed you your ass?"

"I'm not done with you. When this is done, we will meet again, Reaper."

He moved like he was coming after me, but the pyromaniac jumped in the way.

I turned to Dormeuil and said, "Tell your boy the next time he sneaks down to my safe house and tries to hit on me or tries to follow me or tries to do whatever foulness he intended to do, he will end up disarticulated and buried in a cane field in the Scotland area of the island."

Zenga barked, "White nigga bitch."

I opened fire, unloaded the fresh clip at his feet, made that bitch dance in the dirt, and when the clip was empty I tossed his gun back to him, made it land at his filthy feet.

Zenga went Hulk again and tried his best to get to me. The pyromaniac had a hard time holding him back, so Dormeuil jumped in. Dormeuil yelled for him to stand down.

Zenga showed his strength and determination and dragged both of them toward me.

I didn't move an inch. No surrender. No retreat. Too much Reaper in my blood.

Panting like a man gone mad, eventually Zenga stopped fighting them.

Dormeuil panted, "Reaper, Trinidad still isn't resolved. Not even close."

"Man up. You bitches need to man up. Blaming the girl, leaving her out to dry, sticking her in a cell, pretending she's not on your team, treating her like crap, that's a punk move."

"You killed two of their men."

"For the Barbarians."

"That wasn't what you were instructed to do."

"No matter what the fuck I did, they

should've had my back."

"You had a specific target."

"If the Barbarians don't like the way I work, tell them to either get me backup or send in a fuckin' drone. I did it by myself, completed the task, and that still wasn't good enough."

"Walk away and I have to put you down. You know the rules. One way out."

"Then fuckin' put me down. All along you've had three choices. Have my back. Leave me out here on my own. Or put a bullet in my head. No one at RCSI has had my back. They did leave me the fuck out here on my own. So as I walk away, after you kiss my black ass, do your thing, all of you fuckin' cowards, do your thing and shoot me in the back of my fuckin' head."

No hands raised. Another order came. I couldn't hear what was said.

They drew their weapons. Zenga pulled his the fastest. Dormeuil was last, reluctant.

I spat out blood, wiped my mouth.

I said, "Guns and bullets and assholes, oh my. You bitches don't scare me."

"MX-401."

"I'm not MX-401 anymore. I'm Reaper. I'm Goldilocks Reaper, motherfucker."

"You no longer work for the Barbarians?"

"I'm done. I no longer work for the Barbarians."

"You quit?"

"Draw your own conclusion. Record this

convo, shove it up your ass, and push Play."

"Anything else you want to say?"

"Blond is my natural hair color. I prefer the country to the city. I hate the Caribbean. And as of this moment, I am no longer MX-401. I am no longer a Barbarian. Fuck the Barbarians. You think I'm stupid. I'm not. The drug bust here, the dozen I put down, then the drug runner I de-spined and de-dicked the next day, all of that is tied to the LKs. That was LK property being moved by people who worked for that organization. The shipments you dumb fucks stopped in Miami and New York, all of that had to do with the LKs. They will be after you next. Just a matter of time. Let's see who the Barbarians send to back you up. We're deep in some shit and nobody wants to tell the fuckin' truth. I want to know why I had to do a hit in a bank, why the alarm didn't sound when I walked in with a gun, why a sniper couldn't have done that job. I want to know why the fuck the company is broke and I've been stuck here for eternity. I want to know who the fuck do you think I am, Boo Boo the Motherfucking Fool?"

I stood before them, calm. Waiting. Unblinking. Not backing down. Wishing that Petrichor was here, in the woods, her sniper's rifle ready.

Or her bow and arrow ready.

I wished she was here so we could have a

467

shootout, a showdown made for the front page.

I said, "Look at the smoke signals. You'd better get to work before Rasta man burns all the money. The company needs it. Look up in the sky. Guess that was another wasted investment."

Then I turned around and walked away in agony, did my best to walk like a champion.

I felt it. Guns remained drawn for execution. Fat fingers were on slim triggers.

With each step, I anticipated being shot in the back of the head.

Anticipated pink mist.

My eyes looked at the Caribbean sky; each footstep felt like it would be my last.

By the time I made it back to the colorful LIME truck that I had stolen for this journey, I was sweating profusely. Zenga had sucker-kicked me like I was nothing. Before that, each blow was brick. I sat in the stolen van with the air conditioner on high, but it didn't do any good.

A large truck was parked next to mine. Sixteen-foot Chefette truck. Refrigerated. Tandem axle, dual reefer, cold plate. The Barbarians were desperate. If they did like the Germans did during their Hitler days and stacked the dead like cordwood, it could hold one hundred bodies. I had been the last to know. The Barbarians had already hatched their evil plot, had machinated to rid themselves of their Rastafarian problem. This had been planned a long time ago. At least forty days ago.

I drove away, took to the lean roads, again the pathway in the area so rugged it felt like I was off-road, and every time the vehicle was tossed, it reignited the pain that I felt.

The men here were just mindless employees. They probably had no idea that money was in the package they had brought me, had been told to give it to me and they didn't ask questions.

They knew they would deal with squatters, people with brown skin they'd never see as their brothers and sisters, people who had no real weapons. They knew they had arrived to initiate genocide. The Barbarians had kept us separated for a reason. Had given them reasons to dislike and disrespect me before they arrived, so that bit of psychology was in play before our first meet at Six Roads Library. That was why they felt free to disrespect me. They were told that I hadn't earned any respect, regardless of whether I had earned an *M* and an *X*. No one knew where all the land mines were buried. Workers were given a task, did their job, got paid, never met anyone else unless they were forced to collaborate, so there was no chance of conspiracy, and no chance of knowing when your number was up. Your reputation was your job security.

They would come for me. Like the LKs, the Barbarians would come for me.

I was imprisoned on Alcatraz and sitting on death row.

I asked myself what I wanted to do before I died, what I wanted as a last meal.

FIFTY

Parish of St. James, the island's Platinum Coast
He took me from behind, and when I pushed
back up on my elbows, when I pushed up on
the palms of my hands, when I arched my
back and turned to look at him, the blindfolded man reached for me, the silhouette of
his right hand finding my neck, dominating,
squeezing.

He had me. I was weak. Closed my eyes.
He found my hair, pulled my head back, and
that pushed me over the edge. Orgasm. Felt
like I was going to black out.

In the nighttime, smoke continued to bil-
low and float up into starlit skies.

Each stroke was impressive. An orgasm had
come and gone, then ten strokes later I was
close to another orgasm, made intense
sounds, said the fifteenth letter of the alpha-
bet in many octaves. His heavy hand found
my lips, covered my mouth, muffled me, and
I chewed his fingers, panted, put my nails in
his skin. He didn't ease up. We battled.

Grunted. I felt weak. Felt submissive. Then I took a breath and again was fierce and strong.

His stroke lightened; he gave me room to breathe, to recuperate.

He said, "You okay?"

"Cunnilingus included in my duty-free package?"

"All-inclusive. You want it now?"

"Yes, please. Lick me. Eat me. Put your tongue inside me. I need that."

He was good. Deliberate. I gripped his head. Held on. He sucked that part of me like he was trying to give me a hickey. Soon, again, I was loud. Shuddered. Didn't think it was possible to feel the utmost again. That was my first time coming on a man's tongue, putting orgasm inside of a man's mouth. I pulled his face back up to me, pushed him back on the bed, mounted him. Rode him hard. Took deep breaths and rode him, my groove sinuous and intense.

Soon we turned over and I pulled him back between my legs.

I said, "Hard. Deep. Fast. Harder. Deeper. Faster. Harder. Faster. Harder."

Exhausted, suffocating, I coughed, wheezed, and loosened my grip on my rented lover, loosened my legs, legs that felt heavier than osmium. Chest heaving, he ran his hands over my body, groaned as he tried to move, then caught his breath and grinned. The sensation

472

faded and an unwanted reality came back in degrees. With the encouragement from the palms of my hand, he rolled away from me, sweaty, just as winded. The air conditioner hummed. Cool air blew across my heated body like an Arctic breeze.

He whispered, "Shite."

"Yeah. Shite."

I fixed my eyes on the guns I had left on the dresser, then looked at the bruises on my arm, on my shoulder, on my thighs. I took a gun and went to the front door, made sure it was still locked, turned all lights on, saw nothing, only a naked man blindfolded. Then turned the lights off, double-checked the doors again, and eventually went back to the man I owned for a while.

I removed the condom from his John Thomas, flushed it, limped back, took a wipe, cleaned him, flushed that too, then I sat down on the carpet and took a few deep breaths as I massaged my temples. Stress remained. I did push-ups, then sat back and wiped away sweat.

A moment passed. He said, "You're toned. You feel athletic."

"Skydive, mountain climb, horseback ride, kayak, snow ski, motorcycle race, Jet Ski, martial arts, salsa, tango, hip-hop, soca, country line dancing, have done it all."

"I can tell. You have marks on your skin. Felt them when I held you."

"Noticed you have a few marks too. There is a thick scar near your spine. Saw another on your leg and another one on your left arm, behind the right shoulder."

I handed him a fresh condom, impatiently watched him roll it on. Then I made sure that it was on the way it should be on. I stroked him and I squatted over my rented lover.

He sucked my breast as I rode him. He bit my nipple, sucked it hard.

Orgasm came. When it ended, I rode him until another one arrived.

FIFTY-ONE

Air-conditioning hummed, sent cool air over hot, dank skin.

We lay naked without touching. I didn't rush to end my conjugal visit, not this time. Nothing was outside this room but heat, bugs, and death. Weapons within reach, I fed him seedless black grapes and American cherries. I fed him and looked at my injuries, then at his scars. Three deep cuts.

My phone rang. The one I had left on, the one used to contact Big Guy. I left my lover where he was, picked up my phone, picked up a gun, stepped into the luxurious bathroom, left the door open, kept my eyes on my blindfolded escort, on the chilly room.

"Reaper."

"What's up, Big Guy?"

"Bad time?"

"I'm on the way to grab a bite and was just about to send you a text."

"Swing by here. I have your passports."

"How many?"

"I have all eight."

"All eight?"

"Just like you asked for."

"How do they look?"

"Clean. Need to you come to Collymore Rock and pick these up so we can be done."

"What's the rush? Not like you have regular office hours."

"You know about the change in the weather and the storm, right?"

"Been busy. What storm?"

"A tropical storm formed. Now it's racing toward the Lesser Antilles."

"Didn't know. I don't watch local television and nobody BBMs me."

"It's the storm that people have been blogging about for the past couple of days."

"I don't read blogs."

"National Hurricane Center issued an advisory. Barbados, St. Lucia, Dominica."

"Like I said, while it's calm, I'm about to grab a bite to eat."

He paused and swallowed. "Where are you going?"

"Masala Grill."

"How long will you be there, Reaper?"

"Nobody seems to be in a rush and no one is talking about a storm, so I should be here at least an hour, maybe an hour and a half if I meet a sexy Bajan to chat and drink a beer or two or three with."

"Come here when you're done. Would like

to get these passports out of my hands."

"You know what, I'll just order and bring my food with me."

"No, it's fine. Stay there and eat. I'm working on something and need to focus."

"Okay, see you after I eat. Will get there before the storm hits."

He killed the call first. I pulled my bottom lip in, nodded.

Big Guy had said eight passports. I had ordered six.

His voice was smooth, I understood the message. Eight people were there with him. At least eight. That's what he was telling me.

They had linked me to him and they were trying to get my location.

Barbados was a noose tightening around my neck.

Someone was eager to kick the chair from underneath my feet.

I put the phone down, kept the gun at my side, went back near the bed. The money I was saving, my stash, it was down at Six Roads. Wished that I had kept it with me. Wished that I had stolen as much as I could from the dead cricketer's crib. Wished I had been the first one on the island to rob an armored car, three banks, and four gas stations on the same day.

My date asked, "Everything okay?"

I dragged my fingers down my face, grinned at my last meal.

477

He repeated, "Everything okay?"

"Everything is as it should be."

"What are you thinking?"

"A storm is coming. I should leave, but I want to fuck you again before it arrives."

"You're wicked."

"Every fuck I fuck is like it could be my last fuck, so be ready for a good fucking."

I turned on the television, the local news. The world had changed in the last hour. Unending queues at every gas station, all Trimarts and Super Centres overflowing with customers rushing to buy bottled water, batteries, torch lights, and canned food. Buses had stopped running. Workers were being sent home early, especially those who relied on public transportation to get to the other side of the island. Barbados was in a state of controlled panic.

He heard the broadcast and said, "Tomas left a bad taste in our mouths."

"Everyone's trying to be prepared this time."

"Not everybody. Just the smart people. Most won't do anything but play in the water."

I turned the TV off, licked my lips, went to him, and said, "You're not Bajan."

"Guyanese."

"How did you end up with this gig?"

"After the injury, after I lost my job, one thing led to another and I did massages for a while. Randy customers kept flirting and asking for massages with happy endings."

"Female sex tourism. British and American women travel the world to misbehave."

"I was naïve to what women did. Times were bad, was behind on rent, behind on bills, my boys needed money for camp and needed new shoes, and a British woman offered me a large amount of money. She paid me more in thirty minutes than I could make the entire month. Took pressure off me."

"Before this, what were you doing to make a living?"

"Before I was stabbed, I worked telecommunications. Was made redundant. Big men in England cut off our phones and cable and gave us our walking papers without notice. Ruined my life."

"How much time did you lose after you were attacked?"

"Six months."

A moment went by. I gave him another condom.

I turned over, was facedown on the bed, pillow underneath my waist, my hips raised, and he found me, entered me.

I moaned.

He held the edges of the pillow like reins, rode me, my hands grabbing the sheets. I should've done this over forty days ago. Should've done it every day since I'd been here.

FIFTY-TWO

I tied my date to a chair, his restraints not tight but not loose. It was time for me to take my georgie bundle and move on to the next episode. I put my backpack on the bed, took out my gear, began to dress. He sat in the chair, listening to me move, listening to me get organized.

I said, "Thanks for the getaway from reality."

"I like you."

"What?"

"I like you."

"You don't know me. Having sex didn't make us acquaintances. This is business; that's all."

"You're amazing in bed."

"What nationality do you think I am?"

"Ethiopian, maybe Somali, but raised in America."

"You're good."

"I would love to take you on a date."

"You have two kids and an ex-wife who

likes knives."

"She and me, we done. She can fall into a latrine for all I care."

He said that and something inside of me shifted. I said, "You'll never be done. Your sons will always want Mommy and Daddy to be in bed together, like in the movies. They will root for you two to reconcile and remarry. Even if that won't happen, they will still want that. Kids are like that. Even if I dated you, even if I took them to eat at Bubba's four times a week, took them to Casa Grande to play games, to the Harrison caves for kicks, to a different beach every weekend, and did their laundry once a week and cooked their meals three times a day, even if I were the perfect lover to you and sucked your dick like a porn star and swallowed and was the perfect stepmom for them, they would still want you and Mommy together. Kids fantasize unrealistic fantasies, just like adults. Don't be unrealistic. Your scars — someone tried to kill you, marked her territory. You have been cut open and stitched closed."

"You can see my scars, but I can hear yours. Pain in your voice like a chigger has burrowed in your skin and making you itch bad."

"She'll start calling you for no reason, will call early in the morning while you're fucking me good and ping you late at night while you're getting sucked to orgasm, will blow up your phone just because she can, making up

481

emergencies, will do it because she knows you're with someone else, and that disrespect would provoke me, and that would turn ugly. You come across as a father your kids will be more than proud to call their daddy. Sounds like you sacrifice for them. You do this, sell your body, take health risks, compromise yourself, whether you enjoy it or not, and you do it to put food on the table and keep a roof over their heads. You might not be with the ex-wife, might not be fucking her at the moment, but she has her hooks in you, in your life, in your mind, in your wallet. You have to communicate. You're still family, a broken family, like it or not. She has the right to ping you when she wants your attention."

"Is that what happened to you and your ex?"

"New dick never cancels out old dick when a woman is in love."

"Are you talking about me or you now?"

"Was it after sex? Why was she trying to win Deboner of the Year?"

"When she was served papers, she was outraged. She thought it insane that a woman should help take care of the children we made, said it wasn't her responsibility. So I said let the court sort it out so we'd both be clear. She talked to her lawyer. I talked to mine. We had a court date. Then she called me to come over and sort it out, said that maybe we could do this without having to do it in public court, and when I arrived she was calm, smiled, invited me in for dinner. We ate, talked, started a reasonable negotiation. I had my list of custody issues. Nothing extreme. Pick them up a couple of times a week from school. Spend a couple of hours with them. Or keep them overnight and take them to school the next day. She loved to party too much to have the boys overnight. Fine. We went over them one by one. She had excuse after excuse after excuse. Things were tense. We had drinks. You know how it goes."

"So it was after sex. After you had your orgasm, while you were weak, distracted. You're bigger than her, stronger than she is, but once you busted that nut, you were vulnerable, a black-bellied sheep."

"I feel stupid now."

"She played you the way many men have been seduced, sexed, and killed. Pussy and poison, the two weapons a woman has used since she realized she could outwit a man."

"She threatened to kill me if I didn't take her name out of court."

"I bet her name comes up every day. The kids ask for her. They bring up her name in the middle of conversations that have nothing to do with her. Can't break free when you share a kid, not if you're responsible. You and she have two kids. Her name is on the birth certificate. On insurance papers. On school papers. Her name is on every document regarding the child."

"It was really bad for you, the relationship you were in."

"I didn't get stabbed in my sleep. Didn't get cut like a pig in a slaughterhouse."

"I was lucky to survive and I have moved on. I assure you that I have."

"You have kids and you can only move so far. If she's on the island, this small island, you guys are on the same roads, see the same people, have the same friends. You can't move on. You'll run into each other at the grocery store, give each other lights on the road. You can't move on. I moved on. Glad I can pack up my georgie bundle and go on; divorce myself from a man and his lunatic ex and their family and personal issues. Your feet have dried in the concrete."

"All that aside, I'd like to take you out on a date. Just a simple date. It can be fancy; we could go to a restaurant, or we could just go to Oistins on a slow night so we can sit, eat, talk."

"A smart businessman shouldn't become involved with his customers."

"I could make an exception."

"An intelligent woman would never become involved with the help."

" 'The help.' "

"Crazy women. Fights. You are offering what I've already escaped."

" 'The help.' "

"Never processed how I felt in detail, not until tonight. So, thank you for that relief. Also, thanks for the invitation to a front-row seat at your drama. I'm honored, but no thanks."

I went to him. His stiffness was spongy, like cotton. I didn't tingle anymore.

I whispered, "This isn't *Pretty Woman* in reverse."

"I know."

"Sorry I called you the help."

The room felt as cold as my words. Winds picked up. Rain would come soon.

He whispered, " 'New dick never cancels out old dick when a woman is in love.' "

"That's the truth." I straddled him. "You have good dick. Be glad she didn't cut it off. I'm glad she didn't cut it off. I enjoyed it."

He laughed a little. "You're heavier. You feel at least twenty pounds heavier."

I kissed him. Gave him my tongue. We kissed for a long time. It was nice. It wasn't the sex that was worth the money. It was the conversation. I could've fucked anybody. But not many would have given me the conversation that nailed in the realization that what I'd had with Johnny Parker was no good.

I was free from that prison. I'd never ping-ping-ping him again.

My lover's alarm sounded again. That meant my time was up with Orgasm Man. I traced my finger across his softness, kissed his lips, untied one of his hands, then walked to the door.

I said, "All the best."

I walked out the door, into the wind and rain. While we had talked, I had opened my overloaded backpack and put on my concealment clothing, had debated with him as I dressed for war. Two pistol-grip Pepperblasters. Four blades. Handguns were worn in my concealment clothing, .38 rested underneath my left arm, a Glock was strapped to my right hip, another gun on my right side, and a .380 was on my belt clip. There were more toys of death in my weighted backpack.

Again my throwaway cellular rang. The ID displayed Black Jack's contact number, Bajan digits I never should have seen again. Something was wrong. Could have been whoever separated his head from his body and made soup in the plunge pool. Could be the police finally getting around to playing detective. Cops could've had Black Jack's phone and were redialing his last calls.

The island went dark. Lights in every business in the area shut off. Not everyone had a generator. No streetlights. That made the roads shrink, made headlights brighter. Right away, accidents. Everyone was forced to slow down, the abrupt darkness like a total eclipse. The cellular rang again and again. I pulled over to the side of the road at a rum shop. Black Jack's number still flashing on the caller ID. In the new darkness, the digits glowed like a ghost. Reluctantly, I answered.

A frantic, desperate voice said, "Reaper?"

It was indeed a call from the dead, from far beyond the grave.

FIFTY-THREE

The power outage hit St. Lucy, St. Peter, St. James, Michael, and Christ Church while I was on the road. The East Coast might have been just as dark from St. Andrew down to where the Atlantic side kissed the other side of Christ Church as well. The major power outage and Black Jack's call disrupted my nerves. Within minutes, Barbados was darker than the '03 North American Blackout.

By the time I pulled into Sheraton Mall, the car park was a bat's cave, empty of vehicles, the bleak weather a deterrent. I entered the parking structure near Olympus Theatre and found a lone car on the far end of the second level. A dirty Mini Cooper branded with the British flag. I parked fifteen car lengths away, then left my bike facing the car, running, lights on and in their eyes, blinding them to my position. I removed my helmet, took out a gun, and called for them to get out of the car, but not too fast.

At first, I thought I was facing a child, was

being set up Iraqi-style, that a child strapped with a bomb was about to come running toward me, but I was wrong.

I marched her way. "If I hear any sound, see anyone, you're fucked. Understand?"

"I understand."

Her legs were thick, her breasts of a woman's size, her body curvaceous, only she was four feet tall, maybe four-foot-five in her heels. She was a girl with clear skin, hair thick and in powerful dreadlocks. She wore tight jeans, a red T-shirt with a political message: T'INGS DREAD WE VOTING FA DE RED. Nothing was in her hands. No one was in the shadows.

I asked, "Who are you?"

"I'm Hacker."

"Hacker is dead and is a two-piece at Downes Funeral Home."

"I'm not dead."

"Who died?"

She told me that she had been at Black Jack's townhome, had been trying to hack into the LKs' system again, had broken in, extracted information, but a firewall went up. She had enjoyed the game, outsmarting the LKs. Then another girl came over, another UWI student, a Bajan girl that Black Jack was sleeping with. Black Jack hadn't expected her. It was a surprise.

I lowered my gun, said, "She came over and you left?"

"I kept working and they went upstairs to the bedroom."

"When did you leave?"

"Black Jack received a phone call, then asked me to pick up a package, said it was down by the docks, down at Bridgetown Port. He said it was an easy job. I'd pull up, blow my horn four times and someone would put a few boxes in the car and I'd drive off and go back to his place."

"So you were gone when he was attacked."

"Soon as he asked, I walked out the door. It was time-critical. I was lucky."

"Did you see the garbage truck? Bright-red cab with a dull-gray dumpster?"

"They gave me lights when they passed."

"They saw you leave the community, but had no idea who you were."

"If he hadn't sent me to go pick up the package, if the other girl hadn't come over . . ."

"Where have you been since then?"

"Hiding. Scared to death. Constipated and sleeping in my new car."

"Scared."

"Very fucking scared. I saw them dead, before their bodies were discovered."

"How?"

"I went back by the town house."

"Doors were locked."

"I have a key."

"You have a key? Were you sleeping with

Black Jack too?"

Her voice trembled. "Long time ago. Last year. A one-off, became a two-off, became a three-off. We had sex. Two or three or ten times, depends on how you count it. By number of days, three days. Three good days. By number of times, between ten and twelve."

"You and Black Jack."

"We sort of ended up in bed, cuddling, playing footsie, and you know."

"Plunge pool and air-conditioning and home-cooked meals."

"It was the best."

"Okay. But you're not . . . weren't in rotation anymore?"

"I guess we ended up being friends. Guess he did it out of curiosity. Many men want to try to hook up with me, well, because, well, I'm unique and I'm a fetish, so to speak."

"Okay. Why did you go back after they had been killed?"

"The computer was mine. I needed it for university. It was gone. So whoever has it has my information. I'm scared. I found his cell phone. I knew your number was in there, so I went down the line, called everybody Black Jack had called until you answered. Wanted to get this illegal stuff out of my car, and since it was for you, I figured that you should get it all."

We went to the car's trunk. Two boxes too heavy for Hacker to lift. I opened the boxes.

She saw what was in one of the boxes and asked, "Are those hand grenades?"

"Sure are. Grenades. C4. Timers."

"He sent me to pick up explosives?"

"His contact came through. What else did you find when you hacked their systems?"

"Reaper, they're looking for you. Last thing I saw before I left Black Jack's place to make this run was that they had followed you from Trinidad to wherever you went next."

"How do they track me?"

"Two doses of facial recognition software, a dose of luck, and a pound of patience."

"Still not easy to find me, not if I stay in poor lighting, not if I use makeup, not if I keep my head down so they can't get a full profile, not if I keep my sunglasses on, keep my hair long and loose to frame my face, or find one of a thousand ways to partially cover my face and I change my walk. I never have the same walk twice; never have the same posture or body language."

"When you were in a bank, you raised your head for a second. Something about a shoot-out. The video is on YouTube. Saw it. It's posted in a collection of street killings in Trinidad. You raised your head long enough for them to get the information they needed."

"Shite. Yeah. Guy pulled a gun, so I went into survival mode, raised my head."

"They are using a high-end algorithm to analyze the relative position, size, and shape of the eyes, nose, cheekbones, and jaw, then using that info to search for other images with matching features. They went through every passport that left Trinidad. They ran that for about a month, then restarted, brought in another expert, upgraded to software that uses 3D sensors to capture information about the shape of a face. It looks at unique features: the contour of the eye sockets, nose, and chin. They're doing, or have done, a skin-texture analysis as well. They matched the blood vessels in your derma. You're lucky that they haven't found you already."

"Sure it was them? Black Jack had his hands in many things. He was an arms broker, hired contract killers, and I have no idea what else. The hit here, you're sure that it was the LKs and not something else that Black Jack was involved in?"

"Positive. I broke back into their site again, only I did it up at the library at UWI. Two of them flew here and flew right back. Didn't check into a hotel. They flew business class."

"You broke in again."

"As my way of saying fuck you, from a safe distance. I'm smarter. I needed to see what they knew about me. My contact list was synced from my phone, plus I have some personal porn I really don't want anybody to see because if they did I'd have to move from Barbados. Anyway. They have my handle, they know about Hacker, but they thought

493

that they had killed Hacker, so I will let Hacker be dead for now. They came to kill me, Black Jack, and anyone in the house."

"You said you saw the aftermath, saw them beheaded."

"After I spent some time with this guy and he made me bowlegged, I went back around five in the morning, opened the door, walked in, figured they were upstairs bupping the headboard. Then I stepped in something sticky, turned on the lights and saw blood on my shoes, looked up and saw their bloody heads two feet away from me on the counter. I slipped in the blood, ran to the back door, was running to get away and I stumbled. I fucking fell into the plunge pool. I fell in face-first with headless bodies. Face-first. Almost drowned in their meat and blood."

"Wow."

"Be glad it wasn't you he had with him upstairs making bowlegged that time."

"We were all business. I had no interest in letting him make me bowlegged."

"If the other girl hadn't come by, it might've been me up there naked and dead."

"Thought you said those days of bupping his headboard were behind you."

"He was good in bed. I had hopes. I wasn't over there all the time and flirting and working for him for free just because. Sure you weren't sleeping with him?"

"Strictly business. No other interests."

"When did you get there?"

"When the garbage truck was leaving, after four in the morning."

"I left as the truck was arriving just past midnight."

"Four hours."

"Four long hours."

She sobbed. I didn't. I looked at the boxes, at the BMW motorcycle I was rocking.

The rain fell harder. Visibility lessened. The big storm was moving in.

I said, "LKs were booked on two flights to Barbados."

"At least ten were on the reservation list. Others had flown to Grenada."

I inhaled, held it, exhaled, clenched teeth, said, "I'm going to need your car."

"No. I spent all of my money for this car. This is my first true car. I'll drop you off."

"Sure you want to do that? You're a woman easy to describe rocking a car that is easier to describe. If they catch me in the car, again they'll think they have found Hacker. If they catch you riding with me and they are after me, well, they won't give a fuck who you are."

"Will you drop me somewhere?"

"No."

"You're going to leave me in the dark? Alone?"

"If they're looking for you, I'll be in your car. If they are after me, you won't be with me."

"What should I do about getting my car back?"

"You have insurance?"

"Yeah."

"Report it stolen."

"Should I kiss it good-bye?"

"Depends on how you feel about it."

FIFTY-FOUR

Upper Collymore Rock

Five SUVs were in the immediate area. All black. All with tinted windows. One was in the lot at Channel Grocery Store, the one facing the plaza where Big Guy's shop was located. One was across the road at Payne's Plaza. The engines were on. The windshield wipers moved every now and then, wiped away water to yield visibility. The only light came from businesses with generators.

Big Guy didn't have a generator, but at least three people in his space held flashlights.

Phone service was still on. I messaged Big Guy.

IT'S REAPER.

YOU'RE HERE?

LOOK IN THE HALLWAY. LEFT YOUR FOOD ON THE STEPS.

Whoever looked out saw two dead men.

497

One with a knife wound in his heart, the other with his neck broken, his face now facing his back and looking up toward the clouds.

My cellular vibrated.

I knew it would ring. I answered with a smile.

I said, "I hate Barbados, and I really needed those passports."

"Your Kiwi accent is gone."

"Is this better, War Machine?"

"That is a voice I will never forget."

"Does this Kiwi accent get your wanker hard?"

"Who are you working for?"

"Do you want to hire me? I'm a bloody GDI now."

"Who sent you to Trinidad?"

"I was working for the shell corporation RCSI. Ask the guy you're holding hostage. Keep away from his coffee. It tastes like day-old horse-shit, not that I have had day-old horseshit. Tell him I said that it's okay to tell you all he knows, if he's not dead. If you contact the Barbarians, better known as RCSI, they will deny my existence. My association with the Barbarians, that's over now."

"So you're not protected."

"Only during sex."

"Why didn't you stay hidden? Why didn't you run?"

"Since you came this far to see me, I figured I'd show up for the fete."

"Come here. Come out of the rain. Let's sit here and talk."

"No. We should meet. Just you and me, or me and one of your men. Pick a man. Any man. You can pick Appaloosa. I don't give a fuck. He brings one weapon. I bring one weapon."

"You won't win."

"Your guntas like swords. I can handle one. He could bring two swords as long as I am supplied with the same number and of the same quality. Or we could just go toe-to-toe. We meet in Queen's Park or on the field at Kensington Oval and battle like Roman gladiators. I win, I walk away and you stop looking for me, forget I ever existed, take your dead gunta, go back to being whatever scum you were before. You can go after RCSI, kill the Barbarians, I don't care. I just want no part of it."

"I find you fascinating. Come to me. Let's talk this over."

"I'm not going to be bound and gagged and burned alive in a park. Not my kind of barbecue."

"Where are you, Kiwi? Where are you?"

"I'm across the road from you at Payne's Plaza. How many SUVs do you guys have?"

I saw that his men moved in that direction, guns aimed. They were nowhere near me.

I shattered a window, the sole window to Big Guy's office. Men yelled like boys. I threw them a pair of flash-bang grenades to play with. It was enough to shock and disorient the hive of guntas.

I was about to pull the pin on a real grenade, but Big Guy screamed.

He wasn't dead.

The men at Payne's Plaza zoomed to my side of the road. The SUV parked in front of Channel did the same. I threw the grenade toward them, the explosion making both of them veer and stop. Disoriented guntas on my side of the road in Big Guy's office were treated to tear gas. Metal bars were on the windows so there was only one way out, and they fled, stepped out as I stood up high, gun in hand. They felt the sting of hot lead. Weapon-heavy, I was on the roof, soaked in rain. Had come through the Pine, took the flooded back road that snaked to Upper Collymore Rock, then parked in the KFC lot. There were no back doors to the offices on the second level, so they wouldn't need to watch the back of the building, but two men did walk the perimeter. I moved through the rain and darkness, with a silencer on one of my weapons and with two quick pops, the dead count was up to four. I had carried enough stretchable shock cord and made my way to the roof. Without a plan, without a team, without Barbarians in my corner, I had accepted my invitation to be the guest of honor, had arrived, and now the party had officially started.

Guntas fled the building, senses shattered.

I gunned them down, fired and fired and fired, until they regrouped and returned fire.

I dropped down low and rolled, infrareds up to my eyes, reloading, firing. That was what I did until I saw Appaloosa step out of his SUV carrying a large weapon. The winds blew his payload and took it toward Mane Attraction, all but destroyed that building. He had a rocket launcher. A game changer. Fear almost arrested me. Fires raging, I hardball-pitched three grenades at them, hit one SUV and missed the other two, then ran away, bolted across the top of the building and jumped, an explosion behind my back.

Holding on to the stretchable cord.

Hoping I didn't lose my grip.

I tumbled.

I fell into the arms of gravity.

FIFTY-FIVE

I had survived the fall, cut the cord as it stretched, and landed on my feet, but had to roll and rise up running. When I vanished behind KFC, someone else had come up the road in a car. The moment they turned on the main road, the LKs lit them up. Anyone who stepped out into the streets, they were gunned down. They didn't know where I was, if I was alone, so all of Barbados had become their enemy. Then I came out roaring in the Mini Cooper. I hit the main road and passed the poor soul who had been gunned down. They were gunning everyone down. The rear window of my escape vehicle shattered. Glass flew like tiny knives, forced me to close my eyes for a moment. Heart tried to beat out of my chest. Rapid fire came from a dozen guns. The Shell gas station exploded, the projectile sent by Appaloosa barely missing the Mini Cooper. The ground shook as flames, smoke, and shrapnel reached into the dark sky, clawed at the falling rain. Locals had come out, had been on the side of the road like they were watching an action movie, BBMing until they caught fire or were shot. Sobs, curses, and prayers went from their mouths to God's ears. The gas-station explosion caused the LKs to duck for cover, gave me a moment without being fired on. People had already raced outside in the rain and wind. More fuckin' BBMers. Houses were along the main road and people had heard noise and come out. Many caught lead and fell to the ground. I made a hard U-turn, doubled-back by the car that had been riddled with bullets, its driver a victim of pink mist, and took the fight away from this neighborhood, circled though the flaming Shell parking lot, bounced out onto the main road.

LKs recovered from the brunt of the explosion and were in their SUVs within seconds. Adrenaline rushed, flooded my system the way the storm was flooding the roads. I fishtailed, corrected the car, took the anorexic road next to KFC, sideswiped a half-dozen cars as I fled, accelerated through the dark serpentine roads that led into the midnightness of the Pinelands, then was forced into a hard, skidding left where it ended at Pine East-West Boulevard. Streets were slick. Couldn't tell if a tire had been murdered, felt like it had for a moment, the road so rugged at this place, then I was forced into a hard right before Pine Gardens. I shot up the border of Two Mill Hill that fed into and ended at Government Hill. The road curved in their favor and they fired, forced me to make a left. Book Source exploded as I turned. They had anticipated that move. An explosion landed to my right, then the giant iPhone on the right in front of the LIME head office exploded. When I swerved into the next lane, the same happened to the cellular company's car park and lobby. It was a straight shot to Tweedside Road. I killed my headlights, knew that would darken my taillights, and kept my foot from the brake, pressed the accelerator through the floor, zoomed through a red light, and approached yet another roundabout where I would have to decide if I would let it regurgitate me toward Harmony Road or throw me onto Roebuck Street. Headlights were in my rearview, were in both lanes by the time I came up on Sawh's Supermarket. Bombs exploded around me. Rampant destruction testified to their level of anger. More innocent bystanders became casualties. This had too much momentum to stop now. Water gushed from broken mains. Broken glass littered the road. Backpack on the passenger seat, I reached over, found a grenade of my own, pulled the pin, dropped it out the window. Any sane man would have backed off by now.

At my feet, my cellular rang and rang and rang and rang.

Headlights became larger in my rearview, came at me fast, and bullets came faster.

I dropped another grenade and thought I saw an SUV explode, three vehicles back. Headlights kept coming, the bogeymen with xenon eyes turned up high in hopes of blinding me each time I looked in the mirror. I made hard turns, hit snaking roads, hit narrow streets.

They chased me into Bridgetown.

The LKs sideswiped cars parked near St. Mary's Church and the Old Synagogue. The rain put visibility at a minimum, the blackout left me able to see only a few feet ahead, but all they had to do was follow my taillights. Synagogue Lane. Coleridge Street. Magazine Lane. The flooded streets of Bridgetown were my enemy. Explosions were swallowed by the howl of the winds as flames succumbed to the storm. All I could do was try to outrun them, make a turn and lose them, hope the lead car crashed and caused them to pile up. They matched my speed, moved into the delirious winds at over 170 kilometers per hour. My heart rate accelerated, palms sweated, teeth clenched as my enthusiastic hunters came closer, refused to allow their trembling prey to escape its fate.

FIFTY-SIX

From the passenger seat, Kandinsky barked over the roar of the storm, "War Machine."

"Read the readout."

Kandinsky shouted, "Winds near forty. Rain accumulations between two and six inches."

"We've lost more men. We have to recover the bodies and the injured."

"The third team is doing that now. Incredible. The Kiwi will pay."

"Nothing that we do to her will be sufficient, nothing will raise our dead."

"She will pay."

"We will rush the capture, but we can't rush this death."

"Helicopters?"

"When the wind dies."

War Machine and his men had attacked the island of Barbados before they attacked their target.

There was no electrical current and that blackness would obscure all that they did.

Diamond Dust had commanded second-tier guntas to strike the substations at Belmont Road, Government Hill, Pine Garden, and by the Garrison, and they had destroyed them all. Barbados would be dark for many days and nights with no power other than generator power. The roaring island was as dark as the bottom of a grave.

War Machine grimaced, and they accelerated into the winds.

Then he was less than five yards behind the Kiwi, close but not close enough, speeding the wrong way up a one-way street that would end in a *T* at the Bridge House. She would be forced to go left or right, but going left would send her into a dead end behind the Bridge House. The Kiwi would be forced to go to the right, would be forced to slow to make that sharp turn. Slow or slide. Her brake lights flashed. War Machine accelerated and smashed the rear of the vehicle. Contact was strong and dead on point, clipping the left bumper, forcing a spinout to the right. That, combined with the winds, was more than enough to make the Kiwi lose control.

The incensed winds advanced his opponent's skidding turn and blew her vehicle off the road near the docks of Bridgetown, as if the gods had reached down and thrown her, had sent her flying, her battered vehicle airborne and doing a 300-degree turn. The winds and slick road and War Machine's unrelenting speed did him no special favors, shoved his car at least thirty yards beyond his target, the second car in his team on his bumper, sliding and spinning as well, striking him hard enough to make his head jerk backward, ramming him and sending both teams into a second harsh, sliding spin. A few seconds of disorientation was an eternity.

It was long enough for the Kiwi to extricate herself from her mangled vehicle and flee, but not before she had thrown a grenade, one that exploded nowhere near them.

Still, they paused, tensed, anticipated, waited for another.

The winds howled, the force strong. That power delayed War Machine and his men from opening their car doors, but within seconds they were all out, guns aimed, all firing in hopes of a lucky shot, something that would slow if not halt the Kiwi's, that Woman of a Thousand Faces', retreat. The curses of gunfire were swallowed by the storm's incessant roar.

War Machine saw her in the distance, guns no use in the wind.

He led the charge in that direction.

The Kiwi fought her way through the torrent, headed for the bridge and Independence Arch. Boats and catamarans were in the Careenage, but the storm made those of no use. Her only option would be to vanish into the shops and bars in that section, maybe race to the BIDC car park and commandeer another vehicle and try to escape again, but gusts of wind shoved the Kiwi in the opposite direction, toward the inlet, forced her to stay in the open and accept the punishment from the storm. Abrupt gusts that left her holding on to anything that she could use to keep from being blown down, or swept away and tossed into the violent sea.

Weighed down by their weapons of choice and carrying artillery, War Machine and the Laventille Killers battled the same forces of nature. Sweat blended with the rain, with the salty sprays from the sea that were mixing with the downpour. Weapon in each hand, War Machine stood between Appaloosa and Kandinsky. Guerrero, anxious, was reloading his guns. They all gave chase, ran against the winds, fired at will. The Kiwi fled, ran like a track star, at times pausing long enough to return fire. The wind was in her favor and she ran like she was the bastard child of the God of Thunder and an African wind rider.

War Machine growled and suppressed his never-ending rage.

Appaloosa motioned behind them, called out to the rest of the LKs.

Red and blue lights flashed in the darkness, brightened the down-pour, their arrival announced by the scream of sirens. They had company. Five police cars pulled up, each blue and white, arriving on the heels of the one before, arriving with unbridled fear and determination.

War Machine motioned like he was a god that controlled all that surrounded him. His team spread out, opened fire on the officers. They created a dozen widows and countless fatherless children without hesitation. That done, they turned back to their elusive prey.

She fled across a narrow bridge that led to all the shopping areas.

On that side of the main street was a maze of narrow streets, a spider's web of escape routes built in the same style that those across the pond in the UK had used for theirs.

The side of a two-level fast food eatery called Chefette exploded, sending a roar into the storm and purple and golden debris flying into the center of the main road.

War Machine motioned to lower the launcher. His team member did as commanded.

Anger swallowed thoughts as they sweated, grunted, and chased.

The Kiwi had changed her course, cut to her left, moved from Broad Street to Swan Street, ran by stores that sold fabric, household items, jewelry, and clothes. The stores were bi-level, upstairs formerly used as residences, but now being used as warehouses. She sprinted down the pedestrian walkway past a line of shops and malls toward White Park Road. Guns. Flash-bangs. Gre-

nades. She was more resourceful than anticipated.

War Machine ordered, "Do not lose visual."

"What if she drops another explosive?"

"If the Kiwi had any left she would have
used it by now."

"Where is her team?"

"She has no team."

"How do you know for sure, War Machine?"

"She has no team."

The second-level windows at KFC were
blown out.

Da Costas Mall was on fire.

Explosion followed explosion followed explosion.

As they chased, men fell back and guarded
their rear, made smoke and flames rise,
turned Bridgetown into a disaster area, buildings that had been there for decades now
damaged or destroyed.

Town crumbled.

Flames became enormous, ravaged the area
the way a fire had ravaged 20 Swan Street in
the distant past, the way a beautiful and
exotic fire had destroyed homes and acres of
Lower Bridgetown, when the area had been
cleansed by hellfire and nicknamed the Burnt
District.

By sunrise, it would be called the Burnt
District again.

FIFTY-SEVEN

Drowning in rain, I sprinted, feet slapping my butt with each stride. They ran just as hard. Fear gave me wings but determination gave them the power of flight. Bridgetown remained a blur, a maze of death. I cut right at a sign that read START DE TOWN, signage that exploded as I went down the promenade toward marketplaces. Another S.Y. Adam & Son caught bullets, then caught a projectile and exploded. Another explosion made the earth shake under my feet, made me stumble, and I dropped my backpack. Needed it, but couldn't go back for it, ran into the wind, made hard turns into deeper darkness. Heard them. Each block they were closer. Bolton Lane. Mandela Plaza went by. Another close call. Night lit up and debris flew. Sewing World would need sutures. Ran toward High Street Mall and Market. Guntas had fanned out, had run me in circles. Now they were coming from the left, the direction of the National Council on Substance Abuse, so I was forced to go right, again toward Moon Diamond Mall. The front of the mall had been destroyed. I ran inside. Bullets danced across cinder blocks and broke glass that had already been shattered, that shrapnel attacking my flesh.

I tried to get to the top of a three-level beige stucco building, needed to get to the rooftop, had to get to the roof, or die. It was connected to a block of businesses the same height and shoulder to shoulder and I could flee across the rooftops, run to the end and drop down to the main road. Pain made me slow on the second level. Too hurt to move at this pace for long. Looked down. Yellow walls, white tile, stairs with sharp edges. Moved upstairs. Saw Beautiful Tresses Hair Studio. Broke open the doors and fell to the floor. Turned on my flashlight. Pink walls. TV anchored up high. There was no exit. There was no back door. No windows. A cave inside of a cave. Heard them charging up the stairs. When they were outside the shop, War Machine called out. I fired until my clip was dry. They returned fire, firecrackers lighting up the dark, destroying everything in the shop. Ruffians and hooligans never backed off, were too savage and feral. They came into the small room gun by gun, one by one, so close they were one huge shadow, the business ends of guns on me, red dots dancing on my flesh. Eight guntas. Three carried swords. Flashlights on wrists illuminated my new jail and danced on the blades of their toys, barbaric tools that were a tribute to the olden days. They wore grotesque masks like it was Halloween. Masks to conceal their identities. Monstrous masks that were meant to give me horror showed me what they were made of inside. Now they wanted me to give to Caesar what was Caesar's. Couldn't let fear seize my limbs. I had killed a handful of them, and I wanted to take at least one more with me to see Jesus's daddy, maybe play dominoes with me while we sat in the waiting room in the sky. Light reflected in the mirrors over the workstations. They had brought their ugliness and were going to turn this cage into their slaughterhouse, would butcher me and give me their ugliness inside of a beauty shop, would kill me or leave me dying here. Outnumbered. Outgunned. No bullets left. Still I stood in front of them and raised my fists.

FIFTY-EIGHT

The Kiwi.

They had her trapped inside of a beauty shop, a brick jail cell that had no exits.

They had the Kiwi. Wide-eyed. Wild expression. Rabid. Panting for air. She fought. A spinning kick to the gut of one man. A head butt to another. She fought like a demon, boxing, kickboxing, Muay Thai, mixed martial arts, grappling, and karate all wrapped into one, but she was wounded and slow. She was a woman and there were mechanical advantages to being a man, the testosterone, the muscle mass, the size of the hands, the power from the shoulders. She fought like she didn't care about the advantages that men had, didn't care about weight class, fought like she was Changpuek Kiatsongrit.

War Machine watched, Appaloosa, Guerrero, and Kandinsky at his side, winded.

She threw another kick, this one not as fast, not as powerful, her body ragged, exhausted, and her foot was trapped. A second gunta attacked her, then a third, then a fourth, and all struck her fast with a hard fist, beat her until she could no longer defend herself, sent her to the ground. She fought to get back up. The guntas kicked her around the floor until one of them raised her up and hit her with his fist, a powerful blow to the head. She went limp, hit the concrete floor, disoriented, unmoving for ten seconds of their laughter, unable to rise again. They kicked her like she was an animal. All she could do was cover her head, pull into fetal position. Her face was bloodied, as was her body. She had been hit by three shots, at least three, plus her shoulder and side, telling of her rising pain.

She had run for her life, had run injured.

War Machine was impressed.

Appaloosa stepped forward, pushed War Machine to the side; then they lorded over her.

The gigantic gunta ordered, "Cut away her clothing."

Guntas flipped her over on the wet, muddy, and dusty tiled floor, four thugs, dripping of rain and sweat, holding her down, weighing down each limb as Appaloosa came up behind her. He undid his pants, walked to the front of her, showed her his dick, cursed her, threatened her, circled her, and dropped to his knees. He viciously slapped her struggling ass and told her he was about to have her from the rear. She cursed them, continued to fight. Four men couldn't hold her still.

War Machine said, "Get to business and be done with it."

Appaloosa said, "She's done fighting. She's given up. She finally understands. Let her go. I have her now."

Guerrero said, "You don't have her. She's bucked you away."

War Machine commanded, "Flip her back over. Do it rough. Kick her ass. Entertain me."

Guntas picked her up, held her up high, and let her drop to the concrete floor.

Then they stepped back, sea water and sweat stench in the air, all ready for the show.

Appaloosa said, "Golden pussy. King Killer had the golden pussy of a pretend Kiwi."

She was down, in pain, and as the men surrounded her in the cramped shop, as it sounded like thunder and lightning had joined the tropical storm, Appaloosa went after her, the hunter of killers went after the wounded assassin, dropped to his knees, took the general rape position, man on top, pushing his cock close to her cunt, between her legs, but was surprised when she didn't submit, when she exploded, surged, knew how to move, had her arms out straight against his chest, water raining from his immense frame as she grunted and strained and pushed his weight up. Stronger than she looked, her adrenaline giving her power. He grunted and strained and tried to give her all of his weight and strength and tire her out, that wrestle going on as men cheered for him, as she spat and looked like Atlas about to be crushed by the world, as he tried to get better positioned and push down, his weight at least 150 pounds greater than hers, his muscle mass greater, but she shifted, found space, found an inch of breathing room during this endurance test and moved like his size gave her no fear, moved like she knew how to shrimp away, not like the other women, not like the women who had submitted right away, not like the women who saw the LKs coming, saw them, knew how it would end, and submitted. He was forced to regroup. When he pulled his weight back for a moment so he could readjust his position, she moved and struck him, hit him with a fist to the eye, tried to get the heel of her hand to shove his nose back into his brain, fought like a well-seasoned fighter would fight, not with claws, not like a girl, but her nails did still manage to mark his skin, gave him pain, and that pain made him scream in agony. His men cheered. They kicked her as she fought, but she didn't collapse. Appaloosa yelled for his men to back off, angrier now because his men saw him almost bested by the Kiwi, and that motivated him, enraged and aroused him, and in that moment, she managed to get her feet up to his thighs, got him out of the rapist position, one that had been practiced and perfected, and she kicked him hard and strong, kicked him like she was in a cage fight, grabbed his hands, his wrists, reversed the situation and made him the victim, kicked his face, legs bicycled, and she kicked up to his nose, bloodied his nose, kicked his stomach, kicked his chin, kicked him and the big man fell back, fell over, stunned, embarrassed.

Appaloosa said, "I'm going to fucking kill you."

She lay there, on the floor, wounded, growling, each sound threatening.

Guntas raised their guns.

War Machine said, "Spread her legs from Jamaica to Trinidad."

The men attacked her again, flipped her again, Appaloosa outraged, but not wanting to take any more chances. When the men held her facedown, the giant sat on her, then raised up again when she bucked, stood tall and dropped his weight on her lower back, knocked the wind out of her, did that twice. That pain, that level of agony paused the fight in her, and as the Kiwi lay winded, Appaloosa grabbed her neck, pulled her hair, slapped her head, struck her face, then strangled her. He yanked her ass up to him, forced himself inside of an orifice, not caring which, not caring how much she tensed, not caring if she were already occupied or filled with blood, leaving it up to her how she took what he was giving.

She tensed, inhaled and exhaled like a demon, but refused to scream.

He roared, "Oh, I have the Kiwi bitch now. My cock is deep in the Kiwi bitch."

War Machine said, "She's not giving up."

"Oh, I'm loving this. Let her keep fighting. Take this dick, bitch. Take it all."

She fought without stopping, fought and forced him out of her grotto. Guntas watched. War Machine watched. Guerrero watched. Kandinsky watched. Appaloosa beat her in her back, struck her kidneys until she couldn't fight anymore, found an opening, found a place that widened for his erection, and with a grunt he shoved hard. He had her better that time. With all of his power, he grunted and shoved all of himself inside of her, into her slit, widened her gap, breached her, forced his dick inside of her hole. He pulled out and pushed inside again, pushed deep, pushed hard. Most women had broken by then, had cried and uttered loud, harsh cries, become infantile, squawked and bawled, prayed to God or Buddha or Jehovah. He wanted her to yawp to God. He wanted her barbaric yawp to sound over the roofs of the world. Then he did it a third time. A fourth time. A fifth. A sixth. He wanted to break her. Seventh. Eighth. Ninth. Tenth. Not until then did the bitch's eyes open, then they widened as if she could see the other side of the universe, not until then did her back arch, not until then did she stop fighting, stopped moving and tensed like she had gone into shock, then her mouth opened and there was no sound, her mouth wide open, her face in pain, severe pain, and there was no sound, not until she managed to catch her breath, not until her lungs filled with humid air. He pulled out and pushed inside of her again. Then he went for the second orifice. Pushed hard. Not until then did the monster who had come to their land and killed two of their brethren open her mouth and make a sound. Finally, she howled. To the guntas, that cry, her excruciating pain, was like the punch line to the joke of all jokes. She howled that she would kill every man in the room.

War Machine nodded. Retelling this vile moment would please his angered and discontented wife. It would please the vexed and depressed and inconsolable wives of the guntas.

War Machine said, "Barbarians. This bitch is a bloody Barbarian?"

Kandinsky held his gun and his sword and said, "Where are the others?"

Guerrero said, "I hope there are others. I hope there are more for us to kill."

War Machine told Appaloosa, "Be done with it. A queue has formed."

One of the guntas pulled away his shirt,

used it to cover her head, to make her blind, but that didn't muffle her curses, her arrogance, her threats that ended upon penetration.

War Machine thought about his wife, his kids, especially his daughter.

He thought about his dead cousin, the childhood friend he had killed because of this woman. As Appaloosa took the infiltrator of their group, War Machine went to her, outraged, and he punched her, punched her and she went limp, arms and legs spread out.

That was for his cousin. That was for the pain he felt to his bone marrow.

The men pulled War Machine away, but he raised his hands, back in control.

War Machine said, "Fuck her back to this side of the world. Fuck her back awake so I can knock her back out and then you can fuck her back and I can knock the Kiwi bitch out again."

A handful of thrusts, Appaloosa's back arched, and he cried out in pleasure.

After his strong finish, he collapsed on top of Reaper, slapped her thighs over and over.

He rested on the unmoving woman, then pushed up on his palms, drenched, in a room that was a damp oven, all the men that circled him drinking, fanning themselves in the dim light rays of flashlights, sweat dripping. Appaloosa reeled in his cock, his tool of terror, stood, reached for a Shandy, drank it all in one long gulp, belched, and asked who would take the bloody Kiwi bitch next.

The Kiwi lay there like she was dying, breathing hard like she was on the way to heart attack and organ failure. She pushed up on the palms of her hands and roared.

Boiling in anger, she kicked at them from the floor, but she was done.

In a livid, pain-filled voice she said, "You call yourselves men?"

"Don't you ever shut up? What kind of woman are you?"

"Fucking me won't put fear in my heart. And raping. Me. It won't silence. Me."

"This will be the kindest thing my men will do to you. This will be kinder than what will happen before you leave for Trinidad, much kinder than what will happen when you arrive."

They were not done. This was intermission. One of the guntas reached into his bag, not for a weapon, not for condoms, but for Carib Ginger Shandy, Sorrel Shandy, Lime Shandy, Stag and Banks beers, and passed them to his men. They popped the tops and they drank.

They pissed on her the way US Marines had made urine rain on dead Taliban terrorists.

When they were done, she snapped, "That's the best you can do, you disgusting fucks?"

"Just pray you're not lying about being a Barbarian."

"Fuck the Barbarians. You're two sides of the same coin."

"If you're not a liar, many Barbarians will suffer the same way. We know all about RCSI. We have kept our distance, have respected their business, their associations, and not once have we encroached on their territory. We respected the silent arrangement. A silent agreement has been violated. You came onto my island and killed two of my men in the light of day."

"It was an assassination. Your men were collateral damage."

"They had families. They were my brothers. They were off-limits."

"They were off-limits? What does that mean, War Machine?"

"You took a big risk."

"They knew the risks, just like I knew the risks. Why were they off-limits?"

War Machine asked, "Anyone want to fuck this bitch again before we leave?"

Guerrero said, "Not after we've pissed on her. But we should fuck her big mouth."

Kandinsky said, "Make her suck our dicks and shut up, until the storm eases."

Reaper laughed. "Line up. All of you bastards, and all of you are bastards abandoned by their fathers and some by their mothers.

Come on. See who gets their cock bitten off first."

Guntas grabbed Reaper, held her wrists and dragged her from the devastated beauty shop. She fought them. They shoved her down the concrete stairs, and as she lay motionless, dirty, filthy, muddied, they pulled her out of the building, across the flooded streets. They dragged Reaper across new rivers of filth, pulled her recklessly across debris and concrete.

War Machine, Appaloosa, Guerrero, and Kandinsky followed, eyes on the road.

She came back to life, kicked and yelled, "Let me walk. Let me walk with my head up."

Guerrero said, "Still too arrogant. Maybe we should tie her down and tame her again."

Appaloosa said, "Let the come bucket walk to the rendezvous. Make her move fast."

They hauled her to her feet, forced her in front, kicked her, hit her, abused her more, two guntas flanking her, both armed, one with a long bladed knife, the other with at least two guns, one a Glock, and they let her stumble, pushed her bloodied body, again hit her with fists, hit her like she was a prisoner of war, of their war, marched her barefoot in the rain, saw her as naked, broken, and defenseless, this the green mile that all who crossed the LKs would eventually walk.

She gathered a handful of water in her cupped hands, washed her bloodied face.

War Machine said, "You're more trouble than we'd anticipated."

"I guess a simple apology and a Hallmark card expressing condolences won't do."

"Kiwi, your night is only beginning. This will be your longest night."

"It's a little past my bedtime and I was hoping you were done with this fete."

"This fete is only beginning."

"So now what happens? Do I get a last supper before I stand trial? I'm partial to flying fish, macaroni pie, and a big cup of Mauby, but I will settle for a few fishcakes. Then do I get flogged again, maybe get to carry a wooden cross as the mockery continues?"

He spat on her. Then his hand sped through the rain and he slapped her, tried to slap the sarcasm out of her mouth. She stumbled and touched where he had struck her.

She laughed. "It's too late for foreplay, War Machine. Foreplay comes before sex, you moron."

He slapped her five more times. Guntas held her arms and she couldn't hit back. She strained and struggled, tried to pull them all, then eventually ran out of power, stopped screaming threats, pointless threats, and within two heartbeats, became incredibly calm, eerily calm.

They resumed trekking back toward their vehicles, a solid phalanx of armed men surrounding her, leading her. She rubbed her bloodied mouth and looked around.

She asked, "Where is King Killer, by the way? I don't see the crooked-dick prick."

War Machine slapped her three more times.

She said, "Wipe away your sordid expression and tell him I said thank you for bringing me into your group, for allowing me to get an up-close look at the LKs. Tell him I said thanks."

He grabbed her, choked her, spat in her eyes, choked her again. She strained, grinned.

She said, "You're married to your cousin's sister. Why not call it what it is? You married your own cousin. Your parents are brothers and sisters. What, are you preserving the bloodline?"

He let her go, shoved her into the wall, left her gasping for air, stumbling and struggling to breathe. She had seen their files. She knew his personal information. She knew too much.

She said, "Drugs. Guns. Real estate. Oil. Security. Protection. For losers being led by a power-hungry bitch, you've done well. One question, and this is serious. Who eats pussy better? You or the wife? Who eats more pussy at Passy Bay? Heard your cousin-slash-wife does."

He pushed her into a wall again, made her trip, fall to the ground hard, land on her shoulder.

She spat blood and said, "Whatever gets

your dick hard. Whatever gets you hard."

War Machine made her get back up on her own, shoved her, made her limp at their pace.

She asked, "How did you murder your gullible cousin?"

"We will show you. We will show you and you will wish you never knew."

She said, "All of you boys are shit."

"Shut up or I'll shut you up."

"Appaloosa? Now I'm talking to you, you intellectually circumcised behemoth."

"What, skanky Kiwi bitch? Ready for me to put my dick back in your ass again?"

"So valiant. The strong man who assaults women as if it were sport and throws unarmed men from the tops of buildings to hear them scream. To hear the men scream, not the building."

She pointed at him. Teeth clenched, riled, she pointed at him, an empty threat.

She asked, "How does it feel to be first? Tonight, how does it feel to be the first?"

"Fucking you? How did it feel to fuck a bloody bint? I have had better."

"Since you're first to offend me, then you will be the first, so please tell me how penetration feels."

"What did it feel like to make you grunt like a gorilla? What did it feel like to make you squeal like a pig? What did it feel like to make you walk like you're fresh out of labor?"

"I want to know if it hurts, boo. Don't you

want to scream?"

"We've beaten and humiliated you; now you're shell-shocked and delirious."

"It has to hurt."

"What has to hurt?"

"The arrow."

Appaloosa twitched. Blinked. Grunted.

He glanced downward.

Protruding from his jacket was four inches of shaft. Appaloosa frowned, grimaced down at the arrow, pain docking in swells, and he finally had enough air in his lungs to whisper . . .

FIFTY-NINE

"That. Hurts."

Appaloosa fell face-forward, landed in puddles of rainwater that had flooded the narrow, darkened road. A gunta sprinted to him. A second gunta was hit with an arrow, in the stomach and out of his back. He let out a horrific, yodeling yell. He dropped and went into convulsions. The report of guns rose as War Machine directed his men to get into a better position.

All of my talking, all my rambling, all the shouting I had done in the dark had been my GPS. I wasn't making conversation with those vile motherfuckers for sport.

I was in too much agony to move. All I could do was bleed, breathe, and watch.

Guntas yelled they were under attack. At the same moment, another wave of the storm arrived, wind gusts and noise that rang like thunder. The storm had all trapped. The gusts died as fast as they had come, my naked body drenched. War Machine fired at the rooftops, and between changing clips, shouted a command to reconstruct the arrow's trajectory to pinpoint where it came from. They raised weapons and fired in the darkness. I caught my breath, tried to ease away, tried to vanish while they were occupied, but a gunta grabbed my right wrist. I threw a left-handed blow to his face, but he didn't let go. Throwing that haymaker had hurt me more than it had hurt him. Another grabbed the left. Both twisted my wrists, took my arms close to being broken, did that until I collapsed screaming. I blinked water from my eyes, spat blood and saliva to the ground. They yanked me back to my feet again but didn't let my wrists go. I could barely stand. As long as I had been moving, I was fine. Standing still brought pain. War Machine was down on one knee, guntas guarding him as he slapped Appaloosa's face as if he were trying to knock death out of his system. Guerrero and Kandinsky stuttered commands to men who had no idea what to do at this point, men used to attacking but who had never been attacked.

There were more guntas than before. All of them fired up into the shadows.

They had seen the fast-moving silhouette of the enemy.

The two guntas let me go, drew their guns, joined in, and fired toward the silhouette as well. Pandemonium intervened and I dropped to my knees in agony, was left unguarded.

More shattered glass rained down on the road. More fires erupted.

It took all I had, but I panted, put my accumulation of pain on pause, ignored the feeling of unwanted blood, stool, and seed draining down my legs, and I stood, drew back, and grunted and gave it all I had, laid a fast blow to the throat of the gunta to my right, a knife-hand strike, tried to separate his larynx from the trachea. I shifted my weight and threw my shoulder into the gunta to my left, tried to gouge his eyes, crashed into the flooded road and its filth. While he reacted to his gouged eyeballs, I grabbed a blade from the gunta, slashed his arm, and when he grabbed his arm, I used that opening to stab that sword into his left eyeball, attacked him and pushed until the blade exited the back of his skull, my actions as swift as they were brutal.

That left me spent. Had to lean against the wall, ease down on my haunches.

A round of bullets came from above. Two heartbeats later, guntas organized and sent wicked reports that answered rapid volleys, two dozen wild shots that hit nothing but rain.

The first gunta I had attacked surprised me, began to rise to his feet.

Either I had missed my mark or hadn't hit him as hard as I had hoped.

Again I mustered my strength, forced

myself back to my bare feet, clung to my training and the blade, took smooth breaths and attacked the gunta, gifted him with rapid punctures, and when the gangly thug grabbed his pain and tried to scamper away from my rage, I wrestled him, became a tick, a maelstrom on his back. I pulled his curly hair with ferocity, exposed his neck and with a wicked pull I opened his throat. The nonce had struck me and kicked me a dozen times, had held me down, had laughed the loudest when I had been pushed down concrete stairs.

Thirsty for reparations, famished for my own justice, anger owned me and I had an overwhelming edacity for vengeance. This war was our marriage, until death do we part.

Gunshots came from the rooftop, the muzzled fire making the target easy to locate.

It came from the rifle of a Bahamian sniper.

Arrows gave no hint where they had come from, left no burning trail.

Gunfire created its own tracer, displayed its exact origin with every shot, like GPS.

I made it one shop down before they realized what I had done. By then I had two guns, had the guns of the dead men in my hand, and from the ground, we exchanged fire.

Reports came from above as I grunted, screamed, issued shots from up the road.

Then my guns ran dry. Being Winchester meant that I needed to buck the pain and flee for my life again. I tried to take two quick steps.

The agony was too great.

I sat down, almost collapsed. I knew this would be my final time sitting down. Elbows bloody, knees bloody, aching, I wiped salty water from my face, the salt making every wound burn like fire.

As the gods cast stones and pissed on us all, as hellfires danced in the windows of a dozen two-leveled shops, more men with guns stood shoulder-to-shoulder and marched my way.

They came from the opposite direction. Without announcement, they fired on the LKs.

The Royal Barbados Police had arrived and they arrived blazing.

They probably had seen their dead comrades and now were lined up.

The line for revenge was forever growing, was never stagnant.

Again I was surrounded.

There was no way out.

SIXTY

Silhouettes came down Swan Street from Broad Street, stormed through salty rain and harsh wind. They weren't LKs spitting lead at will. I had expected more law enforcement. They weren't the Barbados Defence Force, the Barbados Coast Guard, or the Royal Barbados Police Force.

Barbarians.

They were Barbarians, intruding on my date night.

They'd finished with the Rastafarians and now they were here, locked and reloaded. I recognized Zenga's build, knew that jerk's bulky silhouette as it peeked out and fired shots at the LKs using an automatic weapon. The pyromaniac was in the mash-up as well.

Gunfire came from both sides of the road. A third shooter was in place.

Dormeuil had to be in the shadows too. This was the cleanup crew and I bet their refrigerated truckload of Rasta rotis was nearby and had room for me and a few more bodies. Fear magnified. Barbarians were my enemy as well. They had come to erase me and wipe out the LKs. Laventille Killers were on Swan Street behind me, shouting, shooting.

Barbarians had organized in front of me. They were spitting out .50 caliber rounds and could destroy a target two football fields away. That was what they had taken to the Rastafarians, rounds that could knock down brick walls. A concrete block wouldn't stand a chance. It would go through a door like butter and leave pink mist like no one had ever seen.

One round could cut a man in half. The LKs continued firing. They backed off, but they didn't go away. The exchange of egos continued for a while, two minutes that seemed like two years. The LKs had traveled too far, had sacrificed too much to simply turn and run.

The exchange died down. Fires on Swan Street yielded an eerie glow.

Someone from the Barbarians called out, "Reaper."

Part of a structure collapsed; glass, steel, and concrete fell into the road. Fierce winds returned for a moment, buffeted the noise, pushed debris, made me cover my eyes.

Once the winds died down, they shouted my name again.

I shouted in return, "I'm busy. Take a number."

War Machine called out, gave orders, but I couldn't hear what was said.

I retorted, "Fuck you, you fucking fuck."

A precipice in front, wolves behind me. Swan Street, Roebuck Street, and Tudor Street a battle zone. Somewhere above the mom-and-pop businesses, up on the rooftops, somewhere on buildings made of brick and coral stone, up there was the only person on this planet I trusted.

If one of many dozens of bullets sent her way hadn't found her head.

The LKs fired on the Barbarians. The Barbarians fired on the LKs.

I stumbled into a shop that had been destroyed, its front now the opening to a pitch-black cave, and three guntas appeared, their silhouettes in the glow from the fires. Moved as fast as I could, adrenaline high. They followed my retreat, rushed behind me, but they had failed to pay attention to the shop I had run inside. We played hide-and-seek for a moment. I rose from behind the counter and gifted the first one with the knife I held, then staggered deeper inside the shop. I was in a hardware store. This was where hired guns shopped to buy blades and axes, large hammers, crowbars, and machetes.

Moments later, I emerged panting, holding bloody axes in both hands. Something that looked like rope was on my shoulder. I had left the second gunta on the floor in agony.

When I caught my wind, I turned to him and raised the ax up high.

I brought it down hard enough to make heads roll.

I stepped into the storm facing an assassin carrying an assault rifle.

I emerged facing Petrichor.

She had on all black, hair pulled back, a black-and-purple LIME bandana covered her mouth and nose. She was soaking wet, covered in debris, focused, but on edge, a wreck.

She lowered the business end of her weapon and said, "Goldilocks?"

"Hey, babes. No karaoke tonight, huh?"

She saw me, saw the condition I was in, battered and nude, and she looked infuriated and horrified. She repeated my name. I blinked a dozen times but said nothing.

Her lips moved, but it took me a moment to be able to hear her clearly. There were hissing noises, painful sounds. One glance and she knew. I limped and she knew.

I inhaled deeply, the humid night smelling like seawater, brine, piss, and cake. As long as I didn't smell rotten eggs, that being the scent of propane, this would be my resting spot.

The storm had brought the ocean's moisture and dumped it on top of me.

Face dank, she said, "Muddasik. I was too late."

"You found me, that's all that matters."

"After you dropped the phone, I followed the destruction."

"You told me to get to Swan Street and Roebuck Street. Had car problems."

"I drove as fast and as hard as I could. Cars are flipped over and on fire from Upper Collymore Rock down to here. People were in the roads trying to get to QEH. Broken bones and burns. Dead bodies all over. Saw the turned-over Mini Cooper and their trucks. Saw the dead policemen. Came this way as fast as I could. LKs were all over. Took to the roof."

I touched my swollen face, spat blood, and shook my head. "I'm still alive."

"Your face."

"I still look better than you."

She saw what was being carried on my shoulder. "What else did they do?"

"Don't cry. Snipers don't cry."

"This is my anger overflowing, not tears."

"Serious. No meltdowns."

"All of them?"

We jumped when we heard a round of gunfire, stepped back inside the store. Soldiers, police officers, killers, or clergy on the next religious crusade, some group was marching this way. An ax would do me no good. Needed to upgrade. I dropped one of the axes, the bloodied one in my right hand, freed my gun hand. My hand hurt, nails broken, but it was still functioning. Petrichor changed clips and handed me a fully loaded weapon. She pulled her bandana back up above her nose, took to one side of the shop and I did my best to get to the other side.

From Swan Street someone called out, "Reaper."

The Barbarians had driven the LKs away, at least back down Swan Street, then doubled back for me. They were my enemy as well. Didn't answer. Petrichor prepared to unload her clip.

Then they raised their guns. If they started shooting, death would applaud.

He yelled over the wind and rain, "MX-401."

I yelled, "Who's calling out a defunct Barbarian handle on such a night like this one?"

"It's us, Reaper."

"You need directions to Novel Teas or you came to make more Goldilocks jokes?"

"Do you need help?"

"You come to finish me off?"

"Reaper, do you need assistance?"

"Last time asking, then this gets ugly. Why are you here?"

"Barbarians received intel that the LKs had landed."

"Cut to the chase. You don't have a dog in

this fight. The company and I have parted ways. RCSI sent you here for what purpose?"

"The LKs found you before we did."

"I told them I used to be a Barbarian. Is that what you want to know? I told them that I was sent to Trinidad by the Barbarians, that RCSI sent me on the hit, so get your house in order."

"They got to you."

"No, RCSI got to me. Wish you fuckers had had my back from day one."

"We came to protect you."

"Bullshit. You came to protect the Barbarians' interest in the Barbarians and RCSI."

"We'll get you to safety. We'll sort this out, MX-401."

"I'm not MX-401. You heard my resignation, so stop playing games."

"Look, let me come in and talk with you."

I fired twice. He backed away.

I said, "Call RCSI."

"All comm is dead."

"Rastafarians? They're dead too?"

"Come out."

"I'm not coming out."

"You can't stay there. Island police or military will eventually come this way."

"Fuck you. Fuck all of you. Fuck — shite."

"You okay? Reaper? What was that? You okay in there?"

"No, I'm not okay. Just threw up."

"What's going on?"

"I'm in pain. Leave me be."

"You sound like you're in need of medical attention. Let me check on you."

"Your asshole steroid-eating buddy and the fire-starter, they stay where they are."

"Okay. They are standing guard. Just me."

Glass crunched underneath his boots. Dormeuil came inside the store, soaking wet. Never saw Petrichor in the shadows, her gun aimed, ready to take him out, wanting to take him out. He stopped four feet away, both hands in view, flashlight on my body until he saw my face, until he saw that I was nude, then he turned the light down, looked shocked, embarrassed, stood with his head turned, a man who wouldn't violate a woman, and what he saw was my femininity.

His shoulders slumped and he said, "Jesus."

I stood tall, strong, like I was covered in armor. "Where are they?"

"The LKs broke ranks. They're backing off, retreating."

"They're regrouping. This isn't the end for them; this is only the start."

"Looks like you crawled across barbed wire."

"Be up-front. Be a man; be honorable; be honest. But most of all, just be up-front."

"You're bleeding."

"Most of it's their blood."

"We do have a common enemy at this point."

"We have nothing in common. I was clear."

"They are top status. You should be glad that we caught them off guard."

"Was I your bait?"

"No. Not at all."

"You made them retreat. They didn't know how many guns were behind them."

"We didn't know how many of them were in front of us. Too many of them to chase, not when they were cloaked and shooting. We need to cut them off before they exit the island."

"Still not safe. This storm will keep them trapped here for a few hours."

"The boys up top want to know, so I have to ask. You find out anything we can use?"

"They're almost as evil as the Barbarians."

"Where is their base?"

"We didn't sip tea and exchange addresses."

"How many combatants are left?"

"No idea. I just know that three are dead behind me."

"Three? In your condition, you took out three of them in here?"

"Behind me."

"Damn."

"Shine your light. Look at the pools of blood and draw your own conclusion."

"You're using a pole to stand up."

"An ax, not a pole. A bloodied ax."

"What's that on your shoulder?"

"What does it look like?"

"A spinal cord?"

"That one. I carved a hole in the back of his neck, took out his spine with my fingers."

I let the spine fall from my shoulder, allowed it to crash to the ground.

He said, "You were outnumbered, injured, and you took out three of them?"

"You've seen me. Get your laugh, and report this to your boys."

"I just follow orders for the corporation. You know that."

"That was my downfall. I trusted RCSI. Lesson learned."

"Let me get you some antibiotics from a dispensary before an infection sets in."

"Leave. Return to the theater of war or go home, but leave me as you found me."

"MX-401, get an infection down here in the West Indies and you can lose a limb."

"Fuckin' leave. Leave. Get the fuck out. Leave. Fuckin' leave."

That was when he heard Petrichor in the shadows.

In a harsh Bahamian accent, Petrichor said, "Mister Conky Joe, don't argie. When a woman says go, a gentleman should leave. Walk away or join the stiff-toe gang. When I slap a man, he goin stay slap. If I kill a man, he goin stay dead. First you, then all your friends."

Unarmed, Dormeuil didn't turn toward the voice.

544

He kept his eyes on me.

His men were on Swan Street, other side of the windows, beyond hearing at the moment. He spat, the gobbet of phlegm falling on the dirty floor not too far from his feet, his sweat coming on like a fever, his stench musky and strong, a smell of smoke and gunpowder and cologne and sweat, mixing with the oil scents, the stench of three new deaths that had made three bowels release their stink, his breathing now in spurts, thinking this might be his last breath.

He said, "Reaper, I just follow orders."

"When they ordered you to shoot me, why didn't you?"

"I'm leaving."

"Why didn't you?"

"You're Reaper's kid. I wasn't going to shoot Reaper's kid."

He kept both hands high and backed away. He hurried back out into the storm. He went back to Zenga and the black pyromaniac. They talked, looked my way, debated something. Debated my life. Debated my death. Dormeuil told them about the ax, the dead men.

He told them I had removed a man's spine with a blade and my fingers. He told Zenga that he had gotten off easy. Told the black pyromaniac that I was hotter than fire.

They all took to the rain, followed the way the LKs had retreated under fire.

Zenga moved with a limp. A bandage covered his damaged ear. Band-Aids covered his broken nose. I had fucked him up real good.

Petrichor looked out, saw they were gone, and when it was clear, she came to me.

She asked, "How many of the LKs assaulted you and what did they do to you?"

I searched the shop, grabbed another backpack, picked out more things that could be used as weapons. Knives. Short axes. Rope. Natural hemp rope, hand-twisted. Fifty-foot bundles. I grabbed one of those as well. Packed like I was going to go hunt zombies.

She repeated what she had already said. "How many?"

"I'm going to need you to carry this bag for me."

She cursed, held back tears, then commanded, "Sit."

"I have my second wind. Let's get moving."

"Not naked. You will not walk the roads naked or go into QEH half-dead and naked."

"Not going to QEH."

"Then we go to Holetown to Sandy Crest Medical Centre."

"Petrichor. Listen. Listen well. No one is going to be allowed to examine me."

"Why not?"

"Because I said so."

She said, "Limp over here. Hide behind this case. Hold up this wall until I get back."

Seconds later, I heard her break out the window at a store called Abeds. Everything that hurt magnified with each breath. Seconds moved like days. She returned with an armful of clothing. A black sweatsuit that had two yellow stripes down its sides, and black trainers, all a size too large, but much needed. Light running shoes. Could barely raise my leg. She helped me get dressed.

Gunfire restarted. It came from the direction of Broad Street. Brief exchange. No sirens. No flashing lights. An assassin party.

I said, "The shootout has moved back to the main road."

"I'm in a stolen F-250. A quarter mile away. Circled around and ran from by the Treasury Building and tried to cut them off, but missed you guys when you went inside of a building."

"Was trying to get to the roof and find you. Knew you'd be up top."

"You can barely stand up. Can you walk?"

"I don't need your help. I can walk."

"They sexually assaulted you."

"Focus. I need you to focus."

A spotlight came from overhead. Then I heard the rhythmic thumping sound. A helicopter. A second spotlight penetrated the darkness. Soon a third spotlight sliced into the night.

I said, "Those are Robinson R44s."

"Four-seaters."

I knew pilots who worked for RCSI and they wouldn't fly in moderate winds between ten and twenty-five miles per hour. I'd never seen one flown in a storm, but that didn't mean that it couldn't be done. Because it was being done three times over.

I said, "The LKs broke the bank to get me."

"Let them take their drug money and go."

"They didn't let me go. They showed me no professional courtesy. They had no etiquette, none whatsoever. So I need to catch up with them and be equally as hospitable."

There was no Bajan Air Force or police with choppers to chase them down. They could take to the air and be gone, unchallenged. They could exit Bridgetown in the dark, be back in Trinidad before power was restored. They would have taken me on that short journey, would have abused me from one island until I arrived at the next, then taken me to some faraway place, to one of their torture sites, invited more guntas, and continued their heinous rendition.

I looked into her eyes. Petrichor was gone.

What had happened to me had crushed her.

I asked, "What happened to you?"

"This is about you, not about me."

Not until that moment had I seen the hard-hearted assassin that lived inside of her. Old Man Reaper's Bahamian daughter clenched her teeth, struggled to control her seething anger.

We walked the shopping strip, fired at anything, at anyone that moved. As I passed injured men, LKs that had been left behind, I put a bullet in their heads. I did the same for dead men. One to the cranium and hoped they felt that in hell. When I came up on Appaloosa, I raised my gun to shoot his face but changed my mind, dragged my ax toward his body, kicked him over, raised the ax high, and brought it down on his neck. Made him a two-piece. I promised to return for him soon.

Helicopters remained in the sky, the tropical storm giving them problems — that or they hadn't decided where to land, or their original landing spot had been compromised.

I had dropped my backpack and the LKs had been too busy chasing me to notice. It had to be close to where I had fallen before I had run into the mall. Close to where they had caught me. It was there. In the middle of the road, a black backpack covered by debris.

I picked it up. Grenades and flash-bangs were inside. I had run with it in front of me, just in case a bullet had found me. I had run for my life hoping that I didn't end up exploding.

Sirens were in the distance, barely audible in this weather, but there.

We took the road that fed into KGs Bar and Lucky Seven Slots Arcade. The MMM I Like I Like restaurant was around the corner.

People were in the road. Not many of the people who lived on Nelson Street and in the surrounding areas had come this far, but the curious and foolish had braved the weather. No more than a dozen people were out. All had backpacks, looked lawless, ready to get to Swan Street and loot what they could. We walked by them. They looked at us, but not a word was spoken. A homeless man was in a doorway, shell-shocked and injured, drowning in the storm. He called out for help, said he was hurt and bleeding, and we kept moving. We had come this route on my chase. Marhill Street also corrupted, painted like a war zone. We paused near the Treasury Building, stopped where we could see Bridge Street, Bridge House, the Careenage, where the LKs had abandoned their vehicles in sight.

I asked Petrichor about the landing sites. She rattled off six locations.

I asked, "What's closer? They're circling here, trying to get picked up near town."

Petrichor said a property near Carlisle House used to be leased by Bajan Helicopters.

I asked, "They're closed?"

"Government raised the rent six times over and ran them away."

"Any armed security there?"

"None whatsoever."

"Landing pad usable?"

"It's been neglected. Might have trash and debris, but it would be inconsequential."

"That's where they might go."

"Can't agree. Four helicopters and one landing pad."

"Did you see a fourth?"

"They'd want to get up high. One of the car parks would be better."

"How many are there in this area?"

"Just the two. City Centre parking is five levels. BTI high-rise car park is right across from the landing pad and has three, maybe four levels. Both are tall and have wide-open roofs."

"City Centre is one of the tallest buildings in Bridgetown?"

" 'Suicide Building,' the highest in the area."

"Is it easily accessible?"

"The fifth floor has been locked down since the last big splat."

"What type of lock?"

"A two-dollar chain."

"Guards?"

"They had posted guards on every floor and parking lot, but the top. No one allowed. A night like this, nobody will be there. All the shops are closed. Top level would be perfect for the choppers."

We followed the trail of destruction, ran over debris, sheets of metal, rebar, street poles. My battered hand held on as we rumbled. Courts was on fire, KFC on fire, confirming they had come in this direction. The fire at KFC erupted; a gas line had broken. The eatery spat out flames, puked and shattered the windows at Chefette, made its enemy erupt in fire. Shattered masonry, wreckage, security guard wounded or dead in the road. Helicopters above glowed like alien spaceships, drew people in this direction like the Bat Signal attracted both Batman and villains. Huge holes were in the side of the building. Any car that was out had been gunned down, any driver who had come to this sector, killed. Vagrants were dead in the road.

This was more than the LKs tearing up Barbados; it was more than them being angry at this limestone and punishing her, more than them trying to sink the island.

This was desperation.

Barbarians were fighting the LKs, chasing the LKs, trying to kill them while comms were down and the rest of the LKs knew that RCSI was the bitch to blame for World War III. Pain hit me every time the truck hit a pothole or a bump or turned. A sharp pain came and went and came and stayed, a suffering one that came from the many kicks I had taken to my back and kidneys, and I tensed up, shuddered, held my breath, rode the wave of agony, panted, growled, tried to bite the back of my hand to keep myself quiet, but surrendered and set free a hard groan of agony.

Petrichor whispered, "They gang-raped you like they did the girl in New Delhi."

In a pained, sharp tone, I snapped, "Don't say that. I beg you."

"I smell the LKs on you. I can smell what those motherfuckers did to you."

The other helicopters moved our way. Winds had to be back up to fifty miles an hour, the gusts stronger, wicked enough to give them pause, maybe enough to give us much-needed time.

If I saw them, then in this darkness they could see our headlights as well.

She hit a rough patch of asphalt and I grunted, teeth clenched with the spasms, the waves of pain, the monster agony that refused to diminish. I throbbed. Vicious thrusts had loosened my bowels, had damaged me, gave cramps to my stomach. I shifted in my own filth, in my goo. I bled. More pain.

I shifted, unable to get comfortable, trembled and burned like fire.

We came to City Centre, the entrance next to a flaming Wang Qiu Li vegetarian restaurant. The serpentine car park entryway curved to the left, a sharp curve that ended on a slope at the next level. A metal roll-down security door that covered both the entrance and exit lanes had been rammed over and over until part of it folded and collapsed, but it didn't leave enough space for a vehicle to pass. A handful of black SUVs had been left behind, and behind those SUVs were two trucks. One was a large pickup. The other was a refrigerated Chefette truck. I had seen both earlier in the day when I visited the Rastafarians. They were on foot. Gunshots echoed inside the parking structure. The battle continued. The Barbarians were desperate and the LKs were angry and improvising, had been forced to give up the hunt for now. This wasn't their island. As far as I was concerned, this was my island. I wasn't running away from them. Until my last breath, I would fucking run *at* them. The tropical storm intruded on them the way severe thunderstorms had once spawned a tornado in Washington and messed up the plan by British soldiers and caused significant damage to the city. The LKs were trying to destroy Bridgetown the way the Brits had burned Washington. Heavy rain had helped extinguish the fires that burned throughout Washington; heavy rains and floods would do the same here.

The LKs had assumed coming to get me on this small island would be an easy task.

Petrichor backed out, backed out fast, skidded across debris, and parked on the road.

If she had left the truck there, it could be blocked in.

I said, "Let me go alone."

"No."

"Go back home to your husband."

"You're my sister. Don't you fucking get it? You're my goddamn sister."

In front of the burning restaurant, we stepped out of the truck, weapon heavy, Petrichor carrying the backpack, both of us with our guns trained. I ate pain with each step. I wasn't moving as fast as I wanted, but my adrenaline was high enough to act as a temporary painkiller.

She whispered, "How many?"

As rain fell on flames, spinning rotors sliced though the darkened sky.

The winds. Maybe the chopper pilots weren't as skilled as I had assumed.

A simple evac had turned into a suicide mission, the weather turning on them. Rage fueled me. Had to get to War Machine, if no one else, even if it cost me my life.

Petrichor had flashlight stun guns. Winds shoved us as we moved beyond the damaged door and again it was like running into Harrison Caves during a blackout. Gravity pulled at me, made me want to collapse, my unseen enemy. We heard gunshots, men talking in sharp tones. More gunshots. Massive chunks of stonework fell. The pavement was sticky. Blood. My gut hurt, not from Appaloosa, but from where Zenga had kicked me. Felt like a giant was standing on my gut, made standing upright a Herculean feat. If he hadn't kicked me, I would've been able to outrun them. The pain he had given me had sprung to life and slowed me down. In my mind, I was killing him, making him feel what I felt. Outside, water fell from the roof like Niagara Falls, and after more firepower, glass fell harder than the rain, mixed with the water, became invisible, fell into the curious faces and eyes of the denizens, tourists, and anyone who was stupid enough to gather here, any one of the curious drawn to get a front seat at danger.

A fury inside of me ignited and my walk became a limping trot from the first level until we circled to the darkness of the second. Men were on the next level, engaged in a firefight.

We passed two men, smoke rising. Smelled charred flesh before we saw them. They had been burned alive. The pyromaniac had come this way. The Barbarians had come this way.

A handful of LKs had the Barbarians trapped behind concrete pillars. For neither team was this taking place as advertised by their CEOs. I wanted to kill them all with my bare hands.

Violence echoed, tested men who pretended to be brave, boys pretending to be soldiers.

Petrichor moved to their left and found her position behind a column; I took my crippled body to the right and did the same. Covered, no earplugs, heart pounding so hard it deafened me as well, we opened fire, had clear shots to the back of the LKs. Each shot echoed in these close quarters. Hysterical screams. Howls from the injured. The Barbarians realized they had assistance, and they opened fire on the LKs forced out into the open. LKs fled, inspired by our lead. The LKs were hit from front and back; they tried to return fire in a way that was impressive, but not effective. The dead littered the pavement.

I ignored the pain, but the pain didn't ignore me. I forced myself to focus.

I called out, "It's Reaper."

Dormeuil called back, "Reaper? You're joking."

"Reaper plus one, with weapons."

"Show yourself."

"Fuck you. Show yourself first."

Barbarians emerged from hiding, first Zenga with his weapon aimed, then Dormeuil.

Both lowered their guns. They regarded Petrichor. She had pulled her scarf back up to her eyes. She was a shapely silhouette with gun and backpack, one they had just seen mow down men, reload her clip, and step toward them as if to say fear had no home in her heart.

There were no introductions, no quips, no jokes, just serious expressions.

Zenga and I looked at each other. It was in broken darkness, but we looked at each other. He nodded. He touched where I had taken part of his ear during our hand-to-hand battle. I put my hand on my belly. He nodded again. I didn't know what that meant, but he nodded. I returned the same ambiguous gesture and moved past him. Not allies, but not enemies at the moment, still closer to being the former than the latter, but only one pejorative from being the latter.

The pyromaniac had taken one to the head. Half of his face was gone, the top half.

Dora the Explorer danced with Satan on a muddy hill covered in brown snow.

Three other men were dead. Barbarians I had never met while they could breathe.

Zenga looked at his dead colleagues, rage lines in his face, tears in his eyes.

There was no time to comment, no time to mourn. Dead LKs and Barbarians rotting behind us, weapons high, we continued toward the roof, toward the sounds of choppers.

Dormeuil led the way. I did my best to keep up, refused to be a liability.

I didn't want Petrichor to go, but she refused to turn around and leave me with them.

As it had been for the pyromaniac, this was going to be a one-way trip.

SIXTY-ONE

The campaign continued.

On the top level of the unfinished car park that could accommodate five hundred vehicles, the LKs had shot off the inexpensive chains and opened the insignificant metal double doors that led to the roof of City Centre. We killed the flashlights we carried and an abrupt darkness blanketed us, made the lights from the choppers exponentially brighter. Couldn't tell where men were positioned, couldn't see where the enemy waited, but they were off to the sides giving the chopper room to land, not expecting company at these double doors. They didn't expect us, not up here. We fired on them and they fired on us, but two of them dropped, another three hit, one screamed that his kneecap had been shot. Screams. Rain. Bullets popped like a firefight in Afghanistan. The exchange didn't scare the choppers away. Lights in the dark made choppers glow like UFOs hovering over Little London, so denizens who saw the whirlybirds on this side of the island probably were in awe as if they were witnessing the Concorde land on its final flight. The chopper rocked and landed under pressure. At one end of the roof, War Machine returned fire as he rushed to board a helicopter along with other men. Every time I saw them, there were more guntas, as if they had been stationed all over the island. Maybe some had already been here anticipating this extraction. Maybe those were the ones who rammed the gate and broke the locks. Probably were the same men who had driven the island and killed the power while the others terrorized Big Guy. I was sure that some had already fled in vehicles. Others were trying to collect their injured before they were exposed, and someone had to be out there stacking up their dead. Three guns sent projectiles from the chopper. It had a gunner with a rapid-fire weapon, and the gunner shot hard and fast, chased us back into the dark hallway, made us drop to the floor, scramble across dusty concrete. Concrete walls stopped slugs, but Zenga had grabbed me, pulled me out of the way. I yanked away from him, not wanting his fuckin' hands on me, not even now. When the shots paused, we were back in the door, firing as guntas fired at us. Fewer guntas fired. War Machine's escape vehicle wasn't an R44, but a medium-size Super Puma, the largest of the four. At the other end of the car park Guerrero, Kandinsky, and another gunta were boarded on one of the R44s.

The handful of guntas waiting on the next chopper still had ammo.

We were in the open, exposed both to bullets that fell like rain and rain that fell like bullets. The Super Puma lifted into the winds, lifting into Bridgetown's blackness created by the LKs, was pushed by God and helped by the devil. The four-bladed beast thumped and we were at the entryway to that level, firing rounds. I wanted that chopper to go down in flames. I stepped out as men fired at me, stepped out and fired, fired, fired.

Bullets danced around me while I screamed and tried to kill that bird.

I shouted into the storm at War Machine, screamed into the wind and rain.

Petrichor shouted my name, unloaded her weapon as she came to get me.

I went down on one knee, reloaded, was in too much pain to get up, so I fired from that position. Guntas on the ground returned fire as a second and third chopper landed.

Again fireworks lit up the night.

When it came to war, they were brutes, men with limited vision, no plans, no schemes, just blindly going after what they had been entrusted to trap, dehumanize, and kill.

Gunfire stopped. They were Winchester. That, or pretending.

They raised their hands, but our guns

remained high and kicked out lead.

Petrichor came out and grabbed my shoulder, pulled me to my feet. The Barbarians stepped up, were at my right side. I opened my bag, showed Zenga the grenades. I should have done that the moment we made it to the top level. Pain had distracted me. Zenga did his best to calculate the oscillating wind and threw the grenade and tried to get it to hit a chopper.

Petrichor and Dormeuil fired on guntas and Zenga threw grenades.

I raised my gun and joined in, each recoil sending agony back into my body.

A grenade disrupted the tail of one of the choppers as it took off. Right away, it began to spin wildly. They were already over the edge of the building, and they became an out-of-control merry-go-round. The whirlybird slammed into the bank across the street, erupted into flames, experienced a catastrophic loss of power, and plummeted, began cartwheeling.

We heard the whining, the screeching of metal as it ripped apart. Big bang. Felt the building shake, the rain and winds not muting the sounds, not stopping a big plume of smoke from rising up into the saturated air. Small explosions continued after the big bang, like the Fourth of July.

Fire spread to adjacent buildings, to the front of this structure.

A ruptured high-capacity fuel tank was better than a bomb.

In the distance, another chopper had problems, lost control in the wind. I could tell by its lights, how they rose and fell, more fall than rise. It went up one more time, then nosedived.

It vanished from sight. Then there was an explosion. Flames rose.

It wasn't the chopper carrying War Machine, but one of the R44s. Maybe a lucky shot had sliced through the winds and hurt the pilot. Maybe it was pilot error. Flying in these winds was a sign of desperation. I didn't give a fuck. I wanted all of them dead. I ached from head to toe, bled from wounds and orifices, suffered a living hell. Six guntas had been left behind. Zenga had found two out of ammo, hiding in the darkness. Dormeuil dragged one, the boy with the busted kneecap, to the edge of the building. He made the gunta stand on his good leg, the other guntas captured, at his side. Then Dormeuil grabbed the boy's good leg and flipped him over.

As he screamed, I looked at the other guntas.

They stared at me, hands in fists, stared at the wild woman who was in pain.

I growled, "Jump, motherfuckers. Jump and pray that you grow wings on the way down."

Half-dead, they didn't move. Belligerent warriors. Men born poor and never expected to live beyond twenty-five years, boys pretending to be hardcore, righteous men with guns, abandoned and marginalized children who tried to squeeze one hundred years of living into twenty, not afraid to die, yet wanting to live for an eternity. I shot one in the head at point-blank range, the youngest of the lot.

I took a knife, sliced the back of his neck, and began pulling out his spine.

Zenga said, "Jesus fucking H. Christ."

My hands ached. Had to stop, but with half the spine removed, they got the point.

When I let the body drop, Dormeuil threw the man over the edge.

The other LKs saw their options. Fly or die without a spine. Either way, it was going to be raining men. Like San Salvadorians, they had no hearts, had been raised to be cold, merciless.

Then I repeated, "Jump and hope you land on something softer than a bullet."

They did. They cursed us all, stepped up on the ledge, arms outstretched like they were on a crucifix, and fell backward, did a skydive from darkness into the glow of the fireball below.

I limped and looked over the edge, Petrichor at my side. She held my arm at the elbow, held me as if she were afraid I might fall over, a gun in her right hand, her eyes on the Barbarians. The enemy of my enemy was not her friend, and she didn't pretend they were.

A helicopter's engine was lying on the ground. The helicopter was in a million pieces and each piece scattered up and down the road and on fire to the edges of St. Mary's Anglican Church.

A vehicle was on fire, flames rising, being spat everywhere.

I saw other glows, moving illuminations, the glows from cellular phones being used as flashlights. Plebeians fought wind and rain, came from all directions. People wanted to see. Most sane people were inside their homes, but the insane, those denizens were on the side of the road, maybe wishing they had stayed in their chattel houses and not run into the storm and found their way to a war zone out of morbid curiosity. I'd bet that many were stepping over debris and bodies and looting, bandanas covering their faces, trying to get inside of Courts to steal tele-visions, computers, vacuum cleaners, air conditioners, mattresses. On this side, the crash had broken open the windows on the ground level at Chapel Street. Looters were in clothing boutiques, some grabbing goods from the electronics store.

For both the malicious and the cafeteria Christians, now was the time to come up.

The tropical depression, for some, was a momentary cure for the recession. If Bajans were anything like Americans and Brits, Swan Street was being ransacked at the same time.

There wouldn't be any ambulances. Not anytime soon. Not for all the injured.

Anyone hurt might as well start wining and chipping, wukkup toward QEH.

I needed to be the grand marshal of that cavalcade featuring the walking dead.

Flames here and there. It looked like there had been a terrorist attack.

In some ways, there had been one.

I hoped Barbados had plenty of space at their morgue.

I asked, "Where are the police and paramedics?"

Petrichor adjusted her wet bandana and spoke with a deep, hard, Jamaican accent, spoke like she was a West Indian Batman, said, "Barbados has never seen anything like this. Something happened in Antigua a while back, five or six years ago, but it was nothing like this, not like this shit at all. They are freaking out, overwhelmed. Half are looting and the other half is praying. This shit is awesome."

War Machine and a few others had escaped, vanished into the night. They saw it in reverse. They had defeated me, and I'd escaped. I could hear them cursing in the winds, War Machine cursing the loudest. The woman they would've made their all-night slave cursed into the same winds.

Dormeuil said, "We have work to do. We have a lot of work to do."

I said, "I'm not done. This is only the beginning for me."

Zenga said, "We'd better get moving."

Dormeuil said, "While it's still raining."

"While it's still dark, we need to do as much recovery as possible."

"We need to do some collections. Leave no man behind, dead or alive."

"Have to cover this up the best we can. Low on manpower."

"We still have room in the Chefette truck."

"If it hasn't been stolen."

"We'll have to put our guys in the back with the Rastafarians."

Dormeuil and Zenga had already turned around and started marching away.

Petrichor walked next to me. An Amazon who stood like she was ready to kill the world, seething, so fucking angry, so heated, that each drop of rain that touched her created steam.

I was Reaper, equal parts strong, vicious, driven, dark, unfair, and fucked-up.

Petrichor lowered her LIME kerchief for a moment.

She lowered it so she could spit out her disappointment, then put it back in place.

She was Nemesis. Petrichor wasn't there, only Nemesis Adrasteia.

In that instant, she looked like the ultimate

warrior woman.

With her face cast in bottomless anger, her face was mine, resembled mine.

That was the first time I realized how much she looked like me.

Dressed in black, our frames looked identical to the men.

Which was as irrelevant now as it had always been.

Again I defied my agony, commanded my body to stop aching, to quit bleeding.

I did my best. I failed. Pain exploded. The weapon fell from my hand.

I collapsed, fell hard, fell as if life had been sucked out of me.

Water splashed into my face and I smelled guntas on me.

Someone lifted me up. Lifted me up and carried me. Zenga. I didn't want his help, but I didn't have a choice. I had a feeling I was about to end up in the back of the Chefette truck as well.

SIXTY-TWO

"Don't come back without her. Don't you fucking come back here without the Kiwi. Turn that fucking helicopter around and go back. I don't care. Go back and get the bitch. Go back now."

Diamond Dust cursed War Machine and threw the phone against the wall.

Anger lines grew in her face, made her look thrice her age.

She screamed. Heart-wrenching sobs.

Pain tore through her like knives.

Her children ran to her, saw Mommy's rage, started crying.

She turned her rage, changed from being a brick to a feather.

She held them, smiled a mommy smile, gave them kisses and hugs, told them that everything was fine.

All because of the dead politician needing to become a superstar.

If only the politician hadn't panicked and had done what he was supposed to do.

If he had only killed the Kiwi inside of the bank and elevated his status.

If only her husband's insane idea had worked.

SIXTY-THREE

Zenga carried me down the ramp. By the time we made it to the vehicles stacked up at the crashed security gate, I groaned, told him to put me down. Our journey had been in the darkness. I opened my eyes. Petrichor was there, marching in time, but I didn't see Dormeuil.

Zenga said, "We're not done. Going with us?"

"After this fiasco, you're outnumbered and chasing them on behalf of the Barbarians?"

"We don't know where they are. In a chopper, they could be anywhere."

"They'll be in Trinidad. Might be some stragglers, but they'll go home."

"You told them you were with RCSI?"

I nodded. "I told them that I used to be a Barbarian, that I wasn't anymore."

"Still feel that way?"

"They fucked me over. That will never change. Feel free to record this conversation."

I felt Petrichor's energy. It was strong. She

would shoot them if I nodded.

Zenga paused. "You were not expendable."

"Expendable?"

"What?"

"You said expendable."

"You're one of the best I've seen in this business."

Dormeuil came out. He dragged the body of the pyromaniac to where we were, put him down gently. Zenga walked by him. I assumed he was going to collect the other dead men.

Dormeuil extended his hand. I extended mine and we shook.

Gun in hand, Petrichor at my side, I hobbled into the rain, toward the truck.

Three men ran toward us.

We both raised guns and prepared to shoot.

The men ran by us. All carried flat-screen TVs wrapped in plastic over their heads.

Two women ran by struggling to carry a leather sofa.

We lowered our guns, crossed the flooded road.

Petrichor asked me, "Hospital or medical center?"

"Not yet."

"You're bleeding. You sound like you're dying."

"Not yet."

Parts of St. Michael were under two feet of water, well-paved road turned into lakes.

Along Ronald Mapp Highway, cars were stuck in water. The car park at the Hilton Barbados was flooded.

That was broadcast over station 98.1 as Petrichor drove the flooded road.

We returned to Swan Street, drove over destruction and temporary rivers and found Appaloosa. Blood dripped as I wiped rain from my face and frowned down on his corpse.

When I left the ruined road, flames danced, and parts of Appaloosa traveled with me.

The hair of his bowling-ball-heavy head was slick in my hand as I limped away.

My mind remained filled with riled-up scorpions, stinging, stinging, stinging.

I felt no satisfaction. Rage returned, doubled, made me seethe.

I looked back at Appaloosa's muscular body. Felt what he had done to my insides.

I looked at the body of two other guntas dead in the road.

We heard someone call out. We found three injured guntas, men gunned down by the Barbarians. They saw it was me. They had broken limbs, were unable to hold weapons, were no threat. I studied them. I ached. I bled. I looked at the flames in the buildings.

We took the identification from all the men, living and dead.

Wedding rings were in their pockets. We took those as well.

One of the men had a cellular phone. That was confiscated.

The natural hemp rope, hand-twisted in Romania. Fifty-foot bundle. I tied their legs together, then secured their hands behind their backs. Tethered a rope from the tailgate of the truck to their ankles, tied a stopper knot at the end of the backhand hitch to prevent it from untying by accident. Then redid the knots, did a double sheet bend, a knot that could be used to tow a boat. I told Petrichor to get into the passenger seat, told her she had no choice, and I climbed in, started the engine. Put the vehicle in gear and drove away, the men behind the truck were shouting for a while, for a short while, and the faster I drove across road and pavement, the lighter the load, the less I dragged. A mile of rugged asphalt later, I stopped and crawled out in pain, limped to the back, saw nothing but frayed rope on the back of the truck.

I cut away the last of the bloody rope, pulled myself back into the truck, drove toward the docks, toward where the helicopter carrying Guerrero and Kandinsky had crashed. One of the choppers had cleared the Carlisle Building, but had hit the *Jolly Roger*. The boat was on fire, sinking like the *Titanic*. The *Buccaneer* was on fire as well.

I drove the streets. I found Kandinsky. I found Guerrero.

They were both dead in the road. Either they had been thrown out of the chopper or they had jumped, my mind thinking the former because only a fool would do the latter.

What I had done to Appaloosa, I gifted those men the same way.

Any that I could find I would gift the same way.

Everything I collected was stuffed into industrial-strength black garbage bags.

Petrichor said, "That's enough. Hospital. Now."

"After."

"After what?"

I handed her the heavy bag. "After we get him."

A phone pinged. Pinged. Pinged.

A cellular rang. Not hers. It was the Samsung I had taken from the gunta.

I answered.

It was his wife.

I told her that it was the Kiwi. The one who had killed men in the streets of Port of Spain.

I said, "Killer Kiwi, the one they drew with big tits, small waist, and rotund ass."

I told her that her husband wouldn't be home for Christmas, that he was in line to have a conversation with Jesus's daddy. I told her to tell Diamond Dust that most of the husbands were queued in the same waiting room. I told her to have a nice night, kiss the

575

kids. Then I hung up.

Upper Collymore Rock, Parish of St. Michael
We passed young people carrying old people, passed the old carrying the young, passed the injured, many injured in the rain, saw many transporting the wounded on the bars of worn bicycles, passed secondhand cars filled with people in pain, some of the people crushed, some burned, all heading toward QEH. The flames at the Shell gas station still danced in the wind and rain.

I asked, "What should we expect? The island's version of the National Guard?"

Petrichor answered, "When there is a big disaster, they're slow, but they mobilize. Ambulances from the Barbados Fire Department are also called out. The least injured are sent to polyclinics while the more serious go to the hospitals. QEH might be flooded on the ground level. Was flooded last time it rained like this. Doctors might be on the way to some of the people, maybe starting up by the explosions in Upper Collymore Rock. Sometimes private doctors go to the scene to help in cases like this. Not much they can do, but they will go. People will be on the road driving other people to QEH. Some people will walk five miles to get there. Much people are going to be on the road. Sandy and Cherie Pitt will be busy. *Nation. Advocate.* CBC News. Photographers. Military. If they're not here, they are en route. Dead people will be on the front page of every paper tomorrow and the next day and the next day and the next."

Pain had numbed me and I only heard the first three words she had said.

We were at the plaza where Big Guy had his office.

Gun at my side, Petrichor leading the way, I climbed the stairs to Big Guy's office.

The injured and dead guntas who had been left here were already gone.

LKs had collected some of their men right after the melee started.

I would've tied all of them to the back of the truck and driven them to town.

Big Guy was on the floor in his office, everything turned over and on top of him.

He could only see out of one eye. His right arm was broken. His left leg fractured.

I moved in the darkness and said, "Came to cut your neck."

"Reaper? That you?"

"It's me."

"You got it bad."

"I know. You're about to get it worse."

"Shite." Each breath a deep pant, like it might be his last, each word a groan that trembled in fear, like it might be his last. "They got you and you got mad and came back for me?"

"I came to take your fingers, cut your

throat, then rip your spine out."

"You mad at me? You came back to kill me? What was I supposed to do?"

"Not this time. I was joking. I came to get you to the hospital."

"For real?"

"For true."

He huffed and puffed, crying. "Thought I was dead. The bombs, the explosions."

"Thought you were dead until I heard you scream when the first one hit."

"They made me call you."

"You screamed like a white woman getting her gold snatched at Limegrove."

"You would've screamed too. Scared the shit out of me. Men in wars scream, damn it. I was caught off guard when they came. They were going to kill you, then kill me."

"You snitched."

"They came in here with guns and scared the shit out of me. They knew about the passports. I called you and lied about the eight passports, hoped you'd figure it out, then hoped they didn't."

"Relax. I know."

"I only have three."

"What?"

"I know you wanted twice that, but I only have three passports."

"You have three?"

"Just three."

"Three? You had three passports?"

"They took them. They stormed into my office and took them off my desk."

"Shite."

"They dropped them when the first bomb when off."

"Where are they?"

"On the floor."

"They're in this office?"

"Guy was by the door when the first bomb exploded. He dropped them."

Petrichor used her flashlight, scanned the floor, then said, "I see them."

Big Guy asked, "Who are you?"

"I'm not here."

I used the wall to hold myself up, said, "I have three passports."

He said, "I know you wanted more. Broken or not, I really want to keep my fingers."

"Nobody is going to take your fingers, toes, or nose, not tonight."

"Can you help me get to my car, then put it in neutral and bump me toward the hospital?"

"Your car was destroyed when the gas station blew up."

"Shite. I was behind on my insurance. Goddamn squatters. You still have to pay me for the passports. Don't forget that. They gave them to me on credit, and I need the money."

We helped him into the truck. It was like stuffing a wet elephant into a birdcage. Along the way, we picked up wounded people, young and elderly, let them climb in back and hold on. Winds had died down by the time we trampled into a packed ER, spoke over groans and moans, said we were victims from a melee in Collymore Rock. Petrichor was there the whole time, my backpack at her side, a few grenades in case they were needed, guns in case they were needed, knives and a hatchet in case they were needed. She scouted the hospital hunting for LKs, in case any had been brought here.

Doctors saw me suffering, bleeding, sitting in my own mess, skin ashen, unable to open a swollen eyelid, and either pity or the absurdity of white privilege evoked itself. They rushed to examine me, a Swiss tourist here on holiday, my wealth of injuries the type if broadcast could cause a travel advisory and crush the already weak economy. I told them to tend to Big Guy first, but he told them to take me. Once in the care of a nurse, I said I had been trapped by the bad men, beaten and thrown in the road. Three bullet fragments were in my body. The pain was unbearable. I had to tell them that I had been raped in both orifices. I had to tell them as Petrichor heard denial give way to my vile confession, as she clenched her teeth, cried, and cursed in Bahamian. It hurt her more than it hurt me. She almost broke down. As I lay suffering, they examined me and told me that I had expelled a fetus. Petrichor broke down.

SIXTY-FOUR

Trinidad, Piarco International Airport
The sun was rising, its glow spiritual, the winds calm, the Caribbean Sea beautiful.

Her mood was the opposite of the astounding beauty, opposite of godly.

Thirty minutes after takeoff, Diamond Dust's private plane, an Embraer SA Legacy 650 jet designed to be relaxing and transport up to fourteen people, approached the runway in Barbados. Twelve traveled with her. Four wives. Eight of her council, well-armed men dressed in suits, shades of gray. Her smokeless powder, copper-jacket security. Brutal. Smart. Vicious. They were on red alert. RCSI. The Barbarians. Everyone in her group knew it had been the Barbarians.

The Kiwi had spoken to one of the wives, and the wife had panicked, called other wives.

Wives had the phones of the wives ringing before anyone had called Diamond Dust.

Action had to be taken. More dead husbands. More angry wives.

A second private plane, the twin to the one she was on, was dispatched to America and should have landed three hours ago, hours before dawn. Diamond Dust had entered the plane wearing a beige suit and Blahniks, but when she exited, she wore jeggings, Converse trainers, and a Radical Designs tee.

War Machine and six men waited for her and her entourage outside of customs.

Not many were out. She had come in between the large flights from Miami, New York, and London. With their credentials, her party breezed through customs.

On the soil of Little England, few recognized them; none approached them.

Another cyberattack had originated from here at UWI Cave Hill.

They would access the videos in the library and locate this second hacker.

Her first words to War Machine were, "The Kiwi."

"Let's ride."

"Did you find her again?"

"Area is called Six Roads."

"Where?"

"Five minutes from here in St. Philip, next parish over."

"Two SUVs go with us. One goes to UWI. The others go to meet the Barbarians."

When they were in the SUV, he showed her a roll of money.

She asked, "What's that?"

"Was at her safe house. It's the same money we paid our contact here with."

"The blood?"

"Has to be from when she killed him."

"She killed Scott Pinkerton and robbed him."

Ten minutes later they were at Six Roads, walking through what War Machine had been told was the Kiwi's safe house. Worn mattresses had been flung from the cheap beds, every ragged cabinet emptied, the box-size dwelling in shambles. It was a house that was part of a shell corporation. One of RSCI's well-hidden shell companies. Some clothing had been left behind, plenty of makeup.

War Machine's men had been there, waiting for the Kiwi to return for the last two days.

Diamond Dust inhaled heat, staleness, working-class poverty, and asked, "Fingerprints?"

"None. Nothing. Not on a surface, not on a cup, not on the toilet."

"Anyone talk to the neighbors?"

"One of the men pretended he was her boyfriend, went door to door, said he hadn't heard from her since the tropical depression. No one knows her. She came and went on a motorcycle."

"When did the power come back on?"

"Six hours ago."

"With the damage that had been ordered,

faster than I had anticipated."

"Only half the island has power. The resorts along the West Coast. The landlocked are still living in the dark. With the windows open, you can smell spoiled food rotting in the trash cans. That's what's attracting flies to plant eggs, create maggots, and make more flies."

"What did you and the men do to the Kiwi when you had her in your custody?"

"Standard procedure."

"Standard procedure. Appaloosa went first?"

"It didn't break her. She was as strong-willed as you."

"Did you have her?"

"Stay on point. When we left, she was last seen in a firefight on a rooftop. We had to go, the weather was against us, and the law was bound to arrive soon. She should've been gunned down while we were in the air. She was fucked-up and should've been dead on the roof."

She pulled her lips in. "No remains were found."

"Not yet. None that would be her. We greased palms, walked the morgue."

"I meant the bodies of my . . . our men."

"Missing. That, or unidentifiable."

"The wives are in a severe state of unrest and feel unsafe."

"Within an hour, a team followed our tracks and found nothing identifiable."

"Two helicopters crashed. That was all over the Internet."

"Each had explosives that destroyed anyone onboard and its contents. Nothing pertinent was recovered from either."

"The choppers?"

"Reported stolen from Miami."

"Pilots?"

"Not Trini. None carried identification."

"Our rings?"

"They vanished from our men's fingers. Every ring vanished."

"Looters. Thieves."

"Robbing the dead. A disgrace."

Roosters crowed outside the window.

Diamond Dust looked into the yard. "The Kiwi stayed here?"

"She did. Had been here for over a month."

Diamond Dust looked at every wall. From roof to floor, in every room, in the same handwriting, the same message had been written with a black marker. FUCK YOU, JOHNNY PARKER.

Large and small, it had been written a thousand times a thousand times.

She dismissed the madness. "Why here? Why was she brought here?"

"No idea."

"Take me to the other place. I am ready for the meeting with the Barbarians."

She took her husband's hand, squeezed it over and over.

He asked, "Thoughts?"

"I will cover for you. I have to spend the rest of my life covering for this mistake."

"I did what would have garnered us more political power."

"Your fucking decision cost me my brother. Cost my children their uncle."

"He was my cousin. He was my brother. We will talk."

"If the Kiwi had been killed at the bank, I never would have known."

"Whisper that, and only to me."

Her jaw tightened. "RSCI."

"What about the Barbarians?"

"Our men should be there now, ready to have a business meeting."

"Wife, you went ahead and ordered my men to America unbeknownst to me?"

"Be glad that you are the father of my children; be glad that I live for New Trinidad."

"Just stick to what you do. You have style. You make speeches. You have a flair for that, have an instinct, the ability to mesmerize and have legions of people follow you. No matter what you do, they follow you. I carry the guns and do the heavy lifting. This went bad, and bad things will happen. Mistakes will be made along the way, but that comes with progress. I do the military strategizing, not you."

"What are you without me? Nothing."

"Quite the opposite. You are a speech maker, not a warrior. You put on sexy shoes and vain women want to be like you. Do what you do best; continue the creation of what you want to become — a gynarchy. You can eventually rule all of Trinidad, but it will never be done with a petticoat government."

"Did you forget how I earned my name? I have blood on my hands as well. Much blood."

"Know your place. Know your limitations. I will not make a call and reverse that order to attack RCSI because it will make you look bad, would make me look like I was not in control, would make it look like we are falling apart, so I will support you on that, no matter how it goes, but I tell you this and I tell you this one more time, so fucking hear me: You don't give executive orders. Do nothing without consulting me. Remain a talking mannequin and woo the people with your charm and fashion sense."

"I should have chosen Appaloosa as my number one."

"You didn't."

She said, "Only one of us is replaceable, and that is not me. I am this movement, not you."

"Kings chopped off the heads of old queens and found a new one. They find a younger, prettier queen and the people forget about the old queen. When the king goes away, so does the kingdom."

She reached for his hand. He took hers.

They left the safe house.

Across the field, on the roof of an unpainted block house, there was a reflection. It was but a flash that came and went. Diamond Dust paused, looked across the field, to the roof of that structure, a two-level located one neighborhood over, far removed, but in plain view of the front of the safe house.

War Machine asked, "What's wrong?"

"Do we have other men out in this area?"

"No. Why?"

Diamond Dust looked at that roof again, then said, "Nothing."

Graeme Hall Nature Sanctuary was shut down due to the storm and the power outage. Only the Sanctuary Cafe and Lakeside Lawn and deck area had been open to the public; the interpretive walkways, aviaries, and exhibits were closed to the public due to some issue with the government. Diamond Dust followed her husband and four other men through the closed section, beyond the captive flamingos, exotic birds, and parrots from St. Vincent, took the winding pathway to the back side of the sanctuary and the mangrove swamp. Two Barbarians waited for her arrival. They had waited for forty-eight hours.

The men had been captured, stripped

naked, stripped of wet and battle-worn suits. Dormeuil and Zenga had been placed in narrow rowboats, hands bound to one end, feet bound to the other end. The rowboats were small and the extremities of both men extended beyond the boat. They had been cut a thousand times, small cuts, so the blood would attract bugs, and each man had been force-fed milk and honey until their bowels loosened. Honey covered their bodies, saturated their testicles. They had been smeared with more honey, force-fed milk every hour. More cuts had been added, not enough to die, only enough to make them beg for death. For two days, both day and night, they had attracted every insect imaginable. In pain, shitting without pause inside of the boat, attracting more insects to feast on their bodies, floating in the sun, in the brutal sun with their eyes to the sky. Their eyelids had been removed. Wasps stung the men, insects burrowed into their flesh. Diamond Dust watched, wishing that one had been the Kiwi in front of her with her flesh rotting away and being devoured by worms.

She asked, "What did they reveal?"

"They were in New York. They were in Miami. There were more, but they were there."

She motioned. "These are two of the men who engaged you here?"

"Others are dead. These are the last two."

"The Kiwi was with them in New York and Miami as well?"

"No. They were on the teams that attacked our shipments in both New York and Miami."

"Did they admit that? So that means they were part of the disruption here."

"The muscular one shut down. He manned-up and shut down."

"The other one?"

"Hasn't said a word."

"Not a word in two days?"

"Hasn't screamed. Has shit out loud and suffered in silence."

Diamond Dust's cellular buzzed.

She looked at her phone and said, "Bloody hell. What the shite?"

War Machine said, "What's going on?"

"Someone sent me pictures."

"Of?"

"Us. Pictures of us dressed as we are now."

It was pictures of them at the airport, arriving. Then a picture of a middle finger from the inside of a nondescript airplane, a picture of a middle finger, high above Barbados, the island as clear as it had been when Diamond Dust had landed, only with light clouds in the background.

She said, "It came from a Trini number, from the phone of one of our men."

"Which?"

"One who is on this mission, one who is still missing."

"Someone has his phone. We can assume he is dead."

She read the message. "To the vain, the capricious, the horribly insecure."

It was from the Kiwi. She had his cellular. They had passed her at the airport.

The Woman of a Thousand Faces had passed right by them. She had stood at the airport, in the heat, maybe near Chefette, watching them. The first picture made it look like she was but ten feet away. The second picture showed that she was at thirty thousand feet in the sky.

Diamond Dust said, "She had to be leaving when I arrived."

More pictures came. It was photos of them at the safe house at Six Roads.

The photo was of Diamond Dust looking directly into the faraway camera.

That was the reflection she had seen. Someone had been on the roof photographing them through the lens of a sniper's rifle. Maybe it was the Kiwi, but it couldn't have been.

The message was clear. She was gone. They had failed.

She looked at the Barbarians. It could take seventeen days for them to die from starvation, dehydration, and septic shock. She would love to see the gangrene set in to their extremities.

Diamond Dust ordered, "Kill them. They

are of no use to us."

War Machine nodded at his men, confirming both his power and the order of execution.

As she walked away, as War Machine followed her presidential fury, two guns fired.

Green monkeys ran, fish jumped, and a hundred species of birds flew from the trees.

He asked, "What do you want me to do?"

"Come home. Your children miss you."

"Do you miss me?"

"Don't ask me that."

"Do you love me?"

"You know I love you."

"Do you like me?"

"No."

An hour later, she was back on her private plane, between Barbados and Trinidad.

Diamond Dust glowered at the photos from the Kiwi.

A dozen flights had left since they had arrived in Barbados. That was a dozen planes the Kiwi could have boarded. Flights to other islands. Flights to Miami. Flights to England.

War Machine said, "We'll capture her again, then bring her home."

Diamond Dust shook her head. "No, just kill her. Just kill the bitch."

War Machine said, "She's using his phone."

"We'll track the phone and start the facial recognition again."

War Machine said, "Already started."

"We will know where she lands before we put our children to bed."

They kissed. She straddled him. She pulled her gray skirt up, pulled her thong to the side. She raised her hips, gave him room to unzip his pants and remove his erection.

She said, "Tell me this will be okay."

"This will be okay."

"Tell me again."

"This will be okay."

"I would sacrifice a thousand brothers to make our dream come true."

"I fucked up."

"I will fix it. We will turn our dead into heroes, into martyrs, into champions for our cause."

As the plane descended into Trinidadian airspace, he thrust upward, entered her.

Just like that, as it had always been, she started to orgasm.

SIXTY-FIVE

Toronto, Canada
My flight on Air Canada took me to Pearson International Airport.

Every Bajan on the plane chattered about the destruction to their homeland. Every tourist was happy to get away from the island. They saw me, saw my condition, and the malicious asked me what had happened. It was inescapable. I said that I had been in a car accident, that I was passing by LIME headquarters when it had been destroyed and I was lucky to be alive. I needed to get to Canada to get medical attention. They joked that people could die from a paper cut in the islands.

I sent Diamond Dust a second picture of my middle finger from Terminal 1, on the platform of the LINK train, the people mover. I was 2,500 miles away.

I might as well have been in another universe, and she knew that.

I imagined that I heard her scream.

I made a call. "Hacker?"

"Reaper."

"Everything a go?"

"Yeah. I can make it happen. Download this app."

"Downloading."

"You owe me a car."

"I know. I will work hard and I will pay you back. I promise."

"Waiting on a bus sucks. It's like riding in a can of germs."

Under Canadian skies I became someone else, went to the check-in and bought another ticket, became someone who was in need of aid and was moved around in a wheelchair, an attendant pushing me from security to my gate, my face covered with a scarf, and I caught a flight to Miami. I landed and caught a taxi to the cruise ships, to the hotels on water. Again I was on crutches. A foreign victim of domestic violence trying to escape her psychotic husband.

Three days aboard MCS *Divina,* never leaving the ship as they docked first in Miami, then in Nassau, and finally at San Salvador Island. Then on the Eastern Caribbean for seven days, again staying onboard six of the seven days. I could walk unassisted by then, was back up doing push-ups, stretching. Left the ship long enough to trail a Bajan soca singer to the Flamboyant Hotel and Villas in

Grenada and create pink mist before he attended an awards show. Did another job at Club Opium Nightclub and Lounge in St. Vincent. I did those jobs so Petrichor wouldn't have to leave her husband. I also did them for practice, to make sure that I hadn't lost my edge, that I could still battle, that my trigger finger didn't shake. Next I spent seven days aboard an Alaska cruise line. Never left the ship. The following seven days I was aboard the MS *Veendam*. Back in Miami, I boarded the Oceania *Regatta* for a twenty-five-night cruise. Twenty-five days of running, kicking, punching, lifting weights, preparing myself.

Hot. Humid. Raining. I disembarked at Port of Spain, where it had all begun. Carnival Cruise ships docked in the capital at the Cruise Ship Complex. Everyone was greeted by locals dancing in dazzling Carnival costumes, singing calypso. Some played the steel pan. I walked through the celebration, hair black, wearing white shorts and sandals, an Arkansas-accented woman wearing Jackie-O shades and a gray University of Memphis T-shirt. There were so many women who resembled me leaving the ship that it looked like I had been cloned ten times over.

An empty car waited for me, a car with darkened windows, suitcases in its trunk.

Petrichor had arrived here yesterday, made sure this was handled.

She had been on the roof of a home at Six Roads, had her sniper's rifle.

I could have killed Diamond Dust then. I could've had Petrichor kill War Machine then, but she would've had to escape. I wouldn't do to her what the Barbarians had done to me, send her on a suicide run. The photos had been enough to mess up their heads.

Soca jamming on the radio, I drove toward the Queen's Park Savannah. I parked in front of the American embassy, engine running, visor in the window to block being seen, and I changed, then drove the roundabout to the Carlton Savannah. I checked into the hotel wearing cloth that covered my head and chest and only revealed my eyes, clothing worn by Shia Muslim females. It was an island of many Muslims and Indians, so my attire was above suspicion, my accent on point, the workers never questioning my being alone.

The LKs had been tracking me.

Returning to their soil was my middle finger to all of those motherfuckers.

Thanks to Hacker, they had been thrown off. Thanks to an app I had, I could teleport the gunta's phone to anyplace in the world with two clicks. The app set up fake GPS locations so every other app in your phone believed I was there. I posted on Facebook, Twitter. Took more photos of my middle finger. The LKs thought I was hiding far away, had me fixed at 21.4167° N, 39.8167° E, had me hiding out somewhere near Dar Al Tawhid Intercontinental and Makkah Clock Royal Tower. They thought that I had escaped to Mecca. The arrogant fucks had confused resting with running. They didn't know that if I was running, I was sprinting toward them at full tilt. The GPS on my phone said I was standing at 10°40' N latitude and 61°31' W longitude. Had been a long time since I had seen the beauty of Port of Spain.

I went to the roof of the Carlton. Black Jack's voice inside my head, I stood where the politico had been thrown from the roof, replayed everything that had happened in Trinidad.

The end was always about the way it started.

Sixty-Six

The boy said, "Tobago is the cigar-shaped island. It has a northeast-southwest alignment. I can tell you all about Monos, Huevos, Gaspar Grande, Little Tobago, and Saint Giles Island."

"You're smart."

"If you need a tour guide, me and my father can show you everything. I can tell you about the geography of the islands. I know the archipelago, the reservoirs and dams in Trinidad and Tobago."

"Very smart. You're very smart."

Soon I was a passenger on a small boat riding the waves between Trinidad and Venezuela, a University of Cambridge backpack and luggage at my feet, riding choppy waters, eating bake and shark and sipping a beer. Checked the true GPS. Latitude: 10°42'00″ N. Longitude: 61°42'00″ W. I looked at my arms, my hands, my legs, inspected where scars had healed, where stitches had been removed. I had been on antibiotics for days.

Had been on antifungal meds for days. Was off the hard stuff, but was still on ibuprofen. The boat captain couldn't speak English. However, his teenaged son was fluent and very chatty, trying to earn a good tip. I told him my name was Dr. Jessica Lee. He told me that everyone called him Muppet. He used to watch *Sesame Street* all day as a kid, used to want to design muppets and become famous, like the guy who created Elmo. I was dressed in off-white Old Navy khakis and laced-up hiking boots, long-sleeved cotton blouse with the sleeves rolled up and tied to reveal my belly. An unopened pack of cigarettes was in the shirt pocket. My hair was purple, green, and orange, eyebrows deep-red, many silver and gold earrings in my ears and nose, my accent lazy and horrible North London.

He flirted, asked me if I had gone to college. I told him that I had a degree in advanced physics, had written a book on the theory of dimensionally displaced mass, but was trying something different until I returned to do postdoctoral work. That level of intelligence made him withdraw his application.

We passed by speedboats and yachts, saw fishermen out in the beautiful waters where drug dealing was the rich man's hobby. Then I saw the magnificent mansion sitting at Passy Bay.

It was only one of the homes of Diamond Dust and War Machine.

I took out my binoculars and tried to count the number of armed guards patrolling the dock and the grounds. A dozen women were outside as well. Some private gathering, maybe a small meeting with the top wives and top guntas, was ending, and a mid-size boat was there to take them to the next big social event. Couldn't see inside. Windows wore an embassy tint. Kept me from seeing in and kept the windows from shattering. The private home was cut into the side of the hills and the island was an estimated two miles wide. Behind the home was a tropical forest. In front of the home was the sea.

Muppet saw me looking and said, "Very powerful people live there."

"Priests? Social activists? Philanthropists?"

"Better. Everyone bows down to kiss their rings."

"Your voice trembled. Are you afraid of them?"

"Well, Jessica Lee, I want to be one of them. I want to one day join their group."

"Why?"

"Everyone gives them respect. Look at the crazy speedboat that they have."

"Material things make you want to be one of them?"

"The sexy girls. Sexy like you. The man who runs their business, he has the most beautiful wife in the world. In the universe. I'd get a beautiful girl to be my wife. Maybe get two sexy girls like you."

"Okay."

"I hear they have the best parties. The best parties in the world."

"You admire them with much intensity, almost sounds like you worship them."

"Mrs. Ramjit gave me a bicycle last year. Will never forget that."

"A bicycle won you over."

"No one had ever given me anything. It was stolen, but that's okay. I had it for almost a month. It was the best month of my life. I took my girlfriend for a ride every day. They're kind people."

The home was a technological fortress. Twelve high-def cameras surrounded the house. Those could be monitored from a laptop or a smart phone. A joystick could zoom in.

Diamond Dust and the well-behaved kids left the home, headed toward their private ferry, six armed guntas at her side. There had been more guntas guarding the queen, but I guess they thought I was in Mecca and they were only on yellow alert when they should have been on flashing red.

After what had happened at RCSI, they felt too damned confident.

They had attacked the company, had stormed in like they were in the Matrix, killed many from the guard desk to the main offices of RCSI, but didn't get to the level with the man behind the double red doors. They had put enough deaths in their column to make their members happy.

Since the initial onslaught, twelve had been found dead in the last month.

Binoculars in hand, I saw another woman at Diamond Dust's side.

Her main mistress. Her mistress left with her and their children. Everyone was beautifully dressed. There was a big event tonight. One for the LKs and not open to the public, not open to the press. The beauty and topography of Passy Bay disappeared and in my mind I was back on Swan Street. I had bathed a thousand times and every day I smelled the guntas on my skin.

I glanced at the luggage that I had brought along for this trip, each piece locked.

Muppet laughed, said that maybe later he and his dad would hunt for white lobster.

I said, "Be careful what you fish for. You might catch it."

"You know what white lobster is?"

"Cocaine that's been thrown into the waters while someone was running from the authorities."

"We find some and we can be rich."

For a moment I blanked out, trembled with fear, could hardly breathe, had a shock of PTSD.

Muppet asked, "You okay?"

I nodded.

When I was near my drop-off point, I picked up my backpack. Muppet grabbed my luggage, two metal suitcases on wheels, both with hazard stickers across the top.

Each piece emitted a coldness that could be matched by my heart.

The father made broad sweeping hand motions and said something.

The kid said, "Dr. Jessica Lee, my father wants to know if we can help you with anything."

"You've done enough. I can handle it from here."

SIXTY-SEVEN

Shell casings were all over. Air smelled like
cordite. Heated weapons scattered on the
marble floor. Many weapons. Self-loading
rifles. Armalite rifle. Uzi machine gun. Glock
pistol. Browning pistol. Beretta pistol. A
revolver. Eight magazines. Almost three
rounds of ammunition of the calibers of
7.72mm, 5.56mm, .380mm, and .45mm. I
removed my earplugs, kicked the flash-bangs
I had used out of the way, and started counting the bullet holes in the colorful wall. Too
many to count. It was easier to step over
blood and the fresh and warm Dora the
Explorer art and count the dead men here
and there.

War Machine was unconscious on his
living-room floor, head bloodied from a cruel
blow from my sap. His face battered from the
blows I gave him, my hands covered in biker
gloves. Now his hands and feet were in duct
tape. I grabbed his ankles, dragged him across
the room, down marble stairs, his head

bumping, bumping, bumping. That gave the unconscious man new pain, woke him up.

I paused, looked around, took in what felt like a Trinidadian museum.

He looked up, dazed, confused. Then things became clear.

In a Kiwi accent I said, "War Machine, by jingoes, I love your home. Especially the dunny in each bedroom. I have been working the wrong end of the business. The wrong end, indeed."

"The Woman of a Thousand Faces."

"It's me. The Killer Kiwi. Guess what I came to do? It's in the name."

I pulled away my camouflage bandana, my natural hair exposed.

I said, "Greetings, War Machine. Greetings."

"You're not in the Middle East."

"I'm not in Mecca, only in the mecca of your life."

He looked around as if he expected to see an army, then said, "You're alone."

"I am an army of one."

"Welcome to my humble abode."

"This is like being at 740 Park Avenue, the most expensive place to live in NYC, where the top one percent of the top one percent live. Then again, you are like the Koch Brothers in the US. You have donated to most politicians, have most of them in your pocket, donated to groups, to causes that make mothers weep, given scholarships to colleges and universities. You campaign that your people want their island back the same way the Tea Party wants America, only you have a more forward vision, not one of the past. The moneyed are the real leaders, not the politicians. Excuse me for a moment."

One of the men had moved. I went to him, shot him twice, then went to the window and looked out at the sea. Monos Island. One of the Bocas Islands between Trinidad and Venezuela. South side of the island. Passy Bay. This area was a hiker's paradise. Nearest cities were Maturín, San Felix, and Guayana City. All too far away to hear men scream. Too far away to hear guns and bombs.

I needed to know all of that before I had left the cruise ship to attack a fortress.

Where once upon a time seven hundred million dollars' worth of cocaine was seized in the largest drug bust in Trinidad and Tobago history. More than seventeen hundred kilos of Peruvian marching powder.

I went back toward War Machine. I shot his unmoving men along the way.

I asked, "What was I saying? Breathtaking view distracted me. Lost my train of thought."

Silence.

I went to the back door of his castle, a small nation on a small island next to a larger island.

Four guards were back there, dead, bullets

to the brain. More weapons on the ground.

I said, "Today is my birthday, War Machine. I came to celebrate with you."

I went to the den. Three men were there, in front of five big-screen televisions that were on five sports channels. All the men were dead from the same lead poisoning.

Dora the Explorer was everywhere. A fascinating Rorschach for every wall, wonderful patterns.

He asked, "How did you compromise my home?"

"Abruptly."

Dressed in camouflage, wearing boots, I had hiked over the hills, come the back way.

I hadn't hiked that trail alone. He didn't need to know that. It didn't matter.

I asked, "How do men get to be as fucked-up as you?"

"We are but the reflections of the Creator."

"So you're saying that men are only imitating their father, or the Father."

"Who neglects us, abandons us, and treats us no better than the slave masters."

"What would you know about slavery?"

"I have blood on three continents and all three have suffered, born into a life of suffering, prayed all of their lives, and died suffering. When my people were no longer profitable, no longer interesting, their gods turned away and left them to struggle. We studied history."

"You and your wife."

"We studied the great rulers. Alexander the Great. Abraham Lincoln. Hitler. Queen Elizabeth I. Eva Perón. We studied the greats, we studied the hypocrites. We made a plan."

"That is why you have no behavior and act like you are spoiled gods."

"I am what the Greek gods, Roman gods, Egyptian gods, Norse gods, Hindu gods, Aztec gods, Mayan gods, Inca gods, Celtic gods, and any other god should bow down and worship."

"You're a forgery."

"This from a pretend Kiwi."

"A *killer* Kiwi from the land up under the land down under."

"Where are you really from?"

I imitated my mother's accent: "My ancestors dey Bajan and St. Lucian."

"You're a Douglah?"

Back to my normal voice. "Irrelevant what I am."

"Why don't you set me free?"

"Then? What, shake hands and zip to a pub in your speedboat and throw a few back?"

"We pull swords from my walls and battle to the end, like warriors."

"Now that I have you in a position where I can slash you from stem to stern and remove every bit of meat from your carcass like a pig at a slaughterhouse, you want to have an honorable battle?"

"Let's settle this; winner take all."

"A final battle is what you are offering."

"A final battle."

"Too late. This fox hunt is over. You hunted me. I have captured you."

"We are powerful. Others will come after you and stop you."

"Let me tell you why they never found any dead guntas in the streets of Bridgetown. Why they never found any of your wounded or dead LKs over at Upper Collymore Rock."

"You retrieved our dead from the morgue."

"Your trash was collected and disposed of in the sea, as trash should be disposed of."

"You have touched our dead, disrespected us again."

" 'Disrespected'? Fuck you. I was pregnant."

"My men fucked you like a whore and now you have an LK baby inside of your womb?"

"*Was.* When you assaulted me, I was pregnant. When you beat me, I was pregnant. You kicked me down concrete stairs when I was with child. So, who do you think has been disrespected?"

"You killed two of my men."

"Killing my baby checkmates any-fuckin'-thing you might say."

"The escalation of violence started with you improvising a public execution of my men."

"Blame the assassin. I'm a hired gun. It

could have been anyone from the Barbarians."

"It was your gun that murdered my men. Your trigger triggered all of this."

I paused and whispered, "How is your beautiful family, War Machine?"

He said, "They're off-limits."

"My unborn baby was my family, wouldn't you say?"

I went to my luggage, bags that had been dragged through bush.

I opened both bags, put the iced contents on display for him to see.

I said, "Appaloosa and two others are back home. Say whassup to your homies."

I put the heads in front of him the way Black Jack and the UWI girl they thought was Hacker had been left on display at Ridgeview.

His eyes watered as he stared at his dead brothers.

He stared and saw his fate.

He looked like he imagined himself, his head, on the shelf with his dead brothers.

Then I pulled their spines out of the bag, dropped those on the floor like chains.

His breathing thickened and he managed to say, "Jesus."

"How does it feel?"

"How does what feel?"

"To not feel physical pain for the last time. What comes next, you'll pray to die."

"What's in the needle you're holding?"

"This? Not death. That would be too kind. This is animal tranquilizer."

"Animal tranquilizer. How demeaning."

"Less demeaning than a roofie. The fun starts when you wake up."

I pushed the needle into his flesh, injected him with tranquilizer and whispered, "As thy sword hath made women childless, so shall thy mother be childless among women."

Sixty-Eight

War Machine woke, bound and gagged, naked, a golf ball taped inside his mouth, pillows underneath his belly to force his ass to be up high, restrained, in the position of humiliation. A cold Stag beer was in my right hand. He saw the silver dildo in my left hand. I put the Stag beer down.

He tested his restraints. The restraints won.

The house was cold, air conditioners turned on high.

He shivered and his circumcised cock shrank in response to the winter-like chill.

I mounted his back and inserted the dildo, no lubricant used, shoved it hard, fast, deep, and his back arched. He screamed a muffled scream. His face ripped at the lips. The corners of his mouth had been cut so when he screamed he gave himself a Chelsea smile. I removed the golf ball from his bloodied mouth. I wanted him to hear his own agony.

I pressed a button on a remote control device, and the dildo released sharp hooks.

He pulled at the chains, cried, screamed, made his face bleed, ripped his skin even more. He fought; he begged.

I said, "Don't beg. I never begged. No screaming; no begging."

I yanked out the dildo, let him scream.

Wearing a kind expression, I poured a bottle of alcohol on his wound, watched him suffer.

I took out tools made to break bones, extract teeth, remove fingers, cauterize wounds.

I whispered, "I was MX-401. Was. Did much dirty work, took shit from men like you, endured bigotry like I was in the military, only worse, and I endured, had earned an *M* and an *X*."

He begged. Offered me money. Told me where to find it, said I could have it.

He said, "Then I will tell you the truth about the politician you killed."

"The truth went out of style a long time ago. That's what Raymond Chandler said."

"The truth remains fashionable with me."

"What's the truth? Tell me. Be honest, and maybe you'll live."

In severe pain, he bled, he sweated, panted. "The bank. Where it all went wrong."

"I have questions."

"I'm hurting."

"Why the hell did the bodyguards stay in the car?"

"Those were my orders."

"Why? Why was the metal detector turned off at the bank?"

"Be honorable. Let me . . . too much pain."

"Breathe, breathe. Now, adjust to the pain. Talk."

He panted, sweated, bled.

I asked, "Why did the politician have a loaded gun inside a bank?"

"You are a lucky one. A very lucky one."

"I heard. A preacher told me that, only I doubt if he was a preacher."

"It was as if God was on your side."

"Why did the target recognize me twice, once at the Carlton and the next day at the bank?"

He coughed. "Saved by a priest. You were saved by a gregarious, narcissistic, money-laundering priest who saw cameras and saw a chance to press flesh and steal some publicity for himself."

"I was saved by a priest who was at the right place, wrong time."

He could barely talk. "First off, why were you allowed to walk into a bank with a gun?"

"When I step back, that makes no sense. What would've made sense, and it's something I knew before I was told, was that a sniper could have done that job and never been seen."

"You were allowed to walk into a bank with

a gun because they wanted you there with a gun."

"What was going on?"

"I will tell you. Then let me go."

"Depends on what you say."

The man with the Chelsea smile, the man who was once handsome, had much to say.

SIXTY-NINE

I removed bloodied plastic gloves, wiped my brow, then sat down at one of their computers. I turned it on and contacted Hacker. From there, she could create a remote access and get into their files, could get into whatever computer network was linked to this one. Anything regarding me would be redacted, the rest sent to the news media. Let Trinidad see their saviors as the devils they really are.

Glass of wine in hand, wearing a pair of War Machine's wingtip shoes, leaving bloodied footprints that marked my journey, I toured his extravagant home, touched much Trinidadian art.

The home was an armory by the sea, stocked in preparation for a terrorist attack on Trinidad and Tobago. Emergency power generators, large canisters of propane, bulletproof glass, and each wall fortified to endure an economic collapse, a worldwide pandemic, chaos and the depths to which humanity might sink when there was no law in place. Enough nonperishable food to last six months, maybe nine.

They were ready for an apocalypse, maybe even a major zombie attack.

They hadn't been ready for me, an army of one. The Kiwi killer. After walking through five bedrooms, I went into the master suite. Their sprawling über-king-size bed was a bed/bunker that was bolted to the marble floor, the rest of the room carpeted. Not a bunk bed for a child, but a bed that was custom made and housed a military bunker underneath the mattresses, a king-size metal compartment used for storage, as in one used for the preparations for war, or for storage of weapons and valuables.

Theirs was an immovable safe. It was a bank vault underneath pillow-top comfort.

Hundreds of gold coins, thousands of silver coins, Rolex watches, thirty-six handguns, twenty-seven rifles, ammo, and $125,000 in cash. The first cash that I uncovered was in American money. There was more. Many layers. Underneath that neat stack of cash there also were over 800,000 Trinidad and Tobago dollars. That money was sleeping with 250,000 Bajan dollars, 81,000 British pounds, and 95,000 euro. At the bottom of the pile was over 4 million in Russian rubles, 700,000 in Argentine pesos, 130,000 in Canadian dollars, 700,000 in Chinese yuan,

139 million in the South Korean won, 140,000 in Australian dollars, 1 million in Eastern Caribbean currency, and 800,000 in Swedish krona. My mind did its best to do the math. That might have been close to $2 million US dollars. The money and the jewels.

The cricketer had owned the same style of high-end bunker bed.

He had said there were only two in the West Indies, that the big man he worked for had the second one, and this was the second one, so that double-verified that he worked for the LKs.

I'd bet the cricketer's bed had money under it as well — not this much, but a nice amount.

I'll bet his pregnant wife had no idea she was sleeping on top of a nice amount of cash, guns, and other jewelry, whatever his obsession with material things drove him to buy. I'll bet he had seen the rings that the LKs wore, admired the men of power, then ran out and bought himself three to be like them.

I could see the connection now. I saw a man who idolized another man.

The cricketer had tried to turn his home into a version of Passy Bay.

War Machine was his role model.

The pregnant wife might have been his Diamond Dust without a cause.

I went inside the luxury shower, turned on a dozen shower heads, put the music on, kept guns at my side, and washed away the dead man's blood, washed my scarred skin, and again I changed, decided who I would be for the next few hours, and dressed. While I applied makeup and latex, War Machine's words, his final words, stung. That last conversation as he lay in pain, suffering, bleeding, facing death, made me tighten my jaw, made me want to break and burn everything inside of this wretched home. Once I was dressed, I stood in the doorframe, adjusted my cap, looked at the blood all over the floor.

I stood and looked to the right at his bloodied corpse, then looked to the left at other parts that had once made a disarticulated man whole, stood and reheard his words, War Machine's words, our last conversation played over and over, its ugliness an infinite loop in my head.

Breathing heavily, fear arriving, trying to be brave, he had said, "Reaper."

"Tell me before it's too late."

"You were sent to kill the politician; that was the lie you were told."

"That was the setup. Tell me the punch line."

"That was your task. If you had killed him, only him, it still would have worked itself out."

"If you want medical attention, no matter

how humiliating that will be, tell me every-thing."

"The politician. However that turned out, was fine. That was sanctioned."

"Sanctioned? By whom?"

"By me."

"You knew about the hit in advance."

"I helped with the planning."

"Someone at home was on your team? Is that what you want me to believe?"

"Only, the politician was to kill you while you were here in Trinidad. Not our men. I made the call, took my men out of the bank so no matter what happened, we would suffer no casualties and be unable to be given any blame. If the politician managed to kill you, or if you had killed him, that would have kept us out of the equation because it would have been his choice to go in alone. His choice. His arrogance would have gotten him killed. It would have kept the Barbarians from hav-ing cause to start a war on us."

"He wore a bulletproof vest."

"Because. He. Knew. He was waiting on your arrival."

"He would have killed a woman in a crowded bank?"

"An assassin, not a woman."

"He assumed killing a young woman would be easier. Civilians as witnesses, civilians who would have praised him; it was the perfect setup. They had filled the safe house with everything you needed to make me look like an international hit woman before I arrived. It was all part of the setup."

"The politician knew you were coming. He was armed, waiting. We had practiced with him all morning. He could shoot. All he needed was one shot, but he had never had to shoot under such circumstances. He panicked. The priest stepped to him, you walked in, his view was blocked, but he could see you — saw you coming to kill him. It became a race to shoot, and he panicked."

I paused. "Who sanctioned it on the side that used to issue my paycheck?"

"Someone at the top."

"I need a name."

"I communicated with only one, the one with the power."

"Give me a name."

"There was no name. No one in your organization, no one on its dark side, has a name."

"We all have identifiers. What was his designation?"

He suffered awhile, each breath exacerbating his pain.

I said, "Just when I thought we were getting along swimmingly."

I poured more alcohol over his open wound. When he was done screaming, sweating, and jerking, then he panted and he told me. Still, I didn't believe him. He was desperate to live.

I asked, "Why would the Barbarians work with your organization?"

"Money. It would cost us a lot to have access and the right to kill one of their assassins, one who had status, one who had earned an *M* and an *X*. You were their Modesty Blaise, a secret agent whose hair color, hairstyle, and clothing changed at a snap of her fingers. You were their Lazarus. From what I heard, you were a pain in the neck, impossible to work with. You were expendable."

"Why not a man? Why not kill a James Bond? Why sacrifice me?"

"With your looks, it would have been international news. International fame."

"My curse."

"What curse?"

"My skin is my sin. My gender is my sin. Take your pick."

"What?"

"I live in a world where if a woman asks to be educated, and she presses for that right for herself, she is left for dead with a bullet in her head. Metaphorically, that's what they did to me. Trinidad was a bullet to my head. I was a strong employee, and when I demanded what I deserved, to them I was an uncontrollable bitch. I was a stunningly principled and fearless young woman, a girl who put those barbaric men to shame. If I were a man, I would have been called a maverick and given a corner office."

"The politician was to kill the assassin, the white foreigner, in public — the white woman, the symbol of all things that many have come to both emulate and loathe. He would have saved the people in the bank in Port of Spain, all captured on tape. Then your credentials would have magically been found, and he would be seen as a hero, receive tons of positive press, and elevate his status. He would have been the next prime minister and we would have owned the office."

"And with him in your pocket, every contract that came through would have benefited the LKs."

"Money is power. Politics is power. With both, with him, we would have been unstoppable."

"You were paying well to make that happen. Actually, the second plan sounds better, when you say it. Might be your accent. But the way you say it, killing me in a bank really sounds cool as shit."

"We were paying top dollar to have a top assassin's head on a spike."

I laughed a little. "To be able to kill a white foreign woman who would look good on TV. The Woman of a Thousand Faces. Kill a nobody, and become a somebody. Kill the white woman."

"You find that humorous?"

"You were conned."

"What?"

"And I find that tragic. When they drew my blood and tested my heritage, traced my genealogy, that would have been double hilarious. How much was I being sold for?"

"More money than ninety-nine point nine percent of the people here see in ten lifetimes."

"So, the hit was on me so the minister-of-whatever could look like a national hero."

"It's all part of the game. It's a move on a chessboard, nothing more."

"Not buying it. Sounds good, well thought-out, sort of, but not really, and I am not buying it. What's missing? All you have told me, with the facts you have pieced together, with the time that has gone by, it would be easy to reverse-engineer a bullshit story, an elaborate bullshit conspiracy story like that one."

"Does it look like I knew you were coming here today?"

I pulled my lips in, then I poured more alcohol on his open wound.

His scream echoed throughout the cavernous home.

He prayed for death. He prayed to a God he no longer believed in.

Maybe he was right and was just praying to a God who had no time for him.

I said, "Talk, War Machine."

"I'm in pain."

"I still have two bottles of alcohol left."

626

"No more alcohol."

I shook the bottle, made it slosh. "Talk or I push the dildo back inside of you. Talk or I push the button again. Talk or I will yank it out of you again. Talk or there will be more alcohol."

"Let me catch my breath so I can be clear."

"Talk now or don't talk at all. Take me back to the Caligula party at the Carlton Savannah."

"The minister was expecting you at the Carlton. If he hadn't been unexpectedly delayed, it would have happened that night. If not for Appaloosa and all that came after, it would have been done there, on the roof, in front of many who would spin the story as we saw fit."

"Your misogynistic men didn't know what was going on."

"No. It had to look authentic, and even if the politician had struck the first blow and my men had then drawn and helped gun you down, it would have still been sold as the victory of the minister, an assassination attempt gone bad. Again the press. Again the coverage. Again the elevation of status."

"I'm not convinced."

"At this point, all I own is the truth."

"The woman who was raped for sport, that rape applauded by other women . . ."

"The one woman who refused Appaloosa many times, came with his rival. Came with an old man who brought her to spite him, to rub it in his face, to look down his nose at Appaloosa."

"Appaloosa was a spoiled brat with a gun, corrupted by power."

"He was a smart man, but not much on critical thinking, not when drunk."

"None of you were. At your Caligula party, all of you became typical frat boys."

"I'm hurting."

I said, "Keep going."

"The pain is distracting me."

"You want the pain to stop?"

"Yes, please."

"You want the pain to stop and I want the truth to start."

"You're insane."

More alcohol. Pain sharp and searing. Deafening screams.

Then deep breathing.

I whispered, "Talk. King Killer. He was in on this. He expected me at Rituals."

"He had no idea. If you're wondering if you seduced him, kudos. You did."

"Who sent the drinks?"

"What?"

"Who drugged me?"

"I have to confess. I did. I wanted to assure a victory on the rooftop."

"You drugged me so that when the target arrived, I would be an easy shot. It was you."

"I sent the drink. Yes. It was me. To give

him an advantage."

"You had me searched, weapons taken away."

"Had all chopsticks removed. I knew yours would be filled with poison."

"Then pretended you didn't want me on the roof."

"I played my part. I monitored you, told the politician you had arrived, drugged you."

"You played your part well."

"You should've died on the roof of the Carlton. You should have been thrown from the roof."

"Why did you sacrifice your cousin?"

"There was no other option."

"You led your team into a mission with bad blood."

"It had gone public. Photos of my slaughtered men were on the front page of the fucking newspaper. There was an internal problem. We were seen as weak. Someone had to take the fall."

"He was your Colin Powell, forced to take the blame for what you allowed."

"Colin Powell?"

"Your scapegoat. You blamed your wrongdoings on him, tattooed him with your mistake, did what was convenient, even though it was wrong, not to mention it was an immorality among the immoral, and straight-up cold-blooded. You couldn't have had a meeting with the group and sorted it out?"

"Never felt pain like this before, but it does not compare to killing my cousin."

"The Barbarians sacrificed me, is that what you're selling me? You threw King Killer under a train, and they threw me under a Sherman tank. Connect the final dots for me. One more time. You had a secret partnership of some sorts, is that what, now that the tables are turned, I should believe?"

"At the start, it was for the greater good of two organizations."

"Playing this in my mind. Be patient with me. It went bad; they were about to order me back to the safe house after the bank fiasco, send me there so I could be caught by your crew, but you refused to pay. Your men were dead; you were outraged. The politico had blown it. He was dead. I was alive. No money. So they kept me away, pulled me off the island when you refused to pay, sent me to other islands, had me on hold while you argued, dropped me in Barbados, where I would be close, easy to get to if the money part worked out. When you held strong, refused to close the deal, they attacked you in New York and Miami. I was already in Barbados, so they used me there. They used me to shut down one leg of your business. I was sent to attack you because you didn't pay for not being able to kill me."

"Minor setbacks. Yes, done out of spite when I refused to pay after my men were killed."

"The dots are connecting. The guy I handled at the Gap, he was yours."

"An associate, so to speak."

"He was in charge of your drug shipments there."

"We have contacts on many islands, intermediaries. Go-betweens we used to do things so our hands never get dirty, so our faces are never seen. They work the way the US does its dirty work."

"New York. Miami. Barbados. I have no idea what else they did, but it was all done to get back at you for not paying for the chance to kill me, then not paying after not being able to kill me. Laughable."

"Yes. Laughable. When you say it the way you say it, I do see the humor in the tragedy."

"How much did they charge for allowing a racist politician the chance to kill me?"

"The money we were due to pay them, it is here."

"Here? In this mansion by the Caribbean Sea?"

"It has been here the whole time. My wife discovered it."

"My employer was cash-strapped and willing to sell me to make ends meet."

"Your death would have bought them money and time. They had dealings in Barbados as well. The island has been chopped up and sold off and many companies have businesses there. Those unwise businessmen had a major real estate venture that had gone very bad. They allowed homeless men to put them in a bind. In the end, they were cash-strapped and desperate."

"They sold me to stay in business. You would've used my death to expand yours."

"I had read your credentials. You were perfect. No fingerprints. We could've said you were from anywhere. No blowback for the Barbarians. We could've killed you, shown photos of the Woman of a Thousand Faces on the news, online, all over the Internet and created whatever narrative we saw fit, could've made you out to be whoever we wanted you to be. We would have risen even higher."

I glanced at my hands, at my fingers. He was right. No fingerprints. They could've said I was from anywhere, from any country. I would have been Jane Doe used to further their cause.

I said, "If that's true, you're right, there would have been no blowback."

"Your designation of MX-401 would have been erased from Barbarian records with a keystroke."

"MX-401. You know who I am."

"Kiwi, I know who you are. You're MX-401."

"You could've gotten that off of a license plate."

"You're MX-401. That was all I needed to know. That was what they sold me."

I shook the bottle of alcohol. "You have anything to substantiate your claims?"

"Haven't I said enough? What more can I fucking say?"

"I wish I had killed all of you motherfuckers in Barbados."

He murmured a string of nonsensical sentences, winced, coughed, and ended his diatribe by shouting, "You were not supposed to kill my men."

"I sure as fuck wasn't going to let your men kill me, ya rasshole."

I picked up the golf ball, shoved it back inside of his face, taped his bloodied mouth, wrapped duct tape around his neck. I went to my tools, my tools of torture.

I placed photos of his wife and children so he could see them.

Those would be the last images he saw.

I snapped on surgical gloves, covered my mouth with a surgeon's mask and welding face shield, and said, "Get used to the pain. For Black Jack, for the girl that you thought was Hacker, for the Barbarians you left rotting at the sanctuary, for the baby that was inside of me that you beat until it died and was expelled from my body, this lasts for four hours."

Blade in my hand. Tupperware at my side. Alcohol. Torch to cauterize wounds.

I said, "This is how you earn both an *M* and an *X*. This is how, War Machine."

I told him what few knew, what the *M* stood for, then the significance of the *X*.

I said, "Business is a bullet to the head, that or a knife to the heart."

I held up War Machine's hand, looked at his wedding ring. His prized Wellendorff.

I took it. Would add it to the collection of souvenirs from Swan Street.

I said, "This is personal."

Two hours later, I made it to the hand he had used to strike me. I dropped it into a bucket of used parts. He wished for death. With fire I cauterized his wound to stop the bleeding, the same as I had done with his other extremities. The flaccidity that had once been the stiffness he had used to intrude my orifices without invitation, I dropped it into the bucket as well. I cauterized where it had been.

SEVENTY

I boarded War Machine and Diamond Dust's personal speedboat, a forty-foot Advantage Poker Run named *The Corsair*. Unsettled, I took off into the evening with the rear of the cockpit open. It was like driving a very roomy luxury car on water. I slowed down, stopped, and sent a text, let anxious thumbs open Facebook and guide me to Black Jack's page, then posted a message.

You were right.

I paused, waiting for a reply, knowing one wouldn't come.

I sent a message to Big Guy. Told him I would need him to do some laundry for me.

I sent a message to Hacker, told her she'd get a brand-new car tomorrow.

Then I sped away, a different type of anger below the surface, simmering.

Cold sea spray in my face, I should've felt satisfaction, but there was no satisfaction. There was no false feeling of victory. What had happened to me, it had happened, and would not unhappen. All I thought about ever since was the Punjabi that they had raped before my eyes. I was there and had done nothing. I had been an assassin. Not a savior. I was a killer. I didn't wear a cape. I had watched, allowed her to be violated, humiliated, publicly destroyed. This was for the girl they had taken and abused. This was for the beautiful girl who had been found two weeks later with her wrists slit.

Pyrrhic victory, not broadcast, maybe even pointless, but for her. The last spine I had collected, I threw into the beautiful sea. War Machine's head, I fed it to the Trinidadian waters as well. Then I looked back at the three trunks, all heavy with money from many nations.

The speedboat. The money. This wasn't stealing. This was reparations.

For my goddamn pain and suffering. For making Petrichor break down and cry the way I should have broken down and cried. A bullet to my head, knife to the heart, that would have been fair. I would have lost and had no ill feelings as I sat with a number in hand, waiting my turn to talk to Jesus's daddy.

Live by the bullet, die the same way.

War Machine's confession under duress hadn't changed denial into acceptance, chaos into order, confusion into clarity. I was not stupid. The best lies held some truth.

A man would say anything when death was standing in his face.

I filtered through that conversation, selected what to keep, what to discard, as though I were at a cafeteria of lies; I had no idea how much he had said was true. Some of it was. I just had no idea which parts. War Machine told me that I had been marked for death from the start.

The ill feelings I had hadn't been satiated.

This savage internecine warfare wasn't done.

I wasn't back in Trinidad alone. I had traveled here on the cruise ship alone, and I had been alone most of the evening. I wasn't foolish enough to try to compromise War Machine's home unaided.

A Bajan hacker had compromised the home security system and taken it offline.

A Bahamian sniper had been in the hills as I came down through the bush and trees.

The men up top on the hill, they all were dead with arrows in their chests.

The ones down below had been introduced to lead from a gun wearing a suppressor.

She had helped.

Old Man Reaper's Bahamian daughter had helped.

Petrichor had arrived before me. She had driven north to the safe house I had once used.

It had been empty. She had stepped to the wall, the one with the magic light switch, clicked it over and over. The wall had opened. The blueprints had been taken away, but no one on the LKs' team had discovered the cache of weapons. Many guns had been left behind and the canisters of poison were still there, untouched. We had used those guns to break into Passy Bay. Then Petrichor had left.

She had put on a kitchen worker's uniform and left.

Other things had to be taken care of back on the main island.

Things she insisted be taken care of so I would be able to rest.

Things I couldn't authorize, but I wouldn't stop her from doing.

SEVENTY-ONE

Petrichor entered with the help, most of the women of dark complexion, her accent that of a Trini. Old Man Reaper's Bahamian daughter was at Sunset at Pier 1. Williams Bay. Chaguaramas.

A man's cognitive process was impaired by the sight of a woman in a bikini.

It was destroyed when a naked woman appeared. It was devastated when she wore high heels. The armed guard in the kitchen saw her wassy walk. She began to wine. She began to wukkup, then she began to twerk, showed him the amazing things she could do with her Bahamian boonggy. She made her butt cheeks move one at a time, then in concert. She went into a six thirty, smiled at him from that angle.

She spoke to him using a perfect Trini dialect.

He lowered his gun as his expectations and nature rose. Beautiful brown skin on a perfect frame danced toward him, breasts jiggling.

Unarmed, naked, vulnerable, saying that she was so damn horny.

A palm strike to the bridge of his nose was as effective as a brick to his face, the heel of the hand as hard as a doorknob. Her sperm donor had trained her well. Before the guard could recover, the heel of a stiletto was lodged inside of his eye. Her sperm donor had trained her to make everything a weapon.

She could storm the room now.

She could use her weapons and storm the room.

Tonight called for a quiet storm.

Petrichor kicked away her second stiletto, took the downed guard's rifle and backed the waiter against a wall, threatened to blow his head off. The teenager was terrified. Not a threat. Then she told the teenager she was going to let him live. She reached to her lower back, pulled away a plastic Dasani bottle that had been taped there. She handed him a sixteen-ounce bottle of clear liquid. She told the server to put four drops in every wineglass; comply and serve, or die where he stood.

SEVENTY-TWO

Well-dressed men and women filed into a facility that could accommodate eight thousand, a place with the option of indoor and outdoor seating. Tonight the LKs had taken over Pier 1 for their meeting, a facility equipped with breakaway workshop rooms, lighting, and modern audiovisual equipment, everything necessary for what was the equivalent of their State of the Union speech.

Diamond Dust had married War Machine here. It had been a difficult choice, but she had chosen him over Appaloosa. She needed a man made for the public eye. She walked in and was greeted as if she were more important than the president and prime minister of Trinidad, as if at twenty-four years of age, she was the leader of every island in the West Indies, as if she were the real power.

One day soon she would be. One day soon she would rise to prime minister.

As they filed in, the adults, the leaders, were taken in one direction.

The energetic children kissed their parents good-bye and were taken to their own section, outside where they could have fun, be loud, run and play supervised in the cool areas by the sea.

They would have an ice-cream party. They always had ice-cream parties.

Diamond Dust removed her shades and gazed out over her people.

She had always considered them her people. Hers.

Some were poured Cristal Brut 1990, the "Methuselah." About $17,000 a bottle. Those were for the members of lower standing. The new wives. Others were served Dom Perignon White Gold Jeroboam — $40,000 a bottle. While some chose Pernod-Ricard Perrier-Jouët — $50,000. Diamond Dust drank her favorite Shipwreck 1907 Heidsieck. The cost of hers was $275,000 a bottle. All prices were in US dollars, the currency that set the standard for the world. So her bottle cost $1,765,500 in Trinidadian currency.

She did not share her bottle with anyone other than her husband.

She missed him being at her side. She missed him being inside of her.

Tonight there were no politicians. No public causes. The members of their organization were served the most expensive meal ever sold in Trinidad, prepared by six chefs, and everything was flown in from France, Germany, and Italy. Even as they mourned the dead, the living had to feast.

They gave toasts to their fallen comrades, to their dead husbands, to their murdered leaders, to the fathers of their children, to brothers, to cousins, to lovers, to the men they would avenge, spoke of the guntas like they should all be canonized. She had a power her husband envied.

Diamond Dust had always sounded like the true leader of the guntas, had studied and admired and envied both Argentine president Cristina Elisabet Fernández de Kirchner and María Eva Duarte de Perón — strong women, women born of nothing who had risen to the top and ruled their countries, and she vowed that one day she would do the same, that the LKs would do the same, that this was not the end, only a new beginning, and soon books and movies would be made about them.

She proclaimed, "I live for you. I live for my people. I live for a better Trinidad. This is my dream. You will have to kill me to stop me. We are moving our people from the slums, from violence. We are rising; we will rule this nation properly, as it should be ruled. You would have to kill all of us to stop us."

There was thunderous applause that echoed across Port of Spain.

In the middle of her speech, dryness attacked her throat. She sipped. Noticed everyone was sipping. She coughed. She apologized. Then there was scattered coughing. She felt light-headed. Her drink fell from her hand. She opened and closed her fingers. Numbness. She saw her hands but felt nothing. Everyone coughed, many tones, many octaves, many depths. She heard the echo. Looked out at her people. They all blinked, all looked light-headed, and many dropped or spilled their drinks.

Panic registered in their eyes.

There was a concert of concern and waves of fear as sweat rushed in.

She watched the room. Saw fear. Fear crepitated, ran across every fiber of their being. They rose to their feet. One by one they rose, the women wobbling on beautiful high heels. The first woman collapsed. A woman at the front table fell, lay on the carpet, eyes wide open, not breathing.

Diamond Dust saw another woman lose her footing, wobble on her heels, and fall.

One by one men fell. Men crumbled and fell. It was a death fall.

Diamond Dust didn't panic. She only nodded her head.

One by one, some in groups, she watched them drop, ease into their final sleep.

She sat down, thought of her children.

The children. It was almost time for them to have their dessert.

The children loved ice cream. She had been deprived of ice cream as a child.

High heels click-clacking across tile, the only sound that could be heard in the room, Petrichor went to the stage and sat next to Diamond Dust. Now Petrichor was dressed to fit in. Her wig was one of long, black, kinky hair; her gloves black, her über-sexy dress red, her jewelry gold.

Petrichor sat, crossed her legs, put her palms on her knees.

She whispered, "Checkmate."

Then with two gloved fingers, she reached over and closed the dead woman's eyes.

Petrichor walked away.

Her phone pinged. A sexual message from her husband. She replied: ICE CREAM BLOW JOB WHEN I GET HOME BABY. LOVE YOU. As she passed through the kitchen, the young waiter she had told she wouldn't harm, she faced him. She pulled chopsticks from her hair.

Beautiful chopsticks she had taken from the wall at the safe house up north.

She loosened the end of the red chopstick, rubbed the end and its dampness over his neck, and as the irreversible damage set in, she continued her stroll. No witnesses. He coughed. She kept going, never looked back as the man's nervous system struggled to function.

She paused when she saw the cart. The ice cream. The dessert for the children.

Petrichor looked at the bottle. Half empty. No. Half full.

Plenty was left; plenty of drops were left.

Petrichor went to the cart of ice cream that was for the children waiting in the structure out near the sea. Ice cream for the offspring of those who had raped her sister, of those who had killed her unborn niece or nephew. She pushed the cart, eager to feed the children of the LKs.

SEVENTY-THREE

Humming as she walked, Petrichor went and stood out near the dock. The sun would soon go down. A speedboat cut across the waters, as many had done since she had been waiting, this one named *The Corsair,* like the Barbary or Ottoman corsairs, pirates who worked out of North Africa, pirates who raided towns on the European coast and captured Christian slaves for the European market.

A man was driving the speedboat. A portly man, with blond hair and a Tony Stark goatee, dark sunglasses. The driver wore Dockers and a pink Polo. The moment the boat pulled up, Petrichor boarded. Petrichor carried Diamond Dust's body as if it weighed nothing.

Petrichor asked, "Who are you supposed to be?"

"Well, I ain't Heisenberg from *Breaking Bad.*"

"If I didn't know who you were, I would swear you were a fat man."

"Strapped down my breasts. Fat suit gives me a gut."

"Lose the guy voice, Reaper. That's freaking me out. You look old."

"Makeup. Put some gray in the hair. Gave myself crow's feet for kicks."

"You look like a fifty-year-old tourist from England or Canada."

Reaper helped her lay Diamond Dust on the floor.

"So, that's her."

Petrichor took a bottle from her bag, sat it down, nodded. "That's her."

"The bitch is beautiful."

"Was."

"Still is."

"Looks like she's sleeping."

"Sure was quiet back there at the docks. Saw jumpers, balloons, but no children."

Petrichor wiped tears from her eyes, found a napkin and blew her nose.

"Crying, Petrichor?"

"Allergies."

Petrichor removed her red dress and expensive heels, stripped down to biker shorts, vest, and sandals. She tossed her dress into the sea. Then she pulled her wig away, tossed it, her hair now short and natural. She stood next to her father's American daughter, the woman who, if not for a cruel trick by God, would have been called Petrichor. She felt honored to have her name. Honored.

Now they looked like a rich foreigner and his West Indian prize.

Petrichor asked, "What's in all the luggage?"

"What I'm worth dead, but what I will spend while I'm alive."

"You had a Jessica Lee moment."

"Half of it's yours."

"Twenty-five percent."

"You don't know how much it is."

"I don't care about money the way most people do."

Petrichor looked back toward where she had been. She looked back toward the silence. The bottle, the empty bottle of witches' brew, she tossed it into the sea. She had done what had to be done. No children of the corn would grow on that soil. She was Petrichor, but she was also Nemesis Adrasteia. She had done things her sister would never know about. Things had happened to her that she would never talk about, things that put her on this road. Nemesis, also known as Rhamnousia, the spirit of divine retribution against those who succumb to arrogance before the gods. She had to protect her father's American daughter. This was not a business for the weak. Little LKs would grow up to become big LKs. For their dead mothers, for their dead fathers, many would want revenge. One wanting revenge would be one too many. Maybe Reaper would hate her for what she had done.

Petrichor said, "You know I'm the one whom you call Old Man Reaper's daughter, right?"

"You told me he's your sperm donor."

"Do you have doubts?"

"What's the issue?"

"You're my sister."

"Okay."

"Say it for me one time. Humor me. Acknowledge me as your sister."

"I know you are."

"No, say it."

"You saved my life at Fitts Village. Saved me on Swan Street. Made tonight work. It doesn't matter if Old Man Reaper is your sperm donor, you're my sister. Like it or not, you're my sister."

"He is."

"I believe you."

"Say it."

"You're my sister."

"Thanks."

"That was weird."

"Someday I want to be able to tell people I have a big sister. One day, when the time comes, if the time comes, I want to tell my husband that I have a big sister."

"Someone sounds emotional. Are you pregnant?"

"No, I haven't swallowed watermelon. I have always wanted to have a sister. Is that too much for you?"

"No, it's not."

Petrichor wiped her eyes and said, "Thanks for saying that. Means a lot to me."

"We're family."

"We're a family you don't want to fuck with. I'll kill theirs to protect mine."

"With what I was told by War Machine, I might have to test that out."

"What were you told?"

"Enjoy the view, Petrichor. Enjoy the sunset until I slow down."

"What's the issue?"

"We'll talk."

Petrichor said, "The dead cricketer."

"What about him?"

"Contact came through. Hidden files found on the drive. Got his files encrypted."

"He worked for the LKs. That's where his real money was coming from."

"I have it all with me on my phone." She nodded. "A lot more."

"He was skimming off the top. That's why he had so much cash."

"He did much skimming."

"He was moving much product. They always skim off the top."

"Skimming and fucking and cricket and fucking and smoking and fucking and fetes."

"He had the life."

"All that and a pregnant wife and maybe thirty children."

"More came in?"

"Count's still rising."

Reaper explained what had happened between the Barbarians and War Machine's group.

Then she said, "The Barbarians and LKs were playing chess, but War Machine couldn't make a move without revealing his hand. He couldn't attack RCSI without giving a cause, not without revealing his hand to his people, not without letting them know that he had fucked up, not King Killer."

"Deep shit. What do we do about the Barbarians? We go after RCSI?"

"Let me think about it. Trying to put it together in my mind. Let me think."

"One more thing before I shut up and let you fall into a brown study."

"Okay."

"Guy you met has been blowing up my phone too."

"Orgasm Man."

"Yeah, him."

"Definitely not relevant."

Halfway to Barbados, Petrichor tied weights to the limbs of their dead passenger, then they paused for a moment, paused and fed Diamond Dust to the beautiful Caribbean sea. Extreme beauty sank into deep waters, swallowed by an infinite blackness.

Reaper said, "Too bad she wasn't still breathing."

"Should've kept those Blahniks."

"Would've loved to watch her drown down to the last air bubble."

"Wonder what size shoe she wore."

"I mean the last air bubble."

"Why did you want the fashion statement dumped way out here in the sea?"

"Because of Eva Perón. She had the nerve to compare herself to Eva Perón."

"Okay."

"When Perón died from cancer, some embalmer worked a miracle, took a year to drain the fluids out of her and made her beautiful again, and people love beauty. They love style. Flair. Power. Her people, thousands of women lined up for miles, stood hours to see her remains. Because they had her body preserved, she will never die. Diamond Dust, after what I went through, I would come back and burn down Trinidad if they took her body and preserved that shell for display in a glass-encased national monument, if they drained all of her bodily fluids and replaced it with paraffin wax. There will be no body to fix up like a movie star, no display, and no line of people showing up to mourn."

Petrichor pulled out the bottle of Shipwreck 1907 Heidsieck she had stolen, an untainted bottle, and opened it, wanted to know what it felt like to drink that much money.

She said, "Look up."

"What's up there?"

"The sky."

"Was hoping it wasn't another helicopter chasing us."

"Never been out in the water like this. Stars are pretty."

"Absolutely gorgeous, if you're into that sort of thing."

"I am into that sort of thing. I have never seen them so bright."

"Where I lived in America, it was never this dark."

"So you never saw the stars?"

"Not like this."

"Like I can reach up and grab one from the sky."

"Don't fall off the boat."

"Wish my husband was out here to see this."

"Don't. Fall. Off. The. Boat."

"So, Reaper, what do we do next?"

"Collections, Petrichor. From the Barbarians."

"We're going after them?"

"What, do you think we're a team?"

"What, do you think we're not?"

SEVENTY-FOUR

When the lights along the coast of Bridge-town were in sight, I took out a cellular, checked to see if I had a signal. LIME reached me on the waters. In my mind, for most of the trip, I had been plotting to go to RCSI, guns blazing, shooting my way to the top floor, then kicking open the double red doors.

I had imagined facing the man who sat behind the double red doors. Instead of taking it to their office in the sky, I punched in the digits to the Barbarians. I *called* them. I could have gone to America on the first flight in the morning, walked into their offices, and confronted them, but I called them.

"This is Goldilocks Reaper."

"Goldilocks Reaper?"

"MX-401, when I was a part of the Barbarians."

"MX-401."

"RCSI. Barbarians. Bet you never expected to hear this sweet voice again."

"They thought you were dead. They thought you were killed in Barbados with the others."

"They thought wrong."

"Why are you calling this organization?"

"War Machine told me."

"I don't know what you're talking about."

"Pass this message up to the coward who hides behind the double red doors."

"I don't pass messages."

"If I show up as the messenger, it will be ugly. I don't like being played."

"No one has played you, Reaper. Why would you say that?"

"Because the secret deal between War Machine and the man behind the red doors went bad, because the man behind the red doors still expected War Machine to ante up after Trinidad, because RCSI needed that fucking money to hold them over until the Rastafarians were shoved in a Chefette truck and cash started to flow from that stalled project. Tell them that they failed. Tell them I'm still standing."

"The Barbarians did nothing."

"The money that was used to pay the Rastas, the money they were burning, that money was stolen from the LKs when they were hit in New York and Miami. War Machine didn't pay the cash the company needed to stay afloat, so the company went after his ventures. Am I wrong?"

"There was no money stolen from anyone. We do collections. We're not criminals."

"RSCI will deny it. There is no proof. So, it would be pointless. I'll go up against them one day, just not today. Not while Old Man Reaper is still working for the boys. He keeps you safe from me. In the meantime, the swank safe house in Barbados at Miami Beach, it's mine. I have nowhere to go, nothing worth going back to in America, so I'm staying in Barbados and that seaside mansion will be my new home. Your Rasta problem is over. Your project is breaking ground on the bloodied soil and cash is flowing. Your LK problem is done. MX-401 is done. Your Goldilocks Reaper problem is just starting."

"Is that a threat?"

"My blade is sharp, guns are loaded, and the things I do when pissed off make the LKs look like Boy Scouts. I expect my back pay, every dime, plus penalties and interest at twice the rate of the IRS, and I expect it to be delivered to me within twenty-four hours. Pay me the way War Machine was going to pay the Barbarians: in cash, in multiple currency, same as you were getting from War Machine. Read the papers tomorrow. Read about War Machine. Read about the LKs. Then be afraid. The money and that property. That is nonnegotiable. Then I might walk away. Don't try me. MX-401, out."

"Wait."

"I waited almost two months for my team to do right by me. What am I waiting on?"

"Let me talk to the man behind the red doors. Let me play this recording for him."

"I wasn't supposed to escape the roof of the Carlton Savannah. I did. I know that I was given bad intel intentionally. I wasn't supposed to escape the bank. I know about the LKs' two other drug shipments being disrupted. Two thousand pounds of marijuana, that was what you had me do."

"You're insane. You're stepping into dark, deadly waters."

"Am I? Play this conversation for the man who sold me to the LKs then gave the Barbarians the order to kill me when I refused to participate in the wholesale slaughter of three generations of Rastafarians."

"Sure, I'll tell him you said that. Will ask him to listen to this recording now."

"Step up, compensate, give me reparations, make it right, or I'll make it right."

"He will never agree to any of that."

"This is not a negotiation, so don't talk to me like I'm a squatter. This is collection. It can be done over the phone, it can be done face-to-face, and you know how I do things face-to-face."

He put me on hold long enough to make someone listen to all that had been said, long enough for someone to make international calls to the Land of the Hummingbird.

Hours had passed. By now someone had found out what had happened in Trinidad.

When he came back on the line, he gave the answer from the man behind the red doors.

His voice was different, carried more than respect, carried fear, unfathomable fear, and each word trembled when he said, "You will have to agree to noninterference."

"You treated me like I was Tilikum, like I was just another performing killer whale. You better remember that after cruel treatment, Tilikum attacked, killed its trainer. Until I get a complete confession, a complete apology, one that makes sense, I agree to nothing, but you will agree to my terms."

Nothing would be confirmed. They would never say why they did what they did, why they treated me the way they had. Killer whales at SeaWorld were abused and mistreated, but they were treated better than I had been treated. That was as close to a confession as I would get.

I took a deep breath, steeled myself, and asked, "Where is my father?"

"Safe. On a mission."

"Where?"

"Undisclosed."

"How long?"

"Indefinitely."

"What did he do wrong?"

"Classified."

"Can I join him on the mission?"

"You're no longer part of this corporation."

"I'm somewhat of a bullshitter myself, but occasionally I enjoy listening to an expert."

"Meaning?"

"I want him set free. He's been off-grid too long. You have him imprisoned for something."

"You're not a Barbarian. Remember the first rule of the Barbarians."

I nodded. "One more thing."

"What's that?"

"Big Guy's debt is to be erased. Nobody touches him. Nobody collects."

"You're really pushing it. Push too hard, they'll come after you."

"The LKs came after me. You can come next. Come meet my aggression."

"Surprised you survived."

"You knew all along."

"What?"

"You're surprised that I survived. You knew all along."

"I just answer the phones."

"You take all calls, so you're like the mailman and see all debts, all transactions; you're an administrative assistant of some sort. You're a male Miss Moneypenny, so you know; you're the butler, the maid, the secretary, the fly on the wall. You see and hear and know everything that's going on."

"I just answer the phone and make hot

chocolate."

"I want to know one thing, from you. Why me? Why did they sacrifice me?"

"It was a decision that was made."

"Did it have anything to do with my father?"

"Classified. Sorry."

"I want a brand-new Mini Cooper left in the driveway of my new house."

"Really pushing it."

"I want it there by noon tomorrow. It better be sitting next to a new Wrangler and Ducati."

"The man behind the red doors is already outraged."

"What the fuck do you think I am?"

"You're pushing the Barbarians."

"They pushed first. I'm pushing back. Tell the man behind the double red doors if I have to I will come up there and push, and when I stop pushing, it's because they've fallen over the edge. And tell the man up top this: I have rules too, only three rules. The first rule of Reaper: don't fuck with Reaper. The second rule: never forget the first rule. If you do, there is the third rule."

"The third rule?"

"That one gets told face-to-face, right before you take your last breath."

"Three rules."

"Make that four."

"The fourth?"

"I'm. Not. Expendable. Bitch."

I hung up the phone, then looked down at the trunks of cash, calm, in control.

Petrichor said, "Why would they do that?"

"Maybe because I'm a girl. I'm just a girl."

"Really?"

"Or maybe because I am a Reaper."

A moment passed.

She asked, "You're staying in the Caribbean?"

"For now. Barbados will be my home for now. Until I get sorted out."

"You should've made them buy you a million-dollar condo on the West Coast."

"Should've made them buy me Ilaro Court, ten Chefettes, two beaches, and Novel Teas. Should've made them build me a Starbucks, a Barnes & Noble, Target, Sears, Best Buy, Old Navy, and a Walmart."

"And a Victoria's Secret."

"Fuck yeah."

"Thought you hated it here."

"I hate it everywhere. Hated Memphis. Hated Huntington Beach. Hated Florida. I'm like my mother. I'm just like my mother."

"You're staying."

"Had my first orgasm here."

"Want to see him again?"

"I'll move on."

"My treat."

"Nope. I'll look for something better, or something worse."

"Wait. Hold on. He gave you your first orgasm?"

"First, second, third, fourth, fifth, sixth."

"Serious?"

"Serious."

"How was it?"

"The bomb. That shit was the bomb."

"You don't want a repeat?"

"Someone new can pick it up from there."

Petrichor said, "You're staying."

"For a while. Never been to a carnival. Could check out Kadooment and Foreday."

"We can hang out from time to time, could get a drink at every rum shop."

"Two thousand rum shops, more or less."

"More like twelve thousand, depending on how you define a rum shop."

"I'll have to get used to rice and peas, macaroni pie and chicken. Pudding and souse."

Petrichor said, "We should do the bumper cars at Casa Grande."

"We could do that. We could do that and go bowling."

"We could hang out, try to eat at every nice restaurant on the West Coast."

"Yeah, we'd get fat like Rachel Pringle and have butts like Mother Sally."

"You'd get fat and that bumper would get so broad they'd write a song about it."

"Not the way I train, Child Support Waiting to Happen."

Petrichor smiled. "Does this qualify as the start of girl talk?"

"Probably does. Probably does. If you get me a venti extra-dry nonfat cappuccino with whole-milk foam, sure, we can girl talk while I sip and clean my guns and be ready for whatever."

She looked back toward Trinidad, then in the direction of the United States.

She said, "This isn't done, is it?"

"Probably not. I'll know in a day or two, but probably not."

"It's just on pause."

"Just on pause."

"We need to find my sperm donor."

"Yeah. We need to find Old Man Reaper."

"I'll clean my guns, get my bows and arrows, and be ready too, Reaper."

"Okay. Fine. Child Support Waiting to Happen."

"Stop saying that before you jinx me. Call me Petrichor."

"You have my name."

"Thought it didn't bother you."

"I lied."

Her cellular ping-ping-pinged.

I took her phone, sent her husband a wicked message.

She wiped a tear from her eye.

I asked, "You okay?"

"You're okay. You're safe. I'm okay because you're okay."

"What's wrong?"

"Ice cream."

"What about it?"

"They had ice cream."

"Who?"

"I need to take some ice cream home to my husband."

"Let's go find your ice cream."

"Yeah. Let's go get that ice cream."

Then I looked up at the sky, at the stars.

I said, "Hope Old Man Reaper can see them too."

Petrichor nodded. "We killed them all."

I nodded. "We killed them all."

ACKNOWLEDGEMENTS

O ye faithful reader, here we are again at the end of a marvelous roller-coaster ride.

As you exhale, I hope that the ride was worth the price of the ticket.

Reaper just passed by and Petrichor is in a rush to get back to her boo, so I'll keep it short.

Reaper is angry. I mean, the woman is pissed off. So I'm slipping on my bulletproof jacket.

Okay. Now. Let's all hide under the desk, ignore Reaper yelling my name, and roll.

Come closer. Closer. I'll have to whisper. Closer. Not that close, unless you pop a mint.

Thanks to the NYC family back at Dutton. We've crossed the twenty-book mark. Yay. Eighty more to go. ROFL. Denise Roy, my wonderful editor, thanks for everything. You're brilliant.

Ava Kavyani and the many people working in publicity, much love and thanks to all of you.

Sara Camilli and Ray, back in the Midwest at the Sara Camilli Agency, we've made it to the end of another project, so I'll take a few deep breaths, a thirty-minute nap, then move on to the next one. Okay, I'll skip the nap. Nothing comes to sleepers but dreams. We're all about reality. 'Nuff said.

Karl Planer and Tamala Whittley, my peeps at the Planer Group in L.A., thanks for holding down the fort as I again waved good-bye to the USA, packed up, and moved to another country.

Barbados. Love you.

Hey, look, the third act . . . yeah . . . sorry about the destruction . . . but thangs happen. I will bring a tube of Super Glue and make sure all landmarks are restored by the time this book is published.

Lyn, Lyn, bo byn, banana fana fo fyn . . . Skye,

Skye, bo bye, banana fana fo fye . . .

Book Source in Barbados, Government Hill. I want to give a special thanks to Beverly, Erica, Russell, Whitley, Christina, Jennifer, Gillian, Ashley, and the rest of the Book Source crew. My bro Johan has moved on, but thanks to him as well. Thanks for giving me much support and allowing me to chill out and use one of your offices five days a week. That was awesome. I mean that from my heart. I loved it. You guys are the best of the best. Holla at the fruit guy for me. I need grapes. LOL.

The girls at Coffee Bean Warrens, thanks for being so cool. Y'all kept me laughing and smiling while I sipped my brew, ate, and worked. Same for the girls at Graeme Sanctuary.

Sky Mall. Chefette, Six Roads. Sheraton Centre.

Novel Teas. Thanks for the love, and the teas. Back soon. Everyone, meet me there.

Hugs to the wonderful people at LIME in Government Hill. Thanks for the love, support, and putting up with an American from time to time. I'm heading to the lobby to top up my phone.

John Downes and the crew at the Six Roads branch of the public library, thanks for the support. We still have to hook up and lime down at the shooting range at some point.

Now it's time for me to hitch a ride on the back of a flying fish to the next island.

I have to give a shout to Trinidad. Put the Soca War on pause and listen up. Thanks to Dionne Baptiste for answering questions and letting me get on her nerves from time to time. To my friend from Tobago, shouts to Liselle Des Vignes Quash. (See, I didn't call you a Trini, so put your cutlass down.)

Nigel Khan Booksellers and staff, thanks for the many years of support.

Once again, saving the best for last, it is imperative that I thank _____ for all of their help while I was taking Reaper from the States to the West Indies to Canada, and back to the West Indies. It's between you and Reaper what you did to make this novel possible, but if you want the world to know, feel free to write it here —> _____. :-)

Just remember, Reaper has ears and the man behind the red doors sees all.

Fuck. Reaper is heading this way. Everybody, run. Gotta go, gotta go, gotta go.

Just hope I don't bump into Gideon.

Writing is a wonderful journey. Thanks for keeping me company.

Time to pack my bags.

Thursday, November 7, 2013, 11:31 a.m., PST.

Estoy a: 34° 3' 8" N / 118° 14' 34" W

85 degrees. Adidas shorts, Jimi Hendrix tee, bare feet on wooden floor, CNN in the background.
☺

670

ABOUT THE AUTHOR

Originally from Memphis, Tennessee, **Eric Jerome Dickey** is the *New York Times* best-selling author of twenty-one novels. He is also the author of a six-issue miniseries of graphic novels for Marvel Enterprises featuring Storm (*X-Men*) and the Black Panther, and several short stories.

The employees of Thorndike Press hope you have enjoyed this Large Print book. All our Thorndike, Wheeler, and Kennebec Large Print titles are designed for easy reading, and all our books are made to last. Other Thorndike Press Large Print books are available at your library, through selected bookstores, or directly from us.

For information about titles, please call:
  (800) 223-1244

or visit our Web site at:
  http://gale.cengage.com/thorndike

To share your comments, please write:
  Publisher
  Thorndike Press
  10 Water St., Suite 310
  Waterville, ME 04901